THE LOST
DOOR
A ZIMBELL HOUSE PUBLISHING
ANTHOLOGY

THE LOST DOOR

A ZIMBELL HOUSE ANTHOLOGY

ZIMBELL HOUSE
PUBLISHING, LLC
Union Lake MI
2016

For permission requests, write to the publisher at the address below:
"Attention: Permissions Coordinator"
Zimbell House Publishing, LLC
PO Box 1172
Union Lake, Michigan 48387
mail to: info@zimbellhousepublishing.com

© 2016 Zimbell House Publishing, LLC
© Cover Design by The Book Planners
http://www.TheBookPlanner.com

Published in the United States by Zimbell House Publishing
http://www.ZimbellHousePublishing.com
All Rights Reserved

Print ISBN: 978-1942818885
Kindle ISBN: 978-1942818892
Digital ISBN: 978-1-945967-15-3
Trade Paper ISBN: 978-1-945967-55-9
Library of Congress Control Number: 2016912801

First Edition: August/2016
10 9 8 7 6 5 4

ACKNOWLEGEMENTS

Zimbell House Publishing would like to thank all those that contributed to this anthology. We chose to showcase twenty new voices that best represented our vision for this work.

We would also like to thank our Zimbell House team for all their hard work and dedication to these projects.

Finally, a special shout out to *The Book Planners* for creating yet another great cover design!

Contents

EGRESS

DJ TYRER

"You know, I think there's a doorway back here," said Don, staring closely at the rear wall of the outbuilding.

"Really? I don't see anything," said Kelly.

"Yeah, look here. They've plastered it over, but you can see the outline of the frame, see?" he traced it with his finger.

"Maybe…"

"I'm going to open it up."

Kelly wrinkled her nose. "You sure that's a good idea?"

"I can't see it'll do any harm. We might find a hidden room back there."

"You think so?" Her tone expressed her doubt.

"Oh, ye of little faith. There could be space back there, it's impossible to tell with all that growth out there." The garden was in need of clearing. "And, this is an old building; who knows what might have been forgotten down the years?"

The house they'd just moved into had been built back in the reign of Queen Victoria, but the outbuildings were centuries older, the last vestiges of a monastic farm that had stood on the site before the Dissolution. This building had been full of old, rusted farm junk that must have sat in it for decades and which had taken Don three days to clear.

"Well," said Kelly, brushing a cobweb from her sleeve, "I'll leave you to get on with it, while I decorate the bedroom." She hoped her tone would convey her desire for his assistance, but Don was either oblivious or ignoring it to focus on what he wanted to do.

"Okay, see you…"

Don set to work stripping the plaster away. It proved an easier task than he'd expected; age and damp having weakened its bond so that it fell away in large, flaking lumps.

When he was done, he could see the original stonework of the rear wall and, in it, the stone lintel and uprights that framed the doorway. Within the frame, yellowish brick, quite unlike the grey-blue of the stonework, blocked the entrance.

Don looked at it for a minute, sucking his lip, then nodded to himself and muttered, "Shouldn't take long…"

He set to work with a hammer and chisel, hacking out some of the crumbly old mortar, then inserted a crowbar into the space and began to tear away bricks until he could see a rough wooden door still standing behind it. A faded red cross was painted on it.

Once the brickwork was gone, scattered across the floor of the outbuilding, he tried the door, tugging on the heavy iron ring that served as a handle, but it wouldn't budge. There was a lock, he could see, but even had he had the key he couldn't have used it as the keyhole had been filled with something, putty or wax.

He headed inside for some lunch which, with Kelly having been busy herself, was a do-it-yourself ham sandwich. She joined him a few minutes later.

"Well, I've made good progress on the room," she said archly, as she sat down opposite him with a pot of yogurt and a banana.

"Good. I was right; there is a door there. Somebody sure didn't want it to be open." He proceeded to describe it all to her.

"Very interesting," she said, although to her, it wasn't.

"It is. I'm going to get it open, whatever it takes."

"Good for you. Well, I'd better get going… some of us have productive work to do."

"Yeah. Good luck with that. I'll be up to help you as soon as I'm done with the door."

"Well, don't strain yourself."

"I won't," he joked, waving her off, before returning to the outbuilding and setting to work on separating the door from its lock.

There was a sudden loud cracking sound as the wood finally splintered, and the door swung open.

"What the—?" Don was startled to see, rather than the darkness of a hidden room or the sunlight of the garden, a ruddy glow, a little like that from a fire, coming from the other side of the doorway.

The reddish light wasn't strong and it took a few seconds for his eyes to adjust to it. Through the doorway, he could see a nightmarish landscape that seemed to have sprung from the pages of a book on dinosaurs he remembered reading as a child, or perhaps Mordor, from the films Kelly loved to watch. The scene was dark, a land of black ash that rose to form black hills, beyond which were jagged mountains, all lit by the bleeding rivers of lava that ran from distant volcanoes and the hint of an enormous sanguine sun beyond the dense clouds of smoke overhead.

"Impossible…" It looked real and yet, he knew it couldn't be. He slammed the door shut and looked around. The interior of the empty outbuilding appeared just as it had. Normal. He opened the door again and quickly shut it once more. The eerie landscape was still there.

Should I fetch Kelly, show her? he wondered. *No. I have to be hallucinating… and I don't want to make a fool of myself. Yet, why is everything else normal?*

"Okay," he told himself in a firm tone, as if speaking to a recalcitrant child, "it can't be real. There has to be a room there. If I walk straight forward, I'll hit a wall and know for sure that I'm seeing things."

He fetched a torch from his toolbox and, despite feeling foolish, slipped his chisel into his pocket as if it were a knife. Then, he opened the door. The bizarre landscape was still there. As a precaution, he jammed a fragment of brick beneath the door to stop it from shutting behind him.

Don took a deep breath, flicked on his torch and stepped through the doorway.

The landscape remained, and he heard the gravel crunch beneath his feet. He shone his torch beam about, but it just illuminated the ash as if it were really there. He shivered, and not just from the chill.

He walked directly forward with a regular stride as he counted off his steps. At two-hundred, he stopped.

"There's no way the room can be this big."

Am I hallucinating walking? Is that possible?

Don turned around and could see a stone doorframe standing alone on the plain of ash like a trilithon at Stonehenge.

"I'm going mad…"

He closed his eyes and began walking, counting as he went. At two-hundred, again, he halted and opened his eyes—he was a few feet short of the door. *Surely, if I imagined it, I'd be back at the door exactly, wouldn't I?*

On a whim, Don crouched down and picked up a handful of the gravelly ash, then stepped back through the door. He walked straight through the outbuilding and out into the sunlight, then opened his hand. Black ash covered his palm. He turned his hand over and watched it fall to the grass.

"It's real…" Somehow, the doorway led to some other world. It was ridiculous. It was impossible. It was real. He couldn't believe a hallucination could maintain such detail and integrity.

He had to go take a look around, explore it a little. Of course, nobody would take his word for it, but he had to do it for himself. Still, he could always bring the sceptics here and show them it, couldn't he?

He went back inside. A little of the ash had drifted through the door; there was a definite breeze with a hint of sulphur on it. He stepped through the doorway once more.

Although he could just about see without it, he used his torch to light his way, not wanting to fall down a crevasse hidden in shadow.

Despite the concept of an entirely new world being intriguing, the fact was, that with the absence of plants, animals, ruins, or even any particularly interesting outcrops of rock, it was actually a little boring after a time. Don made the hills his destination, but, while the ground was rising a little, they were even further away than he'd first thought.

A sudden screech announced that there was, apparently, life after all. He shone his torch about, then up as he thought he heard the beating of leathery wings. Then, realising this was, perhaps, a bad idea, he lowered the beam.

A large shape passed overhead, mostly hidden by the smoky cloud. Once more he was put in mind of Kelly's films.

Don waited for it to fly away, then resumed walking, although more cautiously. He halted a few minutes later when he heard a distant cry, a sort of coughed bark, unlike anything he'd ever heard before. Atop a distant hill, he saw something huge astride two powerful hind limbs with a pair of smaller, grasping forelimbs and a heavily-jawed head. It reminded him of a picture of an allosaurus stalking through that nightmare world in his dinosaur book. He decided not to worry as to whether he was a time traveller or on some alien world, but turned and began to run back towards the doorway, desperate for the safety of normality.

He was only halfway back when something threw itself off a boulder at him, slamming into him and bowling him over. Don got the barest look at it, it was about his size with leathery skin, a wide, fanged mouth, cruel eyes and a neck frill. It was a little like a Velociraptor and a little like an Orc and not much like either.

The creature lunged again before Don could regain his feet, grabbing hold of him and snapping at him with razor-like teeth.

For a second, Don was frozen by fear, certain he was about to die, but then the chisel was miraculously in his hand and he was stabbing it through the thick, leathery hide and into the rubbery flesh beneath.

It gave a grunt-like cry and fell slack atop him; Don could feel warm blood on his hand and body. He shoved it off of him and managed to stand, before running back to the doorway and throwing himself through it.

He lay, stunned for a moment, then a high-pitched howl regained him his senses, and he slammed the door shut. He couldn't lock it, but could use fragments of the brick to jam it shut. Then, he could start work on resealing the door so that none of those things could get through. Whoever had first sealed it had had the right idea.

A sudden thought struck him; he had been in that place for some time with the door propped open, and if he could go through it, an ingress also being an egress, then it was entirely possible those things could come through. *What if any have?*

Don ran back to the house, the bloodied chisel still clutched in his hand.

He burst into the kitchen and halted in shock as one of the man-sized creatures looked up from the trash and hissed at him. It lunged towards him. He kicked a chair over in front of it, and it stumbled, and he stabbed the chisel into its side. It slashed at him with one of its clawed hands, gouging three bloody tracks down his arm. He shrieked, but stabbed again. It collapsed, and he kept stabbing it until it stopped moving.

Panting, he leaned upon the table fighting nausea.

Then, there was a sound from upstairs; a crash, a shriek, then the sound of a struggle! He dashed up the stairs and burst into the bedroom.

Don halted in surprise. He had expected to see Kelly being menaced by one of the grotesque creatures, but it lay twitching on the floor, a length of curtain rail impaled down its throat. Kelly stood in a corner of the room, shaking, staring down at it, but seemingly unhurt.

"Don?" She murmured. Then, she shouted, "Don!" and jabbed her finger towards him.

For a split-second, he didn't register what she meant, then it was too late as something smashed into his back, and he fell to the floor. There was a sharp pain as teeth bit deeply into his left shoulder and claws raked his back. He yelled in agony.

Something crashed onto the floor in front of him, and he raised his head a little to see Kelly was throwing bedside lamps and other objects at the beast. It worked, as it let go of his shoulder and changed its attention to her, lunging at her, jaws wide.

Kelly dodged backward, then slashed at it with a craft knife. The creature held back warily, but Don knew that that hesitation would only last a moment before it went for her.

Despite the pain in his mauled shoulder, Don pushed himself up into a crouch and grabbed for its leg, causing it to fall on its face.

Kelly jabbed the knife into its flesh, then jumped back with a shriek as it snapped at her before leaping back onto its feet.

But, Don was back on his feet, too. He grabbed for the chisel, which he'd dropped, and threw himself at it.

It yowled and arched its back as the chisel blade bit deep into its flesh. Don stabbed at it again and again, and Kelly joined him, falling upon it with a terrified mania of stabbing. She stepped back when it fell still, but he kept going until she dragged him off it.

"What the hell are they?" Kelly demanded.

"I… I don't even know where to begin," he said.

Don evaded the question briefly, on the grounds he needed to check there were no more of the things about. There didn't appear to be.

Returning to Kelly, he said, "Trust me, this is something you'll have to see for yourself. But, first, we'll have to get some supplies together, because you're going to help me brick up that door, once again…"

FAIRY MAGIC

SAMMI COX

Amy's face peered out from behind the old, gnarled tree trunk before she was once more lost to sight. However, her voice and her laughter echoed throughout the gardens. "You can't catch me, Aunty Vi!"

Violet sighed. She knew Amy was at that age when she was full of energy and wanted to play all the time, but Violet, thirty years her senior, found she tired far more quickly than the young girl.

This game of hide-and-seek had already lasted an hour, and Amy as yet didn't look like she would tire of it anytime soon. Much to Violet's disappointment.

Violet had come to stay with her sister, Ursula, in her big house in the middle of nowhere, whilst her brother-in-law was abroad on business. In actual fact, this idea suggested to her by Ursula, couldn't have come at a better time. Violet had just broken up with her long-term boyfriend as well as had her hours at work reduced to only a handful a week. Violet couldn't remember ever feeling so down or life being so hard.

However, as soon as her sister had rung, asking her to come and help her with her nieces and nephews—she had two of each—Violet breathed a sigh of relief. She needed to get away from everything. She needed a fresh start. So, she had quit her job and put her things in storage, terminating the contract on the flat she could no longer afford on her own. Then she was on the first train out of the city, heading towards the rolling green fields of rural England.

That had been five days ago. Since her arrival, Amy had constantly sought out her aunt's attention, insisting that she play games with her in the garden, read her books, make-up stories, not to mention help in her favourite activity, looking for fairies.

"Aunty Vi? Aren't you going to catch me?" Amy's light voice called again, as Violet, quite unconsciously, sat down on the bench next to the pond. She couldn't take another step.

"Amy? I bet you can't find me?" she called back, suddenly feeling as if her legs had turned to lead. All this running around was exhausting her.

The next thing she knew, she was lying on the bench, her eyes closing as Amy stood over her, brushing the hair out of her eyes.

"Go to sleep, Aunty Vi. Things will better soon. I promise. All we need is a little fairy magic."

It was early evening when Violet finally woke. A light blanket had been draped over her and a soft pillow placed beneath her head. She couldn't help but smile at the effort someone had gone to make her comfortable.

Walking back to the house, she could smell the soft scent of numerous flowers filling the warm summer air. Lavender, roses, lilacs, jasmine, honeysuckle... she could detect them all, but there were hundreds she could not even guess at.

Entering through the door to the kitchen, she found her sister sitting at the table surrounded by her children. They were just about to start supper.

"Vi, did you sleep well?" Ursula grinned.

Violet held up the blanket and pillow. "Who do I have to thank for the provisions?"

"That would be Amy." Ursula stood up and grabbed another plate from the worktop. "Spaghetti bolognese, salad, and flatbread. Nothing exciting I'm afraid."

"Sounds delicious," Violet took her seat at the other end of the table from her older sister.

The meal passed quickly as the children engaged in friendly banter and the sisters exchanged plans for the rest of the week. When the food was all gone, and the older kids had told Violet about what they were doing at school, they all disappeared, leaving the adults to tidy up.

Suddenly Amy was standing in front of them once more, her hands swinging at her sides and a wide smile spread across her face.

"What do you want this time, Amy?" Ursula asked, worried that her youngest daughter was demanding too much of her sister.

"There's something I want to show Aunty Vi before bed."

"Well, you had better ask her then, but, she might still be tired, Amy. She's not used to running around in this country air."

"Will you come for a little walk with me into the garden, Aunty Vi? There is something I found that I want to show you."

Violet wanted to ask if it could not wait until tomorrow but there was something about the little girl that made her keep quiet. "Are you sure it's only a little walk, Amy?" she asked instead.

"I promise. Cross my heart," Amy swore solemnly.

"All right then, young explorer. Lead the way."

Amy ran out of the kitchen door and into the garden in the time it took for Violet and Ursula to blink.

Ursula smiled. "I don't know what it is about you, but I have never seen her like this, Vi. She's always been so quiet but this last week she is just so…"

"Excitable?"

Ursula nodded as she started to clear the table. "Anyway, you better hurry, before she decides to walk the length of the county."

When Violet caught up with Amy, she was waiting patiently on the swing, singing to herself.

"So what is it that you've found?"

Amy stopped singing and alighted deftly from the moving seat. Taking her aunt's hand she led her along the garden path, but she chose not to explain.

It was the height of summer so it was still light outside. The moon and stars were still a few hours from changing places with the sun in the sky. In the distance, she heard the quacking of ducks as they made their way between the village pond and river.

Although the path continued on, Amy veered to the left and began following a narrow dirt track between the trees and bushes.

"Where are we going?" Violet asked, looking about her.

"You'll soon see," was the only response she was given.

With a sigh and a shrug of her shoulders, all Violet could do was play along.

A little further and Amy pulled Violet to a standstill. Turning to face her, she looked up at the older woman. "Now, Aunty Vi. I found something magical when you were sleeping this afternoon. Would you like to see it?"

"Of course, I would," Violet replied, looking around her, bemused. There was nothing here, nothing that looked magical to her eye, at any rate. Trees and bushes, a few dashes of colour from a flower or two, and some little garden ornaments and that was all. But then she lacked a child's imagination and the ability to conjure anything you wanted from whatever was at hand.

"Before I show you, you must promise that you won't tell anyone about it. I was sworn to secrecy, but I was allowed to tell you."

"I promise, Amy. I won't tell anyone about what you've found. So where is this secret?"

Amy looked left and then right, checking no one else was about, even though she knew the rest of the family was back at the house. Then she carefully stepped aside and pointed at the bottom of the tree trunk that was growing behind her.

"I found a fairy door," she whispered. "A real fairy door."

Violet bent down and stared at the painted ceramic door propped up against the bottom of the tree. She recognised it at once. She had bought it for Amy's last birthday.

"I remember this. So this is where you decided to put it," Violet said, smiling. "When I saw the stall in the market selling them I knew I had to get one for you." She ruffled Amy's hair.

But Amy wasn't smiling. She was looking hard at the door. "Why won't it change?" she asked suddenly, staring up into the face of her aunt. "It changed earlier, and the fairy came out to speak with me." There were tears in her eyes.

"Perhaps the fairy's gone on holiday?" Violet suggested, diplomatically. She didn't want her niece to cry, but the child had such an imagination that it seemed she couldn't tell at that minute what was pretend and what was real.

"He's not gone on holiday. He told me I could come back and bring you with me. Why would he say that if he wasn't going to be here when I came back?"

Violet felt the hairs prickle on the back of her neck. She didn't like it when Amy got like this. She never knew what to say to calm her down. The child was just so insistent.

"Shall we try knocking on the door? If he doesn't answer it must mean that he's popped out for a little while, but we can try again tomorrow."

Amy crawled through the mud to sit in front of the little pottery door and knocked on it twice. There was no answer, but there was never going to be, Violet mused, even though she had waited with bated breath to see if anything happened. There was something in the way Amy sounded that made her wonder, just for the briefest of seconds, if a little fairy man would open the door and step out into the evening.

But there was nothing.

Amy sat on the floor and waited and waited. In the end, Violet decided to pick her up and carry her back to the house.

"I don't understand," Amy whispered into her aunt's shoulder. "He said he would be there."

"Don't worry, sweetie. We will come and call on him again tomorrow."

"Where do you think he's gone?"

"Perhaps he ran out of milk and had to pop out to the shop."

"Do fairies drink milk?"

"Oh yes," Violet said, happier that their conversation was moving towards more comfortable subjects. "Milk and bread and honey… did I ever tell you the story about the little fairy princess who wished away her wings? No? Well, I'll tell it to you now, shall I? There was once a little fairy princess named Harebell, who didn't like to fly, so one night she decided to wish away her wings…"

By the time Violet and Amy got back to the house, Amy was fast asleep in her aunt's arms. In the kitchen, Ursula was pouring two glasses of wine, now that the dishes had been washed and dried.

"I'll just put Amy to bed and then get changed. That glass of wine looks so inviting," she said, before walking through the house and climbing the stairs. Amy, thoroughly exhausted after the excitement of the day, only woke for as long as it took to brush her hair and climb into bed. Then she was lost to the realms of slumber.

Violet switched on the night light and then gently closed the door behind her. At the end of the landing, she could hear the latest pop songs coming out from her eldest niece's room.

Her own room was up another flight of stairs in the converted loft. Spread across two levels, this little guest suite as she thought of it, was perfect for a prolonged stay in the country, with views that stretched for miles across the English countryside.

Violet quickly changed, but as she did so, she noticed her phone flashing on her bedside table. She had quite forgotten to take it downstairs with her when she woke that morning.

Crossing the room quickly she picked it up. Four new voicemails. With a sigh, she decided to listen to them, just in case it was her old boss trying to give her back her job.

But it wasn't. All four recordings were from her ex, Nick. He had been round to the flat expecting her to still be there, even though he had taken all his stuff. Finding her gone, he was angry and wanted to know where she was.

Shaking, she made her way back down the stairs and to her sister and the glass of wine that she now needed to steady her nerves. She had never heard Nick sound like that. He had always been quiet and reserved, not loud and certainly never enraged. What had come over him? He had left her. He didn't want her anymore. He had told her so. So what did it matter to him where she was now?

Ursula had relocated to the living room and was now sprawled out on the sofa, the glasses sitting in front of her on the coffee table.

"In here," she called.

She needed to only take one look at Violet before her sister burst into tears and told her everything. About her job. About Nick. About the messages on her phone. About how disastrous she felt her life had become.

"Maybe he is worried that some knight in shining armour has rescued you and carried you off to his castle, where you will live happily ever after, forever?" Ursula said, patting her sister's hair. "He's just realised what he's missed out on, Vi. He knows he has made a mistake. That's all."

But Violet couldn't stop thinking about how angry he sounded. Nick had changed. In a matter of weeks, the man she had loved had turned into a monster.

So consumed were they with their conversation, neither of them saw little Amy, who, roused from sleep, had come downstairs, only to find her distraught aunt crying her eyes out on the sofa. For a while, she watched and listened before slipping away back up to bed.

After two small glasses of wine, Ursula went to check the children were in bed. Violet, yawning, decided she would head upstairs too.

"Things will be better in the morning," her sister said to her as she bid her goodnight. "Trust me. They will be. Sleep well."

That night, Violet cried herself to sleep. She had thought leaving the city and her old life behind her would put an end to the downward spiral she felt herself moving down. But her life had followed here, and instead of getting better, things were getting worse.

Violet woke to two new messages on her phone from Nick, both demanding she contact him and let him know where she was. Well, she wasn't going to do that. Thankfully, he didn't know Ursula that well, and had never been across the country to her home, so there was very little chance of him finding her.

More than anything, though, a feeling of needing to move on had been awoken within her. Only she had no idea of how she was going to do that. She needed to find somewhere to live. She needed to find a job. She needed to decide where exactly she wanted to be, where she wanted to call home. In her mind, she was a boat cut loose from her moorings, and she was floating aimlessly and directionless on the stormy sea.

Breakfast was a chaotic, hurried affair, as Ursula bustled about the house, readying her three eldest children for school. Amy's school had already broken up for the holidays, so Violet was on babysitting duty until her sister returned from the school run.

"Aunty Vi," Amy whispered, as Violet downed the last of her coffee. "Are we going to go and see the fairy this morning when everyone's gone? You promised we could."

Amy it seemed hadn't forgotten the drama of the previous evening, and this morning she was, if anything, more determined than ever to find out why the fairy door hadn't changed.

"All right, then. Go and put your shoes on. Then we'll go."

Morning dew still clung heavily to the grass as Violet and Amy made their way through the garden. A wood pigeon was cooing in the top of one of the trees. Clouds, light and fluffy, skimmed across the bright blue sky. It was going to be another gloriously warm day.

"You know, Aunty Vi. I've been thinking about what we are going to do if the fairy is still not there. We are going to have to search for him."

"I'm not sure that's necessary, Amy. He might not want to be disturbed."

"But what if something has happened to him? What if he is hurt and waiting for us to find him?" Amy's lip quivered and her eyes filled with tears.

"You are such a sensitive, sweet thing," Violet whispered as she gathered the girl up into her arms. "This fairy is very lucky to have you for a friend."

Violet carried Amy the rest of the way, doing her best to soothe the child. However, she almost dropped her when she reached the tree. Outside the little fairy door, which was now propped open with a stone, was sitting a small little man in a long green coat and black fedora.

"Hell's bells," Violet whispered.

Violet knew she had not slept well the night before. That, coupled with the stress of everything that was going on in her life, was undoubtedly taking its toll on her.

"Good morning, ladies," the little man said, as Amy, now all excited, scrambled out of Violet's arms and across to the doorway.

Violet couldn't move.

"You're back!" Amy exclaimed. "We came last night, but you weren't home."

"You should not have worried yourself, little Amy. I had to go and find a few things I needed. I do believe a spell-casting is on the horizon."

Amy clapped her hands together with glee, before turning back round to her dumbstruck aunt. Taking her hand, she pulled her forward. "I told him all about you," Amy whispered out of the side of her mouth before she began the proper introductions. "This is Aunty Vi, the lady I told you about."

"Right so, right so," the man said, standing up and shaking hands with the newcomer. "It is an honour to make your acquaintance. I'm so glad little Amy brought you to see me."

"You are?"

"Of course, my dear. When she told me how sad you've been, I knew I had to meet you to see if there is anything I could do to help."

Amy coughed and took a few steps away from her aunt, beckoning the little man over to her. "Things are much worse than we thought," she whispered conspiratorially. "Aunty Vi had a bad night."

"Is that so? I'm so sorry to hear that."

"Er… what do you mean, see if there is anything you could do to help?" Violet interrupted. "I'm sorry, I'm just a little confused." She then focused her attention on Amy. "And why, young lady, have you been telling strangers about me? Why have you been talking to strangers at all?"

"I'm no stranger, Miss Vi," the small man decreed.

"Yes, but she doesn't know that," Amy explained. "She is a grown-up after all."

"You're right, so very right. Little Amy is very wise for her years," the man said, smiling. "And it's a good thing too that she came and told me everything." He tilted his hat towards the young girl. "You brought her here at just the right time. Another day or two and she would have been beyond my help."

Violet sighed, rubbing her temples. She knew she was down and that she wasn't her usual self, but she never for one minute would have guessed that she would start to hallucinate! Feeling her legs go weak, she sat down on the path. Very quickly, the man was standing beside her. She was now as tall as he. Then another thought struck her.

"I don't understand how you fit through the door. It's so small, and you are a lot bigger. It makes no sense. None of this makes any sense."

"It's all just a matter of perspective, really. Don't worry, my dear," the short fellow said, his voice gentle and full of compassion. "I don't expect you to understand what is going on at the moment. In fact, I don't expect you to remember anything more than you fell asleep in the garden whilst playing with Amy. And, in the warm sunlight, in an unfamiliar place, you had a bizarre dream. Isn't that right?"

Violet nodded, numbly. That did seem to make more sense than her own explanation.

"Will she be all right now?" she heard Amy ask as her eyes grew heavy. Her voice was full of hope.

"Once I have been able to cast the right spell, she will be, little Amy, dearest. You did the right thing bringing her here, to me."

Amy clapped again. "Oh, thank you! Thank you! I want to hear my aunty laugh again, and smile the way she used to, that made her eyes sparkle like your magic."

"All in good time, little Amy. All in good time. But for now, we wait."

"We wait," she solemnly echoed. "And don't worry. I shan't tell a soul."

"You're going to have to stop falling asleep out in the garden," Ursula chided gently. "You've no sunscreen on and no hat. You don't want to get sunburnt now, do you?"

"Please stop fussing. I'll be all right in a minute," Violet said, sitting up.

My! She had had the strangest dream. A dream of fairy doors and fairy men and fairy magic. And Amy. She had been in the dream too.

"If you say so. I'll be taking Amy over to a friend's for a playdate this evening. The rest are at sleepovers tonight. I'll only be gone for a few hours. Will you be all right on your own?"

"As I said, stop fussing. I'm fine. I'm just exhausted." Violet smiled. "A little quiet 'me' time and I will be as right as rain."

A little while later and Violet was all alone. As she moved around the empty house, wondering how she was going to fill her evening, she couldn't stop thinking about the dream she had, a dream that she could recall so vividly, as if it had been real.

When supper-time came, she decided to eat it outside on the patio. The house, as big as it was, felt too claustrophobic. As she was eating, she got a call from Ursula asking if it would be all right if she and Amy stayed over at her friend's. And so, Violet's quiet evening was turning into a quiet night too.

It was the first time in a week that Violet had been truly on her own. Solitude didn't bother her; she often enjoyed her own company. However, with the way things were, she needed a distraction. She didn't want to dwell on the negative things, but they went round and round in her mind anyway. She didn't want to be a disappointment or a failure, but she felt like both.

As the tears began to fall, she stood up, walked away from the patio and into the garden. Blinded by the tears, she didn't know where she was going, until she suddenly found herself once more by Amy's fairy door.

Wiping her red eyes, she looked about her, thinking of the dream. The door looked exactly as it was supposed to. And yet, she wished it didn't. She wished there was really a fairy that could cast a spell and make everything better.

She sighed as another thought struck her. She could knock on the door, just to be sure. What did she have to lose? After all, there was no one about now. The place was deserted. No one would see her. No one would catch her. There was no one to be embarrassed in front of.

And besides, it would only take a minute to prove it had only been a dream and nothing more. Surely it was worth it to silence the doubt that raged through her?

And so, mimicking Amy the night before, she got down on her hands and knees and crawled across to where the small pottery door was propped up against the tree.

Laughing to herself, she knocked twice and held her breath…

"One minute!" the familiar voice of the little man called out to her, as a light suddenly shone out from the window in the door.

The air around Violet began to tingle and sparkle.

"Hell's bells. What have I done?" She backed away as panic rose up in her. This wasn't supposed to happen. It was only a joke, she told herself as the soft chiming of bells filled the garden.

The edges of the doorway lit up, the colours of the paint changed before her eyes, and then the door swung outwards and out stepped the man of her dream, which she now knew was no dream at all.

"Good evening, Miss Vi. So you remembered then? Good, good. Won't you come in and we'll have some tea." He went back through the door without a second glance.

Violet didn't—couldn't—move. She wanted to go back to the house, but she also wanted to know what was going on. But if she was ever to discover it, she would need to somehow fit through the very small door that was only as big as her hand.

"It's only a matter of perspective," the fairy said to her once more. "Come on now. The kettle's just boiled." His voice trailed away, and she was left alone.

She stood up and took a deep breath in. Then she took one step towards the door, then another and another. The closer she got, the bigger the door seemed to get, until it was the right size for her to fit through it. Holding her breath, she entered the fairy's house.

What she was expecting to find on the other side of the threshold, she had no idea. Logic dictated that a door in a tree trunk gave access to the hollow space behind it. But this wasn't the case.

For a start, the room wasn't round. Neither was it on the ground she realised, as she walked across to the window.

"Where are we?" she asked quietly, taking in the scene. From where she was standing, she could see uninterrupted forest spread out before her.

"We are in the Fairylands. This is the Fairy Forest. It is not of your world, but somewhere else entirely."

The fairy's house reminded Violet of a very large tree house. Everything was made of natural materials. And magic. All that she could see sparkled and shimmered and glowed.

"Fairy custom dictates that I cannot give you my name, though I wish I could introduce myself properly to you." He was now standing at her side, but no longer was he the little man she had met earlier, but as tall as she. Violet couldn't help thinking how handsome he looked. "Crossing over into your world makes us appear different than we really are. It's something to do with the magic, I suppose. But you aren't here to talk about that. Come this way. The tea will be ready now."

They walked around the tree trunk that was in the centre of the room, which held fireplaces and cupboards, and went outside to the balcony. Night was falling over the Fairy Forest.

"We keep the same time as you," he said, pouring each of them a cup of tea. "When it is night where you are, it is night here. When it is day, so it is day here too."

Violet's mind was spinning, with questions she wanted to ask; with questions she had no intention of asking. There was just too much for her to take in.

"Do not trouble yourself, Miss Vi. Things are as they are. That is all you need to know."

"But… I don't understand. I bought that door for Amy from a market. It's not real. How can it open on to a world outside of the one I live in?"

"The portal is behind the door. The door is only a means to access it. Until you bought it for Amy… until Amy placed it where she wanted it, the doorway was redundant and inaccessible. But both you and she changed that, and we are very grateful."

"This is why you've befriended Amy and have offered to help me."

"Exactly. Now… about that…"

Violet woke up laughing. She couldn't remember why or what was so funny, but for some reason, she was smiling and giggling to herself. Stretching, she could hear that Ursula and the children were already home. Grabbing her towel, she headed across to the en suite and showered.

It was then, as she tried to calm down, that things started to slowly fall into place. Casting her mind back to the previous evening, she could see before her the fairy house on the other side of Amy's door, she could hear the voice of the fairy man, she could feel the trepidation that coursed through her as she approached the doorway…

It felt so real.

But it couldn't have been.

Surely it was impossible. There were no such things as fairies, and there was no such thing as magic.

And yet, something was different now. Something about her. The despair she had recently felt was gone and in its place, a feeling of serenity reigned. She was stronger than she had been the day before, and her confidence had somehow been restored to her.

Quickly she got changed. Her phone rang on the bedside table. Without thinking, she picked it up and answered.

"Hello?"

"Vi, where have you been? I've been so worried," Nick's voice crackled out of the handset. "Why didn't you ring to let me know you were all right? I thought you were dead in a ditch somewhere."

"I should have called. I'm sorry," Violet began. "But, there was no need for you to worry. I'm no longer your problem, am I?"

"About that…" Was there a note of contrition in his voice? "I don't know why I left, Vi. I don't know why I said the things I said."

"It doesn't matter now, Nick."

"It does. Please. Give me another chance, Vi. I'll make it up to you."

Violet sighed. She wasn't sure what she wanted to do. However, she knew she didn't need to make a choice right away. If Nick could give her the time and space she needed, perhaps there was still a chance for them.

"Right now, I just need a bit of time away. To think things through."

"But I love you. What more is there to think about?" His tone changed. It was sharper again, like in the messages he had left her. And in that second, Violet had made up her mind, and she was certain she had made the right decision.

"You're right, Nick. There is nothing to think about. We're over. You left me, and I am happy with that. I wish you all the best. I really do. Goodbye." Then she hung up, blocked his number and turned off the phone.

As she made her way downstairs, her step was lighter than it had been in weeks. On entering the kitchen, she spun her sister round and then started dancing with her niece and nephews.

"What happened to you? You look and sound much better," Ursula said, through all the laughing. "So?"

"So what?"

"Something must have happened? Am I right?"

Violet just shrugged. "Where's Amy?"

"She went straight outside when we got home. She said she had to check on something. That it was very important."

A cold shiver went up Violet's spine. Quickly she exited the house, anxious over Amy and something else she couldn't quite put her finger on.

Violet ran through the garden, ignoring everything around her until she came to the tree with the fairy door propped up against its trunk.

Only there was no door there now. It, like the fairy, had gone.

"I guess he did what he had to do and then went home," Amy said, trying to stifle the sobs that were making her shake. Her eyes were red and her cheeks, tear-stained.

"I guess he did. But we won't forget him and what he did for us, will we, Amy?"

"No. Never. Not even when I grow up."

Hand-in-hand, they slowly made their way back toward the house.

"Aunty Vi, will you finish telling me the story of Harebell? Did she really wish her wings away? Did she get them back?"

"Of course, she did. After all, a fairy can do anything, Amy. Absolutely anything."

I'm proof of that, Violet thought to herself, smiling.

FIVE RINGS

ALISON THORNTON

There is a door at the end of the hallway. Charles makes his way cautiously toward it. The door is tall and black and made of stone. When Charles approaches it, the door begins to open. It opens slowly, one inch at a time. It does not reveal anything beyond it. Charles only sees darkness on the other side. He walks slowly and hesitates when he reaches the door; he knows that he must enter.

Total blackness surrounds him.

Charles stands motionless. The door has disappeared behind him. He is afraid to move in any direction. There is no sound, no smell, no breeze. There is nothing but darkness.

A ring of fire violently forms around Charles, ten meters across with golden flames that reach five feet high. Charles is still. He stands in the exact center of the ring. He can feel the heat of the flames on his skin.

"Charlie?"

Charles turns to see his mother standing on the other side of the flames. She is wearing the blue dress that she was buried in. Her dead eyes stare directly into Charles's. Her body slumps with her hands clutched onto her stomach. She whimpers like an animal.

"Mother? Is that really you?"

She stands up straight and reaches out to him lovingly with both arms.

"Sweetheart."

"You shouldn't be here mother, you're dead."

She smiles sadly.

"I know darling. Come to me. Please, I miss you, and I want to see your face. Come close."

Charles backs up.

"I can't mother, the flames are blocking me from you. I'll burn."

"Don't worry about the flames my love. Come to me. I miss my boy."

"But mother, I'll die."

She smiles.

"Then we will be together at last my boy."

Charles doesn't move. He knows that this is a trick. His mother smiles, opens her arms as if expecting a hug and waves for him to come over. Charles stands his ground. His mother's smile changes into a furious frown.

"Get over here Charlie. You were always a disobedient little shit that brought me nothing but pain. You were never there for me, and you left me to die in a goddamned hospital while you ran off with your girlfriend. I never loved you. I have always hated you. You were always nothing but a burden to me. The day that you were born was the worst day of my life. I knew that I would never be free as long as you were around. I knew that from the first time that I saw you. Get over here. I want you to apologize to my face. Come to me."

Charles puts his hands over his ears. His mother claws at him through the golden flames. Her hands burn in the fire. Charles can smell the meat. She shrieks and curses at him. Charles turns his back. He does not want to see her; he knows that she is not real. She disappears.

"Charles?"

Charles turns back around. This time, he sees his kindergarten best friend standing on the other side of the flames.

"Jerry?"

Jerry smiles. He is wearing a high school uniform with his hair slicked back.

"It's been a long time Charles, you look well."

"What are you doing here?"

"I came to see you of course. After all, you never called me or had any sort of contact with me after kindergarten. You were too busy with the cool kids. You left me all alone."

Charles looks down. He knows that this is true, and he is ashamed.

"I am very sorry about that Jerry. I—"

"The worst part wasn't that you abandoned me, it was that you used me to get popular. You used me as the punch line to your jokes when you were trying to make new friends. You ran around telling the entire school stories about me to make yourself look cool. You, my best friend, left me and then you made sure that I would never have any other friends that could replace you. I was so lonely in high school, Charles. Everyone thought that I was a freak because of the things that you ran around telling people. I was beat up almost every day before and after school. I had nobody Charles. I couldn't stand it. That's why I killed myself, Charles. You remember when I slit my wrists in the boys bathroom? You were there that day. You were in the classroom across the hall when I did it. Do you remember what you told me the day before? I was trying to talk to you. I was trying to be nice after everything. You told me to go kill myself. You said that the world would be better off without me. Then you and your buddies all laughed at me. Death was better than my life. At least in death nobody can humiliate you."

"Jerry I'm so—"

"Save it. You turned me into a loser. You did this to me. You beat me down until there was nothing left. I'm dead because of you. What changed in kindergarten, Charles? When did you decide that I wasn't good enough for you?"

Charles steps forward.

"I wasn't like that. What I did to you was horrible. I know that now. I think about it every day, and it fills me with regret. You did not deserve any of what I put you through. I'm so sorry Jerry."

"Come here Charles. I want to see your face. I want you to explain yourself, and I want to see your face. Come to me."

Charles looks at Jerry, and he realizes what is going on. "No, you're not real."

"Come to me."

Jerry reaches an arm through the golden ring of flames. His flesh burns.

"Come to me now."

Charles backs up.

"I'll die if I cross the fire. You're trying to get me to kill myself."

"Maybe you deserve it. After all, you made me kill myself. An eye for an eye."

Jerry smiles twistedly. Then he disappears. Charles takes a deep breath. He closes his eyes for a second, taking a break. He hears footsteps coming from where Jerry and his mother were standing. No, they're too fast to be footsteps. He opens his eyes and sees his childhood dog, Max.

"Max?"

Max barks excitedly and jumps around like a puppy.

"Max, I haven't seen you since I was five! Good boy!"

Max wags his tail and runs in little circles. Charles takes a beat to enjoy this. He misses Max. They were partners in crime. Then Charles's expression changes to sadness.

"Is this the part where you try to get me to cross the flames and kill myself?"

Max whines and tilts his head in confusion.

"It's okay buddy."

Max continues to bark. Then he growls. Then he snaps at Charles, alarming him. Max foams at the mouth and tries to attack Charles through the golden flames. Charles backs up.

"Max what are you doing?"

Max growls viscously. Charles backs up a little more until he can almost feel the hot flames against his back. He turns abruptly. That was a close one. Max disappears.

Charles stands alone in the ring of golden flames once again. He wonders how long this torture will continue. Charles tries to think of anyone else in his life that has died. He can't think of anyone that was close to him or anyone that would have something against him.

"Charles?"

Charles recognizes this new voice right away. It's his little sister.

"Susie?"

"Charles, where am I?"

Susie looks confused and scared.

"Susie, but you're alive. What are you doing here? How did you get here?"

Susie looks at him with tears in her eyes.

"Charles, where are we? What's going on? Who brought us here?"

Charles doesn't know what to make of this.

"It's okay Susie. You're going to be fine. Everything is alright. I will get you out of here. You won't get hurt, I promise."

Susie grabs her stomach and yelps.

"It hurts Charles."

Charles runs forward toward her. They are face to face with the golden flames separating them.

"What hurts, Susie?"

"What's happening Charles? I can't breathe, and it hurts so much."

Charles is frantic. He paces from side to side trying to get a better look at her.

"What can I do Susie? How can I help you?"

Susie screams in pain.

"I'm dying Charles, it's killing me! You have to help me."

Charles looks for a break in the flames that he could run through. There isn't one.

"What do I do?"

Charles runs to the center of the ring and screams at the top of his lungs to whoever may be listening.

"WHAT DO I DO? TELL ME WHAT TO DO! WHY ARE YOU DOING THIS? WHY ARE YOU KILLING HER? LEAVE HER ALONE!"

Susie's screams get louder; she slumps over and falls to the ground. Charles runs back over to her. She has curled up in a fetal position. Charles can see blood coming out of her mouth.

"Susie, what do I do? I don't know what to do."

She looks up at him.

"Help me, Charles. Come here and help me. It's the only way. Come to me."

Charles backs up; realizing. "This is a trick. This was all just a trick. You were trying to get me to cross the flames. You're not Susie, you're not real."

Susie stands up and smiles at him eerily. Then she disappears.

Charles stands for a moment. Stunned. Then he drops to his knees. The ring of golden flames disappears and Charles is alone in the darkness once again. He can hear his heart pounding, and sweat pours down his face. He hears a loud thump directly behind him. It's the stone door that brought him there. It opens slowly. Inch by inch; revealing the hallway of his house. Charles stands up and slowly makes his way back into his home. He goes directly to his bedroom and sits on his bed.

Charles stares at the wall for thirty minutes, then he gets in the shower. After his shower, he finds his best suit and puts it on. Charles combs his hair back and straightens his tie. Then he grabs a line of gold rope from the garage and makes a ring around the end of it. He ties a knot in the ring and hangs the rope from the top of the staircase. Charles cries.

"I'm sorry mother. I'm sorry for not being there when you died. I wish that you were here now. I wish that I could change it. I wish that I was more grateful to you when you were here. I wish that I had told you how much I loved you when I had the chance. I'm sorry Jerry. I'm sorry for making your life hell. It's my fault that you're dead, and I'm sorry. I should have been there for you. I wish that I could be your friend. You had such a bright future, and I ruined it. I know that we were only friends in kindergarten, but you were the best damn friend that I ever had. I'm sorry, Max. I should have given you all the walks and cuddles in the world. I'm sorry that I didn't lock the gate to the backyard. It was my fault that you got hit by that car, Max. It was my fault that you died.

You were a good boy, and you deserved more years than you got. You deserved to play with every dog in the world and swim in any lake that you wanted. I'm sorry Susie. I'm sorry for leaving you alone in this world. I know that you will be able to go on, and I know that you will be stronger than me. I love you. I'm sorry."

Charles puts the golden ring of the rope around his neck. He takes a deep breath and steps off of the staircase.

IN THE EERIE

JOHN VICARY

The side-gate to the Eerie was left open once an eon, usually by mistake. The Mother of Flowers kept close watch most of the time, but occasionally one of the brethren became careless. "You don't understand the danger," Mother would say as she swung shut the offending gate. "You don't know what could come for us."

They didn't know, of course, and so they went about their business with the light hearts of the unconcerned. The swallow fighters bore their needles, and the hunters brandished their screws, and everyone agreed that Mother did as mothers do, which was worry overmuch over nothing.

And soon they forgot, and her words were as seeds cast to the many far winds.

The Eerie had doorways in abundance. The wards held fast, and none had yet been discovered, even those nestled in amongst the barest thistle branches or tucked under loose cobblestones in the market square nor even the one in the leaky downspout of the old church bell tower. Mother sometimes wondered about that one in particular, as it tended to flood in the spring rains, but the wards had never broken, not even at harvest time when the moon was full.

It wasn't a shattered spell but those errant side-gates that caused the Mother of Flowers the most distress. They could be seen by the human eye as a glitter upon new fallen snow or perhaps a sparkle of fresh dew in the morning fields. More than one child had followed the tempting sway of the hawthorn tree too closely, and it was only by dispatching a fleet of White Deer that Mother managed to lead the children astray; times were changing, though, and soon humans would not be deterred by the old ways. Soon they would find the Eerie, and the inhabitants sheltered within, and no petaled distraction would be enough to save them. "Keep the gates closed," she said again. "Do not chance to be seen."

"Yes, Mother," they agreed, but in truth, the thought of a mortal gaze did not frighten them, and so they drifted away into the night, ever heedless and ever careless.

It might have been June or July—they did not keep time by any calendar of human reckoning—when the First Imbalance came to light. It was during flight in the vineyards that one of the swallow fighters noticed a decaying berry. He cried foul on their score, for it was no fair duel, as he'd been distracted by the sight of the mummified fruit dried to the vine that sustained an otherwise healthy patch. The swallow fighters followed a trail of desiccated blackberries sprinkled through the garden path; some were afflicted on the same vine as others that were not. They reported the strange incidence to the Mother of Flowers, who knew a certain chill descended with their words of warning. "Did you leave the Burrow Gate open last eve?" she asked.

They shrugged. "No, Mother."

"What of the Windmill Pane Way? The Leaf Twist? Are there any avenues by which a mortal could have come through to us?" Mother asked. "Have you seen any shadows in the Eerie?"

The swallow fighters shook their heads, their silver plated helmets glinting under starlight.

Mother bit her lip and kept a long watch over the heather, but she saw nothing for her efforts. A cold wind arose from the west, but it might've just been a storm brewing, so she veiled her face and crossed her arrows over her chest to await in vigilance the coming dawn.

It was the Hunters who discovered the Second Imbalance. They were gaming in the forest primeval when they came across the remains of a deer mouse. It was not so out of the ordinary to find dead things in the deep woods, but this one was unusual in that it had no marks upon its corpse. The Hunters poked at its fur with their screws. The skin and muscle gave way under their steel; it was a fresh kill, but the absent predator had left its trophy to rot. This broke the fundamental rules of nature as the Hunters understood them to function. Nervousness began to unspool in their guts. The unblinking eye of the deer mouse stared back, a sheen of unshed tears still shining in its unseeing gaze. The Hunters turned to find Mother. On the way home, they encountered the lifeless body of a pheasant and the unmoving form of a rabbit.

"Are you quite sure?" Mother asked. "All dead? None rotten?"

"None, Mother," the Hunters said in unison. "But dead as can be. What does it mean? What shall we do?"

Mother did not look at them but kept her chin raised and whispered secret summons to the creatures of the air. "We shall do what we can. We shall call the Master of Hares."

The Master of Hares practiced the gift of prophecy. He straddled the gap between worlds, and for that reason the brethren avoided him. His affectations were not easily understood by denizens of either realm, but Mother had a special twinge for him. If their kind loved, it might have been called that, but they didn't so it wasn't. Still, she watched him appear out of the mists in the east, and her chest warmed at the sight of him. "It has been an age," she said after a moment or three.

"It has," he replied. "I hear from the bees that you have need of me. I am ever at your service."

The Mother of Flowers saw that he had aged; his time away from the Eerie had cost him in ways that she would never quite be able to understand. His whiskers were not as bristled as they once had been, and his white hair was beginning to gray. He had taken to wearing a suit at all times now, she noticed, not just while he walked in the world of man. It suited him, she was surprised to see. His hands remained the same, she noted with relief. They were not rabbit's paws, but long-fingered and pink and still unlined. They gave her comfort as few things could. She nodded to herself. "I believe there has been a breach."

"Oh?" His voice was steady, betraying no sign of the curiosity he must have been harboring. "Why do you say that?"

"There have been two signs thus far," she said. "I expect the third in short order."

He cleared his throat. "I see. And you have brought me to verify."

"And to counsel," she said. "As only you can."

The Master said no more but brought forth the bell jar of his trade. He stared straight into the glass for what seemed like years, but as they did not measure time in the Eerie, there was no way to measure how many minutes slipped by. Finally, he blinked the clouds from his vision. "Yes," he murmured. "I can see that it is indeed thus."

The Mother of Flowers bit back a gasp but said nothing.

"There is much to be feared," the Master said, still looking at his empty jar. "The situation is dire."

"What can be done?" Mother asked. "What do you see?"

The Master waved his hands as if to chase away some unseen spirits that plagued him. "Princess Squirrelhair in the North has already begun the evacuation, but it will not be enough. I foresee a Crossing, but the earth is barren, and the sea is dry. All is ruin. All is despair. You are too late, Madam. There is a child in the Eerie, and the change has begun. Don't you feel the fester around you even now?"

The Mother shook her head. "I can't believe it. I won't! There has to be a way. You must foresee a way!"

The Master looked again to the vacant glass before him. "There is something, though it pains me to tell you."

"Tell me!"

"You must go to the child and make an offer of your most precious gift. I see a great loss for you and also for her, but only in this way can balance be restored. Any other action brings the third sign," the Master said.

"You must be mistaken," Mother whispered. "There must be another way."

The Master of Hares pocketed his oracular jar. "I'm sorry, I am most sincere in this vision. All other avenues lead to the black sunflowers. I am afraid that by any choice, this is to be our final parting." A keen viewer might have discerned a tear glistening behind his coarse lashes, but the Master was never one for overtures of emotion. He merely lifted his hand in farewell and so turning, retreated into the mists from whence he came and was gone.

The sounds of the Eerie were lost to Mother for time immemorial as she recalled the image of that hand and watched the seasons spin around her. The chatter of the brethren fell silent as the truth of the Master's words could be denied no longer. Mother pulled her black veil over her eyes and knew what must be done. The tug on her soul led her to the bramble border, where the thistle gate stood gaping in the gloaming. The dark silhouette of the child could be seen in the haze of noxious fumes she brought into the Eerie with her mortal presence.

Mother knew she had wasted too much time in indecision. She could ill afford another second, that province of humanity in which she was forced now to deal. She plucked from her breast the flower of life and held it in offering. She could not speak, or the poison would overwhelm her before the deed could see itself accomplished.

Who is to say what the child saw in that minute? A bright rose, a dew-laden lily, it was an enchantment that caught her attention and drew her to the calling blossom. She plucked the bud, and the gate swung shut, entrapping her and protecting all within. Her eyes washed clear of the sheltering magic, and she saw before her the true visage of the mother whose crown she had stolen, and she was unafraid.

The Mother of the Flowers was now the mother of nothing. With the loss of her animating seed, she grew beyond the height of even the stoutest brethren. Her wings shriveled into husks, and her antennae stubbed and broke. The Eerie leached from her bones until she dried into a towering monument of ash to be dispersed as a rain of dark flakes in the next easy zephyr to pass. The child sighed, and the old mother was carried into the Eerie on that very exhalation to rest as a part of all living things forever.

The child tucked the flower to her breast and stood sentinel as the sun set and rose too many times to count. She didn't know how long she stood there, perhaps it was a month or perhaps it was a year. She understood that time had no meaning here. After an epoch, she noticed the gathering of the White Deer, the Hunters, the Swallow fighters. They watched her from a hill beyond the heather. They waited for her to come to them.

She took hold of the bees and let them carry her home.

INFINITY STARTS HERE

EMILY LEEDHAM

Rushing.

A rushing and a rustling and a rumbling, punctuating by a humming so deep and heavy in her ears that she moved to cover them, but she couldn't move her arms, couldn't feel her arms, where was her body? And a thought broke through—through the rushing and the humming—a thought that made the blood that she couldn't feel, but that must have been inside her run cold.

But the humming silenced it, drowned it out, drowned everything out, until she was floating in a sea so black and endless it stole her breath—which had to be there. She had to still be breathing. How else would she be thinking?

And suddenly a pinprick of light appeared, rushing towards her. Or was she rushing towards it? There was no tug in her gut, no insistent pull of gravity and motion to guide her, only a sense of nothingness, and still, the light approached, closer, closer, closer, until it enveloped her, and inside she was surrounded by white—too hot, too bright, too—

She opened her eyes to a cloudy sky, the scent of dying leaves, solid earth against her back. Sitting up with a start, she whipped her head back and forth, trying to get a sense of where she was. An ancient, weather-worn stone wall surrounded her in a tight ring that stretched well over her head, with a single opening directly in front of her. Tendrils of ivy crept along the walls with the sole intention of smothering them, the dark green leaves the only spot of colour. The sky hung thick with smoke-grey clouds blurred together into an unending fog that matched her thoughts.

Where was she?

She tried to think, tried to remember, but her mind wouldn't cooperate. Her thoughts hung just out of reach, flitting away like startled birds whenever she reached for one. Her birdcage mind had opened without her knowing, and, try as she might, nothing would return.

But there is one, sharp and cold and hard as diamond, but it is confusing, and she doesn't want to dwell on it. Bright lights and crunching metal and a voice she thinks she might recognise, but in the same way that one confuses dreams with reality, she can't be sure. But she remembers the voice, and more importantly the scream, of a name—probably—a name that might be her name, but she couldn't make it out for the sheer terror in the voice.

What was her name?

She couldn't recall, but what was most disturbing was that didn't really bother her too much. Lethargy gripped her, body and mind, and insisted that everything was fine and that she should just close her eyes, lie back on the ground, and sleep for an eternity.

It was then that she noticed the sign hanging on the wall by the exit, and her muddled mind was certain that it hadn't been there earlier. Made of a single piece of worn wood, it had a message scrawled on it in white paint.

She read it out loud, half out of habit and half out of a desire to hear something—anything—other than her own breathing:

"You have one hour. Don't touch the walls."

One hour until what?

Would the walls close in around her? Would the ground open up and swallow her?

Where was she?

She didn't know, couldn't think, couldn't get her stupid brain to wake up and focus on the present, and the world tilted as a wave of dizziness overcame her. She pressed a hand to her head, shut her eyes, and waited for it to pass as nausea boiled her gut. Finally, it stopped, and she stood up on shaky legs, taking a step forward.

One hour. She had one hour.

Don't touch the walls.

Five steps and she was through the opening and into a passageway that curved away at both ends. Around her, air swirled, pulling at her clothes and hair as if trying to suck her back to the ivy-covered clearing. A great rushing began behind her, and when she turned around, there was nothing.

The clearing was gone, replaced by a black void that moved like a curtain in a breeze. She did not know how, or why, but she knew she did not want to touch the black.

Picking one path at random, she hurried away.

She was in a labyrinth. There was no other word for this twisting, turning mess of paths. She had walked for who knows how long now; time passed differently here. Seconds felt like hours, minutes felt like seconds, and she was at once rapidly approaching her one-hour time limit and creeping towards it like how frost slowly overcomes the ground.

An eternity ago, she had left the clearing.

A millennia ago, she had stopped trying to figure out who she had been before she woke up.

A moment ago, she had heard the huffing of smothered laughter.

She was being followed, had been being followed almost since she left the clearing. It didn't scare her as much as she knew it probably should.

Giggles followed her as loyally as a shadow, had been with since moments after she hurried from the void. Bright, clear laughter—like bells.

Laughter, a sudden scramble, and something pulled on her hair. She shrieked and whirled around, but saw nothing save the stone wall, crumbling and barren. Along the edge of her vision, shadows crept, always just out of sight.

More giggling.

She had had enough.

"Hello?" she called, her voice too loud in her ears.

"Hello," replied a voice, tinged with mirth.

Her skin prickled, hairs standing on end. Something hid in that voice, something that she had no part in hearing. Darkness and trickery and hunger, strong enough to devour her.

The air filled with whispers like crackling leaves, and she wondered how many there were, waiting and watching. What were they waiting for?

And what did she have to lose, really?

"Where am I?" she asked, and the whispers stopped instantly.

"Somewhere between everywhere and nowhere," it laughed. She tried not to let her confusion and frustration show.

"Is there a way out?"

If there was, she hadn't found it, and probably wouldn't in the time she had left.

You have one hour.

"Oh yes," it said, "Provided you touch the walls."

Don't touch the walls.

"I... I'll keep to walking, thanks," she gasped, and hurried away.

Laughter followed, but this time, it sounded like the cackling of madness.

As she walked, the labyrinth changed. The stone walls here were crumbling, lined with cracks and punctuated with crevices. Whole chunks lay broken on the sides of the path. More than once, she had to gingerly step over broken bits.

Don't touch the walls.

She wasn't taking any chances.

The voices still followed her, but quietly, with barely a scratch against the walls, as if they were simply watching, waiting for her to try and touch the walls, but she knew better than to take advice from something that she couldn't see.

She had a feeling that someone had taught her that, although she couldn't be sure. The further she walked into the labyrinth, the less her mind cooperated.

It was rather vexing.

Still, she walked on. But as she walked further and further, and the walls grew older and older, she began to wonder if she was walking towards an exit, or if she was walking towards the heart of the labyrinth. And what would she find at the end?

The sky was changing. In the distance, a darkness bloomed, like a storm, creeping over the horizon. Shadows grew at the foot of the walls and stretched out onto the path.

She made sure not to walk in them.

It must have been an hour. But why had nothing happened? No lightning had fallen from the sky to strike her down, no monster had appeared to slowly tear her to shreds, no hole had appeared in the ground to suck her down, down, down into the dark—nothing, save the brisk wind that curled around, lifting her hair and tugging on her clothes. She shivered and wrapped her arms around herself, but that did little to stop the cold that seeped into her bones.

"Cold?"

"Not terribly," she murmured, not turning around to the source of the voice. She knew that she would find nothing there, anyways.

"You could warm yourself up if you touched the wall," it urged, voice right beside her ear.

And she tripped.

Stumbled over her own feet in surprise and fell, arms swinging wildly as she instinctively tried to stop herself.

It was an accident. A simple slip-up. She didn't mean it.

Don't touch the walls.

She did. Just a brush of her fingers.

Inconsequential. Or at least it should have been.

In an instant, the labyrinth disappeared, replaced by an unending sea of black. She could still feel her finger, just barely grazing the stone wall. Warmth spread up her hand and down her arm to pool around her chest, where it swirled around pleasantly. As she watched, an image appeared, sepia-toned and grainy, the edges blurred.

The image moved, and she stared at it in wonder as someone's childhood played before her. Three years old, a birthday with a chocolate cake. Five years old, a family at the park, all the faces blank slates of flesh. Seven years old, holding a hand much larger as they walked to school in the rain.

Ten.

Eighteen.

She watched the girl age, shooting through the years like a comet hurtling into infinity, the images blurring together until she couldn't understand any of it. Her stomach rolled threateningly, and she pulled her hand away with a gasp. The labyrinth returned, with her sitting in the dirt.

"See anything interesting?"

"No," she replied briskly, dusting herself off and standing up. "Nothing at all."

The voice laughed knowingly, and she hurried away from it.

She did not recognise that girl, did not feel a tingling in her gut, her chest as she watched her grow up. And she did not want to know what happened after eighteen, even if she couldn't understand vestigial memories that tugged at her mind with a growing insistence.

"It's been almost an hour," the voice called. "You'd best hurry."

"So I am looking for an exit?"

"Maybe. Or you could just touch the wall again," it suggested, ignoring her question. "Don't you want to know what happens next?"

She didn't want to know.

And she did, too.

"No," she said and kept walking.

"Not long now," it crowed and said no more.

Her hour was up. She knew it when the ground shook, when the walls shot skyward, and when the voice returned, its laugh coming from everywhere to wrap around her throat.

She ran.

Stumbling and tripping and leaping—her legs moved of their own accord, arms pumping, and feet trying to stay underneath her. The stone walls of the labyrinth grew, twisting and turning and warping as they created new paths, and she hurtled down them, turning when they threatened to crush her. The cackling followed her, chased her down the paths. Something swiped at her hair, her clothes, her fear, and she screamed, breath short and gasping, eyes swimming, head pounding.

And then there, directly ahead of her, a bit of blue.

In the deep shadows cast by the walls, she ran from the darkness that threatened to swallow her. The walls closed in, and she sped up, sprinting, jumping, flying through the opening. In an instant, she went from being surrounded by black to being surrounded by blue. Brilliant blue, vibrant blue, a thousand different shades all at once.

A tug on her gut and she was falling, wind ripping at her face. Through squinted eyes she watched as the sun rose and set, the sky blooming with sunset after sunrise on an eternal loop. Clouds zipped past, forming as fast as they dissipated, lit up pink and orange and purple, and she fell through them.

Her freefall slowed, became more controlled, and she stretched out her hands, trailing vapor streams from her fingers. Hair floating around her, she watched as the ground neared, and as she stuck out her legs to land, she blinked—

And opened her eyes to a forest.

She stood on a thick carpet of moss, surrounded by lush undergrowth. Ferns, bushes, and long, swaying grasses all clambered for space and crept up around tall, spindly white trees with peeling bark and fire—bright leaves that slowly floated to the ground.

And a sign, much like the first, on a post before her.

"Don't leave the path," she read. What path? She stood in a grove of birch, trapped on all sides.

"Made it by the skin of your teeth."

"You're still here?" she asked, sighing heavily. She glanced to the side and saw a black blur perched on the lower branches of a tree. Its edges faded and darkened, like curling smoke, and the constant pulse reminded her of a heartbeat.

"I'm hard to lose," it said. "I never really leave, you've known me for a long time."

She opened her mouth to respond, but the ground rumbled, and a path of emerald moss appeared, snaking between the trees.

She, by now used to this business of appearing in strange places, started off.

Birds twittered above her head, their songs impossibly sweet, but hollow, and a little bit unsettling.

"This is a strange place," she murmured.

"This is a wondrous place," the voice replied, from a tree branch above her head. "Brilliant lakes, secret groves, quiet glens—all for you to discover."

"No, thank you."

"Untold riches, unimaginable creatures, impossibly sweet fruit—"

"I'll stay on the path," she said firmly, and the voice grumbled.

"How dull it must be, to follow the rules."

"How dull it must be, to spend your time bothering people," she countered.

"But are you really still a person?" it asked. "Have you stopped to consider what's going on?"

"I'm walking on the path."

"But where are you going?" it persisted. "Have you never stopped to consider that? Where does your path go?"

She shrugged. It felt right, walking along the mossy path, even if her footsteps crunched when they should have been silent. A soft breeze caressed her face, blew through her hair like gentle fingers. Warm light touched her face, and she breathed in the cool fresh air.

Where had she been before?

She couldn't recall.

"I don't really care," she replied. She found it hard to be afraid when she was surrounded by such beauty.

"You probably should."

The moss was growing thicker, the forest denser, and her footsteps louder, but her eyes stayed pointing straight ahead to where the path disappeared into the trees as if trapped. And her thoughts, like mist, floated over the shallows of her consciousness.

"Ever wondered what that crackling is?" the voice asked.

Instead of answering, she shook her head. Her mouth seemed stuck, throat closed off to any words. Her mind was not her own, trapped by falling leaves and beams of light.

But the voice persisted.

"Why do you let yourself be led?" it asked, with mounting frustration. "Why do you not fight back? There are other ways."

She shrugged.

"Fight back," it urged.

Her eyes wouldn't turn, her body wouldn't cooperate. Against her will, her mind was waking, struggling to the surface, out of the dark. Her consciousness whispered sedition, her legs shouted conformity, and refused to bend, refused to break stride for even a moment.

"Fight back."

She began to wonder for how long she had been trapped like this. Since she started walking?

And where had she been before?

Why couldn't she remember?

"Turn around."

Her mind raged, screamed, spit curses at whatever held her back.

"Turn—"

She did.

Her path—her lush, vibrant, living path—stretched behind her brown and dead, with her footprints etched in harshly. Death and decay seeped from the prints and into the forest beyond; black mold and fungi covered the once silvery birch trees, brown ferns crumpled in on themselves, and bushes sat squat and forlorn, stripped of their leaves. A black haze hung in the air, and heavy clouds covered the sky.

"Wh… why?" she asked, voice wobbling and cracking like the dead branches before her.

"You tell me."

This trail of death she left in her wake staggered her. She almost wished that she hadn't turned, hadn't rebelled. Almost.

"I'm dead," she murmured.

There could be no other explanation; the missing memories, the strange forest, the death she left in her wake. When she realised it, her thoughts cleared, although her memories never returned.

She suspected that was a result of dying.

"Afraid so," the voice said gleefully. Beside her, it followed along, shadow floating through the air. It was clearer, edges more defined, and she could just make out something in its centre, a purplish light that pulsed softly.

Perhaps she should have been upset, or even angry, but all she could feel was a sort of acceptance, a sort of "That's Life," ironically.

"I see."

She didn't see, not really. How could she understand the finality of death when she couldn't remember living?

In truth, all she really felt was a little hollow, a little sad in an unspecified way.

"You're lucky, you know," the voice said. "Not many people remember."

"What happens now?"

"Nothing. Sorry to disappoint, but death is dull like that." Its purple heart pulsed in time with its words.

Kicking her feet as she walked and watching how the moss wilted before her eyes, she hummed in thought.

"Are you some demon?" she asked, "Meant to lead me astray?"

"I could be, depending on your point of view," it said. "What am I leading you astray from?"

"Heaven, or something similar, isn't it? Eternal paradise?"

"Depends on what you think is paradise."

"Will this lead me there?" She tapped the path with one foot, and death shot out from under her shoe like spider webs.

"I don't know, but you're going somewhere, aren't you? And somewhere is better than nowhere."

Around her, the forest was thinning. Trees grew in smaller and smaller clumps, and she could see splashes of blue and white between them. Even her path was shrinking, fading down to a trickle that meandered through the long grass.

She did not understand this voice, this creature; her travelling companion. It was a contradiction, a hypocrite, a talking enigma.

"Why did you want me to touch the labyrinth walls?" she asked.

"To see what would happen," it replied cheerily.

"Haven't you heard that curiosity killed the cat?"

"That's a human expression," it chastised, "And it has no place here."

"And where is here?"

"You're dead, aren't you? You tell me what it looks like."

"A forest?" she said hesitantly.

"That's usually the case," it mused.

They walked on. Or, she at least walked on; the voice floated along beside her before finally coming to settle on her shoulder with a small huff. Strangely, she could feel it—almost. Maybe she imagined it, but it felt like a feather, almost non-existent, but vaguely warm. Almost comforting.

Her forest petered to nothing, and she found herself with a choice. Her walking stuttered to a stop.

"Arrived, have you?" the voice asked. As it spoke, its body hummed, like thousands of tiny wings fluttering at once. "What does it look like?"

"Difficult," she grumbled. This being dead business was beginning to wear on her.

A decision stood before, served as a mountain and a tunnel. To one side, a staircase carved into the rock snaked its way up the slope, its steps smooth and overgrown with grass. It climbed up and up until it disappeared around a corner, overgrown with pine and cedar. Snow blanketed the top half of the mountain, and she couldn't tell how high the staircase went.

To the other side, a sandy path, banked by grassy dunes and leading down to rolling grey water. Sea air breezes caressed her face and covered the scent of rot behind her. She imagined walking down to the soft sand and burying her feet in it and not moving for a long while, with only the waves as an accompaniment to her breathing.

But there, hidden away at the foot of the mountain, a small cave disappeared into the rock, its mouth smooth and curved. Moss and lichen grew along the rock, and a simple dirt path disappeared inside. Something told her she shouldn't have seen it; the air around it hung heavy with disquiet.

"What do you see?" the voice insisted, floating off her shoulder to hover in the air before her.

"Mountain path and a trail to the ocean."

"Ah, a choice," it mused. "They do love testing their beloved dead."

"They?"

"The one who runs this world. They have many names."

"And they're the ones who didn't want me leaving the path or touching the walls?"

"It disrupts things," the voice explained. "The self-aware don't always do what they're supposed to."

"Well, what do you see?" she asked. The shadows surrounding the voice had finally lifted, like fog over an inlet or sleep from her eyes. Before her floated a purple flame, rolling and flickering and flecked with violet and lavender and hints of indigo.

"Endless sky and a starlight road and you, a flicker against the darkness."

"Poetic, are you? What ever happened to the nuisance that wouldn't shut up in the labyrinth?"

"Not many dead people have heard me. Or answered."

A lonely fire, waiting for someone to talk to. She glanced behind, to the dead forest.

There was no returning.

Ahead, a choice to be made. Snowy mountain top or seaside.

Down, to a small ring of violet light.

Her choice was made.

"There's a third option," she admitted. "A tunnel under the mountain."

"Shouldn't be," it said. "See? Self-aware dead disturb things."

"Come on," she said, beckoning with a tilt of her head. "That tunnel looks dark, and dying hasn't given me night vision."

The fire shot sparks excitedly. "It may be a long journey."

"I'm dead," she replied, "I have all the time in the world."

Into the Dark of Night

Jon Alston

Rain tapped Edwin's sliding glass door to his bedroom, he was half asleep. Gray clouds darkened the evening sky. An occasional shoe or backpack left on the floor. The walls had been left nearly bare, containing only a single poster of a pair of Siberian Tigers over the head of his bed. Outside he could hear the low rumbling echo of distant thunder off the hills that surrounded his home. As the night progressed, the storm grew more violent; wind thrashed against the house, great flashes of lightning lit up Edwin's room followed by the crashing of thunder.

This did not really bother him much; he had always liked the sound of lighting and the smell of the rain when it soaked into the ground. Everything always felt fresh after a good storm, like a warm pair of socks just out of the dryer. He took off his glasses, placed them on his nightstand next to his alarm clock and a stack of books he was currently reading, and rolled onto his left side to go to sleep.

Edwin jolted upright in his bed. An exceptionally loud crack of thunder had startled him from his deep sleep, the sound resonating in his chest. He sat rubbing his eyes with his fingers, trying to wake them up too; he was wide awake now, and there was no sense trying to get back to sleep. After he had put his hands down from his face, he noticed something move at the end of his bed, but it was too dark to make anything out. Frightened, he picked up his glasses and put them on, pushing them on with the middle finger of his right hand. He looked again, but still nothing. He thought he could hear a low, heavy breathing, like that of a large tiger, but it was too soft to be certain.

"Who's there?" he said loudly. There was no response. He took a book from his nightstand and threw it at the shadows; all he heard was the dull thud it made when it hit the floor. The hair on his arms and neck began to stand on end, as if the wind outside had blown in and chilled his spine.

He tried to move, but his body would not obey him. Edwin started to breathe heavily, the weight of the shadows pressing in on him. The room began to shrink, and he knew that if he did not get out of his bed, the darkness would eventually consume him. This was the end for him. He did not know why, but he could feel it. A shiver slithered through his body causing him to shake uncontrollably, though he tried with all his strength to stop it.

A sudden flash of lightning illuminated the room and Edwin's heart nearly stopped. Sitting on the floor at the end of his bed was a very large light-gray creature, obviously wet from the pouring rain. Time had stopped as he stared into its large ice cold blue eyes. It had a face somewhat like a dog, but more slender and elegant with a much shorter muzzle. Two giant wings were folded against its sides, stretching to what Edwin thought would have spanned at least fifteen feet. Its body was covered in thick hair, including its wings, and it had two very long, pointy ears that stuck straight back off the sides of its head.

From his bed, Edwin could not see its feet or legs, but was certain that they too were as magnificent as the rest of its body. His mouth had fallen slightly open as he continued to stare into the creature's eyes, falling into a sort of trance.

"Edwin," it said, "I have been waiting for you." Its voice was soft and deep, yet full of great power. He was jolted to a conscious state again, taken aback that the creature had spoken to him; his heart began to pound rapidly. It was only now that he realized what he was looking at. It was something foreign he did not know, something that could kill him. Fear started to creep into his thoughts—*it knows my name?*

"How long have you been there?" Edwin asked, his voice trembling.

"Not long."

There was a pause, and neither said a word.

"Who… or, er… what, are you?" asked Edwin, trying to sound confident.

"That is unimportant. All that you must know is that I have come here for you, and we must leave quickly."

Come for me? What is going on here? Edwin thought. *I must be dreaming, please say that I am dreaming.* He pinched himself just to make sure he was really awake. He didn't know how that was supposed to tell him whether or not he was asleep, but he did it all the same. And of course, he felt it. He opened his mouth to speak, but only a small squeak came out. For a moment he paused and then he said with a stutter, "How do you know who I am?"

"All know you where I come from," it replied.

"All who know… wait, what?" Edwin could not believe what he was hearing.

"I have been watching you for years, Edwin. Ever since you first stepped into our forest, I have been ordered by the Queen to watch you."

"'Our Forest?'" He thought for a moment. "Do you mean the trees out by the school?"

"The same."

He had played in those redwood trees for as long as he could remember. Never once had he ever seen anyone else there before, not even a squirrel. Edwin did not know what to say or what to do. Certainly, if he were to get out of his bed the creature would attack, he had no doubt about that. But even if he managed to get away, what would he do? Surely his parents would not believe him that a gray flying dog-of-a-thing was sitting in his room, that it wanted to take him away. He started to panic, sweat building up on his forehead, his hands clenched tight around his comforter. Every other second he would glance at the door as if he were waiting for the right moment to run.

"Why do you want me?" Edwin asked, his voice still trembling.

"You have something that we need."

"What?"

"You do not need to know now, but you must come with me immediately."

"Not unless you tell me why first."

"I was told to come and gather you, and to say nothing of it to anyone—including you. I have already stepped over my bounds in conversing with you thus far. So I ask you again, come with me now," it said as it walked along the right side of Edwin's bed. Another shudder ran up Edwin's spine as he watched the creature coming closer to him. It sat next to him, staring down into his eyes. He had noticed as it moved, that a bushy tail of about four feet trailed behind it, swishing slightly back and forth through the air as it walked.

What is it that they could possibly want? I don't have anything. And who is this 'they' anyway? Maybe they want to sacrifice me or something? But why would they do that? Or maybe they are cannibals, and they want to eat me? Why me, though? There are hundreds of other kids, much fatter than I am they could eat. For a few moments, more thoughts of horror and death flashed through Edwin's mind as he wondered why this thing had come to him this night and not to someone else.

"What if I don't want to go?" Edwin said at last, though his voice lacked all confidence.

"Then I will take you with me all the same."

"Well, where will you take me then?"

"I will take you to our Queen."

"But where is she?"

"In the deepest part of the forest, as I have already said."

"Oh… but why me? I'm only fourteen, I don't know anything, I don't have anything." The creature just stared at him. Edwin could sense that it wanted to tell him precisely why it was there, but that its duty was far too important to break the orders that it had been given.

"There are things that even I do not understand, but I know that you are very important to my Queen. Terrible things are happening, and it is you that we must have to stop them."

"What do you mean terrible things? What is wrong?" Edwin started to feel a little less frightened by the beast as he began to feel almost sorry for these 'people,' although he did not know why; he started to sense that maybe the creature was not too dangerous after all.

"I cannot say. There are eyes that see and ears that hear that I know not of in this place. None but the Queen is supposed to know that I am here to see you, but we cannot know this for certain."

"What do you mean? There is no one else here."

"You know nothing of what is here and what is not. There are many things that appear not, that are."

"What?"

"You know nothing of my people and the Queen, yet we are. I was before I came to you, but you did not know of me, yet now you see me here. I have watched you every day in the forest since the first, but you never knew of me." It paused as it looked around the room. "The enemy watches from where you cannot see, and hears the same."

Edwin started to talk in a whisper. "So then what do you want from me?"

"I must bring you back to the Queen; she is in need of you."

"Yes, I know, but why? Please, just tell me."

"I have already told you I cannot speak of such things to you, especially not here. If you come with me, she will tell you all that you must know," it said tersely as it continued to survey the room.

"I don't know. Why should I trust you?"

The creature heaved a sorrowful sigh and then brought its eyes to meet Edwin's. He could see the pain worn on its face. It looked as though it had not slept for days, and Edwin began to feel that the creature was much more important than he could have possibly imagined. "I cannot make you believe. I know that this is hard to understand for you, b—"

"Hard to understand?" Edwin yelled, then continued in a whisper, "Hard to understand? This is way beyond 'hard to understand!' There is a six foot tall… thing in my room, talking about some 'hidden kingdom' in the woods that I've played in all my life but have never seen! No one else knows about it because no one else has seen it either, but you say it's there, and you want me to come with you though you can't tell me why. What do you expect me to think?"

It took a deep breath and said, "I do not know." It dropped its head lower so that it was level with Edwin's. "Forgive me my trespass my lord. I will tell my Queen that I have failed her." It turned away slightly and started to mumble to itself. "Another must be chosen, though I fear there is no other to be found."

"I thought I was the one you needed?" Edwin said defiantly.

"This is true, you are. But you are not willing, and I will not waste the Queen's time here if you do not agree to come and converse with her."

"Wait… but you said that you would take me anyway, even if I didn't want to go?"

"I did, but that was said with a hope that I would convince you of your importance to us. You have shown me, however, that you do not wish to accompany me back to the Queen or to help my people. Perhaps the Queen was wrong in thinking that you could help us," it said and turned to head out the sliding door that lead to the backyard.

Edwin did not know what to do. *Why don't I help him?* He thought. *They need me, don't they? Whoever they are. And besides, it's not like anyone needs me here. But what if he is lying to me? Perhaps he wants to lure me into the woods to eat me? Why would he waste all this time on me, though? I'm not the only thing he could eat.* He only stopped going over the creature's words when he heard the sliding door open, and the footsteps of the creature's large paws splash in a puddle in the backyard.

"Wait!" Edwin yelped. It stopped midway out the door and turned to look at him over its left shoulder. They stared at each other, Edwin not sure what to say. "What… what will happen to me if I go?"

It started to grin at him, closed its eyes for a moment and answered, "I will die before any harm comes to you, young master."

Edwin hesitated, apparently trying to make a decision. His eyes darted back and forth as he frantically tried to make up his mind. It felt as though hours had gone by before he spoke again.

"Okay," he said at once, his voice still hesitant and shaky, "I don't know why, but I will go with you." The creature's smile widened, and it came back into the room much more relaxed as though a heavy pack was taken from his back. Edwin got out of his bed and quickly opened his closet. He grabbed his raincoat, a pair of hiking boots, and a red beanie and hurriedly put them on. After fumbling for a few minutes with his boots, he said, "I guess I'm ready."

"Very well; get on," it said, bowing down on its front legs.

Edwin was not sure how to get on the creature's back without pulling out its hair, so he hap-hazardously threw himself over its side. Its fur was softer than the smoothest silk. It was the softest thing Edwin had ever touched, and he dug his hands and face into its side, holding it tightly around the middle. A low humming came from inside the creature, as if it were purring, though it did not sound anything like a cat. Edwin pulled the rest of his body up, throwing one leg over the top of the creature, straddling it much like someone riding a horse for the first time.

"Shall we leave now?" it said.

"Uh… I guess," Edwin said, still trying to find a good position to sit in on its back. Without warning the creature lurched forward into a full sprint, running out the open door and through the yard. Just before they would have crashed through the fence, the creature opened its large wings, pushed them down with great power, and the two of them lifted off the ground. Higher and higher they went with every flap of its enormous wings, Edwin trying to hold on as best he could. The wind was cold, and the rain stung his face like a swarm of aggravated wasps. A dark blanket of clouds filled the sky so that not even the moon was visible.

Edwin was cold and wet as they flew, but he did not care. The smell of fresh rain was in the air, and he felt completely weightless as he sat upon its back; it soared as effortlessly through the sky like a fish swimming through a calm pool of water. He had never felt so free in his life. It must have been like a dog being let out of a carrier kennel for the first time in years, running wild in an open field. That moment could have never ended, and Edwin would have been more than happy. All of the troubles and cares of the silent little world below him could not bother him up so high, and he wanted to keep it that way. But as soon as he became comfortable up in the darkened sky, they were landing softly down on the ground again. Its hind legs settled down first, followed by its front. Edwin could hardly tell that they had hit solid ground the landing was so exact.

"We must walk from here," it said. Edwin looked puzzled at the creature for a moment, until he saw where it was they had landed. They were standing at the foot of the forest that the creature had been talking about. The trees were tall, standing much higher than any of the buildings in the city behind them. Many of their trunks were so big around at the base that a Volkswagen Bug could have driven through them with ease. The beautiful dark red bark was much softer than most trees, feeling much more like rough fur than a hard shield of protection. Among the redwood trees were large green ferns. They stood two feet tall and covered the forest floor so that almost no dirt was visible. There were fallen snags that lay randomly within the ferns; Edwin knew that they had been dead for quite some time because of the little plants and moss that had grown all over them.

Edwin slipped off the creature's back and began to follow it through the sentinel trees that stood as guards on the outer edge of the forest. The two walked in silence, Edwin trailing behind having no idea where they were going. They continued in silence for over an hour; as they walked into the darkness, Edwin slowly began to become afraid again for his life.

He was sure now that this creature would not harm him, but he still had no idea why it needed him or what it was going to do with him once they had reached the Queen. Regardless, he followed slowly wiping his sweaty hands on his now damp coat. It was much quieter in the forest than it was in his room, the canopy of branches blocked out the sound of the storm and the city. Every twig breaking or swoosh of a plant sounded like gunfire. He was completely aware of everything around him, his senses more acute than usual because of the frightening silence.

Then Edwin suddenly stopped; his legs would no longer move. A hollow feeling grew inside his stomach as though someone, or something, had been standing right behind him ready to strike. Frozen to the spot, he tried to yell to the creature, but nothing came out. He tried again, but there was still nothing. As he stood there, mouth open, unable to move he started to panic.

"Edwin, we must continue," the creature said as it stopped and peered back at him. He said nothing for a moment, and it started to walk back towards him. It looked at him intently, then said, "What is troubling you?"

"I... I just can't... I just... I need to know," said Edwin, his voice shaking as if he were about to cry. A tear slid down his cheek. The creature looked all around, making sure that there was nothing else in sight.

"Hmmm, very well. But know that I cannot say all for even I do not know everything that you must desire."

"Okay." Edwin looked down at his feet for a moment before he started again. "What is your name anyway?" he said, though he did not know why he had asked that. The creature gave Edwin a small smile.

"You may call me Lorendor."

"Lorendor... well, it is nice to finally meet you," said Edwin as he stretched out his hand to stroke the top of Lorendor's head. Again it made the purr-like sound as Edwin pat him. He hesitated shortly again before asking what he had intended to in the first place. "Why me? What do you need from me? I have to know. No one has ever needed anything from me." He dropped his gaze back down to his feet. Lorendor put his left paw underneath Edwin's chin and raised his head up so their eyes met.

"You are a very special boy." It placed its paw back on the ground. "You have something that none other of your kind has."

"But what is that?"

"The memories of this forest."

"What?" Edwin wore a puzzled look on his face. "That is why I am so important? Because I have memories? I am sure loads of other people have memories of this place."

"I wish that were so," Lorendor's gaze saddened as he said this, gazing blankly at their surroundings. "If it were we would not have need of you... our world would already be safe."

"Are you saying that nobody else has a single memory of here?" The two of them began to walk again slowly along their previous path, Edwin placing his left hand on Lorendor's side.

"Since I have watched you for the last ten years, the only others that have come to these woods, come to cut them down."

"I don't believe that. Someone else has to have come here like me."

"There was a time, yes, when others like you loved the trees, the quiet, the solitary beauty. Some have even seen our kingdom, but that time has long since passed." Lorendor stopped to look at Edwin. "Now, you are the only one that can help us."

"But what do my memories have to do with anything? How does that help?"

"They are everything. Our world slowly dies as your world grows. With the passing of each year, more of the forest is lost as your people cut it down to build up your kingdoms. The memories that you have, the experiences you have had here, contain a powerful magic that many know not of. If you were to give us your memories, we could protect these woods."

"What? Well, if all you need are memories, why can't you use your own?"

"Because it is not that simple." He sat down among the ferns and beckoned Edwin to sit on a large stump beside him. "We have memories of here, that is true, but this is our world. We did not choose to be placed here, though we do love the beauty that surrounds us, much like you do. But you, however, you chose this place over the world that you come from. You have loved these woods more than your own home, and for that, your memories contain the power that all the memories of my world combined could not match."

Edwin placed his hands on the sides of the stump as he leaned forward. "So if I give you my memories of this forest... what does that do?"

"Everything." Lorendor looked up at the branches above them. "I have heard the Queen say, that with the power of your memories, she can use her magic to create a protection for our entire kingdom so that what is left of it can never be destroyed."

Edwin had loved that forest more than anything. Never had he thought about what had been happening to it all his life. He knew that the city was always growing, but he had not considered that in order for his world to grow, the forest had to die. He could not let the place where he grew up be destroyed, this much he knew.

"Okay, so what do I need to do?" said Edwin, a feeling of confidence flooding through him. For the first time in his life, he felt important, like he had a purpose in life.

Lorendor looked back at him. "The Queen will have to extract your memories."

"Okay, fine."

"It is not that simple, dear one. If you give them to us, you can never have them back."

There was silence. "What?" Edwin started to stand up.

"Your memories, once we have taken them and performed the ritual, they cannot be returned to you."

"You mean you can't just borrow them? I thought you only need their energy or something?"

"Not exactly. The spell used in conjunction with your memories will, in essence, destroy them."

"Wait, so you are just going to blow up my memories!"

"No, not at all. As you said, we need their energy, and the energy that they contain is immensely powerful. With the Queen's magic she can, according to the legends, take that force and transform it into a barrier that will cover this forest and protect those who dwell within it. This will, however, most likely consume all that was your memories, though I am not certain. This is magic that I have never seen used before." Lorendor looked at Edwin reading the conflict in his face.

Edwin did not want to give up his memories. He loved the forest. But because of that love, he also knew that he could not deny Lorendor and his people the power that he contained. *What should I do?* Edwin thought, kicking his feet against the stump he had been sitting on.

"Will... will I ever be able to get the memories back?"

"I do not know. This is ancient magic even for my people, but I do not believe that you will."

"Is there no other way we can do this?"

"No."

Edwin hesitated, frantically trying to decide what to do as he rubbed his hands together nervously.

"Okay… I'll… I'll do it." A sense of relief covered Lorendor's face as he wrapped Edwin in his wings like a mother putting a blanket around her shivering child.

"I thank you, Edwin. You have shown true courage tonight. Come; let us make haste to the Queen."

"Wait. Can you do it now? My memories I mean, can you take them now?" Lorendor looked at him puzzled.

"It is not my place to do so; it is for the Queen to do."

"Please, can you just do it now? I won't be able to do it if we wait, I will probably change my mind or something. I am already too scared of what is going to happen, and I can't wait to meet the Queen. Please Lorendor, can you just take them now?"

He looked at Edwin like a father watching his son having his leg amputated, wanting so badly to comfort him but not knowing how to do so.

"Very well. If that is what you wish. Come lay your head in my paws." He leaned back on his hind legs and took Edwin's head in his two front paws as they faced each other. Each paw was placed over Edwin's ears like a pair of wet gray earmuffs. "Are you certain that you wish me to do this?"

"Ye… yes. Just… do it quick." He saw Lorendor close his eyes, and so he did the same. Though his paws were wet, they were warm on Edwin's face, covering it almost entirely. Slowly he could feel Lorendor taking them away from his head as he muttered something under his breath; Edwin knew that this must have been some sort of spell that was going to extract his memories.

At the very thought of that, he felt a sharp pain in the back of his head, and he screamed in terror. It was as though two large hooks had clawed somewhere inside his head and were trying to tear his mind out through his ears. Harder and harder they pulled, feeling as though they were ripping his flesh. The pain grew as Lorendor continued the spell. It was not long before Edwin could not hear the muttering over the sound of his own screams. His mind was being torn to pieces like a leaf of paper in a shredder. Everything started to swirl around him as the pain became worse, and he tried to open his eyes to find a focus, to keep his balance. But it was as though a thick fog had settled in his brain, and Edwin's vision was so blurred that he could not even make out the shape of Lorendor still standing in front of him. Edwin soon felt that his legs would no longer support him, and he fell to his knees. He just wanted it to end, but the pain did not cease, it only grew stronger causing him to become nauseous. Everything kept spinning as he fought to stay conscious. If the pain did not end soon, Edwin knew that his head would burst from the pressure that was ripping his mind from his head. The ground started to slip away from him as the pain became too great for him to bear; an envelope of darkness covered his eyes, and he fainted.

Edwin woke the next morning in his bed, the storm from the night before having ended, the sun peeking out from around some of the remaining clouds. He sat up, took his glasses from the nightstand and put them on. He knew he had been dreaming all night but could not recall exactly what it was about. For a few moments, he tried to recall what the dream had been, but could remember nothing. Edwin looked outside the glass door at the colorful morning sunrise. The forest was in perfect view from his bedroom—he stared blankly at it. A large gray bird flew out of the middle of the trees, and Edwin wondered what it could be. He had never seen anything like it before; it was much larger than anything he had ever seen.

"Hmm," he sighed to himself, "someday I need to go into that forest…"

MERCY

MATTHEW MCKIERNAN

Elohiir crashed onto the ground, after taking only one sip from his silver goblet. It slipped out of his hand, spilling wine everywhere. Elohiir saw the tent spinning; he could not breathe. Every inch of his body felt like it was being crushed. He could not speak or move. He could not do anything, but think.

Is this death? No, I am not dying like this!

Elohiir found that he could still tap the tips of his fingers against the ground. That was enough to show him that he could fight against the poison and that he could live. He squeezed his eyes shut to stop the world from spinning. *How could this have happened?* If he could figure out what caused this situation, it would be the first step to overcoming it. He needed to think. He needed to keep his mind working in order to stay alive.

Poison! Of course, the Zassern would use poison, those damn cowards!

Elohiir's mind was racing. He had no idea how they had managed to sneak into his camp and poison his goblet. He needed to get outside. Otherwise, he was going to die alone inside his tent. The Zassern normally poisoned their enemies right before they attacked. Elohiir had no idea whether or not he could save himself, but he had to warn his comrades and give them a chance to prepare.

His left hand brushed by the sword encased in a silver scabbard attached to his right hip. Normally, his armor and weapon felt so light that he never noticed their actual weight. Now it was as though a mountain of steel covered his body, but Elohiir would not let that stop him. He clawed his way up to the table until his entire torso pressed against it. His legs wobbled as he took a deep breath and tipped the table over. Standing on his own two feet was almost impossible. Elohiir could not even feel the ground beneath his feet, as he turned around and stumbled outside of his tent.

He kept his eyes closed because everything was still spinning. It was pouring, and the rain felt icy cold. That was good because it would keep him awake. He had to keep his mind focused. Losing focus would lead to certain death before the poison did. Elohiir growled and slowly clenched his right hand into a fist.

I'm an elf, and I will not let this poison cloud my wits. Even if my body fails me, my mind will not!

Elohiir's long white hair waved through the swirling wind. It was going to storm tonight. He could hear howling in the distance. His pointy ears twitched, and his blue eyes shot open. The Zassern always sent their hounds to attack before they did so themselves.

As some of the elves were leaping out of their tents, those keeping guard helped to assemble them. Elohiir noticed many elves were stumbling, while others were not even leaving their tents. The wine diluted the potency of the poison for some elves, but not all.

They poisoned so many of us. I swear to the Gods that as long I am breathing, I will keep on fighting until I am dead. The Zassern will not be free from my wrath!

Elohiir ran, or at least he tried to. He almost tripped. It had been raining every night for the past week. Therefore, the ground was like mush. He drew his sword, and raindrops danced off the blade as the hounds attacked. The elves formed ranks, and the hounds struck for their necks. The hounds of Zassern were horrible, like their twisted masters. They rushed at the elves as they raised their shields in defense.

A hideous beast that was as black as the night and foaming at the mouth attacked Elohiir. The hound tried to bite Elohiir's face, but only bit his blade. He wrestled the hound to the ground and stomped on its neck with such great force, that it snapped like a twig.

The moment Elohiir pried his sword free from the dead hound's jaws, another hound lunged at him and closed its mighty jaws around his right arm. Elohiir's steel armor kept the hound's teeth from piercing his flesh, but the beast's grip was ironclad as it tugged with all its might. Through his foggy mind, Elohiir felt his joints snap as his right arm was dislocated.

Elohiir did not show a hint of pain as he pulled his right arm free. He put his sword in his left hand and kicked the hound with such great force that he knocked the beast onto its back. Elohiir stabbed his sword through the hound's skull and then slashed his blade across the face of the next hound that charged him. At that moment, Elohiir realized that the more he fought, the more he wore the poison down. He was starting to feel increasingly better.

All of Elohiir's comrades were now busy fighting the hounds off. The sounds of drums banging rumbled throughout the woods. The Zassern always used some sort of noise in order to mask their numbers. Elohiir was not going to let the Zassern confuse his mind. He quickly bent down, dropped his sword and popped his right arm back into is socket. He got back on his feet as the Zassern charged.

The Zassern were a human tribe that dressed in the skins of mountain lions, wolves, and sometimes even the skins of bears, all of which they skinned alive. They also wore the bones of their slain victims as armor. They had started this war by raiding and pillaging just for the fun of it. The bloodlust and sadism of the Zassern were legendary, but so was the military discipline and strength of the elves.

The Zassern charged. One of them threw a spear at Elohiir's head. He caught the spear in his left hand and flung it into the skull of his attacker. The Zassern fell dead on the ground. Elohiir picked up a more worthy spear, an elfin spear, from the grasp of one of his dead comrades. He ran and stabbed the spear through the chest of a Zassern, who was swinging an ax at him while slicing his sword across the neck of another Zassern that was attacking him with a dagger. They both fell dead on the ground.

The elves, while being overwhelmed, were still holding strong. The Zassern did not know how to fight in formation and form ranks. They would just keep charging at the elves repeatedly until they overwhelmed them. The battle raged on as Elohiir and his fellow elves managed to drive the Zassern back. Many elves still felt the effects of the poison while stuck up to their knees in mud. Yet they gave it their all. The elves managed to get the Zassern to retreat.

Elohiir ran with his companions after the Zassern. The storm raged on, and he swore he saw lighting strike a Zassern, who got back up, shrugged it off, and kept on running. Elohiir would not let the poison stop him. If tonight were his last night, he would make sure that the Zassern remembered him.

Elohiir and his companions found themselves splitting up, chasing after the Zassern, who were retreating in countless directions. He ran after the Zassern who had been struck by lightning. The lighting stuck Zassern met his end after tripping over a rock and Elohiir stabbing his spear into his throat. Elohiir now stood alone without a fellow elf or Zassern anywhere in sight. The night was young, and the battle was not even half way through. Elohiir took a deep breath and closed his eyes as he listened to his surroundings.

Elohiir was able to hear all the chaos going on around him. He ran north until he heard leaves crunching behind him. He spun around and found himself crossing blades with Hadrian, the general of the River Elves. Elohiir and Hadrian lowered their blades.

Hadrian spoke in his usual soft, but stern voice. "Elohiir."

"General."

General Hadrian was an inch taller than Elohiir. His hair was a silvery gray, and his eyes were piercing. General Hadrian looked into Elohiir's eyes, noticing that they were severely bloodshot. He could see that Elohiir had fought off the poison. He would have expected nothing less from him. Elohiir stayed on alert. "How bad is it?"

General Hadrian replied, "A disaster, very few of us escaped being poisoned. Thankfully, this poison is not as potent as the Zassern's normal brew. Still, it has confused everyone, making them spread out instead of staying in rank."

"Chaos is the Zassern's greatest weapon."

"Indeed, listen we need to find everyone and regroup. The Zassern want us to be out here running around like blood-crazed wolves so they can double back and burn down our camp."

"We can't let that happen," Elohiir replied.

"It will if I don't restore order. Now let's go."

Elohiir and Hadrian ran through the woods. They encountered many of their fellow elves lying dead against trees and in ditches. The sight of his dead comrades sickened Elohiir; so many of them had fought through the poison as he had, just to be cut apart like cattle. Suddenly, Elohiir heard the sound of a whip cracking.

The whip wrapped itself around Elohiir's right arm and yanked him to the ground with great force. Hadrian drew his sword but did not have the opportunity to swing it. The Zassern lunged at him and stabbed him in the shoulder with a dagger that was dripping with black ooze. Elohiir yelled, fought against the Zassern's grip, and managed to free himself. He swung his blade and took the Zassern out with one blow. He then bent down next to General Hadrian and examined his wound. The dagger had barely grazed him, but the poison had still entered his veins. Despite it being a very warm night, Hadrian was shivering. Elohiir helped the General back onto his feet.

Hadrian grunted to hold back the pain. "It is no use. My legs are as lifeless as stone."

Elohiir replied, "If I leave you here, you're as good as dead."

"As long as I can still draw a sword I will live. I order you to lead us to victory, Elohiir, and to only look for me when it's all over."

Elohiir nodded and gently set Hadrian against an oak tree. He ran with a determination sharper than any blade in existence. He managed to rally his fellow elves. The battle raged on until daybreak. Many brave elves died that night. When the slaughter was over, the rest of the elves stood as victors with their camp untouched. Elohiir had won; the battle was over. He managed to fight off the poison and live to have the warm glow of the rising sun wash over him.

Elohiir found Hadrian where he had left him. He was still alive with six slain Zassern scattered all around him. Hadrian was deathly pale, and he was lying on the ground shivering and in pain. Elohiir carried him back to camp and placed him in the healing tent. The sound of elves dying from the same poison that was killing Hadrian echoed throughout the camp.

Elohiir knew Hadrian would not yell out in pain. He would never give his enemies the satisfaction of showing any weakness. Many brave elves had died that night, but the army was still strong, and reinforcements would arrive soon. Everyone wondered whether General Hadrian would be alive to lead them in their next battle.

Elohiir spent the whole night praying to the Gods. They had granted him the strength to survive the poison and granted the elves victory against all odds. He knew it would be foolish to ask for any more than this. Nevertheless, he had no idea what path his life would take if Hadrian died.

After he finished praying, Elohiir waited outside the tent. The healer walked out and gave a quick shake of her head. Elohiir knew this was it and walked back into the tent. Every elf that was lying on a cot was dead, either from their wounds or from the poison. Hadrian still lived, but the flame of life that had always shone in his eyes was fading quickly. Still, Hadrian managed to turn his head and look Elohiir right in the eyes.

Elohiir stood firm as always. "Morning General Hadrian…"

"There is no more need for formalities, Elohiir."

Elohiir nodded. "Understood Father."

He bent down by his father's bedside and grasped his hand. Hadrian held onto Elohiir's hand with his remaining strength. General Hadrian took a long, painful breath. "I am sorry that I did not have the strength to fight off this poison."

"You had enough strength to kill six Zassern without the use of your legs; few elves could say the same."

"True, you live hundreds of years and go through countless battles and you know you'll probably die someday, but when the time comes, it catches us all off guard. It makes you wonder about things you did your best not to think about."

"What do you mean?" Elohiir replied.

"I wasn't there for your childhood. I missed far more than I had any right to. I thought that becoming a grandfather would give me another chance to do it right, this time, that's not happening now."

Elohiir tightened his grip around his father's hand. "You made me the soldier I am today, and I will always be grateful for that. If my first child is a son, he shall have your name. I have always been proud to have you as my father and my leader."

Hadrian hissed in agony, as a wave of utter pain flowed through his body. Gathering his remaining strength, Hadrian uttered. "I have one last order to give you my son."

"Speak it."

"Dying by poison is not a death worthy of any elf. I would rather die by the hand of my beloved son than my most hated enemy."

Elohiir almost burst into tears with what his father was asking of him, but he had no right to deny him this request. "As you wish Father."

Elohiir stood up and raised his sword up high. He held it right above his father's heart. General Hadrian's face was a mask of pain. "Wait, I want to see it coming."

Elohiir nodded and pointed the edge of his sword against his father's right eye. He stabbed his sword through his father's skull. Blood rushed out of Hadrian's head covering the pillow. Elohiir tightened his grip on the hilt of his sword. He did everything in his power to keep from weeping. With his father dead, by the laws of the caste system, he was now the General of the River Elves. He had no idea what he would do next, but he swore that after all the Zassern had done, he would show them no mercy.

Elohiir walked out of the tent with his father's blood dripping off his sword. Every elf able to stand was waiting for him outside the tent. They all knew that Elohiir was their General now. He stood tall and proud as his army saluted him. There was no time to mourn his father or even think of his own future. Now it was time to show his rank by giving his first order. Elohiir spoke with as much authority as he could gather. "Bring forth the prisoners."

It was law among the elves that the highest-ranking officer judged all prisoners captured during a battle. Of the seventeen prisoners, three were women. This did not surprise Elohiir, as all Zassern were killers. The men fought with weapons while the women used poison. These women had brewed the poison that had almost killed Elohiir and slain so many of his fellow River Elves. He already knew the sentence he would impose upon all of them.

Elohiir did not hesitate. "Death!" The elves cheered as Elohiir passed sentence. He would carry it out himself as his father had done. He showed no hesitation, as one by one, the Zassern prisoners met their end by his sword.

Finally, only the women remained. Two of them were quite old, with gray hair and skin that sagged from age. The third woman was somewhere in her early or mid-twenties, with wheat-colored hair and countless facial piercings. She looked at Elohiir with a smile on her face, as though she knew something he did not. Elohiir would not suffer a hint of humiliation during his first day as General. She would have to die now. As he raised his sword against the woman's head, she started laughing. She had nothing left to defend herself with and yet, she acted as though she had won.

Elohiir spoke to this wretched woman. "Why do you laugh?"

"I know your laws elf! You can kill prisoners for being your enemies. But you cannot slay those who have done you no harm." The Zassern woman replied.

"What do you mean?"

As she stood up, Elohiir could see the roundness of her belly. His wife's belly had been slightly rounder the last time he had been home. Elfin law forbade the killing of children too young to fight, babies and women with child. He would not be able to kill this woman until she gave birth. It was wrong beyond all measure, that while his father and comrades were rotting, this terrible woman would have a stay of execution because of her condition.

Elohiir held back his rage and spoke to the woman with as much indifference as he could muster. "Due to your condition, you will be moved to Fort Elk Wood, where you will be kept well fed and healthy until your child is born. Once your baby is born, your execution date will be set."

"Do not speak to me like I am nothing, Blade Ears. I am Vinra, the maker of death. I crafted the poison that killed so many of you, and I will not let you take my baby from me!"

"You are our prisoner now. Once your baby is born, we may do whatever we wish. Get her out of my sight."

The guards took Vinra away, while Elohiir killed the last two prisoners. Afterwards, the crowd dispersed, and Elohiir went to what once had been his father's tent. He then read a letter containing his father's orders, his orders now. Fort Elk Wood would be his new command post. He knew he had a difficult task ahead of him. This war still had no end in sight, but dealing with Vinra would be worse than any battle. She would be a constant reminder of the death of his father.

After a few weeks, Elohiir decided to visit Vinra. The prison at Fort Elk Wood was in the tallest tower. The elves believed all prisoners had the right to sunlight. The tower prison was a small room with nothing inside except for Vinra. Her wrists were tightly chained to the wall. All she wore now was a huge brown sack that went all the way down to her feet.

Her prison cell was spotless. The elves prided themselves on cleanliness, so even their prisons did not have a speck of dirt in them. Elohiir figured that Vinra was cleaner now as a prisoner than she ever had been as a free woman. He had also made sure that she was adequately fed.

Vinra looked as confident as ever as she pulled on the chains to stand up straight. "Have you come to gloat, General?"

Elohiir replied, "No. I am just here to inspect things."

"You didn't come here to see if you can get me to talk?"

"The only way anyone can get a Zassern to say anything of value is through torture of the most extreme variety. However, since you are with child, you cannot be tortured. Once you give birth, I will remedy that."

Vinra snickered. "What a lovely people you elves are."

Elohiir moved some loose strands of hair that were covering his right eye as he responded. "We are a race that knows honor. All humans are dishonorable and spiteful. However, your tribe is monstrous. You show no mercy, empathy, or remorse. You are a blight on all that is good in the world, and I pray for the day when the Zassern are gone and forgotten."

Vinra gave her chains a playful twist. "We will be remembered for our deeds forever. Sneaking in and poisoning your wine as you all slept, that is a tale for the ages. For if crawling under the nose of one elf is an incredible feat, what do you say of crawling under the noses of thousands of elves? We have done and will continue to do things so horrible that no one will be able to forget them. No matter how much they want to."

Elohiir could not deny that Vinra was right. No one ever forgot unspeakable acts of evil. It gave those who committed these deeds power beyond the grave. He decided that Vinra had taken away enough of his time. Elohiir could always remind her that being born a Zassern had landed her in chains.

A few days later, Elohiir received a letter. He tore it open and prepared to read it without a second thought. He had seen and signed more letters in these past three months as general than he had in his whole 172 years of life. He was bored to tears from reading all of them. However, when he read this letter, his life changed forever.

Elohiir smashed his hands against his desk until they bled. The letter, that damn letter. He collapsed to the ground sobbing, wishing he had never opened it. His wife had died after giving birth to a stillborn son. Born dead, cursed never to know a moment of life. Perhaps, seeing she had given birth to a dead baby had made Elohiir's wife lose her will to live. That did not matter now. They were gone. There was no one he could blame, no one he could kill to get revenge for them.

Tragic events like this happened, but never did Elohiir fathom anything like this could ever happen to him. If he had been there, he could have tried to save them or at least done something. Instead, he was hundreds of leagues away while his wife had died, heartbroken and alone. Elohiir's hands grasped the hilt of his sword. He wanted to throw himself on it, end his life, and join his family.

He knew he could not end his life to be with them. Despite his desire for death, he was the General of the River Elves. He would not betray his men by ending his life over a personal loss. Instead, Elohiir stormed outside through two feet of deep late winter snow and hacked away at the first tree he spotted. He slashed his sword against the tree until his arms were numb and tears had frozen on his face. Elohiir spent the next few weeks living in his chambers. His men avoided him. They could all tell his soul was broken from grief.

A few days later one of the prison guards told Elohiir that when Vinra had overheard him speaking of the death of his wife and child, she began cursing them. Elohiir could tolerate Vinra cursing his name and the name of his father, but his wife and stillborn son had done no harm to the Zassern.

Vinra was sleeping peacefully when Elohiir kicked open her cell door. He wrapped his left hand around her throat. "You dare mock my wife and son. Damn you! My wife harmed no one, and my son did not enjoy even a second of life. What right do you have to curse them?"

Elohiir released his hand from Vinra's neck. She took in a large breath of air. "I say whatever I want to elf. Your family dying gives me greater joy than you will ever know. All whom I love have died thanks to you and your kind. I only regret that it was nature and not my poison which claimed their lives."

Elohiir struck Vinra across her face with such fury that his chainmail scrapped her left cheek tearing it open. He hit her repeatedly until her face was bloody. Her eyes were so swollen she could barely see, but the fire of defiance was still there. Elohiir grabbed Vinra's hair and pulled on it so hard he almost tore it out of her scalp. "I hope to the Gods your baby is born dead!"

Vinra spat out a mouthful of bloody spit into Elohiir's face. "My baby…"

Her words left her as her face contorted in pain. Elohiir's beating and her own rage had put her into labor two months early. Vinra cried out as blood started dripping down her legs. Elohiir let go of her hair and took a step back. Vinra clenched her chains as the pain increased. She forced back a scream. "I shouldn't be giving birth now! Please, Elohiir get a healer or a nurse, get somebody!"

Elohiir could easily get someone to help Vinra through her labor. However, he was not going to do that. He was content with having her give birth alone like a wild beast. If the baby lived, it lived; if it died, it died. Either way, she would not be raising it. Vinra's ability to speak left her as she went fully into labor. After several hours of heavy breathing and struggling, Vinra's baby was born.

It was a boy. A beautiful baby boy whose cries filled the cell, the moment he entered the world. Elohiir saw that he was smaller and skinnier than a full term infant. Besides that, he seemed perfectly fine. He could not recall the last time he had seen a baby. Since the elves had been fighting many successive wars, births were rare.

My own son probably didn't look much different from him. Only he is born quite alive while my son was born dead. That is not fair, but I cannot hate this child no matter how much I wish to. He is innocent and completely helpless like any other infant.

Vinra had passed out from the pain of giving birth. Elohiir did not bother to wake her. Instead, he dashed out of the cell and came right back holding a small knife, some cloths and a sky blue silk blanket. He used the knife to cut the baby's umbilical cord. Then he cleaned the baby gently with a white cloth and wrapped him up in the silk blanket. This blanket was supposed to have been the first of many gifts for his son, not the child of his enemy. However, that did not matter now.

Elohiir rocked the baby in his arms until he went to sleep. Then Elohiir sat down against the wall, completely drained from all the events that had just happened. He wondered what should be done with this Zassern baby. He did not have any Zassern tattoos or scars on him. He could leave the infant in any human village or give it to any human couple.

For this child to be saved from his evil bloodline, he needs stronger guidance and discipline than any human could give him. *There are many who will be against it, but I should raise him. I will show him the proper path and free him from the sins of his ancestors.*

Elohiir stood up. As soon he was almost out the door, Vinra woke up. Elohiir glanced at her with eyes free of anger. "It's a boy."

"Let me hold him. Let me hold him!"

Vinra could barely stand; nevertheless, she struggled against the chains. No matter how hard she tried, she could not free herself. Elohiir turned around and spoke in a voice of utter detachment. "Your poison took my father from me. I think it is fitting that I take your son from you. I shall raise him to hate the Zassern as much as I do. He will know nothing of you, not even your name."

Elohiir walked out of the cell, while Vinra thrashed and shrieked like a dying hawk. As long as Elohiir lived, he would not forget the sound of her screams. However, they would not haunt him. Instead, he would treasure every single one of them. They would be constant reminders of his victory over her and would fuel his mind for a grand plan of vengeance.

Thirteen Years Later

Hundreds of Elohiir's men gathered in a gorgeous green field to witness the execution of the prisoner. Cadeus stood at Elohiir's side ready to prove himself. Cadeus was a strong lad, with a head of messy red hair and soft brown eyes. Adopting a human as his son had caused quite a scandal. One of the benefits of inheriting his father's command was that Elohiir had inherited his father's very influential friends as well.

With a few promises and promotions, Cadeus was his. Elohiir had brought up Cadeus with a proper hatred for the Zassern. He had told Cadeus that he had found him in a small human fishing village, the only survivor of a horrible Zassern raid. The best lies were the ones that were mostly true. The fishing village was real and so was the massacre; there had just been no survivors.

Cadeus had been quite shocked when his father had asked him to be the one to perform the execution. His skill with a sword and spear were decent, but he had never killed a living thing. Today he would for his father. When Elohiir saw that all of his men were standing in attendance, he smiled and shouted, "Bring forth the prisoner."

The guards dragged Vinra out of her cage; chains bound her hands and feet. She looked as though she had aged thirty years since Elohiir had last laid eyes on her. A haggard and thin-haired woman, whose tongue had been cut out so no one would have to hear her screams. That was after she had suffered countless whippings, beatings, and burnings to tell all she knew of the plans of her fellow Zassern.

They tied Vinra to a huge stone block. Elohiir twirled his spear and handed it to his son. Cadeus carried the spear with confidence but looked unsure at his target. Elohiir decided to have some last words with Vinra. He walked over to her. Vinra was terrified of Elohiir. She whimpered more and more with every step he took towards her. Elohiir noticed her eyes glued to Cadeus, and he spoke to her in a harsh whisper. "That's right, Vinra. Cadeus was your son; now he's mine and today you will die by his hand."

Elohiir gave Cadeus the nod and Cadeus tightened his hold around his spear. With trembling hands, Cadeus aimed the spear at Vinra's heart. One good thrust and she would be gone. He had dreamed of killing a Zassern, but he always imagined that his first kill would be a man on the battlefield. Not a defenseless woman tied in chains.

"Father..."

"Yes, Cadeus?"

"Never mind..."

Elohiir crossed his arms and smirked. Thirteen years was less than a snap of a finger to an elf. Still, he felt that this day was a long time coming. Vinra was trying to say the word son, but without a tongue and with many missing teeth, it was pointless. Elohiir smiled to himself. This was a fitting end for her.

He looked into Vinra's eyes and his heart froze. Elohiir had looked into the eyes of the countless elves who had died by her poison; none had shown the suffering he saw in her eyes. Elohiir could see his reflection in Vinra's eyes, and he saw a monster. The Zassern had never done anything as cruel as this, making a son kill his own mother.

As all this was going through Elohiir's mind, Cadeus put the tip of his spear against Vinra's chest. The poor boy looked to be on the verge of crying. He did not want to do this, but he had to make this father proud. As Cadeus was about to thrust the spear into Vinra's flesh, Elohiir grabbed the spear tightly. "A man's first kill should be on the battlefield; otherwise, he'll never know true courage."

Cadeus nodded as his heart flooded with relief and he handed the spear to Elohiir. "Thank you, Father."

Elohiir gave his son a brief smile. Then he looked Vinra in the eyes and mouthed the words, "I'm sorry."

Elohiir stabbed the spear into Vinra's heart, ending her torment. He did not know whether his actions against Vinra had been right, but he had shown her mercy in the end.

PILLARS OF MARS

MIKE EVIS

What on earth? He swiftly corrected himself. *This isn't Earth,* he thought, *you're on Mars, the fourth planet, somewhere you've always wanted to go and here you are, you've made it at last after all those years of training.*

What he was seeing was clearly impossible. Ahead of him were two pillars, dark and tall, looming up from behind the rocks, standing in stark contrast to the red sand around. They were far too perfect to be natural, but they couldn't be man made. No human had ever been here before. This was why Doug's expedition was here, exploring this area, simply because there'd never been any probes or rovers sent to this area. Unless the Russians, Chinese or the Europeans had landed something here they didn't know about.

He steered the rover round to the side of the rocks, where the strange, impossible columns poked upwards. It had to be some sort of illusion, perhaps some unusual rock formation. As Doug rounded the other side, he could see the sand stretching smoothly ahead for miles, like a calm red ocean.

"Base, are you getting this?"

The cameras on the rover should be transmitting everything he saw.

"Affirmative. Lovely view, Doug. What is it?"

"I don't know. Can you check if anything has ever landed in this area—not one of ours, but maybe the Russians or somebody. Or God knows who?"

"Yeah, will do."

Static burst through the speakers on the radio as he brought the rover to a stop. Then silence, the pure silence that had lasted unbroken for billions of years on Mars before humans arrived on this barren planet.

He'd always had a hankering for Mars—that tantalisingly close neighbour of Earth, shining like a red beacon in the night sky—and as a teenager had devoured all the books that speculated and fantasized about it—the long dead fantasies of Edgar Rice Burroughs, with their vivid descriptions of a dying world, peopled with exotic races, beautiful princesses, glorious cities, and empty canals, the Mars Leigh Brackett had written about set a million years in the past, through to Robert Heinlein's 'Stranger in a Strange Land'. Years before he was born, though, those dreams of Mars had been shattered for good by the Mariner probes, and then later probes too, all of them showing a cratered, airless world as lifeless as the Moon.

He had to go and see for himself. There was a whole world to explore, perhaps not as large as the Earth, but as big as Africa. And what if there was something there, after all, waiting to be discovered?

"Base, I'm getting a closer look."

"Okay."

"Switching to the camera in my helmet."

"Roger that."

Nothing on Earth could compare with the sheer emptiness and the loneliness here, except perhaps the snowy expanses of the South Pole. Back on Earth, there was nowhere left to explore. It had all been done. Here, go less than a mile or two from the base in any direction and you would be walking where no human footsteps had ever been before.

A shiver went down his spine as he climbed down from the rover, and in strict contravention of the rules, jumped down the last few feet from the little craft. Loose sand flew a few feet in the Martian air.

The radio squawked.

"Doug, are you okay? We picked up a lot of wobble just then on your camera."

"No problem, base, I probably got off a bit awkwardly."

"You just take care."

The twin columns lay directly ahead. They stood, alien and out of place on this vast plain of red sand. They must have risen to over forty feet high, and were roughly ten feet apart. He felt a further shiver run down his spine. There was a burst of static on the suit radio.

"Doug, base here. We ran a check, and as far as we know, no probe, or lander, or anything else has been here before."

"Thanks. Close up, it doesn't look like that sort of thing anyway."

"We're trying to analyse it from this end, and we'll get Ground Control to take a look. You're the guy on the ground, though."

He tried to consider the possibilities. Some natural piece of hard rock, perhaps sandblasted over millennia? Or a secret mission of some kind that no one knew about, leaving behind this monument? For that was what it looked like, nothing other than a monument. He shook his head at such a crazy thought.

Another burst of static. He stood about ten feet away now. The pillars towered over him, in a way that struck him as menacing. *No, that is stupid,* he thought, *how could they possibly be menacing? You're a scientist, try and stick to facts, what you can see, not what you feel.* It was just their sheer height, that was what made him feel uneasy. And the fact that the pillars weren't natural, and that they weren't made by the human race. In which case, they could only have been put there by aliens…

"I'm about five feet away now. This artefact, natural rock formation, whatever the hell it is, is now high above my head."

He turned his head so the camera would capture the landscape all around the columns. To him, it looked like the pillars had just been arbitrarily deposited here on this plain. Perhaps the idea was to make them stand out. They certainly did.

"We're getting occasional breaks in transmission," said the voice on the radio. "Can you repeat?"

Now Doug knew what the pillars reminded him of. Standing in front of them it was like when he'd visited Stonehenge. The awe he'd felt on Salisbury Plain at those huge standing stones, the sense of vast antiquity and unknown purpose—it was exactly the same, except that the pillars could only be far, far older. Just how long had they stood here, waiting to be discovered? And, crazy though it seemed on this dead planet, he couldn't help feeling an immense sense of the spiritual and the vast Beyond.

"Doug, are you okay? We're still getting periodic glitches in transmission."

"Yeah, I'm fine, just taking in the view."

"Let's hope your camera is picking this up okay."

He walked forward a few more feet. The pillars were round, completely dark, pitted with tiny indentures, coming from thousands of years of desert sand being blown against them, he guessed. As he walked, he tried to describe what he saw for the benefit of his audience. For all he knew, they might be showing this live back on Earth. Live given that it would take long minutes to get there.

"The pillars are about nine inches in diameter, a bit dull and pitted all around, eroded by the sand. Far as I can tell, they are the same diameter all the way up. Both pillars are identical."

He paused. The sun was almost directly overhead now, a sun distinctly smaller than it appeared from Earth. As he bent to look more closely at the pillars, he saw that despite their roughened surface, they gleamed in the sunshine. That surely wasn't quite right.

He gulped.

"This doesn't look natural to me."

"We've still got things to check at this end, but we read you, Doug."

He looked up to the top of the pillars. There was no way this was natural.

"I think this is definitely artificial. But who built it? It certainly wasn't put here yesterday."

Around the base of each column, the sand was piled up inches high. There were no footsteps here, and over millennia the drifting sand had erased any sign of their construction, had there been any to see. The only marks around were Doug's own steps leading from the rover. The columns had stood here for a very long time, judging by their pitted surface.

"Doug, what do you think it's made of?"

"Metal, I should imagine. That's what it looks like."

He put his glove on the surface of the nearer pillar. Through layers of insulation, his hand felt the rough surface and—was it his imagination, or was there a slight warmth coming from it? *Probably just where the sun had warmed it*, he thought, feeble though its power was here.

"You want me to get a sample?"

He rummaged for his hammer in the pouch of his suit.

"Yeah… no, wait."

Another huge burst of static. *Where is that coming from? The sun?* If there'd been solar storms on the way, surely the agency would have warned them. He continued to examine the pillars. Incredible though it seemed, it was beginning to sink in that he had discovered evidence of extraterrestrial life. And he was the first person ever to do so. Unless this was all a very elaborate hoax played by his colleagues.

No footprints, though. And how would they have smuggled two forty foot pillars onto the ship, or else cobbled something this large together on the base, when supplies were always at such a premium? No, that didn't really make sense. But when the alternative was so incredible you had to think of all the options.

"I'm walking around the outside of the two pillars now. They look identical in every detail, except for the sand erosion. No markings, otherwise."

"Doug, we're sending some of the others out. Stay put until they get there."

"Affirmative. I'll just walk around a bit…"

Another burst of static nearly deafened him. He peered at the pillars again, closely. What secrets could they hold? Was he really the first man to discover an extraterrestrial artefact?

He stepped between the two pillars. For a second or so, he had the strange sense that something had pushed back against him, and then it was gone. He shrugged, then an even louder burst of static sounded in his ears, so loud that, despite all the years of training, he came close to taking his helmet off.

Then everything changed. Suddenly he felt himself falling. And where were the pillars? They were gone; instead, he saw black space, filled with stars and galaxies, gently revolving in front of him. Like a film run at the wrong speed, everything was getting faster. Colours swirled and unknown, unimaginable images sped past his eyes. Was there a hidden hole in the desert he'd fallen into? He could be falling hundreds of feet down into a deep pit, disguised by the drifting sand, between the two pillars.

There was nothing but static on the radio now, though thankfully it was quieter than before.

"Base, can you hear me?"

Nothing.

"Base, are you receiving?"

"Base, this is Doug. Something odd has happened. Do you read me?"

Still nothing.

He had stopped falling but still everything whirled around him. Stars, galaxies, black space, all dissolved and reformed in front of him at a maddening speed. In time the images changed, now he saw fragments from memories, but they so vivid they were more than just memories, he was actually reliving real events: he saw his many goodbyes before the mission, culminating in the pained farewell to Lorraine and the hurt in her eyes, then time jumped backwards and he was still in training, he saw an old girlfriend, long before Lorraine, then time moved back further still, and he was reliving his childhood. On and on it went and he became dizzy and more and more disoriented.

With one final grasp at sanity, he tried the radio again.

"Base, this is Doug."

Static.

What the hell has happened? Why is no one answering? Has something... a solar flare perhaps, knocked out all communications? Or, worse still, perhaps a planetary dust storm has wiped out the base camp, is that what has caused all this? Still, the visions continued, accelerating further. Memories, both recent and long past, darted vividly before his eyes, alternating with images of strange and beautiful things he could hardly comprehend. He felt a great weakness and weariness. With his last thoughts before he succumbed to unconsciousness, he realised it must be the oxygen level in his suit. The tanks must be empty, there was a leak, and he had run low. That was the only explanation. *Odd that the alarms hadn't gone off, though.*

He came to. How long had he been out for? The sun—he could tell from the sun. Odd that it seemed so much larger and brighter now, though. But he was alive, he was breathing, and the oxygen levels were okay. He still had several hours of oxygen left. Unless of course, this was still part of his hallucination. *Blocked tube, that must be it. It isn't a leak. That's what caused it all, simply a blockage. Happens every now and again.*

He sat up, still feeling a bit drowsy and weak. The plain of sand stretched, just like before, on to the horizon. He turned round to see the pillars. Odd. They were slightly further away than he expected. Strange, but he must have walked, or crawled away from them. *Well, I'm alive. And breathing. Better get the suit checked out when I get back. Still static on the radio, though.*

"Base, are you—"

He never finished the call. Something struck him on the back of the head. It must be his crew mates. They were playing a prank on him. The whole thing was a prank. Involuntarily he heard himself saying "Come on, knock it off—"

Then another blow, even heavier. The suit was designed to withstand some impacts, but he could see a large crack spreading across its visor now. *Jesus—* he was a dead man with the helmet ruptured.

Turning, he saw a man, but it couldn't be a man, not with skin such a shade of blue. Doug hardly had time to dwell on it, noticing instead the huge polished sword the man was wielding. Its blade must have been two or three feet long. That was what had hit him. And he was ready to strike again. Somehow, Doug remembered his fitness moves, and his training, and rolled quickly to one side. The cracks were still spreading in his helmet, but he managed to pick up a handful of sand and throw it in the face of the blue man. Temporarily blinded, the man wheeled round. Doug felt the sword slash right across the chest of his suit, cutting right through the material and draining blood from him. *This is it, I really am dead.* He had minutes at the most while the oxygen leaked away, maybe even less than that. Except, why didn't he hear a hiss of air as it escaped? And come to that, how was this ferocious blue man breathing without a space suit? He had to be an oxygen starved hallucination. *Is any of this real?*

There was no question that the painful cut across his chest was real, that was for sure. And the ache in his head, that was real too. No time to think. He grabbed more sand and threw it at the blue man. Clad only in some kind of animal skin, though what kind of animal Doug didn't care to think, with dark red striped fur, the attacker stumbled. Doug went to grab the sword. It was obvious the blue man would kill him given half the chance.

Despite the suit impeding him, Doug reached with a strength he didn't know he had and grasped the sword from the man's loosened grip. Pulling with a sudden movement, he yanked it out of the surprised blue man's hand.

Still half blinded, the man tottered forward towards Doug, and Doug brought the sword crashing down onto his head, staggering back himself from the impact and the weight of the sword. The blue man fell onto the sand, and lay there motionless, a trickle of green liquid running away from his head. His hair was matted and unclean. *Are there others? Maybe I can get away.*

He examined the sword. It was a silvery colour, with rust marks in places, and strange markings, like no language or script he'd ever seen before. He was still alive. Surely all the oxygen must have leaked out of his damaged suit by now; his helmet was cracked, and there were several long gashes in his suit. Was this man's first encounter with an alien? If so what had he done? The alien lay dead on the sand. What a mess, but there was nothing else he could have done. No time to think about that, he realised. He needed to get away. He hefted the sword. It might yet come in useful.

The sensible thing might be to head back to the pillars. But where were they? He looked all round. The plain was featureless, the sand stretched away in all directions. There were no pillars in sight. Surely they couldn't have gone that far whilst they were fighting? He looked all round again and saw nothing but the endless plain of sand. And nothing in his training had prepared him for any of this. A crash landing; damage to the spacecraft in flight; depressurisation, they'd thought of everything, but not being attacked by a mad blue man with a sword.

Maybe this was just the last few minutes of an oxygen starved delirium. In which case, it would all soon be over. He started to walk away. *Will they track my footsteps?* All he could do was walk. There were no features to be seen so it didn't matter which direction.

The sun was low in the sky when he stopped. The oxygen level had been empty for hours. In any case, with all those leaks, there couldn't be any left, could there? So how was he breathing? What was he breathing? On Mars, they'd always taught, you'd asphyxiate within a matter of minutes if you didn't freeze first. But it didn't feel cold, not even with the holes in the suit. Somehow, with his suit ruptured, and a sword wound, he'd survived. He waved the sword in the air. It left his hand and sailed up into the sky before gracefully, slowly, falling to the ground. Well, that was one familiar thing then—the gravity was the same.

So if the oxygen was out, and he was still alive, he might as well take his helmet off. It went against all he'd ever been taught, it was like breaking a taboo, but the only thing that made sense was that the air was breathable. If it wasn't, then everything would soon be over.

He slowly unscrewed the helmet, his fingers feeling uncertain and wary. There wasn't even a gasp of air as it came loose. The tanks and the suit were empty. There was probably some oxygen in the emergency reserve but what use was that? A few minutes that was all that would provide, and he'd need the emergency oxygen mask too. He certainly didn't feel like he couldn't breathe. There was just something a bit strange, something so small you could hardly notice, about the smell of the air. It was a hint of a metallic smell. Or was it simply that he'd breathed canned air for too long? *Hang on,* this still didn't make much sense. He couldn't possibly be breathing air, this was Mars. What was happening? The pillars, the strange experience when he'd stepped between them, the ferocious attack by the sword-wielding blue man. None of it made any sense.

There was still power in the radio. He tried it again, convinced nothing would happen.

"Base, this is Doug, do you read?"

Just static. It was never going to work. Nothing but static. He was on his own, completely. He stood there for a moment, hands by his side in dejection. The helmet, cracked and broken in several places, lay on the ground.

This featureless and endless plain perhaps wasn't quite as endless as he'd thought; in the distance he could see a mountain range, shimmering slightly. And that wasn't right either, on Mars, there wasn't enough air to cause any shimmering. He shrugged. Nothing was right now. Nothing was believable. Everything was wrong except the gravity. The sun looked too large, the air was breathable and what about that strange blue man that attacked him? *This is crazy, just crazy.*

He sat down on the sand. The ground felt surprisingly warm through his suit. He had food in the form of emergency rations. That would see him through tonight, maybe the morning. *And then?* He shrugged. *No use worrying about that, is there?* The emergency rations were all God awful semi-dried stuff, but if you took some water with it, it was just about bearable. The water might be more of a problem, especially in this desert. He had barely half a bottle left.

The sun glistened above the distant peaks. *Like nothing on earth,* he thought, and then laughed to himself. For it was nothing on earth. Shadows were lengthening, and the red of the sky was slowly turning to a darker hue. In a minute the first stars would be out. *Analyse,* he thought as he chewed on his rations. That's what he'd been taught way back in training, analyse. Well, he'd like to see them try that here. The pillars, the blue man, what did it all mean?

And now there was something seriously wrong with the sky. As he watched, something impossible happened. A vast ghostly shape was rising in the far distance, where the plain stretched to the horizon. It wasn't one of the tiny Martian moons. Nor was it Earth's moon, even though it had been some years since he'd last seen moonrise on Earth. No, this was far too large, like a grotesque balloon or an enormous lantern. Pale red, as he watched, minute by minute it rose sedately free of the horizon as if mocking him.

I have to keep my sanity, he thought, as the huge globe drifted higher into the sky. He shivered. Minute by minute the sky grew darker still and that impossibly big moon grew brighter and rose higher. Now the stars began to come out. Maybe if he tried to recognise the constellations that might give him a clue. Above this endless plain, the stars hung brightly in this vast sky. He searched the sky for patterns, but there were so many stars it was almost dizzying to see. He had to look away and then look back, to try to make out from the teeming millions of stars the familiar Northern Hemisphere patterns: the Plough, Orion the Hunter. There was nothing he could recognise at all. There was a strange zig-zag pattern of stars near the mountains, but it wasn't Cassiopeia, it was too large for that. And where was Polaris, the Pole Star? Nothing was recognisable.

Hang on, he thought, *on Mars, I'd been in the Southern Hemisphere.* So that was why he didn't recognise any of the stars. The Southern Cross, that was the thing to aim for. He scoured the sky but, despite it being distinctive, he had to admit he couldn't find that either. He shivered again, as a horrible thought began to dawn on him. If the constellations weren't familiar, that must mean he wasn't on Mars. Or anywhere close by. *But how can that be?*

It was the pillars, had to be. Something had happened when he stepped through them. He'd seen all manner of hallucinatory images, memories, and visions. *What if…? Could it have transported me somewhere?* No, that was too incredible. But then, so was what he'd experienced. Just how far would you have to travel before you didn't recognise any of the star patterns? Some distance, he guessed. Surely a few light years away—even tens of light years away—they'd still look vaguely the same. Had those pillars somehow transported him across space? So he was no longer on Mars, but somewhere else entirely, somewhere millions of light years away?

But space and time weren't separate, he thought, so could it be that he'd travelled in time too? He could just as well be millions of years in the past—or the future. *My God.* He should have stayed close to the pillars. He lay down on the warm sand, under that alien sky, even though he knew sleep wouldn't come easily. Were those unknown stars of the far distance, stars of the past, or stars of the future? Where had the pillars sent him?

There were theories, not proven, of so-called wormholes in space that could connect wildly different regions in space and time. *Is that what the pillars did?* Even more outlandish theories talked of other, multiple universes, of our own universe being merely one amongst many, and of these universes being separated by something far less than a hair's breadth. The thoughts whirled round in his mind, as the silent stars shone down from that alien sky.

It must have been towards dawn that he slept, for he had a vivid dream. The blue man had tracked him down and was sitting on him, about to strike with his sword… He woke with a shock, in a cold sweat, to find he couldn't move. Something was pressed hard against his throat. He squirmed; from his position all he could see was the sky, starting to glow red in one corner. Squirming some more, he was able to see…

It was a woman, blue-skinned like the man who'd attacked him earlier. She wore a cloak made of light blue coloured fur. She stood above him, with a boot made from the same animal skin planted on his throat. He realised the mistake he'd made, for it was his sword she held in her hands. *This world is mad indeed,* he thought, *perhaps I should never have woken up.*

Realising he'd seen the sword, she moved her foot from his throat, replacing it with the tip of the sword. She spoke, but in no language he understood or could even imagine. The sounds were guttural and urgent. As he looked up at her, she sounded increasingly irritated, jabbing the sword at his chest. He shook his head, but that just made her voice louder. *Was everyone here completely mad?*

>◊< >◊< >◊<

"Play that over again, only more slowly."

Stefan Gosston sat in the main building of the small base camp, a prominent worry frown on his forehead. His voice was deep and commanding, suiting his role, and his pale freckled skin contrasted starkly with his thick red hair and beard.

"Okay, now, let's... yeah, slow it down. Right down. As much as you can."

The video footage showed Doug walking around the two mysterious pillars, with the plain stretching away into the distance. As they watched, he moved slowly around the pillars. Soaring into the sky, the pillars jarred unnaturally with the flat, featureless landscape. Doug leaned in close, peering at the surface of the columns, cautiously touching them with his gloves. There was nothing out of the ordinary at all, except for those towering metal pillars.

"Here's where it begins," said John Hudson, his thick fingers repeatedly pressing the console buttons with surprising dexterity. Shorter than Stefan, clean shaven, he was more solid than the commander's wiry frame. "Watch now."

Now, slowed down, the footage was nearly frozen in time. Each step Doug took round the pillars, slowly moving round until he began to move between the two, appeared to take long minutes. Finally, the screen showed him right between both pillars. Still, nothing out of the ordinary happened until the final few seconds of footage. A bright spot appeared in the middle of the screen, between the pillars, and very quickly grew to fill the entire screen, until all that could be seen was white light. As quickly, it began to fade and shrink back. But Doug was no longer there.

"What the hell happened there?" said Stefan.

"We can try enhancing it."

"I'm not sure that's going to help, but... yeah, okay, do that."

"Was any of this footage sent to Earth?"

"No, it's just us that have seen it so far."

"Okay, let's keep a lid on it so far, for now, but we need to let the agency know, sooner or later."

"Fine… you're the boss."

Stefan patted him on the shoulder. It was good to have a team you could trust. But what had happened out there, in the desert? It had all been completely routine until Doug found these mysterious columns. As soon as Doug first reported what he'd seen, Stefan had sent Janna and Eric off towards the area. After Doug's disappearance, he quickly ordered them to wait, and not get any closer until they had a better idea of what they were dealing with.

"You think he's dead?" said John.

"I don't know. We have to assume that, I guess."

"What do you think the pillars are?"

Stefan shrugged.

"Some sort of weapon, a force field, a defence he triggered, who can say?"

"Let's look at the helmet footage we captured. Might show us some more."

They watched long minutes of footage showing the pillars' scarred surface close up as Doug examined it.

"They've been there some time, I'd say."

"Yeah, you wouldn't get sand damage like that overnight."

As they watched Doug's patient examination, there was nothing at all to indicate what might happen next.

"Okay, slow it down now. This is where he's going to step through."

Again the screen showed the barren desert landscape that lay beyond the twin columns. Closer, closer to the space between, went the view. Then they saw the image shimmer, the distant sands wavering in a way that was impossible on Mars with its lack of atmosphere. A pale white light shone up from the base of the pillars, intensifying, and then it was as if a curtain had suddenly been drawn back, revealing the perfect blackness of deep space. Stars appeared in the darkness, and then, as quickly, the images were gone, and they were left watching nothing but static.

"What was that?" said John.

"I don't know," said Stefan. "I'm going to send Janna and Eric in closer… but not too close."

"Janna, Eric," he radioed, "You can go closer, but do not, repeat, do not under any circumstances go right up close to those columns. And don't touch. In particular, do not step between them. Got it… do not step between them. Concentrate on looking for Doug, wherever he is."

"Is this wise?" said John.

"I don't know, but we owe it to Doug. We've watched the footage, but is there some way the camera could lie? Could he be behind the pillars somewhere? Or somehow hidden from view? Maybe injured somewhere?"

John shrugged. "I suppose so, but it doesn't look like it from the video footage."

"I know. I hope Janna and Eric are careful."

"You're being overprotective."

"I know. But we may have just lost a crew member."

"You did impress that on them."

"I'm responsible for them. Are there are any other explanations? Anything we can think of?"

John sighed. "I can't see any myself."

"We have to assume he's gone."

"What will you tell Earth?"

"That's what I need to think about. We'll decide after Janna and Eric have taken a look. What about radio contact?"

"I've seen no further radio contact from Doug at all, absolutely nothing."

"What about his transponder?"

"Like the radio, it's been completely silent since whatever happened."

"So he's either incapacitated… or…"

"Yeah."

"Let's see what they find."

⊱•⊰ ⊱•⊰ ⊱•⊰

He was able to lean forward a bit now. She'd taken her boot off his neck and was pointing the sword at his chest instead. And now he saw there was someone else with her; an older, shorter man with a beard, another of this blue-skinned race. And curiously, there was no sign of him carrying a weapon, so was he leaving all the fighting and sword play to her? Odd, though worth bearing in mind. Clad in a pale orange animal skin, the old man looked on, his bearded face betraying some amusement. That was a surprise to Doug, given his encounters so far with the natives.

The blue woman kept the sword firmly held against him, whilst jabbering away in a guttural language he couldn't even begin to place. It was like nothing he'd ever come across. Doug could only presume she was trying to question him and with the pressure on his throat released, he was able to speak.

"Who are you? Why are—"

She looked at him with what he took to be bemusement. She beckoned the older man over. They jabbered away in that unearthly tongue, keeping their eyes on him the whole time. The older man made a gesture with his hands and then knelt down beside Doug. As the woman stood there, her long golden hair flowing down onto her cloak of pale blue, the older man put both his hands on Doug's head.

My God, what the hell are they doing now? At least they hadn't killed him just yet.

⤞◈⤝ ⤞◈⤝ ⤞◈⤝

"Afternoon, everyone," said Stefan. He sat at the head of the small conference table, arms comfortably laid on its fake wooden surface.

"I've called you here so we can all go through everything that's happened, recap what we know, and see if there's anything we can think of, anything we can add, before I have to contact Earth. We can't keep a lid on this much longer, and to be honest, we shouldn't... As it is, I'll probably get court-martialled for this, but as the nearest court is a hundred million miles away, and the next space ship isn't due for a year and a half, I'm not too worried."

He looked round the table. They all nodded.

"So, let's start with what we know. Doug disappeared whilst investigating two strange metal pillars, origin unknown, found in the plains about five miles from here. These pillars appear to be artificial. John, describe what we saw on the video footage."

John raised his eyebrows quizzically.

"Hell, you've all seen it, right?"

They nodded glumly.

"Footage shows Doug walking around the columns and then walking right between them. As he does so… he vanishes from view. The helmet streaming stops then too. Stefan and I have been taking a closer look at the footage."

"Did you… I mean what does it show exactly on the footage, does he just disappear? How?" said Janna. She was a short, slightly dumpy woman in her thirties, with bitten nails. She looked nervous.

"When you slow it right down you can see there's this momentary flash."

"That's all?"

"Nothing after that."

Stefan cut in.

"No radio contact either since then. We've repeatedly been calling, and there's nothing. Just static on his frequency. No signal from his transponder either."

"Janna and Eric, could you tell us what you found?"

They looked at each other. Janna motioned to Eric, a man with a moustache and beard which his broad smile seemed to hide behind.

"In brief… nothing."

Stefan looked sharply at him.

"Go on."

"We had a good look all round the columns, taking care not to get too close. We used the camera to zoom in. There are some rocks nearby, but a little way off. Otherwise, the sand stretches away, for miles, completely smooth. The landscape is dead flat. Anything would stick out like a sore thumb."

"Like the columns," said Stefan.

"Yes," said Eric ruefully.

"Okay," said Stefan, "so there was no trace of him?"

"None."

He ran his hands through his thinning hair.

"God knows what they'll tell the family. That's not our job, though. Any signs of a struggle, signs of something happening, parts of a suit?"

"No. No, we had a good look around."

"And the pillars?"

"Nothing."

"Anything odd happen when you were there?"

He and Janna looked at each other.

"Not to me," said Eric.

"There's this odd feeling you get near the pillars," she said.

"An odd feeling?" said Stefan.

"Just something not right."

"You imagined it," said Eric. "I didn't feel it."

"Hmm,' said Stefan. "Well… maybe that's just due to what's happened."

"We could see," said Eric, "it was exactly as he described."

"And like we saw in the video," said Janna.

"The spooky thing is—" said Eric.

"Let's try and avoid language like that," said Stefan.

"All right, the strange thing is, you can see his footprints."

"Oh."

"All round the outside. That sand hasn't been disturbed for millennia otherwise. And then we saw one set of footprints leading off towards the pillars, I mean between them. We didn't go too close, but as far as we could see when we zoomed in with the camera, there were no footprints that came out the other side."

"Could he have jumped over?"

"Hardly. Those things are forty feet high."

"So something caused him to completely disappear."

"Off the face of the earth," said Janna.

"Off the face of Mars," said Eric.

"So he's dead," said Stefan.

"How?" said John.

"Vaporised?" said Eric. "There's that tiny flash when he disappears from view."

"Hmmm," said John. "But you didn't see any sign of that, you said there was no debris, nothing like that. Surely if he were vaporised, the sand would be scorched, there'd be material left behind. There'd be some sort of clue."

"You're right," said Janna. "The sand was undisturbed. We didn't go in that close, but we'd have spotted something if it was there. Just rocks and sand, that's all we saw. Aside from the pillars of course."

"So no residue, burn marks, nothing."

"I don't think you should talk about Doug as residue."

"Sorry. That was insensitive."

Stefan looked thoughtful. "That flash could just be a machine glitch."

"So what are we left with?" said John.

"How about this," said Janna, "could the pillars have destroyed Doug so completely nothing was left behind, nothing at all? Converted him into pure energy, like fusion? Wouldn't that be totally clean and leave nothing behind?"

"No," said John. "There would be a massive burst of energy and radiation affecting everything nearby. The whole area would be fried. And even if we didn't see signs of it, the High Martian Orbiter would have detected it."

"It'd be like a nuclear explosion," said Eric.

"Yeah," said John.

"We're back where we started," said Stefan. "He's vanished, that's all."

John turned round, his eyes excited.

"You're all assuming he's dead. What if he isn't?"

In contrast to John's excitement, Stefan looked sombre.

"Eh? Look, we all saw the video, and Janna and Eric have searched the area. He's just vanished. Look, something happened at those pillars that we just don't understand. And anyway, this isn't Earth. You can't just vanish, or if you do, you're most likely dead. He's nowhere to be seen, we've had no contact, and whatever happened, I'm sorry, but we've got to face it, Doug's dead."

"Suppose," said John, "those pillars are actually some kind of machine. I mean some incredible machine, advanced far beyond anything we can understand. And suppose it isn't a weapon or a defence mechanism, but something else entirely."

"What are you talking about, John?"

"I'm talking about a machine that opens up a portal."

"To what?"

"Who knows? Another space or time—maybe even another universe."

Eric smiled.

"John, this is crazy. You've been taking those old science fiction books you read too seriously."

"But think. You didn't find any debris or anything like that on the ground."

"No, but what's that got to do with it?"

"Either it somehow vaporised Doug so cleanly and with no remains of any kind, no explosion, no effect on the desert, no radiation, absolutely nothing and that's impossible, or else it's some kind of gateway. Both are beyond our science."

"We can't give false hope," mused Stefan. "That would be wrong. This is just speculation. And we've no way of proving it, or even if it were true of getting him back. If he is still alive somewhere," he said, quietly. "Look, I've got to report back to Earth pretty soon now. Anyone want to add anything?"

They shook their heads.

"I'll mention your theory and comments, John," added Stefan. "For what's it worth. What they'll do about it—"

He threw his hands in the air.

"It's a damned odd business."

"But if what John says is true, that it's a machine, doesn't this mean real evidence of aliens?" said Janna.

"God, can you imagine the headlines?"

"Let's not get ahead of ourselves," said Stefan. "And let's hope the agency can keep this whole thing under wraps for a bit."

"I AM IN YOUR HEAD," boomed the voice, so loudly it seemed the ground and the distant mountains would shake and crumble.

"I MUST UNDERSTAND YOU," it continued.

This was it, Doug thought, now he really was losing his mind. Well, if nothing else, he had to admire his mind's inventiveness: that strange journey through the pillars and beyond, that ugly blue man attacking him and smashing his helmet, the rather more attractive blue woman standing above him with the sword, and now this.

He tried to shout but couldn't, tried to move but found he was completely paralysed. Surely that old man didn't have this sort of strength. Try as he might he couldn't move at all. The blue man had laid his hands on Dog's forehead. His head was so close, Doug could see every one of the few yellow hairs on his balding head, could smell his breath— and it wasn't nice.

"DON'T RESIST!" boomed the voice, echoing inside his skull. Round and round it echoed until Doug's mind became overwhelmed and he knew and heard no more.

When he came to, his head was no longer echoing. Instead, there was complete silence, and the old man no longer held Doug's head. Doug was still lying on the ground, and the blue man and woman were jabbering away in that strange language. The woman saw him open his eyes and smiled at him.

This was his chance, surely, to escape this madness, he thought, as she looked away again. She still had the sword, but if he was quick... He shakily sat up.

They still weren't looking. And if the gravity was the same as Mars... He leapt to his feet, moving faster than he'd thought possible, and sailed yards into the air, knocking the old man down, and somehow, he didn't know how, grabbing the sword from the blue woman's hand. Something was wrong, though; as he brandished it in front of her, blade flashing in the bright sunlight, she didn't look surprised. Instead, quicker than he could think, she launched out with her right foot and kicked him hard in the stomach. Taken by surprise, he collapsed in pain, and she grabbed the sword. Bent double as he was, he was unable to resist as she pointed it at him, forcing him to the ground.

Well, he thought, *I'd never have got far in this damned suit. And there are two of them. But at least I'm not hearing voices anymore, even if I am mad.* The blue woman sat on his back, handing the sword to the old man, who was now standing up, though winded. Now she grabbed Doug's head in both hands, forcing it back. He winced with pain.

This is insane, isn't it, he thought, as he lay, stomach still aching, with a blue woman holding his head, his eyes staring up at the red sky. At least she didn't have the bad breath of the old man. And, considering she was bright blue, she wasn't unattractive either. Was it his imagination, or had some expression flickered across her face as he was thinking that?

The voices in his head started up again. But this time, they seemed softer, more feminine.

"We scared you," said the voice, in a tone that was quiet and soothing. It didn't seem likely to shake the ground or the mountains.

This time, he spoke back to it.

"Who—"

The voice said nothing, but something in her eyes told him.

"You?"

"There are techniques for healing minds and imparting learning. Languages especially."

Again he couldn't move. He could strain as much as he liked, but his body was ignoring him.

"I am not as proficient at this as is Sasak."

Once more he strained, applying all his strength. He felt himself sweating with the exertion but nothing happened.

"It was necessary to immobilise you. Sasak managed to establish contact and make your mind receptive."

He felt sheer terror then. What were they planning to do with him? He felt her take one hand away from his head and then gently smooth it.

"We will not hurt you. We needed to find out if you were a bandit or not. The desert is full of them."

She was staring into his face.

"I decided to continue, there were signs you were rejecting Sasak."

"He was a bit loud and rough," said Doug, in his mind. "And his breath smelt."

Was that laughter in her voice when she answered?

"He means well. He is an old man, but a very wise one. He is my trusted companion."

She added, "I do not blame you for trying to attack us and escape. I would do the same. You are brave. If you are happy for me to continue, then you can speak our language, and we will not need to do this in the future. It will not hurt. And you will not have to put up with Sasak's breath."

Afterwards, he wondered if he had imagined what came next.

"I will continue. Do not forget I can read your mind, when you are thinking how pleasant it is to have a beautiful woman so close. Even if she is blue. Now relax," she said, and it came easily, much easier than it did with the old man and his foul breath.

A strange sensation this, it felt his mind was a huge mansion, and someone was tiptoeing through rooms kept shut for years, their contents covered in dust and cobwebs, and that same someone was carefully opening doors long closed, to reveal daylight, uncovering long forgotten memories. It was all done with great sensitively, though, especially as intimate or hidden thoughts were stirred to the surface. He could do nothing to stop it, but was dimly aware of her gentle view as she slowly stepped around the abandoned places of his mind, like a librarian handling valuable old books, rather than some voyeur peering at secrets. He began to admire her soft touch, so at odds with her physical strength and swordsmanship.

At memories long forgotten she paused, and he fancied he heard a soft murmur; many evoked puzzlement and confusion, but at times he felt sympathy when she unearthed painful memories. Eventually, he felt a deep weariness come upon him, and his mind began to dim and darken. And did he really hear a soft, "Goodnight. Sleep," as he faded into oblivion?

Sometimes the communications time lag with Earth was a complete nuisance. The simplest conversation took ages as you waited for a reply to what you'd said several minutes ago. But there were other times when it was more useful. *Like now,* thought Stefan, when you were facing awkward questions. Before him, the face of Christine Foreman showed on the screen, her lips pursed, her hair pulled back tight, giving an appearance of steely determination. He'd learned from experience that was the real her, her outward polite and reasonable manner being nothing more than a mask. Quickly, he realised he'd let his thoughts wander, and tried to concentrate on what she might ask next, while he still had time.

He nearly jumped when she spoke again.

"What do you mean, disappeared? How can that be? You need to explain this. Surely this is impossible, Commander? I want a full explanation of this episode." Her eyes narrowed and hardened.

These bloody bureaucrats, he thought. They've never been out there in space, in completely alien environments, they know nothing at all. Just as I know nothing about pen pushing, the demands of politicians and the public, and dealing with the media.

"I'll send over our video footage. It appears to show Doug Henson examining the artefacts and then, well, you'll see. He just steps between them and vanishes. We sent a team out to check, and we couldn't find any sign of him. We think the pillars must be some kind of machine and..." he swallowed hard, "vaporised him or something like that. But, Ms. Foreman, we think this is real evidence of aliens. Those pillars are some kind of alien technology, way beyond our capabilities. It needs checking out, but we can't see any other explanation. No probes, no landers have ever been in that area, we checked with the Russians, the Chinese, everyone."

He stopped. He'd probably already told her too much. Like any bureaucrat, this would just spark off more questions. Well, there was nothing for it. On the screen, her expression remained unchanged; after a minute or so she turned to someone he couldn't see, and muttered something too low to hear.

"Commander," came the reply, after a further two minutes, "this seems to be nothing but pure speculation, all this talk of fantastical machines, aliens, mysterious disappearances and so on. We need facts. We need to know what's happened. This is your job. I want a full report on this. You need to conduct a thorough investigation into what happened. And you will send us all available footage and transcripts. Everything–is that clear? And I must have your entire team available to answer questions. In the meantime, you must not, repeat not, talk to the media Earthside without my express authorisation."

He shrugged.

"With respect, we've searched all around the area where Doug disappeared. It's on a large featureless plain, there's hardly anything to see except desert. There's simply no trace of him, his transponder isn't sending a signal, but there's nowhere else he could go. It's a—"

He stopped himself. He had been about to say 'mystery' but thought better of it.

"We're sending you everything we've got. We've a couple of ideas about what happened. We'd be grateful of course for any useful suggestions."

He paused.

"The team will be available to you. They're all a bit shaken. I presume you will be informing the family?"

"Thank you, Commander. We will be talking to Astronaut Henson's family as appropriate. I have to go in to a meeting now. I will contact you shortly."

The screen went blank.

As appropriate, he thought. What did that mean? Were they going to hold off telling the family until they'd come up with a suitable story? Not tell them at all?

Well, the family wasn't strictly his concern, but that didn't mean he felt good about it.

He wondered what story they would concoct; some sort of accident, he guessed. And what about the pillars? The footage and the truth would surely break out sooner rather than later, and when it did there'd be hell to pay.

They were talking nearby. That was the first thing Doug heard as he opened his eyes. They both turned towards him realising he had woken. The light was different, it must be morning. His head ached, and he felt a great weariness.

"Is this the next day?" he asked, not thinking. Of course, she wouldn't understand a word he said.

She turned to him, her mane of golden hair shining in the fresh sun.

"Yes," she said.

"Wait… I can understand you."

"And speak our language."

"How?"

"Sasak connected with you and implanted the knowledge to do so. It has taken time to work. That is why you were so tired."

It was true. Just as he could understand what they were saying, he could speak to them in their own language. It just seemed completely natural, as if he'd been speaking the language since a child.

He gasped.

"That's amazing."

She smiled.

"Sasak is a wise man."

The old man made a strange gesture to them, some sort of acknowledgement, Doug mused.

"I don't know your name."

"I am Gotissa. But you can call me Goti. I know your name, you are Doug," she smiled shyly. "But there are also many strange things in your head we do not understand. Not even Sasak, and he has seen many mysterious and wonderful things in his life."

"You know all about me."

The old man spoke. "Doesn't mean, as Prin—as Goti says… we understand it."

"You came from the pillars," she said.

"Yes. But don't ask me to explain. I don't know how and I don't understand. It doesn't make sense."

"We knew you weren't a bandit or a barbarian, from your clothes," she said. "We saw you lying there. Had we left you, you might not have made it 'till morning. This desert," she spat loudly, "is full of bandits."

Sasak spoke. "The pillars are unapproachable, guarded day and night."

"I was attacked when I first arrived. I managed to fight him off." He thought for a moment then asked, "Could you help me get back there?"

They looked at each other.

Goti spoke first.

"The pillars are taboo. There is something we need first. We are on a quest, a mission."

"What kind of—"

"Will you trust us? We will explain all, but will you trust us first?"

He shrugged, or rather, that was what he meant to do, but it came out as an entirely different movement. Instead of a shrug, he leaned his head to one side. It had to be yet another translation, this time cultural. Had his brain been completely rewired?

She went on.

"We could have killed you. I could have done. I have fought many warriors in my time and battled many beasts too."

"I don't doubt it. I would like to return to the pillars if you can help me do so. But, Goti, I will help you first."

"Good." She smiled.

Sasak spoke. "Your memories are strange, but they cannot lie. They speak of you coming from elsewhere, somewhere I do not know. Yet, as I say, they cannot lie. Ancient legends tell of the pillars leading to other worlds where strange people and beings live. That is why they have the Guardians there to kill anyone or anything that comes through. You came through and survived. You are lucky, Doug, to be alive."

From a bag made from a substance like leather, Goti produced a red bottle. She pulled a stopper from it. A pungent smell, with hints of roses, wildflowers, lavender, and mint hung heavily in the still desert air. Yet it was none of those. A white vapour rose from its neck.

"We drink deeply to show friendship. Will you drink with us, Doug of the Pillars?" she asked, taking a deep draught. The vapour surrounded her lips, obscuring the blue of her face. *It looks for all the world that she is smoking,* Doug thought. He tasted the red liquid, then took a deeper draught. It was intoxicating. Cool and with a sweet taste, it brought to mind spring mornings on Earth, the ultimate cold of deep space, and the freshness of mountain air. He knew he would never be able to describe it properly. He went to take another draught, but Goti put her hand over the bottle.

"Not too much, it is dangerous to drink too much."

She handed the bottle to Sasak, who made a loud belch after he'd taken a long draught. Goti gave him a pained look, but Sasak just looked at Doug, smiling.

"A wise man has to have his vices."

"If you must," Goti said, taking the bottle and stopping it up.

"Thank you, Doug of the Pillars," she said.

"Is that my name?" he said.

"Yes."

She gave the air, Doug thought, of someone used to being obeyed and getting her own way.

"What is that stuff?"

"It is called grivak. It comes from the Mountains of the Two Empires. You liked it?"

"I did like it. I can't describe to you what it does."

She laughed. "No one can describe it properly. It has a different effect on everyone because it summons up personal impressions. No two people will ever feel the same drinking it."

"So where are you heading, Goti?"

"We must get off the Desert of Lost Souls as soon as we can. I have some provisions, as has Sasak, but they may not last long in this place. There are few plants or animals in the deserts, and too many bandits and barbarians. So we need to set off again very soon. We cross the Mountains of Desolation, past the Plains of Eternity, and then we come to Jasanna. Ah, the city of Jasanna, Doug! What a glorious sight! Half as old as time itself, if not older, the city shines deep red in the morning light, with its great towers, its teeming streets, and its markets crammed with exotic goods from half a world away. In the evening a breeze blows in from the sea and when the moon rises the city gleams violet in the cool of the evening."

"It's on the sea?"

"Yes, after the desert is the mountains, and then after that the plains, and Jasanna by the sea."

"And your quest… your mission?"

Sasak looked over. "Prin—"

"We will talk of that later. First, we must cross the desert safely. There are other perils too."

"I have food," he said, lifting a flap in his suit, by now gone grimy and off colour, pulling out three ration packs. "Just add water," he said.

Sasak took one and peered at it.

"Why this is marvellous," he said. "You mean you just pour water on it?"

"Yes," said Doug.

"Looks disgusting," said Goti, pulling a face. "I'm not eating that."

"You might have to."

"I'd rather catch a sand worm. Or a tendril grabber."

"What?"

"Just kidding, but I'll be able to catch us something else much better."

"No, what's a tendril grabber?"

"Oh, we won't see any of those. They live much farther north. You really do come from a strange place, don't you?"

They were going to eat before leaving, Doug realised.

Goti pulled out something that looked like mushy bread from her bag except that it was bright yellow in colour, and held it out to Doug.

"Unless you'd rather eat your dried food?" she said.

He noticed the old man was already tucking in.

"I'll try it," he said. It didn't taste like bread, instead, within a few seconds, it felt like his entire mouth was tingling. It was a strange, unexpected mixture of tastes: there was salt and spice and something mushy and an odd tang that reminded him of Marmite.

The sun had risen higher in the sky now but was still not that far away from the horizon, swollen and huge. Odd to see such a gigantic red sun in the sky, but then what wasn't odd about this world? It hit him then, he was somewhere so incredibly far from Mars, and from Earth, that all his friends, his parents too, might as well be dead. Just as they probably thought he was dead. And that was without wondering about whether he'd crossed time as well as space.

For all he knew, everyone he had ever known might be long dead— or yet to be born—in some distant future. He thought of Stefan and Janna, Janna with whom he'd once had a fling, and who had been so very grown up and matter of fact about it afterwards. He'd been embarrassed at first, but she took him aside, in a very matter of fact Scandinavian way and said, "Doug, we all have to live together on this base." After that, they never talked about it again, and she became a good friend. He smiled, thinking of John too, with his wild scientific theories, and the piles of experimental devices he was always building and tinkering with in his study. John's skills came in handy when equipment broke down, and they needed to repair it. He was the only repairman for millions of miles.

Would any of them have any inkling of Doug still being alive? *No, he thought, at best they'd just think I'd vanished.* And surely his disappearance would be overshadowed by the discovery of the pillars.

He could feel his eyes welling up, and he struggled to stop them doing so. Goti watched him.

"Don't be sad, Doug of the Pillars. We will help you."

All three of them got to their feet and started walking. The Desert of Lost Souls looked the same to him in all directions, except for some distant mountains far off on the horizon. *Those must be the Mountains of Desolation,* he thought. The sand lay level and flat otherwise as far as the eye could see.

After several hours, a few stops and some refreshment from both his bottle and Goti's bottle, the sun was well clear of the horizon. Its glare now made it impossible to look at. No longer was it just a dull glow on the horizon. Once it had risen free of the desert floor, it was as if someone had turned its power up rapidly. Under its fierce glare, the red sand still stretched on into the distance, and the Mountains of Desolation looked no closer. Yet now there were small orange plants poking up through the sand, here and there, and the sand was looser and less firm under their feet. Goti and Sasak stopped, looking troubled.

"Have we gone wrong?" she said.

"The desert sands can shift over time," said Sasak, scratching his head.

Doug wondered who was in charge; Goti had an air of authority, despite being far younger. She seemed used to leading and being in authority. Yet at times, she deferred to Sasak's age and knowledge. And Sasak had a natural air of being listened to.

"We can refill our water, at least," she said, marching up to one of the plants and slitting a hole in one of its bloated leaves. As she held a bottle underneath, a dribble of liquid trickled from the leak, and the plant began to deflate as they watched. Within a minute or two, half a bottle was full, and the plant looked withered.

"What do you think?" she said. "Sasak, shall we carry on this way?"

"It is what my senses tell me," he said. "Yet—"

The plants were getting thicker now, and some reached as high as a foot or two.

Goti looked concerned.

"Are these tendril—"

At that moment, Doug trod on one of the orange leaves lying on the ground and felt something grab onto his foot. As he bent down, to free it from the plant he'd stood on, something long and thick-lashed out from the ground and fastened itself round his chest, tugging him to the ground. As he struggled, something else fastened itself around his feet, and he realised they were being tugged down below the sand. Now he was struggling to breathe, gasping for each breath. Behind him, Goti shouted, "Tendril grabbers!" and he could see, as the long tendril wrapped itself tighter still, that she was caught hard too.

He was glad he didn't have to put up with the full media storm that had erupted on Earth since they'd gone public about Doug. Even so, Stefan had to take a number of interviews with reporters that the agency had arranged before all this blew up. They hadn't been able to wriggle out of them, it would look as if they were avoiding the press. Worryingly, he'd seen some of the more lurid headlines and reports, talking about space monsters and aliens planning to invade. *Really, such rubbish has been out of date even by the middle of the last century,* he thought.

He tried to focus his mind, as he was in the middle of an interview right now. Originally this would have been a pretty dull nuts and bolts account of their usual day to day activities at the base, given to a junior reporter to cover. But now both he and the reporter had been catapulted into fame.

"So what do you think happened to Doug?" said the reporter, a fresh-faced young Malaysian woman.

Keep the party line, thought Stefan. There was a part of him that was beyond caring; they were going to get him for this, whatever happened.

"We don't really know. But I'm afraid we have to assume the worst."

"We understand there is some video footage of the event."

"That's right. It's still being analysed, but it seems to show Doug stepping between the pillars and vanishing. We conducted a detailed search and found nothing."

"And the pillars? They're evidence of aliens, is that right? Are they still on Mars? Could they be coming for us next?"

Stefan smiled. "The pillars are definitely artificial. And as far as we know, also not man made. So yes, they seem to be evidence of extraterrestrial life. But they are very old. We've never come across anything like this on Mars before, and we've never seen any other evidence of any extraterrestrial presence here."

"Could they have come from elsewhere in the Solar System?"

This is certainly more fun than a 'normal interview', he thought, before remembering Doug. Fun wasn't exactly the word to use when it involved the death of a colleague.

"We've also never seen any evidence of that. Like I said, the pillars could have been there for a very, very long time. There are signs of that, the surface of each pillar is pitted with marks from sand and dust. It wasn't put there yesterday. It's very, very old."

"But it's definitely the first evidence of intelligent alien life."

He swallowed hard. "Look, I'm sticking my neck out here, but yes, I'd say so. It has to be. And credit should go to Doug for finding it. Wherever he is."

"How are you and your fellow crew members dealing with Doug's disappearance?"

"It hasn't been easy for any of us. Doug was a great team member. He was well liked. We all just want to get to the bottom of it now."

"Getting back to the pillars, what are they? Some kind of machine? Have you been able to investigate them?"

"Yes. We think they may be some sort of incredibly advanced machine, far beyond our technology, but a machine all the same. We don't know exactly what its purpose is. We do know it caused Doug to vanish. And because of that, we're having to take great care, so I've not allowed anyone else to get too close yet. That has limited our investigation, both of what happened to Doug, and also into the pillars."

This was great, compared to press conferences he'd done on Earth, where they kept interrupting you. The delay helped, of course, it meant you couldn't be interrupted, and you could talk on, unimpeded, to your heart's content. The PR people on Earth would probably blow a fuse, but there.

An idle thought entered his head, *how long before the politicians back on Earth got wind of this? They'd all want to go to Mars to be interviewed.*

"One last question, Commander Gosston. How do you personally feel about what happened to Dr. Henson?"

"We're all very upset about what happened, and our feelings go out to his family. Our thoughts and our prayers are with them in this hour of need."

He looked dead ahead at the tiny camera, keeping his expression serious.

"Dr. Henson was a brave and dedicated colleague… and a friend. His ambition had always been to go to Mars one day and to explore it. He made it, but sadly, it seems he gave his life. He will be remembered for a great discovery… perhaps one of the greatest discoveries ever in human history."

After the screen went blank, he sat for a minute or so, gazing out onto the dead, rocky landscape beyond the window. *Dead, or maybe not so dead,* he thought. There were mysteries here. Something had been here, untold ages ago, and left those pillars there, for what purpose, God alone knew. He radioed Janna and Eric. He'd sent them back out again to take a more detailed look.

"How's it going?"

Janna replied. "Hi, boss. We've taken detailed video all round the pillars—"

"Not inside! Don't go inside!" he shouted into the radio.

"No, don't worry. We've not been inside."

"And you're keeping well back?"

He felt a shiver. What the hell were those pillars and what could they do?

"Yes. No need to mollycoddle us."

"Sorry, Janna. Sometimes commanders have to do that. You understand, nature of the job."

"We've sent one of the robots in quite close to take pictures. That might help. I wondered…"

"Go on."

"Should we send the robot in between the pillars?"

"Hmm. Good question. It would be interesting to see what happens, but can we afford to lose it? We only have four robots, don't we?"

"Three."

"Only three?"

"One of them failed, not long after we landed and even John couldn't make sense of the diagnostics."

"I'd forgotten that. Let's see... if we send the robot in and lose it, those bureaucrats back home will moan about why we lost such an expensive piece of equipment. If we don't send it in, everyone else will ask us why we didn't try it."

"Would be useful, wouldn't it?"

"I agree. Let's see what it does," he sucked his teeth. "And Janna?"

"Yes?"

"You and Eric... keep well back when the robot goes in. I don't want to lose anyone else. That clear?"

"Yes."

"We don't understand what the pillars are or what they can do, so we can't predict what might happen."

"How did the interview go?"

"Oh, some interesting questions came up. Though there was a lot I couldn't answer, and nor could anyone else. God knows what the media frenzy back home must be like."

"Maybe it's just as well we're here."

"Okay, carry on. Take care."

As he watched, Goti was sinking deeper, the black tendrils rising higher as she was pulled down. Doug looked on with horror as first her legs vanished into the sand, and then her upper body started to disappear too. Soon just her head was left and already that was being pulled slowly underneath.

The tendrils were tightening and pulling all the time. It was becoming incredibly painful around his legs and torso, and the pressure was immense. It felt like hot knives were sticking into his skin. Was this how these things worked, wrapping themselves ever tighter, like pythons crushing their prey?

Sasak, somehow, had escaped this fate and was rummaging in his bag. With a turn of speed Doug was surprised at, Sasak sprang forward clutching a small flask. Carefully standing to one side of Goti, her head now barely visible, he poured the contents of the flask onto the tendrils. Was it Doug's imagination, or was there a sound like a stifled shriek?

Then he heard it again. It was real, but he had no time to worry about that, for now, his legs were completely under the sand, and the pressure and pain were immense. He was sure he would pass out and then that would be that. He closed his eyes, but something forced him to open them again. In the corner of his eye, he could dimly see Sasak next to him, pouring an acrid foul smelling liquid onto the tendrils grasping Doug. The stench filled his nostrils; like the pain, it too was unbearable.

But instantly he felt the pressure on his legs and chest relax. The tendrils loosened their hold, and again he heard that stifled scream. To his left, he saw Goti struggling out of the sand, and with that dreadful grip now released, he was able to pull himself out too. Sasak smiled at him.

"You see, I may not be a great swordsman, but a wise man has other means."

"Thank you," said Doug. "This world of yours has many surprises. What are these plants? And what would have happened to us? What is that stuff?"

"It's concentrated sap from the jazzabera tree. It is the only known substance to combat them."

"Are the tendrils animals, plants, or what?"

Goti walked over. She made a strange half bowing, half kneeling gesture which Doug took to be one of appreciation and thanks.

"I was telling Doug," said Sasak, "that a wise man may not know how to fight with a sword, but can fight in other ways."'

"Very true," she said.

"What are those things?" said Doug.

She turned to Sasak.

"They live in areas near the edge of the desert. No one can say if they are plants or animals."

"Does it matter?" said Goti. "We just know they are dangerous."

"And they'd have killed us?"

"Yes. Then eaten us."

The perils are never-ending on this world, thought Doug.

Goti turned to Sasak.

"Thanks, Sasak."

"You are welcome, my la—" he started, but went on "Gotissa."

Doug could have sworn he had been going to say something else.

"Let's move away before any more of these wretched things attack us," she said.

They were nearer the mountains now, and the sands of the desert were beginning to give out. Great boulders lay scattered around like the discarded playthings of some outsized child. Soon they were climbing loose scree and gravel. Their feet knocked small stones loose, and they saw them rolling down for hundreds of feet before coming to a halt. Now half the sky was covered with the immense bulk of the mountains above them, rising so high they blocked out the sun.

"At least we're safe from those tendril things here… aren't we?" said Doug.

"There are other hazards in the mountains," said Sasak gravely. "Snow apes and many other fierce creatures live up here. Your pale skin may protect you, though. You may not be seen against the snow."

"That's a cheerful thought," said Doug.

Far above, the higher peaks gleamed white with snow. They looked icy, chilly and forbidding.

"We're going up there?"

"It's the only way through," said Goti. "But once we're up there, you'll be able to see the Plains of Eternity and the golden city of Jasanna lying, gleaming in the distance. The climb and the hazards make it worth it. They say you should see it once before you die."

"I've already nearly died several times," said Doug.

"It certainly is a splendid sight," said Sasak. "I never weary of it. How long has it been?"

"Since the old emperor died," said Goti.

"Are we going through the mountains tonight?" said Doug.

"No," said Sasak. "We'll stop for the night quite soon. It's cold and treacherous up there, we're losing the light already, and we need our strength and wits about us in the morning."

It was true that the light was fading. The swollen red sun of this world was sinking behind the mountains, and already there was a chill in the air. They had been walking all day.

They reached a shallow plateau, no more than thirty feet across, and the same in width. It was full of small, loose rocks and some large boulders.

"Shall we stop here?" said Goti.

"How high are these mountains?" asked Doug.

Sasak named a figure and a measure Doug did not understand. All he knew was, they were high. Now the old man produced a small metal cylinder from his sack. He twisted something, and as Doug watched, the cylinder almost immediately began to glow red, and soon Doug felt it give out heat too.

They sat around the metal cylinder, its heat fighting against the growing chill in the air.

"Look, Doug," said Goti, "the stars are coming out."

The sky was almost completely dark by now, and the stars were as vivid and plentiful as they had been down in the desert, perhaps even more so. *Not like the polluted skies above Earth's cities*, thought Doug. As the stars became brighter, he gazed with no recognition at those unfamiliar star patterns.

"Do you have names you give to groups of stars?" he asked.

Sasak answered, "Indeed. If you look over there," he pointed vaguely across to the sky above a nearby mountain peak, which loomed malevolently over them, "right there is the Great Throne, and over there," he waved to the left, "is the Thawn of Wekoot."

Doug couldn't see exactly what he'd pointed to, nor see anything resembling a throne.

"What is a Thawn?"

"A giant bird. We might see one in the Plains of Eternity, though I hope not. They do not usually attack people, but they are big enough to carry off a man."

"Though not a fighting woman," added Goti.

Doug was again struck by how far he was from home. Tears welled up in his eyes, despite his attempts to stop them.

"Are you sad, Doug?" said Goti. "Are you thinking of your own world?"

"Yes, and how far away it might be."

"Tell us more about your world, and this strange clothing you wear. I will buy you some new clothes when we get to Jasanna. The markets and bazaars are wonderful."

"Yes, tell us all about it, Doug," said Sasak. "I have only picked up bits and pieces from your mind…"

"I picked up more than that," said Goti, "but then I have a better way with me than you do, Sasak."

"As you say," said Sasak, looking wistful. "I am always eager to learn."

"The mark of a wise man," said Goti.

"And of a wise woman too."

"I believe, unless all this is a dream…" said Doug.

"I am not in your dream!" said Goti.

"You were in my mind, though."

"Carry on," said Sasak.

"Unless this is a dream, those pillars transported me a vast distance across space and time to your world."

Now the giant moon had risen, slowly peeping out above the mountain like a great illuminated lamp, its serene light casting eerie shadows across the landscape.

"My world," said Doug, "is not where I came from."

They looked puzzled.

Sasak made a gesture with his hands so quickly Doug could not make it out.

"I do not understand," said Sasak.

"I mean, the world I travelled from, the world the pillars took me from, is not the world where I live."

Still, Sasak looked blank.

"'How can this be?"

"I will explain. We travelled in a ship, a kind of ship, that is, not a ship that sails the sea, but a ship that can travel between worlds. We came through vast distances to get to this world. We were exploring it. Like travelling to your moon," he pointed to the great moon, now rising free of the mountain top, "but much, much further. Many times further. The world we travelled to has no air. That is why I was wearing these clothes, the ones Goti admires."

"I do not!" she retorted. "We're changing them once we get to Jasanna."

"The clothes provided air that I can breathe. As you can see, one of the Guardians did some damage to it."

"Do you understand this, Sasak?" said Goti.

"Some of it, I think, my—"

"It sounds to me the sort of thing a storyteller might tell our children."

"Remember," said Sasak, "there are many strange and wonderful things in this world. And we know the legends of the pillars."

"Like this world," Doug went on, "it has desert. It's full of deserts, in fact. Sand and rock everywhere. I was exploring when I found the pillars. I walked around them, and then, when I walked through them, something happened, and I found myself here."

"And your own world… it is very distant, you say, from the world where you found the pillars?" said Sasak.

"Yes…" said Doug, and he found himself struggling to find the word equivalent to year. What was it?

"It was a very long journey. It took us hundreds and hundreds of days to travel there."

"Hundreds and hundreds of days? That is indeed a long voyage. Beyond the edge of the world," said Goti.

"Many times beyond the edge of the world," said Sasak. "But tell us more about your world."

"I'll see if you have the words for it. It has air like yours, vast oceans, jungle, deserts, mountains, and in the far north and far south are great ice caps. There are great cities, all kinds of different peoples and animals. It's hard to describe…" he trailed off.

"There are jungles and great cities and seas here too. This desert, as you see, does not last forever."

"Talking of going on forever, I am going to get some sleep," said Goti.

"She is young and headstrong," said Sasak, laughing.

"I heard that," she said.

"And strong too. One day, Doug, she may even be wise."

"Hmph."

Doug stayed awake for a while, under those unknown stars. The giant moon bathed the rocky landscape in brilliant white light, a hundred times brighter than any Earthly moonlight.

"Don't get any closer, Janna!" cautioned Eric.

"What with you and Stefan looking after me!"

But she moved a few paces back.

"We don't even know what a safe distance is."

"Very true. All we know is that Doug triggered something when he stepped in between."

"So we won't step between. Are we ready to try the robot?"

"Let's hope we don't lose it… the agency will blow a fuse."

"Okay, let's get back in the rover so we can make a quick exit if we have to."

Doug's rover was parked here too, but neither of them mentioned it. For now, they were leaving it where it was.

They sat in silence, side by side in the rover, the unforgettable sight of the twin pillars rising high against the Martian sky, a hundred feet ahead. Like Janna and Eric and Doug before them, the pillars were also outsiders in this place. Janna and Eric watched the little robot inching itself forward across level ground on its tracks, adroitly avoiding some small boulders on one side, Janna controlling it through the rover's console.

"Let me have a go," said Eric.

"Men and their toys!"

"The way you're going you'll probably crash into one of the columns."

"Bloody cheek."

She stopped the robot around ten feet away. The pillars stood there, as they had stood for centuries past, inscrutable. Hard to believe that, only a day or two before, Doug had disappeared into thin air on this very spot.

"Anything unusual?" said Eric.

"No. Nothing at all. Shall I go on?"

"Yes, just don't knock one of the columns over."

She playfully punched him.

"Ow."

"Serves you right. Anyway, we'd be court-martialled if we did. I'd tell them you did it, of course."

"I bet you would. Okay, take it slowly."

The little robot slowly trundled on its caterpillar tracks closer to the pillars. A screen next to Janna, in the middle of the console, showed the robot's camera view.

"Four feet... three, two."

She stopped the robot again.

"Anything?" said Eric, peering as intently as she was at the console.

"Nothing our instruments can detect. Taking it to one foot."

The robot was now so close that little more than a small section of each pillar was visible now in the camera's view.

"Something ought to be happening..."

"Go on... no, wait."

"What is it?"

"It's gone now," said Eric. He pressed several buttons, frowning at the console. "Let me just replay it. Yes, there it is... a sudden electromagnetic pulse."

They looked at each other.

"A glitch?" she said.

"I don't think so. I think something just woke up."

"Maybe it's probing what's going on."

"It didn't last long. Must have come from the pillars themselves... or something buried beneath."

"Let's take it through the pillars then, very slowly, and see what happens."

The robot lurched forward and then stopped.

"It's right between the pillars now."

"Nothing. Nothing happening at all. Let's go on."

The robot moved slowly on. All its camera showed was the scene of the desolate plain beyond the pillars. Janna guided the robot out the other side.

"Still nothing."

They radioed Stefan.

"Did you see that?"

"I wasn't watching, I've been doing some more interviews. Anything interesting going on?"

"We were about to take the robot through the pillars," said Janna, "and we got a strange electromagnetic pulse. But that was all. Nothing happened. No more pulses either."

"Maybe," said Eric, "it's only interested in living things?"

"I'm not volunteering to find out," said Janna.

"You mean the robot came out unscathed?" said Stefan.

"That's right," said Janna.

"At least I don't have to tell the agency we lost a robot. But let's be clear… neither of you is going through in person to check this out. We can't afford to lose anyone else, and I'm not going to."

"Could be it only works at certain times, under certain conditions," said Eric.

"Possible, I suppose," said Stefan.

"It's all guesswork," said Janna. "We should keep trying, though."

"With the robot," said Stefan. "I've got to talk some more to the higher ups. Keep at it and I'll talk to you later. And don't take any risks. That's an order. Is that clear?"

"Yes, boss," they chorused.

The three of them slept close together for warmth. Now that the sun had gone down, the temperature had plummeted too. Sasak lay on one side, Goti was in the middle, and Doug on the other side. *Just as well,* thought Doug, as every now and again the old man snored heavily.

Something woke him in what he guessed was the early hours of the morning. The ghostlike shape of the large moon hung over the desert below, and he found his arm draped over Goti. Sleepily she nursed it, muttering something indistinct. Was it something like 'protect your Princess'? Whatever it was, it didn't make sense. *Princess indeed!* Doug smiled as he felt her stroke his arm. That girl had a high opinion of herself, no doubt about that.

By morning, the moon had long since set, and it was not quite daylight when they began to move.

"We need to move now to have a chance of reaching the city before nightfall," said Sasak.

The going was treacherous. Loose scree lay everywhere on the slopes, and the ground was uneven and rough. He wondered how Sasak and Goti would cope with their animal skin boots. His spacesuit boots seemed tough enough to cope well with this terrain.

"Doug, look behind," said Goti.

He turned. They were now high up above the great desert plain, and the view was magnificent. "What's that glistening over there?" he said. Beyond the plain, there was something twinkling far off.

"The sea," said Sasak. "The Ocean of Storms. Looks fairly calm today."

As they climbed higher still, Doug felt himself fighting for breath, but the others showed no discomfort. The rocky ground began to be covered with snow and ice, at first a light covering, but as they pressed on it wasn't long before the snow lay inches deep and their feet crunched with every step. His teeth began to chatter.

"Don't worry, Doug, we'll soon be at the summit and from then it's all downhill," said Sasak.

Doug began to gasp for breath. It was like every breath was hard fought, as if it were his last. *Am I dying now,* he thought? *Maybe this is all a dream, a fabulous dream, but a dream all the same?* His breathing became more and more laboured.

"I can't... I can't go on," he said, bent double, trying to force air into his lungs.

Goti stopped and leaned over him.

"Doug... what is the matter?"

"The air. Too thin. Can't breathe."

Sleep, he thought, *that's what I need, sleep, just let me sleep here. Just a few minutes, just let me rest.*

"Doug!" she shouted. "You can't sleep here. You mustn't."

But sleep was all he desired. A slap to the face from Goti brought him back to a dim level of consciousness.

"Oxygen," he murmured.

"What is he saying?" said Goti.

"Oxygen tank, turn it on, see if any left. Put mask on."

"What do you mean?" shouted Goti. "I don't understand you."

He pointed at the emergency bottle of oxygen and its mask. There was no way of telling if it still worked; if it did, then that was all the oxygen he had left. It might be enough.

But Goti was exasperated.

"Your words are meaningless," she said, throwing her arms up.

Sasak grasped the meaning. Striding purposefully over the snowy rocks, he made sense of Doug's frantic gesturing and found the oxygen valve and the mask. He quickly placed the mask over Doug's face and opened the valve. Doug felt a rush of pure oxygen seeping into his lungs. Some of it would go to waste, and it wouldn't last long, but it was better than nothing. Breathe, that was all. *Breathe.*

He panted for breath, gasping, "Thank you."

"So that's what he wanted," said Goti.

"One day," said Sasak, "if you behave yourself, you might be as wise as me."

She made a sign with her fingers that Doug presumed was very rude. Sasak sighed.

"You know my dignity and position won't allow me to respond."

Later, Doug would remember this. Dignity, yes… position? What was his position exactly? But at that moment he was still gasping as the fresh oxygen revived him.

Doug turned the valve back to low and removed the mask. With luck, it would hold whilst they traversed the high peaks of the mountain. And, with his breath back, they continued on what seemed to him an endless journey. *Surely it has to turn downhill soon,* he thought.

At last, as they walked through a narrow pass, snow piled and drifted on all sides, a pale sun faintly visible above the rocks, Sasak announced, "Any moment it will be downhill."

"Thank the Great Warrior for that!" said Goti.

They walked through narrow crevasses in the sheer rock, crunching on deeper snow, to find themselves perched on the edge of another vast view.

Like the view from the other side of the mountain, down below a vast plain stretched into the distance, but unlike the uniform red emptiness of the desert, this plain looked like a mad artist had splattered paint everywhere. There were myriad colours to be seen, overloading both eye and brain. And beyond the plain, shimmering like a vision, domes of gold and slender towers glittered in the sunlight. Periodically, points of light flashed out from in and around the towers.

Doug strained to see more clearly. "What is this?" he asked. "Is it a mirage?"

"No mirage," said Sasak. "Below you are the Plains of Eternity, and beyond that, the city of Jasanna."

They stood on the ledge of rock and stared at the magnificent vista below, regaining their breath.

But they were still high up in the mountains, and when they resumed walking, the snow seemed even thicker, piled snow lying feet high on all sides.

Doug twisted his valve back to release more oxygen.

Sasak looked wary.

"I don't like this—" he started, but was interrupted by a scream.

Impossible as it seemed, one of the piles of snow on one side had come to life and was moving. Ten feet tall, white, with giant teeth, to Doug it looked for all the world like a huge polar bear, or perhaps an Abominable Snowman, though one with razor sharp teeth. It was Goti that had screamed, for it was heading straight towards her. Snarling, it grabbed her with a thick furry arm before she had a chance to reach for her sword.

Doug reached for his own sword and ran over to the creature. It turned and snarled as if mocking him. Holding Goti fast with one arm, it reached for Doug with the other, giant claws flailing in the air.

"A snow ape!" shouted Sasak. "Take care! This is exactly what I was fearing."

"I've got to save Goti," said Doug.

The creature still looked on with what looked like amusement as Doug advanced with his sword. Before he could plunge the sword into its chest, it thrust its enormous arm out, and digging its claws in, left a deep, painful and bloody gash across his chest. He fell back from the shock and pain. It lunged again, and he staggered back as its claws cut another deep gash.

It was too much for him. He fell to the ground, seeing blood seep from his chest. The pain was unbearable. Sasak rushed over to him as the creature turned, satisfied Doug was no more threat to it. Turning, the creature roared and stomped off through the snow and rock.

"Never mind me, we've got to save Goti," said Doug.

"You need patching up," said Sasak, "or we'll never save her."

The old man knelt down, pulling out strips of cloth from his bag. Doug was convinced his last moments were upon him. Having survived so many adventures now, this was it. He was going to die here, on this distant planet, amongst strangers, far from everyone he'd ever known, killed by some unknown monster.

Yet, Sasak's bandages did the trick. Within minutes the blood had stopped flowing, and the pain was lessening.

"They are infused with a special plant, we call it pluthener, which promotes healing," explained Sasak.

The old man sat on a rock.

"I will be beheaded if we lose Goti."

"Why? It's not your fault—"

"She is not what she seems. But it doesn't matter. There's not a moment to lose. We need to find the snow ape's lair if we are to save her."

They followed the giant footsteps of the snow ape, trudging through the snow after it. Doug couldn't help seeing visions of Goti torn to bits under the snow ape's vicious teeth as it devoured her. Sasak's next words gave rise to an even more fearful image.

"They imprison their prey in huge cocoons. They wrap them around, hanging them up in their lair. Gradually their prey becomes paralysed. No one can escape the cocoon without help. Hopefully, we can get there in time."

"How are we going to fight it?" asked Doug.

"Surprise," said Sasak. "That's all we have on our side."

They'd sent the robot through the pillars, round the pillars, over and over, but except for that first electromagnetic pulse, there was nothing at all. And no sign of the robot vanishing.

"It knows it's seen it before," said Janna.

"Perhaps it's biding its time?" said Eric.

"Well, I'm not walking through," she said.

"The boss would kill you anyway." Eric consulted the console, his face concentrating. "Does look like there's something buried under there."

"Under the pillars? Is that what the scanners show?"

"Yeah. Could be the machinery that does the business."

"Wouldn't it be fascinating to see it?" Janna bit her lip.

"But could just be a large lump of iron ore."

"You're the geologist, how likely is that?"

"It's possible."

"Well, watch the instruments, I'm going to try something."

"Eric, remember what Stefan said."

"I'm going to try throwing a rock, that's all."

He got down out of the rover. The pillars were a hundred feet away but still he felt the sheer strangeness, the wrongness even, of these twin columns straight in front. He walked closer.

"Don't go too close," cautioned Janna over the radio.

"I'm not going too far, but I just need to get a bit nearer." He stopped at fifty feet.

"You'd better stay there," she said.

"I'm going to. I should be able to throw a rock from here."

He bent down, selected a large boulder, as big as spacesuit helmet, and hurled it between the two pillars. The rock sailed through, flying on through in the low Martian gravity for another fifty feet before falling to the ground.

"Any reaction?" he asked.

"Nothing. No, wait. There was something, let me check. Yes. Almost too low for the instruments to read, but a minute pulse, just lasting a millisecond or so."

He looked around for another rock, picked up a smaller one, around the size of a man's fist, and threw that. Again, it flew through the pillars with no impediment.

"No pulse this time."

"Nothing?"

"Nothing at all."

"I think it's analysing and learning."

"I don't know what to think."

Stefan was sitting with John watching a screen showing a large conference table at the space agency, back on Earth. Christine Foreman was chairing, but aside from her most of the attendees were technical people: engineers, astronauts, flight controllers, plus the original designers of the ship and the Martian bases.

Stefan spoke while Christine looked on, her face tense.

"So far we've sent a robot through the pillars and nothing's happened. Obviously, we won't be sending anyone through until we understand what's happened."

"You will not send anyone through, period," she shouted. "Do we have any idea of what the pillars are and what they do… other than being responsible for Dr. Henson's disappearance?"

"We think they're some kind of machine, purpose unknown. We detected structures buried in the ground under the pillars. And we've also detected short bursts of power coming from the same area."

"A machine. An alien machine. This sounds incredible, too incredible for words."

Stefan shrugged.

"That's what it appears to be."

"Whatever it may be, we can't take any risks with it. It's already killed one person. We have to be very careful. There are already questions about funding. But if it's a weapon the military are going to be very interested."

"Well," said Stefan, trying to curb his growing anger, "John here has a different idea. I'll let him speak for himself. It sounds a bit unusual to me, but you hear what he has to say."

"We don't know Doug is dead," said John, to Christine's blank stare. "We don't know the machine killed him. You're making the assumption that it's a weapon but what if it's something else entirely? What if it's some sort of transporter? What if it's not killed him, but taken him elsewhere?"

When the message reached them, she immediately said, "No, no. That's preposterous. That simply cannot be. Impossible, utterly ridiculous. We have to assume Dr. Henson is dead."

But there was a murmur behind her, and the camera view swivelled to show several people in earnest discussion. A young woman with long black hair addressed the screen directly.

"You mean something like a wormhole? Connecting distant regions of space or time? It's a theoretical possibility, way beyond our capabilities, but maybe—"

A bearded man next to her cut in. "And why would aliens go to all the trouble of building a killing machine in the middle of nowhere? Doesn't make any sense."

As they followed the giant snow prints, Sasak motioned Doug to halt.

"Luckily for us, they are solitary creatures… they live in huge caverns, with all the prey kept cocooned as a food supply, stashing it up for ages."

"Goti, is she…" Doug swallowed hard. The thought of something dreadful happening to her was almost too much to bear. He hadn't known her long, but already he felt a certain fondness for her. But there was no time to think about that. There was no time to waste.

"Not if we can get to her soon."

"And what if it gets us?"

"Then we'll all be cocooned together. Till we're eaten. Are you with me?"

"Yes," Doug said, without hesitation.

"You are a brave man," said Sasak.

"So are you," said Doug. "As well as a wise one."

"We need to… ah, here's where the tracks lead."

The snow ape's prints led into the mouth of a cavern as Sasak had suggested. It was hard to judge how large the cave might be from outside, but the mouth itself was enormous. *Not surprising,* thought Doug, *the creature itself is huge.*

"Are we going in?"

"It's fairly safe, the snow ape will be sleeping now."

"How do you know all this?"

"In my younger days, I often used to explore these caverns."

"You amaze me, Sasak."

"I only had to fight off a snow ape once. Maybe twice."

The cavern was dark, sunlight and reflected light from the snow only reached a short distance inside. Sasak started up the metal cylinder he had used to provide heat the night before, but this time, it gave a cold, penetrating white light, projecting eerie shadows that seemed to move onto the walls of the cavern.

"Be very quiet," said Sasak.

"Look!" Doug motioned to a ledge, leading up from the cave floor. What looked like gigantic spiders' cocoons, in all manner of shapes, were grouped along the ledge.

"The snow ape will gather whatever it finds for its food," said Sasak.

The cocoons were all still, except the very last one, at the end. Having climbed onto the ledge, they inched their way to the wriggling cocoon. Doug gasped. Bound inside its silk-like form was none other than Goti. She shook and quivered, her mouth opened and closed, but no sound came out, nor could she struggle free. She was held fast by the cocoon.

Doug couldn't help but notice the other cocooned shapes close to her, as he brandished his sword, alert for danger. The binding around all the others were thick and dusty, there was no movement from within, yet what was inside was not decayed, for he could clearly see the shapes of exotic creatures with claws and stripes, some still bearing the fierce expressions they'd must have made during their last minutes fighting off the snow ape.

This is nothing more than a huge larder for the creature, thought Doug. *And Goti is just one item in its larder.*

He hacked away with his sword at the semi-transparent binding. It was tough going, whatever the cocoon was made of was like glue, sticking and impeding the metal of his sword, but after a few anxious moments, he began to hear Goti's muffled voice.

"Is that you, Doug?"

"Yes, keep still. I don't want to hurt you."

Finally, the last cord was cut, and she stumbled free, nearly collapsing onto him. She turned to Sasak.

"He is my champion."

"You know what this means!" said Sasak gravely.

"Well, I don't," said Doug. "What are you talking about?"

"Look," said Sasak, "there is no time to waste. We'll explain, but we need to get out. But Doug, just know you have done great work."

The whites of Goti's eyes shone in the semi-darkness.

"He has. He is a truly brave man."

In the distance, they heard an inhuman groan.

"Come on," said Sasak. "We need to get out now."

But it was too late. In the white light from the cylinder, they could see the huge white ape approaching. Snorting and snarling, it raised its arms and bellowed, a sound that echoed and re-echoed throughout the entire cavern. They were caught.

"What!" said Stefan, switching the video link off, "did you have to do that for?"

"What do you mean?"

"I mean raising their hopes like that, talking about Doug being alive."

"You said to speak about my ideas…"

"Yes, but not wormholes, gateways in time and space, that's bad enough, and then to start suggesting Doug's not dead. What's his family going to think? We can't go raising false hope like that—"

"I was just saying—"

"As if this wasn't a big enough mess already, with the media circling around like vultures. We've had Doug's disappearance, Doug's death, evidence of aliens, an alien weapon… and now we're going to face another storm… Doug could be alive, but we're not going to do anything to get him back. What a mess. What were you thinking of? Nobody's going to realise you were just coming out with ideas. They'll all think he's alive now."

"Oh."

"Yes, see what you've done."

"I suppose I just got carried away."

They lapsed into silence, looking out of the window at the calm, serene Martian night, the stars hanging over the horizon like brilliant diamonds set in a jet black sky.

"Sorry."

"It's okay. She's determined to get me for something anyway," said Stefan. He paused. "I'm sorry, John, I'm just a bit unnerved. I know you didn't intend it like that. I know we're all shocked by what happened to Doug and believe me, I wish as much as anyone he were alive. But I guess we have to face facts. He probably isn't. How could he be?"

Doug began to wonder if their luck was running out. They were still on the ledge, they'd saved Goti, but for what? Now it looked like they faced certain death. The giant ape, its hairs bristling, its mouth slavering, was between them and the cave mouth. They were trapped. Its roar shook the cave and reverberated through their bones. It had found them in its food store, stealing its food. In the next instant, it would be on them.

Doug pushed aside Sasak and Goti.

"I've an idea." He began to loosen the cocoons from the ledge, pushing them over one by one.

The snow ape paused, unsure whether to save its food or attack them. As it hesitated, it bellowed at them even more furiously.

"Push the rest of them over!" shouted Doug. "In the diversion, we can escape."

Within seconds, a huge pile of cocoons lay shattered on the cavern floor in front of the snow ape, between it and the mouth of the cave. As each one toppled over, a huge spray of foul-smelling dust flew up into the air, blinding the ape. Dust filled the air, creating a thick haze so they could no longer see the ape, just hear its increasingly frantic bellowing.

"Now run!" shouted Doug, as he toppled one final cocoon over the side. As it fell, the carcass inside was revealed, a strange green and yellow patterned beast faintly reminiscent of an Earth tiger, but with the size, colour, and shape all wrong.

"Run!"

They were outside the cave now, panting and looking all around. Distant bellows could still be heard inside the cave, as dust billowed out, making them cough.

"Up here," said Doug, climbing up above the cavern mouth, lending Goti his hand. Hers was a surprisingly warm and strong grip. Within the snow ape's lair, they could still hear it blundering and roaring, blinded by the dust.

"You saved me," said Goti.

"You're welcome," said Doug, "but let's make sure and get out of here first."

They kept moving, taking turns to nervously look around, but the snow ape wasn't following them. Soon its cries became fainter and faded from hearing.

"I'll be happier when we get below the snow level," said Sasak. "The apes prefer the snowy regions, as they can blend in perfectly with their surroundings."

The snow was firm but drifted and piled, with loose rocks and scree underneath. They were all wary now of any piles of snow. It was hardly the best terrain to move quickly around in, but they were conscious that at any moment the snow ape might reappear. Yet already patches of bare rock were poking through the snow. They were leaving the region of snow behind.

"We should be safer now," said Sasak, panting heavily.

They went to sit on a large, almost rectangular rock, but to Doug's surprise, Goti immediately prostrated herself on the ground in front of him, before getting up.

"Doug of the Pillars," she said. "You saved me. That means you are my champion."

Sasak turned to him.

"You are a stranger, Doug, so you may not understand. By saving Goti, she recognises you are due a great honour. And now is the time to tell you more. We have not been open with you about who Gotissa is. But we trusted you and we knew when the moment was right… She is a princess, Doug. And by saving her, you may yet have saved her empire."

Doug looked at Goti and then back at Sasak. "Princess?"

"Yes," said Sasak. "I am her advisor. We are in exile, but we hope to regain her empire."

Doug turned to Goti. "Is this true?"

She smiled. "You're probably the only person in this world who doesn't know who I am. You're a stranger, so why should you? But, Doug of the Pillars, will you accept the honour of being my champion, sworn to protect me but also to be protected by me?"

The words were out before he even thought about it. "I will."

"Good."

"But I have many questions."

"Let us talk of those as we travel, if that is acceptable. We will explain everything."

"And Sasak… your advisor?"

"Not only advisor, but friend, wise man, and most trusted counsellor."

"I knew it!"

"A very wise man indeed."

"Only a fool would argue with that."

"And you will see it all when we get to Jasanna. For now, trust us and you will have your reward, as we trusted you with our lives. When I called you my champion, that was my formal declaration."

"I am honoured."

"Doug," said Sasak. "I saw into your mind, and I saw many things, some of them strange and unusual, but chief amongst them what I saw was goodness and honesty and bravery."

"You certainly are a wise man," said Doug.

"I saw that too," said Goti. "Except I saw more, because unlike you, he did not throw me out of his mind."

Doug turned to Goti. "And must I call you Princess? Princess—"

"No, no titles for champions. Goti. Just call me Goti."

"How are you feeling?"

'I am fine, I felt weak at first. The cocoon is strong; as you struggle it grows stronger, and you grow weaker. It begins to absorb you."

"I could see lots of other animals captured there. Some quite ferocious looking beasts."

Sasak looked uncomfortable. "Perhaps I am wrong. Maybe the creature does roam further afield than I thought, down to the lush plains below for its hunting forays, if there is such a variety of animals as you suggest. But surely its fur is far too thick for that."

"How far is the city from here?" asked Doug.

"It looks tantalisingly close, from up here, but it's about a day's journey. When we get there, though, we can rest, wash the dust off, and dine like nobles," said Sasak.

"Or princesses," said Doug.

Was that a blush spreading over her face?

Doug felt a sense of relief as they descended from the mountain onto the lush, variegated vegetation of the Plains of Eternity. He was sure the others did too. That encounter with the snow ape had shaken them all up. This was certainly a world of danger, dangers he was completely unaware of unlike the others. *Maybe it was just as well,* he thought.

The Plains of Eternity were like another world entirely; neither the harsh heat of the lifeless desert nor the cold and desolation of the mountains. On all sides, strange plants sprouted to heights of six, seven, eight feet, in a wild profusion of colour. Red, blue, yellow, green, the plants showed all the colours of the rainbow. Yet, as Doug, Goti, and Sasak pushed their way through the dense growth, they saw no sign of anyone else, nor any animals.

"Are there no creatures living here?" said Doug, hoping for no more encounters like those with the snow ape.

"They know better than to show themselves to us," said Sasak.

"And they know we'll eat them," said Goti.

As they walked further, they came to the beginnings of a track, if it could be called that, consisting merely of broken down and trampled leaves and plants. Gradually it became wider, and they were no longer forced to walk in single file. The path was now bare earth, between a tunnel of huge purple bushes overhanging the path. Once they even met a solitary blue man sitting on a great fierce looking beast with six legs. Horned and with bristles around its mouth, it opened its jaw to reveal huge fangs, and a blue tongue, as it roared at them.

It certainly isn't as elegant a way to get around as riding a horse, thought Doug. It's six feet made it look ungainly, and unlike a horse, it was stout and wide, looking more like a hippo or rhinoceros. The rider struggled to control the beast as it stamped and roared at them.

"I must apologise," shouted the man, as it lurched from side to side, nearly pushing them off the road, and brushing its rough hide against Doug as he went past.

"She is still young and not yet fully tamed."

Behind the beast was a cart, made of some purple wood-like material.

"What was that beast?" said Doug, as cart and rider disappeared from view in the tunnel of dense vegetation.

"It is a kankaram," said Goti. "Used to pull heavy loads."

If it weren't for the fantastically varied and colourful plants, the journey would have been endless. But as it was, every few steps revealed plants, unlike any Doug had ever seen before, and the sheer variety was so great you could never get bored with it.

By the end of the day, the height of the plants seemed to be decreasing. Now Doug could often see tantalising glimpses of the landscape beyond, revealing rippling leaves and stems waving far off into the distance. Then he caught a glimpse of something else, but what was it? Far off in the distance, almost at the horizon, he could see the gleam of something red, shimmering and wavering in the air.

"What is that?" he said.

"It is the city wall of Jasanna," said Sasak. "Built untold ages ago, it is the oldest and most beautiful city in the world."

"In your world," said Doug. "Though maybe indeed anywhere."

As they drew nearer, for a long time, the vision of the city on the edge of the plain stayed persistently out of reach, getting no closer. But after some time, more details became gradually visible. Glittering towers, slender, and shining with gold or silver were visible above the walls. Ornate spheres capped the towers, and slender bridges spanned the spaces between.

Doug gasped on seeing it. "It's beautiful."

Goti placed her hand on his shoulder. "Wait till you see it closer."

"It is often called the City at the Edge of the World," said Sasak.

"Why?"

"Because it marks the boundary. Where we've come from is the realm of barbarians."

"How much further?"

"An hour, perhaps two," said Sasak.

The city was breathtaking when at last they approached its walls, after an endless walk through land cleared of high vegetation, all plants shorn were at two to three feet.

"The plants are kept short to stop cover for invaders," said Sasak. "And for food. Though the only way to invade is to come the way we came. You see why it's called the City at the Edge of the World."

The walls were solid metal, polished and reflective, rising high above them to perhaps a hundred feet. Doug felt dwarfed by the immensity of such walls, below which people were little more than minute figures. He could see great walkways, beyond the walls, spanning the space from tower to tower. People were walking across them, hundreds of feet above the ground. And wide staircases, built of some lustrous yellow stone, led at angles up and around the towers. The towers themselves were unbelievably slender, as fragile as delicate flowers. No two towers were identical, they were all of differing heights, colours, and materials too numerous to mention. He counted gold, silver, red, blue... He had to look away, it was almost too much to take in. For, as the last light of day gleamed on the precious materials of the towers, the whole scene looked exquisite and magical; it was like a dream hovering just beyond existence. He half expected it to vanish if he looked away.

A quote from Shakespeare came to his mind, 'And, like the baseless fabric of this vision, the cloud-capped towers, the gorgeous palaces... shall dissolve.' But when he looked back, the vision was still there. It was real.

"This is the Gate of Weary Travellers," said Sasak. "There are another six vast gates like this around the city."

A seven-foot tall purple-skinned man, stout and solid, wearing something akin to a tunic, in red, made from some unknown beast's hide, stood by the entrance beneath the city wall, stopping everyone as they approached.

Before he could stop himself, Doug couldn't help blurting out, "He's purple!"

The guard heard but merely gave a strange smile. Doug saw the three-foot sword resting by his side.

"Welcome strangers. Jasanna welcomes all with good intentions. Even," and he looked keenly at Doug, "those of strange pale skin. But what is your intention?"

Sasak was about to answer when the giant continued, "I fancy I recognise your company. You look familiar my lady. Why, you could be the image of the Princess of the Far Sands."

They fell silent. Goti made a gesture, half bow, half wave. "You're very kind," she said.

"Enter," said the giant, making the same gesture in return but bowing far lower.

Inside the city walls, the streets were bustling, raising a perpetual haze of red dust. Doug wondered if that was why the people lived in those tall towers, high above the dirt of the streets. Yet there were squat buildings too, almost as beautiful as the towers in their own way. They hugged the earth rather than soaring to great heights. In sparkling white stone, tiled with precious stones, they were decorated with fantastical beasts. Doug wondered how many of those beasts really did exist in this strange world? Here anything seemed possible.

There were certainly enough exotic looking people here. In just a few minutes he'd seen skin in all the colours you could imagine: purple, red, blue, green, orange, grey. It was hard not to imagine the city as a great meeting place, a city lying at the end of some immensely long trading route, like the old Silk Road back on Earth.

With every step he took, Doug marvelled more at what he saw. If he were dreaming, then this was some dream. Mars had proven to be a dead world, and the fantastic worlds imagined by Burroughs and Brackett and many others had turned out to be just that, works of the imagination. *But what would they make,* he wondered, *of this world if they could see it?* He watched as a huge balloon drifted by overhead, with a small silver craft slung underneath. People were crammed against the windows as it lazily floated towards a tower of black and gold, a tower that soared so high it hurt his neck to see up to the top.

He'd nearly died, he'd seen many dangers and fierce foes, but this strange beauty, he wouldn't swap this for the world, any world. He thought of Stefan, Janna, and Eric, John too, on that desolate Mars that now seemed so remote from this world, so devoid of the exotic life teeming on this one. He took a deep breath. This was his world now.

◦──◦──◦

"Sounds crazy," said Stefan, "and I'm as crazy for listening."

"No, it's true," said John, leaning back in his seat.

"This is what those engineers at the conference told you?"

"That's right. They think we can trace where Doug went."

Stefan shook his head. "How is that even possible?"

"They want us to try tracing Doug's transponder."

"Through the pillars?"

"Yeah."

"I don't suppose it can do any harm. I don't suppose it'll work either."

"I'll put some equipment together. And…"

"And?"

"If we locate him, there's something else they'd like to try. They've got a prototype they've been working on."

"What type of prototype?"

"When we locate him—"

"If."

"If we locate him, we could try… there's a chance we could bring him back."

"Bring him back? Are you serious?"

"If we can find him. There's no guarantee."

"I take it this is all unofficial, under the radar stuff."

"Yeah."

"If the agency finds out…"

"It's got to be worth a shot."

"Mmm. Let's face it, Doug's probably dead."

"But if he isn't…"

"Hell, I'm finished anyway when we get back to Earth. Losing a crewman… that's the end of my career. But until we get back…"

"You mean we can try?"

"What have we got to lose?"

⪥◇⪤ ⪥◇⪤ ⪥◇⪤

They stopped in front of a stall selling vases of all shapes and sizes, ornately decorated and coloured in exquisite detail. The stall holder came up to them.

"For you, lady… this vase here?"

Goti looked pleased.

"But… I don't have any money on me."

The stall holder made a motion Doug realised meant this was not a problem.

"For a lady as beautiful as her Excellency the Princess Gottissa, this is an acceptable gift, no?"

They walked on, Doug carrying the vase.

"I can't thank you both enough," said Goti.

"It was Sasak—"

"It was Doug—"

They both spoke at the same time.

"Well," said Goti to Sasak, "you are my wisest counsellor," and turning to Doug, "but you are my champion." She smiled. "For now and always."

Right there, in the centre of the alleyway, she prostrated herself. The bustling crowds merely stepped aside, as if this was an everyday occurrence.

Doug looked around, embarrassed yet secretly pleased.

"Not here!" hissed Sasak.

"I couldn't help it," said Goti, getting to her feet and embracing Doug. Touching his cheek, she kissed him.

"There is much to do, Doug of the Pillars, but I want you by my side."

Doug held her tight. Sasak coughed discreetly once, then again. *This is unbelievable,* Doug thought, *Goti, a princess of another world, is embracing me!* He sensed a new life beckoning him. There was no way back to the old life anyway. There was, no doubt, much to do, and they still hadn't told him what their quest was, and why they were in exile, but he would be by their side. He would be by her side.

He held on to her tightly, but as he did so, something odd happened. He felt queasy. She seemed to be growing insubstantial. He tried to hold her tighter still, but there was less and less to hold on to. It was like putting his arms around mist. Lights flickered in the corner of his vision, and strange visual effects like veils of coloured light wafted in the air. Shimmering points of light cascaded down in front of him, moving faster and faster.

All the time, the market, the city, and even the sky above were fading to pure grey. Goti and Sasak took on a ghost like appearance. Their voices too grew distant as if heard from the bottom of a deep well. He tried to move, but he was paralysed, could only watch helplessly as everything started to fade away.

He heard Goti shouting, "Doug! Doug!" and saw Sasak's horror and puzzlement.

He shouted, "Goti!" at the top of his voice, but it seemed to amount to little more than a whisper. Then he was shouting into an empty void.

The shimmering gave way to whirling coloured lights, circling round and round, faster and faster. He could no longer feel Goti, no longer see the bazaar, or smell its scents, or hear the cries of the merchants. His eyes hurt from the strong lights, and a loud buzzing was in his ears. It grew louder still, as the light grew brighter, and he thought his skull would split in two. The images he'd seen before, when he first came through the pillars appeared again. He was going back through again, that was what it must be. Somehow the pillars were taking him back. But this time, the visions he saw were those of Goti and Sasak and that empty desert. For a second he heard her cries of, "Doug! Doug!" but he knew it wasn't real.

Now he was falling, falling down into a black void, a void of such total darkness that it couldn't be imagined. He was endlessly falling, on and on for hours, until at last, he heard a rushing noise in his ears. *For God's sake, what new torment is this?*

The rushing noise grew louder. Stars appeared, yellow stars, galaxies, and then a huge red star filled his vision. *Just stop,* he thought. Finally, when he thought he could endure it no longer, the oncoming rush of images began to slow and the sense of falling decreased. It was coming to an end. He saw white all around. *I must be dead now,* he thought, *this is death.*

Instead, he heard applause and a voice—oddly familiar—speaking, but he couldn't catch the words. He lost consciousness.

When he opened his eyes again, he still saw that blinding light all around him. Wait, if he squinted a bit he could see. *Isn't this the base on Mars? That is Stefan and Janna, and over there… Eric and John.*

They were talking, but he couldn't understand the words. And what were the gestures they were making? Something was wrong, horribly wrong.

"Goti…" he wearily said.

He heard Janna speak, but it wasn't words, it was just a series of guttural sounds, nothing he could make sense of. She wiped his brow.

"Goti!" he shouted.

They were all clustered around him now, making those strange gestures. And Stefan too, Stefan was making the same sounds Janna had. In his mind, there was some distant memory, of what those noises might mean, but it lay beyond reach. Instead, maddeningly, they kept making those guttural sounds that were meaningless to him. With horror, he realised his mind had been rewired when Sasak and Goti taught him their language. He screamed.

RUIN

ALMA SINAN

"Don't ya be goin' up there, Kathryn! That ruin on the hill is evil!"

"How can a bunch of old, broken columns be evil?"

"Those old columns trap ya like the bars of a jail cell."

"I never took you to be superstitious Grandma."

"Superstitious? A bunch of quaint, Irish folktales, is that what you think I'm tellin' ya? Well, I'm not out to tell ya daft stories of leprechauns or faeries or such nonsense. What I'm tellin' ya is real. It happened to myself."

"Okay, Grandma, tell me what happened."

"I was once nineteen years old, and all piss and vinegar like yourself. That's why your ma shipped ya out here, thought we'd relate. But now I'm thinkin', this is probably the worst place she could have sent ya."

I'd just gotten out of rehab and Mom had decided to get me out of her hair and away from my heroin-addict friends. So she sent me 'back home' to Ireland; even though it was never my home, and I told her that. Made me feel sorry for Grandma, though, the way Mom unloaded me on her like that.

"Well, I'm here now, and I want to hear your story. The ruin…"

"Yes, the ruin," she paused as if to gather strength enough to tell the tale. Her green eyes glistened with some remembered pain.

"'Twas once a cathedral, centuries old, that fell most like due to ancient tantrums of wars long past. Your grand-da brought me here as his bride when I was about your age. I recall how he looked that day, the sun shining through his red hair like someone set it alight. But it was his eyes, as blue as cornflowers, that made me lose my mind with love for him. We moved here from Donegal, and I was with-child and still in love with your grand-da. But all that changed the moment we saw that ruin on the hill."

"How could everything change, just by looking at an old ruin?"

"Truth be told, I was part to blame. My da was vehemently against the Catholic Church which was so busy forgin' haloes for those who'd placed coins in the collection plates and instilling fear into the minds of those who didn't. We were hated, my sisters and I, 'cause everyone knew we were atheists. They only put up with us because our da was the sole doctor for miles about. And he never forgave me for marrying Thomas Murphy, who was about as Catholic as could be."

"But… the ruin?"

"Keep your alans on, I'm gettin' to it. Thomas and I had only just arrived and were takin' a dander on the road. I looked up at that ruin perched on the hill and laughed sayin' it was as useful as a lighthouse on a bog and how it was the perfect metaphor for the Catholic Church. 'Twas then your grand-da struck me plain across the face and called me a hoor's melt. He yelled at me, 'Show some respect, woman!' Well, I slugged him right back, I did. Told him I'd rob the eye from his head if he ever laid a finger on me again."

"I can't believe he hit you!"

"He never did again, to be sure. He provided for us well enough. Times were hard then, but my Thomas was ambitious. He'd sell the steam off his own piss if he could get a shilling for it. He opened a pub with Henry O'Shay.

"By that time, of course, the polish of infatuation had worn away, especially after your ma was born. I hadn't forgiven Thomas and rarely took him to my bed. A man needs that, a woman's touch, and I denied it to him. 'Twas wrong of me, bein' so stubborn and harsh, but by then so much damage had been done, I knew not how to mend it between us.

"Every day after work, Thomas would take a bottle of gin and go to the ruin. Then I started finding blood on Thomas' shirt when I did the washin'.

'What in the hell, you doin' up there?' I demanded.

'Ask me arse. It don't concern you, woman,' he'd always say.

"So one day, I went up there myself… and what I seen child, ya'd think I was off my nut. I ne'er til this day told anyone what I saw."

I leaned forward. "What did you see?"

"It was early mornin', and Thomas had been gone all night. I left your ma with the neighbor and I headed out to find him. 'Twas a steep climb. The rain the night before had left the path as slick as wet leather, and I had to keep grabbin' roots to pull myself along. By the time I reached the top, I was drenched in sweat and muck. Slowly I climbed a flight of seven stairs, carved in the rock, and the jagged arches of the ruined Cathedral came into view.

"The roof and two of the building's walls had crumbled away, leavin' the interior exposed. 'Twas as though the centuries had devoured that church and had spit out the bones; those remainin' arches jutted like a skeleton's crooked ribs. The two walls still standin' were clasped in ivy. Leaves fluttered with each passin' breeze making it look as if the stones were breathin'.

"I stopped in front of what once must have been the doorway, but now was only half an arch and a bit of wall. A gargoyle sat upon a pedestal on top of the door frame. He jeered at me, his stone tongue protrudin' from his mouth, and his lizard tail poised obscenely between his legs. Made me wonder why anyone should want to carve such a vulgar creature at the entrance of what was supposed to be a holy place.

"As I crossed the threshold, the smell overwhelmed me. It was like walkin' into a sealed room where a couple had been at it for hours; that musky-sweet scent of sweat and body fluids. And it was wrong that smell, like I told ya, the place was exposed to open air."

I shifted uncomfortably.

"I heard 'em first, makin' animal noises, ruttin' and moanin' and whimperin'. I picked my way across the broken tiles and chunks of masonry. Then I saw 'em…" she paused and looked at her hands.

"Grandma?"

"My Thomas with that creature that lives up there. They lay together upon the marble altar that was green and slick with moss and slime. On that day, she was the most beautiful woman I'd ever seen. Her thick, black hair flowed down her back and my Thomas, lay naked and thrashin' beneath her, held in the wanton grip of his own lust.

"I stood there, horrified, unable to speak, unable to stop what was happening, Thomas begged her to cut him again. 'Twas then that I saw wounds that looked like crimson wrinkles all over his body. The creature ran one of her blood-stained fingernails across the tender underside of his right arm. His cry knifed through the silence, from ecstasy or pain, I knew not which. Blood dripped like a slow river down his arm and then trickled off his finger and into the ground below the altar. The creature opened its scarlet mouth and laughed.

"I finally found my voice. 'Thomas Murphy!' I yelled. He and the creature turned and stared straight at me and it 'twas as if the world froze in that second. Then a wind blustered around me, blowin' grit and sand into my eyes. When I opened them again, the creature was gone.

"For a few moments, I thought I'd imagined it all. My eyes darted to every crumblin' corner of the place, searchin' for the woman. The Cathedral was deserted, except for a raven sittin' on top of a broken column, its claws and beak stained with blood. It rustled its plumes and flew away in a whisper of beatin' wings.

"Then I turned and ran to Thomas, who was blatherin' nonsense. He tried to pull me close to kiss me, no doubt thinkin' I was the dark-haired creature. I felt sick with jealousy and disgust over what I'd witnessed but knew I needed to help him. I coaxed him up, all naked and shiverin', and bloody as he was.

"'Well you certainly made a holy show of yourself,' I said, but I struggled not to cry. I threw his trousers at him. 'Here! Put your cacks back on, I'm takin' you home.' I threw his bloodied arm around my shoulder and somehow managed to get us down that hill."

"What happened to him?"

"He lay in the grip of fever, ravin' wanton phrases for the colleen with long black hair. I tended his wounds, wishin' I could do more for his mind. Seven days after I brought him home, I called the priest to administer the last rites. We were but three years wed when he died.

"The night of the wake, my Thomas came to me in a dream. He sat on the side of our bed and looked at me with such love I'd scarce seen since our weddin' day.

"He said, 'Sorry Maggie for treatin' you so poorly. I'll never forgive myself for hittin' ya, and for what happened in the ruin. But it be evil, that place; it gives ya what you most yearn for in exchange for your blood. 'Twas only you I wanted, Maggie, but when you wouldn't have me, I started yearnin' for another. Will you forgive me?'

"Of course, I forgave him. When I awoke, my pillow was drenched in tears, and I realized that the whole thing had been a dream.

"I took myself to the parlor, where Thomas lay in his coffin. His red hair hung limp, and his face was creased with worry like an old man's.

"Suddenly, a raven flew in through an open window and lighted on Thomas' chest. Its claws and beak were stained with dried blood. Rage climbed through my heart and up into my throat. 'Go on with ya!' I screamed and grabbed the broom by the hearth and chased it around the room. I heard your ma cryin' upstairs, but I couldn't stop until the raven was dead. It flew back out the open window and me, in my nightdress, pulled open the front door and chased after it; left the child cryin' in her cot, all by herself and her da downstairs layin' in his coffin and the house wide open.

"I fought my way up the hillside, the raven every so often, landin' on the path in front of me, chiding me with its gritty voice. This infuriated me more, and I struggled harder to get up the hill. By the time I reached the seven stairs leadin' to the ruin, I was knackered and had to crawl the rest of the way up to the threshold. The raven was nowhere in sight.

"I picked myself up and looked at the wall, expectin' to see the lewd gargoyle stickin' his tongue out at me, but saw a stone angel in its stead. Its wings were outstretched, and someone had carved it so expertly, I could see the tendons in its neck as if it was truly blowin' the trumpet raised to its lips.

"Silver mist wreathed the inside of the cathedral. I could smell the scent of frankincense, the fragrance as thick and heavy as repentance. The mellow churnin' of the fog revealed more marble-winged acolytes rimming the two remainin' walls. Why hadn't I seen them before? I walked in further and noticed the broken stained glass windows still confined in their casements.

"Then I heard a male voice murmuring Latin verses, and I glued myself to where I stood. The consecrated language entered my mind and formed pictures there, and I could almost understand what was bein' said.

"The mist parted, and I saw a priest, standin' by the altar, dressed in black vestments, his ebony hair like a dark halo around his head and draped in radiant humility. As I drew closer, his cornflower blue eyes gleamed, and he stretched his arms out in welcome.

'You've come, Maggie,' he said. 'We've been expectin' you.'

"A fire, that I'd quelled since childhood flared in my heart. All the longing I'd ever had to know God, in spite of me da's upbringin', burned bright within me. I recalled how, in my youth, I'd watched with envy, the devout, returnin' home from church, with hidden knowledge and serenity glowin' in their eyes. How I longed to join them and taste the sweetness of belonging! I approached the priest with tears streamin' down my face. 'So it be true? God exists?' I asked.

'Oh yes,' he said and assured me that heaven wasn't just an empty tomb perched above the world; that it was a mansion filled with beings of light. 'Would you like to hear them, Maggie?'

"All I could do was nod like an eejit. The priest picked up a golden chalice and a thin, round wafer from a silver tray restin' on the altar. 'Are you ready, Maggie?'

"Again I nodded and opened my mouth to receive the Holy Communion. As soon as the wafer touched my tongue, I felt it turn to flesh. Then the sweet, ruby wine filled my mouth, and I tasted it turnin' warm and salty, as only blood could taste.

"Canticles rose up from the invisible pews and the melody ached through me. I heard the rejoicin' of angels singin' their praises to God. I was listenin' to the harmony of all creation.

'Beautiful, isn't it?' The priest asked, and somehow his voice sounded clear through the strong Gregorian voices.

"I stood transfixed; couldn't remember my Thomas, my child or my own name. And then the priest reached out, and I saw dried blood beneath his fingernails. He touched my hands and feet, and my blood burst forth as if there were nails being hammered into them. I felt everythin'… the pain and the warmth of my blood spillin' from me into the ground by the altar."

"Stigmata." I breathed the word. Grandma nodded and showed me the scars on her hands.

"There I was, bleedin' into the ground and bein' assaulted by canting, ethereal voices, when the priest, he threw back his head and laughed. 'Twas then I recalled how the creature with the long black hair had bled my Thomas and laughed in the same chilling way. And I remembered that the ruins would give you what you most longed for, in exchange for your blood.

"When I came to myself, I screamed as loud as I could, 'Go way outta that! I'm Margaret Murphy, and you'll have no more 'o' me.' Everythin' stopped dead. And then the wind blew sand and grit into my eyes. I ran out of there, half blinded and crazed with what I'd seen and heard.

"At home the door still stood open, the mirrors all draped, my Thomas still in his coffin, the woman who lived next door held my child in her arms, and the room was filled with neighbors. I rushed into the parlor, in my blood stained night dress, then the world went dark.

"I awoke in an asylum, a week later. I never even got to see them lay my Thomas to rest."

I took a deep breath. Up until that point, I'd almost believed everything my grandmother had said. She'd had me going there, talking about ghosts and shape-shifters and now she was telling me she'd spent time in the nut house! Maybe she was crazy! Maybe they put her away because she was having hallucinations and harming herself. Or worse;

maybe they put her away because she was the one responsible for my granddad's death.

"'Twas a good year later that I came back, collected your ma from the neighbor who was keepin' her, and returned to this house."

She searched my face.

"I can see you think I'm blaggardin' ya."

I opened my mouth to say something but found I couldn't. Then I thought about Mom, and how she'd sent me here, to stay with grandma, who was either making up stories or really nuts.

"Well don't look at me that way!" Grandma continued. "I'm just warnin' you, Kathryn, I'll give ya' a toe in the hole if I ever find out you've takin' it into your head to go up to that ruin!"

As I climbed the seven stone steps that my grandmother described to me the night before, I felt my heart racing.

There, just as she'd described it, stood the arched doorway. But instead of a gargoyle or trumpeting angel, I saw a sculpture of a monk, hunched over and flagellating himself, his marble hand bore a many thronged whip that spread out like flames across his back.

Slowly, I crossed the threshold and saw ferns soaked with rain and drenched mushroom caps sprouting between the crumbling marble tiles. There stood the two walls covered in emerald ivy and the broken windows, tracery still clutching bits of colored glass.

Then I saw him.

He was dressed casually, in jeans and a cable-knit sweater. His eyes were as blue as cornflowers, his hair as dark as a raven's wing.

Laid out upon the altar, were the tools I'd come to know so well: a bottle of water, citric acid, a cigarette filter, a belt, a lighter, a spoon, a syringe, and the heroin.

When he motioned to the altar, I saw the dried blood beneath his fingernails. He smiled. "You've come, Kathryn! We've been expectin' you."

RUNES OF TIME

E. W. FARNSWORTH

Professor Ola Halvarsson was a rune collector and archivist. He was also a full professor and teacher at Oslo University. On weekends he would take groups of students to do field work at likely sites for new discoveries. They would camp overnight and cook picnic-style meals over an open fire. Most often they verified and photographed runes scholars had already discovered. On rare occasions, they discovered undocumented stone carvings that contained both runes and pictures.

He and his students had combed the area in the south of the country so well that Halvarsson offered a monetary prize for new discoveries in that region. To the far north so many sites remained to be explored, Masters Theses and Doctoral dissertations were cordoned off by lots the students paid for. So it was that Ingrid Hansen the Swede heiress and doctoral student began her survey of the runic stones on the north side of Ufa Fjord.

The site Ingrid had purchased the rights to research was forty acres abutting the cliff that plunged down half a mile before the fjord water and another mile below. Picturesque and untouched by tourism, the site was ideal for her purposes. From her first days, new discoveries abounded.

Having first gridded off the forty acres into twenty-five-meter squares, she further subdivided her find into five-meter squares. She used a computer graphics program to map her site and its subdivisions. As she made her painstaking way from square to square, she kept a diary of her discoveries. She hoped the diary would become her dissertation. Each night she sent Professor Halvarsson an email progress report. He would review her report and send back comments and suggestions.

In the twenty-fourth report of her current expedition, Ingrid noted the discovery of something she had never found in her prior voluminous research: an underground crypt with runes on all the interior walls comprising what seemed to be a history. Ingrid managed to take cell phone photographs of some features of her find, which she sent as attachments to her daily reports. Then unaccountably her reports stopped altogether. Professor Halvarsson was alarmed and feared she might have become sick. She was his prize student and something more than that to the professor. He took emergency time off and flew north to pick up her trail.

Halvarsson knew exactly where to begin his search because of Ingrid's plan and sequence of reports. He went straight to the square where she claimed she had made her find. He found her camp, but she was not present. Frantic because her camp was so close to the cliff that overhung the fjord, he radioed the Norwegian Navy for assistance in finding his missing person.

So while the Norwegian ships and divers searched the fjord for her body, the professor continued an inch-by-inch search of the pertinent square for any sign of the crypt Ingrid had found and photographed. He reasoned that she may have become trapped in the structure and could not escape.

On his first, careful pass, which took a full week, the professor had no luck finding the entrance to the crypt. He found runic inscriptions aplenty, some of which his student had recorded in her diary. Before he began his second pass through the area, he reviewed Ingrid's emails and their attachments for clues. Nothing in the landscape indicated that a crypt lay below the surface. Could one of the stone monuments contain the secret of the crypt? The professor had no idea.

After the tenth day, the Norwegian Navy called off their search for Ingrid's body. They reasoned that the girl had not fallen into the fjord. That was a relief to Halvarsson, but he knew no human could survive ten days without food and water in the rugged landscape above the fjord.

The professor, whose grief was inconsolable, continued his search for the entrance to the crypt for the next fortnight without positive results. Finally, he wired the girl's parents she could not be found. They declined to visit the site of her disappearance but sent a private investigator to assist with continued search for the girl's body. The investigator, a no-nonsense detective named Olaf Lukasson arrived in the area and went over all the data the professor had amassed.

With Halvarsson, Lukasson went inch by inch over the landscape to discover the entrance to the crypt, without positive results. Lukasson then read through the search reports of the Norwegian Navy. He spoke with the leader of the maritime search team. The detective's report on his findings indicated that the authorities and the professor had done everything humanly possible to find Ingrid. They had not failed because of dereliction. There was no evidence of foul play in Ingrid's disappearance. It remained to be seen whether she had stumbled on some sort of hidden trapdoor leading to her death.

Lukasson departed the area, but the professor remained convinced he could find Ingrid somehow. This time, he reviewed the runes she had found just prior to her disappearance. He went to find each stone and verify its inscriptions. Her discovery of five stones in succession preceded her disappearance. The stones were arranged in a quincunx pattern, like the dots on a die for the number five.

Halvarsson became convinced that those stones were the key to the mystery of Ingrid's disappearance. Strangely, no ratiocination about those stones appeared anywhere in Ingrid's emails or diary. He could find among her things no hand-written record of her thoughts about those stones.

The professor now limited his search to the area in which the five stones lay. He moved Ingrid's tent so it lay within that area. He tried to move each stone in turn, but they were firmly embedded in the ground as they probably had been since the Third Century A.D. when they had been inscribed. By day the professor continued his search. By night, he dreamed and hallucinated about the stones and their inscriptions.

The runes on the stones described warfare between the Norse tribes and foreign soldiers. Halvarsson thought the foreigners might be Romans or Swedes. They were more likely the former since at the time the Romans were ascendant in England and broadening their scope to the Scandinavian Peninsula.

Some inscriptions on the stones were runic but transliterated Roman words. The Roman alphabet was not apparent, but the transliterations indicated the Norse tribes on the fjord had communicated with Romans regularly. In fact, indications were that some Romans had interbred with the Norse tribes.

This insight gave the professor a new approach. He theorized that some Romans, whose empire was then fragmenting, might have settled in Norway. That would explain the proliferation of stone monuments from the third century forward. It would also suggest that Roman engineering might have influenced whatever constructions had been made during that time. In a dream, Halvarsson envisioned Romans building secret fortifications underground to hide themselves and their families from predation by their own kind. Such fortifications would have been repositories of gold and silver as well as other valuables.

The professor began thinking like a gifted Roman soldier in those chaotic end-times of the empire. He wondered what he would have done to hide his wealth and family on the cliff over the fjord. The Romans might have come by sea up the fjord, but they never would have scaled the cliffs to reach the plateau that lay above. The Romans might also have come up the Norwegian coast, passing each fjord until they arrived here. They would have looked for signs of their own deserters hoping to crucify them as examples.

The professor asked himself, "What underground structures might the Romans in Norway have built for their own security?" He was aware of Roman soldiers having escaped to China and to India. He suspected Romans had gone deep into Africa from Alexandria as their empire crumbled. The professor conjectured that four or five generations of survival would have placed the Roman settlers in Norway beyond the reach of their countrymen. Only much later was Christianity introduced. By then the Roman blood would have been entirely blended with native Norse blood.

The professor reviewed the pictures Ingrid had taken of the crypt. Seeing in the photos a sequence of twenty descending steps, Halvarsson deduced the underground cavity's floor was from fifteen to twenty feet below the surface terrain. The walls of the underground structure were as solid as the five stones used for the inscriptions.

He asked, "Is it possible the five stones actually came from excavating the subterranean chamber?"

The professor measured the five stones and used a computer graphics program to determine how they might have fitted together. The program showed that the five stones might have been hewn from the same great rock formation. In that case, the excavation might have penetrated the surface in an open excavation like a modern strip mine. Reviewing the cell phone pictures again, he noticed that the ceiling of the crypt was not like the walls. The stone ceiling had been laid over the large opening caused by the excavation. Like the Pantheon in Rome, it had been created to radiate its thrust sideways, not downward.

Halvarsson began looking for a low domed structure like a slight bow in the surface of the land. He found such a pattern, with the five stones in its center. Certain that he was near to a solution, the professor did a meticulous spiral search outward from his camp site, well outside the area where the five stones lay. As the sun set, he reached one side the cliff's edge over the fjord. He had to wait for morning to examine the cliff, but he was now convinced he had the answer. The opening to the crypt was on the cliff face somewhere near the edge where he was lying.

The professor spent a restless night tossing and turning. He had visions of what he might find when he penetrated the crypt conforming to the pictures Ingrid had sent him before she disappeared. He awakened in a cold sweat when in a nightmare he found his intern's decomposing body. No archaeological find, he thought, was worth a human death, particularly the death of his favorite student.

At daybreak after having a quick repast, Halvarsson drove pitons into the rock just above and behind the overhang of the cliff's face. On ropes, he rappelled over the side, his rock hammer on a string attached to his belt. He descended eight feet, then ten and finally twelve feet before he saw a ledge cut into the rock face. The ledge was visible neither from above nor from below. It was the perfect foothold for someone in hiding. The professor saw runes written across the rock.

A quick translation of the runes was encouraging. They read, "Man is dust. To dust, he will return." This ancient saw was associated with early pre-Christian burial sites throughout Norway. He looked for signs of an opening or entryway. He rested his foot on the ledge.

A lever was activated by the professor's weight, and a giant stone door opened inward. The professor swung himself into the entry and let his ropes dangle as he scrambled down the stone stairway into a large cavern. It was the same as Ingrid's pictures had shown.

The professor stood where Ingrid snapped her photos. He realized that she had captured the essence of the crypt. He could not have done better than she. He surmised that she had successfully ascended to the surface to transmit her images. It would have been unthinkable for her to do anything but return to her discovery the next day. But she had disappeared.

Halvarsson explored the crypt, using his cell phone's torch. Ingrid's body was not present. He wondered whether she had found another doorway hidden inside the crypt. With that premise, he pressed the walls looking for a hidden door.

In the farthest recess of the crypt he saw the inscription, "Seek and you will find what you are looking for."

He pressed the rock at the center of this runic inscription, and two things happened. The entry that had admitted him closed cutting off all external light. A new entry appeared in the wall he had pressed. Using his cell phone torch, he descended the stairs to the second chamber.

The second chamber was fitted like a catacomb, with rock recesses formed to accept bodies of the dead. The professor counted over one hundred recesses, each lined with limestone and filled with human remains. By the clothing, he saw that some were female, some male and others children. He searched each compartment for Ingrid's body but did not find it. He did find evidence the men had Roman artifacts buried with them, Lares, gladii and beads characteristic of the Second Century empire. He used his cell phone camera to record the crypt. Then he searched for a third entry behind it.

Having discovered two entries in the space of an hour, he thought finding the third would be trivial. It was not so. The Roman minds that had created the structure made each level an intellectual challenge harder than the previous one.

After attempting to penetrate the far side of the crypt, he came back to the stairwell and looked for a trapdoor to a level below where he stood. He reasoned he was looking for a stone lever since wood long since should have decayed. The bottom step proved the key. Standing on the far right side, the stair gave way, revealing a trap door and a continuation of the stairs below the surface. The professor did not want to wait. He shone his torch and stepped down into the third chamber.

He did not need his light for long. The chamber had a light of its own. Instead of a crypt, this cavern was full of enormous jars and piles of gold and silver. Statues of Roman gods and goddesses were also present. A throne room lay at the end of the cave opposite the stairs. Seated on the throne in a robe of gold embroidered silk sat Ingrid, very much alive and smiling.

"Well, professor, you found me. It only took you two months. Anyway, I'm glad you came."

"Ingrid, I'm so glad to see you alive. Your parents and I have been worried to distraction. We thought you were dead."

"I am as you see me. Come see the fourth cave. This is only the third."

Behind the throne, she pressed on two stones simultaneously. The great wall opened. Ingrid stepped through the opening and gestured for her professor to follow. When he did, he noticed that the entrance to the third chamber had closed, and the entrance to the fourth chamber also closed.

"Now we are in a realm our academics never figured on," Ingrid said. "Here I've found my destiny. I'd like to introduce you to my new friends. They found me and fed me when I was about to despair."

She clapped her hands three times. Niches appeared in the walls, and giant figures advanced from their confines. They were purplish green and heavy with muscles. They had short, knobby ears and sharp teeth showing over their swollen lips. Immediately the professor knew they were trolls. His hair stood on end, but he decided to brave it because Ingrid did not seem to be afraid in the least.

"On your right, professor, is the Troll King. On the left is the Troll Queen. We are in their realm now. We live or die at their pleasure."

The professor had not seen their thrones yet, but he did when the two trolls walked to their thrones and sat down.

Ingrid introduced her professor to the troll monarchs. Then she expounded on what she had discovered.

"Professor, the short version is that Romans, who fled to Norway when their empire collapsed, made common cause with trolls. Runes were the result of collaboration between trolls and Romans. Just as Caesarian code is one-for-one substitution, so the runic alphabet is a one-for-one substitution. We have runes because of the collaboration. The Romans trained trolls in their engineering arts, so this crypt complex has designs well known from ancient architecture. The crypt was perfectly secure because no Romans could ever find it. After Rome fell, the Romans were no longer useful. They were killed and eaten by the trolls. Vestiges of Rome remain in these underground structures and the runes themselves."

"You learned this from the trolls?"

"I learned part of this from the trolls and part from my observations of these monuments. The entire story is told in the runes of the outer cavern." She smiled. "Don't you think what I've find is worth the doctorate I was seeking?"

The professor thought for a moment. "Yes. If properly written up with documentary evidence in the form of pictures, your dissertation would shake the foundations of architectural history."

"If only I could tell the tale! Of course, the trolls object. Isn't that correct, Troll King?"

The Troll King nodded. He said, "Trolls need security. You are both prisoners here because you know too much. Centuries ago the Romans came. They assimilated into the surface villages. Then they and their descendants became useful for us trolls. When they were no longer useful, they were killed and eaten. So it shall be with you."

The Troll King's voice resounded in the cave. As if to punctuate what he had said, the walls opened and revealed a troll army, fully armed and ready to attack.

"For now, you are our guests. You'll tell us what you can do for us. If we agree that you can help, we'll let you live. If not, we'll do to you what we did to the Romans. While you're thinking, eat and drink as much as you like. Sleep or work as you please." The Troll King burped contentedly and sat back in his throne. This gave the Troll Queen a chance to talk.

"Humans, you've come at a good time from the trolls' point of view. We need new blood. We'll have it in breeding or in eating or in both. Ingrid has made her choice. She will marry our troll prince, my son. You, professor, must choose wisely. I have a troll princess, my daughter. She needs a mate. Marry her, and you'll live. Spurn her, and you'll die in anguish."

The professor saw no way to escape. He looked at Ingrid, who only smiled at him as if to say, "It's up to you to choose. I can't help you."

"I'd like to meet your daughter, Troll Queen. Is she available?"

The Troll Queen clapped her hands twice. A beautiful female troll, with features exactly like Ingrid's, came out from a recess in the wall. She stood beside Ingrid so the professor could compare them. He could see no difference between the figures. This gave him an idea.

"Your majesty, your daughter is beautiful and graceful. Is she also intelligent?"

The Troll Queen liked his question. She decreed, "Command her to do whatever you like. See what she does. Then judge for yourself."

"Troll Princess, lead Ingrid and me to the surface world so we can show you our camp and sleep with you under the stars."

The Troll Princess snapped her fingers. The professor, Ingrid and she were suddenly outside Ingrid's tent on the surface. Believing they were free, the professor decided to be rid of the Troll Princess.

"Now return alone where you came from and leave us alone."

The Troll Princess snapped her fingers twice and disappeared.

"So, Ingrid, we are back where you started before you descended the cliff and found the crypt!"

Ingrid smiled shyly. "Do you think trolls are so stupid they cannot penetrate your fraud? You've made yourself clear to them. Now we'll have to flee."

The professor agreed. Instead of breaking camp, they gathered what they could carry and ran. At the nearest village, the professor rented a jeep that took them to Oslo. There the professor emailed Ingrid's parents. Attaching a selfie photo of himself with Ingrid, he explained how he had found her alive in a subterranean cavern near her site. Her parents emailed back immediately. They were ecstatic and overjoyed about his having found their daughter.

Ingrid stayed with the professor for the next month. They worked together to pull together her ideas for her dissertation. They took pains to include only what could be deduced from the received tradition plus the cell phone photographs he and she had taken. They decided nothing in the dissertation would make reference to trolls. The Roman history angle was sensational enough to make Ingrid's name among foremost archaeologists.

Ingrid received her Ph.D. She navigated her exams and orals without divulging anything about trolls. After she had processed to obtain her diploma, the professor, she and her parents had a quiet celebration dinner.

There Ingrid told her parents the whole story, leaving out no detail. Her parents were alarmed, but they were also overwhelmed their daughter had earned her terminal degree. They thought nothing more about the matter. They were, however, concerned by what people would say about her consorting with her major professor openly. They hinted strongly that the pair should be married, the sooner, the better.

The professor proposed to Ingrid later that same evening. She accepted his proposal. Their engagement lasted a month. They were married in the Lutheran Church. They spent their two-week honeymoon in Belize swatting black flies on the white, sandy beaches before returning to Oslo to teach.

Ingrid's dissertation was a worldwide success. Publishers vied to give her a generous contract to retool the work as a book. Now Ingrid was faced with the difficult decision of keeping on track with the Roman story or broadening its scope to include her information about the trolls. She kept with the original intent largely because her husband felt that way.

The professor and she, who had lecturer rank at the time, continued to catalog the runes of Norway, but they avoided going anywhere near the forty-acre plot where Ingrid had made her discovery of the crypt and its access to the troll kingdom.

When Ingrid conceived her first child, the couple was delighted. They planned to name the child Ola if it was a boy and Ingrid if a girl. The child turned out to be male, so Ola Halvarsson was christened in the church. The child did not much resemble its father. In fact, his parents felt his closest resemblance was to the Troll King. Halvarsson was distraught.

"Ingrid, I strongly suspect magic has been at work. The trolls have conspired to make our offspring a troll."

"Ola, I don't know what you're complaining about. I think our child is beautiful. This troll business has you obsessed. Calm down and get a new perspective."

The professor was not consoled. He began to suspect his wife had a dark secret she had not revealed to him. He brooded on the matter. After weighing all possibilities, he became deeply frustrated.

When he could no longer constrain himself, he asked his wife, "When we escaped from the cavern, who came back to Oslo with me? Was it Ingrid the human? Or was it the Troll Princess disguised as Ingrid?"

Ingrid burst into tears. She accused her husband of verbal abuse. She threatened to leave him if he didn't come to his senses. She even went to the pastor of their church for counseling. The pastor was nonplussed by a man who thought his child was part troll. Examining the child, the thought the professor might have a point. Still, a divorce on the grounds of a child's appearance was hardly sustainable. The husband and wife had no reason to suspect adultery. So the couple stayed together and made the best of their situation.

When Ingrid became pregnant with her second child, Ola dreaded the day of its birth. He prayed fervently and bought magical charms to assure the best outcome. He engaged their pastor to compose special prayers and sermons to ward off curses and demonic influences, like trolls.

The child was a girl, who was named Ingrid after her mother. Like her brother Ola, she had troll as well as human features. Ola was now convinced that his wife was not human but a troll who had taken human form. He did not complain. Instead, he bided his time waiting for his revenge against the trolls.

When the children were in their early teens, at the professor's instigation, the archaeologists decided to revisit the forty-acre plot that had determined their fates. They took the children along on their camping and exploring expedition. They pitched their tent where Ingrid had pitched hers before her descent to the crypt. They enjoyed a night around a fire under the clear Norwegian sky where the color of the Aurora Borealis shone green.

The next day all four rappelled down the cliff face to the ledge where the entrance to the crypt lay. They entered the cave and progressed through the second level to the third. There the image of Ingrid met them with two children who were identical to the Halvarsson's children in every respect. They were half troll and half human. For Ola, this was proof that his theory was correct. He had married a troll princess. The real Ingrid had married a troll prince. The children, evidently half troll and half human, were the proof.

The Troll King and Troll Queen appeared and sat on their thrones looking very pleased with the outcomes.

The Troll King intoned in an authoritative voice, "We now have four grandchildren who will enrich our bloodline. We are most pleased."

A murmuring of approbation arose from the armed trolls who lined the walls.

The Troll Queen taunted the professor, "You thought you could deceive us, but we turned your trick against you. We kept our secret and gained what we most desired. Of course, we cannot allow you to divulge what you know. Because you are family and the father of our daughter's children, we cannot kill and eat you. I'm sorely tempted to make an exception to our rule of eating in-laws. Nevertheless, from henceforth, you shall be deaf and mute. When you think of trolls, you will substitute Romans for trolls in your thoughts."

The Troll King said, "Now for a while, go back to the surface with the Ingrid and children of your choice. Come whenever you like and exchange any of them for their counterparts." He clapped his hands twice.

The professor found himself once again on the surface with Ingrid and the two children. He did not know which versions of each had been transported with him. He did not care at the present which they were. When their camping vacation was over, they went back to Oslo to recommence their normal lives. Because he could no longer speak or hear, the professor, who had been awarded emeritus status anyway, left off lecturing and devoted himself to writing scholarly articles and providing reviews of books in his field.

Now that Ola and Ingrid were teenagers, their being half troll caused them endless grief among the other children. They were persecuted and ridiculed. The professor was mortified at accusations that either he or his wife must be a troll. One day he could view their whining and complaining no longer. He took them camping at the fjord without their mother. He returned to Oslo without them.

"Where are little Ola and little Ingrid?"

Since he could not hear her, she had used their special sign language to ask her question.

"They're staying with their grandparents," he signed in return.

"They're not with my parents," she signed.

He smiled at the implication and signed, "They're with their Roman grandparents."

His wife broke down and cried. That night they slept together and conceived a child. Ten months later, a baby boy with no apparent troll characteristics was born.

The professor was very pleased. He signed to his wife that she had not borne a Roman child.

She had to admit she had dreaded bearing another Roman as he was so appalled by the idea.

Ola and Ingrid agreed to name their new child Magnus. It was a Roman name, but it sounded good to them. They presumed the name would remind them of what might have been.

Not everyone had forgotten about the couple's other children. People sometimes asked Ingrid where little Ola and Ingrid had gone. Ingrid informed them the children's grandparents had assumed responsibility for raising them abroad. So Magnus soon eclipsed the shame that his half-troll siblings had brought to his family. He was an exceptionally brilliant boy with a knack for Classical languages and a love of history, particularly Roman imperial history.

Magnus was acutely aware that some of his family did not communicate with his parents. This did not bother him because he was totally immersed in his studies. Increasingly, he gravitated towards the study of Dio Cassius, Suetonius, and the other late Roman, decadent historians. Since his mother and father were renowned archaeologists, he was determined to follow in their footsteps. Instead of studying Norse runes, however, he chose to study physical anthropology and modern DNA technologies to trace the Roman incursions into Norway through genetic forensics.

Magnus's initial findings were profound and disturbing to the keepers of the received tradition. Through bone DNA, he did statistical studies of the intermarriage of Romans with Norse tribes. He detected in the DNA strands an early incursion of a third DNA tribal strain he could not immediately identify. He named the unknown tribe Anonymous. As the Roman Y-chromosomes diminished, Anonymous Y-chromosomes increased ultimately to achieve parity with the Norse Y-chromosomes. The new balance within the male population continued from around the seventh century to the present.

Because he used strictly scientific evidence for his articles, Magnus's findings were thought to be unimpeachable. Then jealous competitors remembered that Magnus's parents had borne other children with suspicious characteristics. In their commentaries on Magnus's writings, they opined that his findings had been purposely skewed to legitimize the presence of troll DNA in the bloodlines of Norse peoples.

Magnus confronted his parents about this. His mother explained the family history as best she could. Instead of this settling the matter, her son vowed to find his siblings and discover the truth for himself. He badgered his parents until Ola signaled to Ingrid that it was time for them all to visit the troll kingdom so their son could see how things stood for himself.

Once again, they camped out on the forty-acre plot above the fjord. Ingrid carefully instructed Magnus about her research and the crypt that lay below the surface. Ola, Ingrid, and Magnus descended to the ledge and entered the system of caverns, which were fascinating to Magnus on account of their roots in Classical antecedents.

Finally, they stood in front of the troll version of Ingrid and the four children who were part human and part troll. The troll Ingrid withdrew in repulsion from Magnus, who saw in a flash what must be the truth. He had brought a syringe and six ampoules for blood samples. He took the samples from the four children and the two Ingrids. Meanwhile, the human Ingrid caught up on what had happened since her departure from the troll kingdom.

The half-troll, half-human children, said they were happy living in the troll kingdom with their mother. Little Ola and little Ingrid definitely did not want to return to Oslo.

Professor Ola, the human Ingrid, and Magnus were conveyed to the surface world after their visit. They returned to Oslo where Magnus did the DNA analysis that proved conclusively the Anonymous tribe was, indeed, trolls.

The enfant terrible of archaeologists refused to be bound by promises that his parents had made to the Troll King and Troll Queen. Instead, Magnus published his findings in the obscure American journal,

Everything Trolls. The publication was hailed among rebel anthropologists as a breakthrough and among traditionalists as a fraud.

Magnus also published on the engineering mechanics of the troll caverns. The contentious critics were savage in condemnation of his 'shoddy research and specious logic.' When Hyram Phthodius, the greatest Roman architectural historian then at the University of Rome, agreed with everything Magnus wrote, the tide of opinion turned. People began to pay close attention to Magnus's research. They took him seriously. So it was that Magnus was appointed Chair of Roman Antiquities in Norway, a chair funded by his mother's wealthy Swedish parents.

From that august position, Magnus Halvarsson sent forth students throughout Scandinavia looking for Roman artifacts and DNA forensic materials. His teams' collective research proved the troll lineage was specific to Norway. Romans and their offspring, however, had migrated throughout Scandinavia to an extent never before acknowledged.

On the basis of Magnus's research, satellite-based ground-penetrating radars were pointed at lands surrounding all the fjords of Norway. On the basis of the radar imagery, numerous areas were designated as possible Roman subterranean sites. Magnus's students used those sites to do excavations and write their dissertations. As a result of this intensive archaeological research, some troll contacts were reported. Other troll contacts went unreported. The stigma of consorting with trolls continued.

Magnus and his students discovered one consistent pattern in the Roman excavations: the ingenuity of static and dynamic stone engineering in a time before the mechanical revolution of Nineteenth-Century Europe. Matching that was the science of hiding entrances to secret places in plain view and of hiding entrances within those structures for concealment and defense.

Magnus never wanted to return to the troll kingdom to visit his extended family. He was much too busy publishing and teaching. His mother worried about his ever finding a good match for a wife. She wanted him to have some normalcy in his life. Otherwise, he would not experience the joys of a family and child rearing.

When she and Ola went to Rome to see the Pantheon, they met a young woman who seemed to Ingrid to be perfect for her son in every respect. Her name was Claudia Secura. She worked at a special Vatican library for archaeology. Ingrid invited her to visit Oslo soon for scholarly discussions.

Ingrid knew her son well. Once the woman was in Norway, Magnus fell completely in love with Claudia Secura after only a week of close proximity.

His father signed, "What makes you so sure you love this woman?"

Magnus signed in reply, "She is the perfect Roman woman."

Ola had no argument against that. He resolved to be happy with his son's choice.

Within four weeks the two were engaged. They married within a year. Magnus and Claudia were married in a double ceremony with Lutheran and Catholic concelebrants. They honeymooned for two weeks at an archaeological dig in Denmark and returned to teach and study in Oslo. There she had been granted a professorship of Classical Roman music, funded by Magnus's grandparents on his mother's side.

Magnus and Claudia had a son within a year of their marriage. His was named Claudius, after the Roman emperor. Ola took one look at the child and went white with terror.

He signed, "That child is pure Roman!"

Claudia was most pleased.

Ingrid, however, looked closely because she knew when her husband signed "Roman" he likely meant, "troll." In Claudius's features, she plainly discerned troll signatures. She held her peace and tried to comfort her husband. Fortunately, he was now emeritus and retired from the university. Ingrid encouraged him to focus on his writing and to leave his new grandson alone.

Magnus never made an issue of the fact that Claudius, his son, was half troll. The only indication that he was the least interested was a small monograph he wrote, "The Incidence of Anonymous Y-chromosomes in Certain Catacombs of Ancient Rome."

The fact that Romans, Norse, and trolls had interbred was clear to Magnus and widely published. It was becoming abundantly clear to

Magnus the exponents of interbreeding had returned to Rome and the continuance of those strains, including trolls, extended to the present.

SCRATCHING IN THE DUST

BETTY GABRIEL

I slipped sideways on a loose pile of iron shavings and concrete shale as I crested the final mountain of debris, jarring my knee. Sucking in my breath in annoyance, I paused to stretch my leg out and catch my breath. Ahead of me lay the market—what remained of it—and beyond that the grey rubble of the ruined city sprawled in every direction.

I wheezed and hacked, and coughed up a wad of thick infected phlegm, spitting it to the side of me with a grimace. The dust was ubiquitous, and it was ruining my lungs. I suppose I'd been one of the lucky ones, though, at least I remained alive. These days, everyone's life expectancy had been severely curtailed. Most of us would be lucky to make it past forty. I had eight years maybe.

Twenty years after the war, and over 80% of the population had perished. The maternity rate continued to be negligible. We humans were a dying breed. It had been the poisoning of the water after the initial onslaught of bombs that had been the final straw. Everyone needs water to survive, regardless of the make of car they once drove, how many mistresses they had kept, or how deep the bunker they had dug.

I didn't want to stay up here for too long. The stench of rotting flesh had dissipated years ago, corpses and carcasses had been picked clean by carrion, but occasionally, the putrefaction of something long buried far among the shifting rubble beneath my feet inveigled its way through air pockets and made me gag. I hefted my backpack, and carefully started to slip and slide my way down into the dip, the location for the daily market.

I'd had a good day at Gulliver's where I was employed. All the new industry took place outside the city now, in abandoned factories and warehouses. I worked as a 'cleaner'. Not that anything was clean, or even a close approximation. I suppose a better term for the job I did was a dismantler. The foragers brought in mechanical items or anything that could be stripped down, and my job involved carefully taking things apart and filing each component, no matter how tiny, into the correct storage bin to be sold on to our Overseers and their team of engineers. I'd dismantled a vacuum cleaner and a hairdryer this morning, and an old fashioned radio this afternoon. I preferred the really antique stuff, the parts were complicated and intricate. It made the job more interesting, albeit fiddly, whereas twenty-first-century hair dryers were simply constructed from plastic. Nobody wanted or needed plastic anymore. The damn stuff was everywhere.

My boots crunched on the ground as I headed into the market. It was a covered area, dulled plastic sheeting had been roughly tied over scaffolding, and warped wood had been laid out to serve as counter tops for the twenty or so stalls here. Merchandise was minimal, though, and what there was of it was limp and grey, coated with dirt. As we all were. This was the state of the world we inhabited.

I kept my chin down and eyes on the floor, so as to avoid the looks of resignation, boredom or pure desperation from the traders I didn't frequent. The market wasn't busy, so I had little opportunity of blending into obscurity, and while none of them were looking at me, I knew they all saw me. I headed straight for Joanne, as usual, an old acquaintance, she would treat me well.

"Lucie," she greeted me. "Good day?"

I nodded shyly, then lifted my hand and uncurled my fingers. A number of old coins nestled dully on my filth encrusted palm.

"Not bad," Joanne agreed, and her lips curled slightly.

"I have this too." I offered her my other hand. "I snuck it out." She reached for what I held, but I pulled my hand back in alarm. She jumped. "Sorry. Sorry," I said in a rush. "Be careful. It can bite you."

Puzzled, she indicated I place the item on the counter. I did so: a thin sliver of wood and a couple of pieces of metal.

"What is it?"

"Gulliver told me it's an old fashioned mousetrap. It's spring loaded. Look," I demonstrated how to pull the lever back. "You load food here. The mouse tries to eat it. The pressure of him doing so makes the trap slam shut, and he can't get out. See?"

Joanne laughed in delight. "Ain't that quaint?"

"A forager found a whole box of them somewhere and brought them in. I swiped this one. You want it?"

Joanne shrugged, but I could tell by the twinkle in her eye she did. I didn't. I happily traded to give the awful contraption a new home.

"I could use it, I guess. Beats laying poison everywhere, don't it?"

I nodded and looked at what she had on display, a pitiful collection of odds and sods. Joanne hastily picked up a few potatoes and a turnip. "I got these," she said, "and there's these lentils. You like lentils. And here, you can have a few twists." Joanne twisted salt, pepper and any other herbs she could get her hands on into tiny packages and sold them at her stall. They were a godsend, really helped to flavor the mundane day to day vegetables and bland rat meat we had to survive on.

I accepted what she offered. I wasn't unhappy with the trade, given so little choice. I packed the goods away in my backpack. Joanne watched me as I started to walk away then she stopped me.

"Wait," she said in a low voice. "Have this. Put it away, quick." She passed me a small round tin, cool to the touch. Hurriedly I stuffed it in my pocket and scuffled away. If she didn't want anyone else to see what she had given me, I wouldn't betray her confidence. Not so long ago, before The Organization took charge, people were killed for morsels of food. I remembered those days and remained watchful at all times.

I trudged homewards on what passed as a road. The rubble from office blocks and shops—destroyed during the war—towered above me on both sides; towers of concrete, twisted metal, and rusting iron that blocked half demolished buildings from my view. The foragers occasionally picked through the piles here, and although less and less was of any use to us, I still found the occasional treasure: twisted teaspoons or bicycle wheels with rusted spokes, so I scanned the ground as well as the horizon.

A small quick movement down one of the intermittent alleyways drew my attention. I wouldn't normally have dared to look, but whatever had caught my eye moved low to the ground. I paused and peered into the shadows. The thing moved again, watched me watching it. A dog.

I tutted and moved on. Dogs were rare these days. Straight after The War, they had roamed the streets in huge numbers, but they—like everything else—needed water to survive and dogs and humans alike had been poisoned or gone mad with thirst. Those canines that had managed to survive had been hunted down and used as meat until the farms had been established way out of town beyond Gulliver's. Maybe dogs were making a comeback. I didn't care. I continued my walk home.

The dog followed me. I studiously ignored it. It would be seen, and that would be the end of it. It would be someone's dinner.

A quarter of a mile further on, I ducked down another alley and followed a twisting path through the rubble. Beneath the overhang of a ruined Victorian hotel, I found the dwelling I called home. I pushed the door and peered in cautiously. Little point in locking up when I left, I had nothing worth stealing.

I dropped my backpack and turned to push the door closed. The dog stood on the front step watching me. I scowled.

"Go away," I said, and then felt cross that I'd connected with the damn thing. It tilted its head and stared at me with soft brown eyes.

"No." I shook my head. "I have nothing to give you. And I don't need you here."

The dog stood and padded into my room, climbed onto my bed and curled up there. I watched in disbelief.

"Are you kidding me? Get off there. You're filthy."

But that was a lie. The dog was relatively clean. I could see his brown and white coat clearly. He was cleaner than the faded throw that covered my bed.

Puzzled, I approached him and put my hand out tentatively. The dog didn't move. I held my breath and touched him. His fur was soft, a little gritty, but otherwise clean. He smelled fresh. He'd had a bath recently. Where had he found enough water for a bath? Or who had given him one?

I grunted and turned away. I needed to eat. I started a small fire in my fire pit, and poured some of my own precious, rationed water into a pan, rubbed the worst of the dirt off the potatoes and turnip with a rag, then cut them up into small chunks and dropped them into the water to parboil them. While I waited, I swept my little home, as though that would make much difference, and carefully rearranged the small collection of trinkets and treasures I had scavenged: A Barbie doll, a plastic train, a few books. It was my one connection to my old life, before the war, when I had been a child.

Only twelve when the war came, everyone I knew died—my parents, my little brother, my friends. I sought shelter with other survivors, and I'd been lucky. There had been lawlessness. People were traumatized by so much death. But I survived, thanks to the kindness of strangers, my biddableness, my instincts, my ability to pick out good people, like Joanne, and by keeping my head down.

When the potatoes and turnip had softened, I threw them in a frying pan to finish them off. Remembering the tin Joanne had given me I picked it out of my pocket. It had no label. It would be potluck then. I located a rusted tin opener among my treasures and with some difficulty peeled back the lid. It was fish of some kind. Tuna probably. It had been a long time since I'd eaten fish. I added it to the frying pan. Tonight I'd enjoy a proper feast.

I ate out of the pan using a spoon. It was good. Different. The dog eyed me, patiently waiting for me to finish. I didn't save him any. I didn't want to encourage him to stay. But as I stood to scour the pan clean with some sand, I relented and set the pan on the floor so that he could lick my leavings.

"You have to go," I said as he finished. I opened the door. He trotted out obediently, then looked back at me. I closed the door on his gaze.

The following evening, he was waiting for me as I left the market. Once again he had been hiding in the alley. For a moment I didn't know whether to feel exasperated or pleased. I decided on the former and walked on. The dog yipped quietly behind me. I stopped and turned back. It had never made a sound the previous day. Drawing attention to itself was a dangerous thing for it to do, but I didn't expect it to understand that.

The dog and I regarded each other and then it ran back down the alley. Hesitating for a moment, I decided to follow it, at least for a way. I scrambled down the rubble into the alley, my boots slipping on loose chunks of concrete and shale. The dog trotted to a door cast in shadow at the rear of the alley, and I quickly caught up with it.

I stood and gaped. In front of me was a green wooden door, the paint fresh and bright. I reached out, my dirty fingers caressed the sheen of the paint, expecting it to be wet. It was dry and looking closely I could see a thin layer of dust covering the door. It had been freshly painted recently. I wondered who would live here and why they would bother to paint a door that would be grey within days.

The dog whined beside me and sat, looking up at me expectantly. It wanted me to go in.

"No," I said, imagining someone on the other side armed with a machete or similar weapon. The dog whined again. He was placing me in a quandary. What if his owner had been hurt and needed help? I should help if I could.

I tapped nervously on the door. There was no response. I tapped harder. Again nothing. The third time I rapped noisily, but no-one came. I huffed my cheeks and considered. The dog scratched the door. There was nothing for it. I turned the old fashioned knob. The door opened easily, swung inwards with a satisfying whoosh. I stepped forwards into a small bare room, containing a mop and bucket, a broom cupboard, and some wellington boots. It was clean. I could smell the soap. I inhaled deeply, it was the headiest of all perfumes.

The dog trotted happily in beside me and walked straight to the cupboard. With nothing to lose, I pulled that door open too.

And gasped in shock.

It wasn't a cupboard at all, but an opening into a dream or something half remembered. Outside, behind me, the world was rubble and grit, grey dust accompanied by the putrid stench of decay. But here, inside, color lit up the world in every shade, the cheerful chirruping sounds of contented birds, and the sweetest and lightest of scents drifting towards me on the breeze. Heaven blossomed in a garden such as I'd never imagined.

I stepped forward into paradise. My heavy boots sank into a sponge-like ground, and when I looked down, I marveled at their clunky ugliness, compared to the delicate daisies of a neatly groomed lawn.

"You can take them off," a high pitched voice nearby suggested.

Startled, I clenched my fists and whirled around.

"Sorry, I didn't mean to frighten you. Only, if you want to, you can take them off." A young boy of about eight or nine years jumped from a wall to the right of me and landed softly on the grass.

"Who are you?" I demanded. He seemed oddly familiar, but I couldn't quite place him. I knew most of the survivors in the vicinity, as well as their families.

"I'm Derek. You're Lucie."

Puzzled, I stared at the boy. He wore blue knee-length shorts, and a t-shirt with some cartoon character emblazoned across the chest. His knees and cheeks were smeared with mud, and his clothes had grass stains. But his dirt was clean and fresh. It wasn't ingrained through years of toil in the acrid city beyond.

Derek. The name rang a bell. And he knew my name too.

"Where are your people?" I asked. I couldn't see anyone else around. Just us and the dog.

He shrugged. "They come, and they go. Thank you for bringing Bailey back. He runs off."

"I had a dog called Bailey once," I said. The words came out of me in a rush. Memories that tasted warm and loving. I bit them back. No point in remembering what happened before. "You shouldn't let him run off," I said coldly. "What are you doing here, anyway?" I gazed around, deeply impressed by the quality of the soil here, everything seemed so abundant. The farmers would love this place. I thought of the superiority of the goods they could produce. I wondered why they didn't know about it.

Derek shrugged. "Playing," he said.

Playing. Such a simple concept, but I was awed into a stunned silence. No-one played anymore. Perhaps cards to while away the late evening, but mostly we all worked, and then we ate, and then we slept. We didn't do any of that particularly well. But that's what it meant to survive.

"Would you like to play," Derek asked plaintively. "I haven't had anyone to play with for a long time." He skipped away from me, followed a winding path down the bank, Bailey trotting nonchalantly at his heels. After a moment's hesitation, I followed.

The garden was huge. As a child, my family had visited a stately home, and I had romped in the garden there. Like that one, this space had been divided into sections; an enormous lawn, glades, a meticulously laid out kitchen garden, and most incredible of all, a small maze. But the sight that stopped me in my tracks was a small lake, surrounded by reeds and tall flowers, their heads drooping lazily as they studied their own reflections in the clear water.

And yes, the water was clear. The sun reflected off the surface, and I fancied I could see the sandy bottom. Minnows darted here and there, gliding this way, then shooting off quickly in the opposite direction. I edged closer and reached out to dip my hand in, but instinct held me back.

"Is the water poisoned?"

"Poisoned?" Derek frowned.

I folded my arms, tucking my hands out of sight, away from temptation. The water could be pure acid for all I knew. Perhaps the minnows were an adapted species.

"It's not poisoned," Derek said, and plunged his hand in up to the wrist, agitating the water and surprising a number of spectacular blue dragonflies. I backed away, fearful of being splashed by the toxic water. Derek watched me. I could see from the wary look that drifted across his face, he thought me odd.

But he was a child, and artless. "Would you like an apple?" he cried. "Look, the ones over here are ready to drop. Come on!" He raced away. After a second I followed him, lumbering clumsily in my great boots, as he dashed sprite-like ahead of me.

The apple tree was huge and old, gnarled and twisted. Branches bowed under the weight of the heavy, ripe fruit. Derek reached up and pulled at an apple, and then threw it my way. I lunged for it awkwardly and missed. It fell on the grass with a thump. I scooped it up quickly and stared at in astonishment. It was firm in my grasp, hardly marked at all. I lifted it to my face and sniffed. The light delicately perfumed fragrance made my mouth water.

I dropped my hand. "I can't." Everyone knew the only food safe to eat should be grown in the sterile environment of the undercover farms beyond Gulliver's. It was foolhardy to eat anything that had been exposed to the radiation in the atmosphere.

"Don't you like apples?" asked Derek, and pulled one off the branch for himself. He opened his mouth and bit deeply into the green skin. I gasped in shock. Derek stared at me as he chewed. "It's good," he said, his mouth full of creamy flesh.

I turned the apple over in my hand. I wanted to taste it. How I wanted to.

I gaped at Derek as he munched noisily. Then I lifted my hand and brought the apple to my lips. It was smooth. I caressed the skin with my tongue, so smooth, and then opened my mouth wide. It took more effort than I remembered. I bit into it, the sweetness exploding in my mouth, the crunch reverberating in my ears. I sucked on the juices, chewed, waited for something bitter to replace the taste sensation, but nothing did, and so I swallowed. I finished the apple in 30 seconds flat, and Derek handed me another one with a smile.

"You must be hungry!" he laughed in delight. I found myself smiling back at him.

After that, I toured the garden in Derek's wake. He showed me raspberries, and tomatoes, green beans and pots full of herbs. Fascinated by them all, I sniffed them, tasted them, turned my nose up at the sharpness of the raspberries, but ate my fill of tiny tomatoes, sweet and red and firm.

"Who looks after all of this?" I asked the boy.

Derek considered the question with all of the gravity he possessed, but the question flummoxed him. "I don't know," he said. "Maybe we do."

Maybe we do.

We don't, but maybe we can do, I thought later. I had returned home as the light began to fail, aware of the curfew, and tired from all the fresh air. I didn't understand how the garden had not been discovered by the foragers, and I couldn't get my head around the fact that such a glorious place existed. Derek had elicited from me a promise that I would return, and I intended to.

The next day at Gulliver's, my fingers were scrabbling among the muck and scratching in the dust as was customary. As I unfastened bolts and prized joints apart, I detected a sense of urgency and excitement in my movements. For once, I had something to look forward to at the end of the day.

I had no intention of spilling the secret about the garden. It being too special. Its mere existence filled me with joy and hope, two emotions I hadn't experienced at all during the past twenty years. I practically bounced with excitement when Gulliver finally let her workers go. We filtered off in every direction. I walked the two miles back into the city, climbing the mountains of debris—small lumps of concrete skittering in all directions—with a renewed vigor, anxious in case the garden had been a dream and didn't actually exist at all.

But there it was, through the green door still bright and shiny, and then through the cupboard door, mundane in the extreme. The sun shone on my face as I moved out of the shadows. It warmed me. Greeting Derek and Bailey, I divested myself of my boots, painfully peeled three layers of socks away from my stinking, wrinkled feet, and stood barefoot on grass for the first time in two decades. Derek stared down in barely concealed disgust at the grey flesh of my feet and my curled yellow toenails. He shot off in the direction of the lake.

Stems of grass tickled the arches of my feet and wormed their way between my toes. It felt extraordinary. I hadn't realized how much my feet ached until I experienced the coolness of the earth against my skin. It seemed to draw the pain from my muscles. It was agonizing but sensational at the same time.

I hobbled after Derek, both afraid and exhilarated as I drew closer to the water. Derek had perched on the edge, sitting on the grass. He patted a rock, and I sat down awkwardly next to him.

"What's wrong with your feet?"

"I haven't bathed them much," I said, meaning not at all. Not since I'd been a kid.

"Is the rest of you like that?"

"No," I smiled at his temerity. "Not so bad, I think."

"You should get in the water."

"I can't swim."

"Just put your feet in then. It won't hurt. I do it all the time. Look." He slipped his shoes off and jumped into the lake. I watched him, recoiling from the splashing.

"Why are you so scared?" he asked. The disdain in his voice hurt a little. I didn't have many friends. Didn't want them. Derek was just a little boy, but I wanted him to like me. That was dangerous for me. I couldn't risk becoming emotionally entangled with anyone, even a kid.

I stood abruptly. "Let's get some apples," I shouted and ran for the tree, forgetting the pain in my feet momentarily. I heard Derek laugh and then he ran too, overtaking me with ease. I thundered after him, my breath wheezing in and out of my ruined lungs. I halted at the tree, bent over, coughed and coughed as phlegm worked its way up and out of me, infected and bloody. I hacked into the long grass, trying to avoid Derek seeing. When I had myself under control, I turned back to him. He held out an apple.

"They say an apple a day keeps the doctor away," he offered, and I nodded, my eyes prickling with unshed tears. The old sayings. Things my mother would say. I shook the memories away.

"Where are your parents?" I asked.

Derek didn't answer, just chewed on his apple. I bit into mine, enjoyed the crisp, tangy sweetness, glad when it washed away the metallic taste of blood from my mouth.

"Let's play on the swings!" demanded Derek and away he ran again, Bailey barking and leaping at him as he went. I plucked another few apples from the tree and followed at a more sedate pace.

The play area was wild with dog daisies and yellow-wort, nodding their heads in the tall grass. Butterflies danced from flower to flower, and bees buzzed lazily among them. I couldn't recall seeing butterflies and bees for many years, but here they were thriving. A neat path had been mown through the grass, and a pair of swings hung on chains from a tall metal skeleton, freshly painted the same shade of bright green as the front door.

"Someone does look after this place," I said, more to myself than to Derek, who didn't seem to care. He had climbed up onto one of the wooden seats and was already pushing himself backwards and forwards.

"Come on!" he shouted. "Let's fly!"

And I did. Tentatively at first. I let my feet do the work, before my stomach muscles—unaccustomed to the action of pushing— instinctively took over. I settled into the rhythm, drawing back and then flowing forwards. Higher I flew, the blood rushing through my veins in exhilaration. Backwards and forwards, to and fro, higher and higher. I soared through the air, as free as a bird, and all I could see was the garden, fresh and green and alive all around me. No dust, no dirt, no debris.

But suddenly if felt alien and wrong. I slammed my bare feet painfully into the ground, slid to a stop and flung myself from the swing. The momentum catapulted me into the long grass where I retched uncontrollably, the apple I'd eaten quickly regurgitated, and then I started dry heaving.

I felt a small hand on the center of my back. "Are you okay?" Derek's concerned voice came from far away.

How could I tell him of my fears? How afraid, how desperately frightened I felt. Not of the water, or the apples or the swings. But because these things didn't exist in my world and it was easier to live without them—and without the hope they actually existed—than to know of them, to experience them, and to fall in love with them, and have them cruelly taken away. Everything I had loved in my life had been stolen violently away at some stage or another.

What if somebody else had followed me here? What if someone stumbled across the door? What would the organization think of this place? What would they do to it? They would turn it into a farm, try to feed everyone. It would become contaminated, and it would fail. It would die. I couldn't bear it.

Derek's hand pressed firmly on my back. I shrugged him off, pushed myself to stand and walked away. Away from the swings, past the maze and the apple trees, past the raspberry bushes, the vine tomatoes, and the lake. Dragonflies hovered curiously in front of my face, keeping a perfect distance, and then zipped off. Derek called to me. I didn't look back, simply collected my heap of socks and my boots and strolled on.

Stony face, I pulled the green door firmly shut. Behind me was the sunshine, in front of me, only shadow. I turned for home and walked barefoot among the rubble of a ruined civilization.

"You're pretty sick," Joanne said to me one evening months later, as the sun dropped steadily to the horizon, and I wheezed my way up to her sparse stall.

"I'm alright."

We all got sick. Joanne wasn't immune. She and I were more or less the same age, but if I looked as old as her, I knew I was in trouble. I handed over my day's takings, and she passed me a pile of dried out root vegetables and three tiny green tomatoes, too soft now to ever ripen. I gawped at them, remembered the sweet tomatoes, as red as blood, I'd eaten in the garden.

"New from the farm. You could probably do with a fair few of these to get some vitamins inside you." I shrugged. No chance of that. No point in speaking of it. I turned to leave, but Joanne stopped me. "I heard that someone caught a dog or something. They're cooking it in the square now. Maybe you could get some? Meat would do you good." She offered me some of my coins back.

My stomach rolled, and I looked at Joanne in mute shock. It was the kind of news I'd dreaded since I'd discovered the garden. What if the dog in question was Bailey? I wheeled around and stumbled out of the market.

In order to get home, I had to pass right through the square where a small crowd was gathering around a fire pit. I could smell roasting flesh, so I held my breath, and averted my eyes, not wanting to see the small animal strung up on the spit, being turned slowly as onlookers drooled in anticipation. I walked away rapidly, the vegetables tumbling from my grasp as I went, the tomatoes exploding as they hit the ground.

What a waste. Such a waste. I felt heartily tired of it. The death, the destruction, the futility of picking out a life in the rubble and the dust. I stepped up the pace to get away from the stink of the dog on the spit, but my lungs burned with the effort of trying to walk through the loose concrete chippings too quickly, and I slowed down in order to prevent a painful coughing fit that would see me leave half a lung in the gutter.

I drew level with the alley where I had first seen Bailey and reluctantly looked for him. I could see no discernible movement through the twilight gloom. Casting a wary eye around me, I picked my way through the alley, under the overhang, through to the dead end. No sign of the dog. I would have liked to pretend that I had never thought of him, or of Derek, in the intervening months since I'd walked out of the garden, but that would have been a lie. I didn't dwell on them because that would be too painful, but I carried them in my memory and in my heart. Something I had never intended to do. Thinking of them took me home. Back to the past. Back when I had a family. I missed them. I missed them all.

I paused in front of the door. The bright green paint had faded to grey now, lost under thick layers of dust and filth. I scraped some away with my finger, exposed the color. Wrote my name, Lucie, considered it my epitaph, and turned the handle. The store room seemed much as it had been before, just a little mustier, the faint scent of detergent masking something old and long forgotten.

I caught my breath and reached out for the handle of the cupboard door. It was cold in my grip. What would I see beyond? I feared it would be an extension of the world I had left behind me and not the garden I remembered. I held the door, inching it forward, then let it spring fully open. I was momentarily blinded by bright midday sunshine. It was always daytime here.

I stepped out onto the grass, the earth spongy beneath my feet and damp with recent rainfall, the trees bowing under their sodden foliage. The air smelled fresh and clean. Relieved, I breathed as deeply as I could without setting off my cough. Somewhere ahead of me I heard a child laughing. Derek. And the answering bark of a dog. My spirits lifted. All was well, then. We could be together.

I wanted to feel clean inside and out. I wanted to divest myself of fear. I headed for the lake, and there at the edge I impatiently unlaced my boots and threw them into the water. The water didn't bubble and froth and dissolve them, the boots simply bobbed for a moment and sank out of sight.

I ripped the clothes from my body. Layer after layer. Rag after rag. Methodically at first, desperately at the end. My pale grey flesh disgusted me, thin and unwholesome and difficult to look at, but I was determined now not to hide from my own gaze. Not my memories, not my fears, not my hopes, and certainly not my physical reality.

Naked, I plunged waist deep into the lake. I expected to be burned by the water, but instead found myself stunned and exhilarated by the sharp coldness of it. Shivering I walked further in until the water lapped at my breasts.

I heard Derek calling my name joyfully, and I smiled. It filled my heart with an unknown warmth to hear his pleasure. How good it is to love and be loved. I dropped backwards, lifted my feet, let the water carry me, surround me. I lay my head back, and the water pulled me down. Eyes open, I studied my surroundings, watched as the minnows dashed this way and that among the reeds. I sank lower, breathed out, watched the bubbles escaping, heading for the sunshine at the surface.

And breathed in.

THE ATTIC DOOR

JEREMY KRATKA

There are times in our lives where we go through terrible traumas. During those times we pretend that we are fine, and we try to hold ourselves together. Though friends and families ask if we are doing okay, we numbly say yes. Alicen Carter, a young woman at the age of twenty-five, has lost a newborn, James, and had her husband go missing all within the past four months. She has held a funeral that no mother should ever in their lives have to hold, been questioned and had her time of mourning intruded upon by police, and even had a falling out with her family. If anyone is walking numbly through life, it's her.

Alicen walks through her home, a home that has been barely kept up since her life came shattering down. Vodka and whiskey bottles cover the counter, and now old moldy plates soak in the sink. As she passes it, swarms of fruit flies ascend and quickly settle back down as she leaves her once proud kitchen. Without a word she quietly curls up on the couch in her living room. She doesn't look at the clothes tossed about, nor does she look at the piles of past due bills and unopened condolence cards from people she hasn't seen or spoken to in years. All she looks at is a very dusty TV playing old reruns of a show she used to watch as a kid. It's clear that she isn't even watching the show, just taking solace in a faint glow of a fictional show where no true horror has ever struck this happy family of seven. The sound and the laugh track break what would be a very depressing and eerie silence.

Alicen doesn't want to fall asleep tonight. She knows all too well of the terrible life that she has been leading for a few months, and she knows that tomorrow is going to be even harder. The savings account has been overdrawn for a month and bills are becoming overdue. She needs to go back to work. A very privileged job for someone her age and anyone that wasn't in her situation, herself included before everything happened, would be excited to have a high paying job at a stable company. But for now, she numbly falls asleep.

Occasionally during the night creaking would disturb her sleep. It always came from the attic, but she would have no idea what it was. She had the landlord go up and check it out. He would come down with no news. All that was in the attic was a few dusty old boxes, some hers and her husbands and some the other tenants but then there were some old antiques that belonged to the landlords mother who had passed. Everything in the attic had gone untouched but still the creaking continued. It wasn't the sound that you would normally hear from an old house that is settling deeper onto it's foundation but as if a silent visitor was trying hard to rest for the night. Alicen couldn't shake the feeling, and it didn't help that the news was reporting about such a visitor that was living in an unknown room in someone's house only a few towns over. So her nights would become restless and fearful.

In the morning, a very tired Alicen woke to the warm embrace of the sun shining down on her. What should have been a comforting hello for her was now an unwelcome annoyance. She made her way into the bathroom where she looked at her untidy hair and sad face. She sighed as she turned on the water to the shower. She didn't want to go back to work. She didn't want to feel the piercing stares from her colleagues, hearing the loud whispers of what they thought and the unwanted sympathy. She tried to follow her old morning routine. After she got out of the shower, she would brush her dirty blonde hair.

Tying it into a bun, she would proceed to put on some makeup. She wouldn't apply a lot but enough to brighten her already naturally glowing skin. While today she didn't glow as she used to, she did bring herself to what she considered to be human looking. After that, she would turn to the walk in closet and press play on the radio that would be playing a song she enjoyed. Though music didn't bring the same joy as it did before. She put on her clothes, a very professional looking skirt and blouse topping it with a light sweater. Today instead of heels she decided for some flat dress shoes. She took one last look at herself in the full mirror in the closet. A faint smile crept onto her face. A natural beauty, Alicen felt the smallest spark of something normal in her life. She looked at the different person she had become used to seeing. She wasn't the disheveled stranger that had invaded her home, and if it weren't for the horrible mess behind her, then she would have, if only for a moment, forgotten about the last few months.

Grabbing her keys, she made her way outside. A sunny eighty-seven-degree day met her. Wincing at the bright unexpected sun, she got in the car and put on the news talk station that she liked to listen too. They were discussing the upcoming mayoral election. The drive to work went as it typically did. She stopped at the coffee shop for her favorite iced coffee blend. She drove into the city and saw the street performers starting their daily routine. Pulling up to the guard gate at the business complex she showed the gentle old guard her badge.

"Ah, Alicen," he greeted with a relieved smile "it's always a pleasure to see you doing well."

"Thanks, Isaac," she replied forcing a smile. She knew he didn't mean any harm, but she also felt uncomfortable with the idea of 'doing well.' She couldn't be mean to Isaac though. He was a sixty-seven-year-old, retiree. He was always kind, always smiling.

Alicen reached her parking spot and exited her car. She turned and looked at the mountains that met the horizon. Everything felt as if nothing happened. The thought of this gave her mixed feelings. On the one hand, it helped the transition back to everyday life. On the other, it hurt because she was still grieving. She turned toward the office building and scanned herself in. Something did change which made her return feel as if she landed on an alien planet. The lobby furniture was rearranged, and a new blue couch had replaced the white and pink floral pattern couch. The plant had been completely removed, probably placed in the courtyard to enjoy the summer months, and the art on the wall had been replaced by, in her opinion, better more modern art. As she was taking in the drastic change to her workplace, an excited voice of a middle-aged woman came from a corner office that read Nancy Carrington: Assistant Manager.

"Alicen! Oh, my word, I can't believe you are back!" the jubilant Nancy exclaimed in a louder voice than she probably intended. The heavyset woman ran over and embraced Alicen in a very welcoming hug. "Please, come into my office."

Without a word Alicen followed her into the moderately sized office. She took a seat in front of the desk as Nancy closed the door. Alicen worried this would hopefully be the worst part of the day as Nancy is a bit nosy but she also needed to fill her in on what she missed in the last four months. The temporary worker's last day was last Friday and from the discussion on the phone, he didn't make Alicen's return very easy. He wasn't very organized.

"We are so excited for you to come back, hon," Nancy started. "We have a lot to cover."

Nancy started off by talking about Alicen's job. How the temp was horrible at his job. By the way things were described, Alicen couldn't decide whether he wasn't good because he was just bad at the actual job or if he just didn't partake in the typical work drama you know most jobs have. She was part of the decision to hire him instead of the four other qualified candidates, so she couldn't imagine that her intuition was off. After that, Nancy went into four months of drama. Gwen caught her boyfriend cheating and Rick, Gwen's freshly dumped ex, became engaged to Gwen's cousin. Alicen didn't care, but she automatically nodded her head. Though somethings she just couldn't understand, like why Gwen would be the maid of honor to her cousin who ruined her relationship.

They were in the office for an hour before emerging back into the lobby. Alicen looked as if she just barely survived a torture session and the smile on Nancy's face clearly showed she wanted to talk more drama. They walked down the hall together. Alicen kept getting greeted by her fellow peers, only to hear the rumor mill going into overtime as the hushed whispers weighed heavy on Alicen's ears. That sick, sinking feeling churned her stomach making her feel worse than she did yesterday.

The walk to her office felt longer than it should have. She and Nancy said their goodbyes and Alicen closed the door behind her. Her office looked just as she left it. An L-shaped desk tucked into a corner of the room that was very well organized. A book shelf with a bunch of accounting books as well as some personal trinkets for decoration and three filing cabinets with a bunch of private records. During her first days on the job, she took the time to reorganize everything to a precise order. This was the way she enjoyed things. She sat down in the computer chair and powered up her computer and monitors. She started her day by reading through the past four months of reports.

The next seven hours had suddenly gone by. Alicen didn't realize how fast the time had gone before Nancy came in to say goodbye for the day. She gathered her things and went back out to her car. She used to enjoy the drive home because the setting sun would turn the sky some shade of pink or purple. She always thought it was nature's promise that tomorrow was going to be a better day. During the summer, however, this isn't the case. The sunsets are much later and during the day overcast clouds rolled in. Dark clouds tumbled through the sky as the winds picked up. She was lucky to miss the rain before she got home.

Entering the quiet apartment was eerie. While she had turned the light on she was returning home to the ghosts of an unwanted past. She looked around at the mess that had become her life and almost out of instinct called out to her husband. She hesitated and stopped as she realized nobody was there.

The police investigated the disappearance of her husband for a good month before moving on to more urgent matters. They never closed the case making the matter even worse. When he disappeared, they had a fight. One month after the passing of what was supposed to be their first child and start of their family. While no one was to blame for the unexpected passing of their child, he blamed her. Alicen could never forgive Nathan for that. He started drinking and going to the bar on a daily basis. She urged him to stop, but he just didn't listen to her.

As an heir of his father's money, Nathan was always the 'do as he pleased type'. That was until he met Alicen a few years ago in college. Their romance was almost out of a storybook. She was working as a waitress trying to earn a little extra money for school, and he was out with a few of his buddies when they literally bumped into each other. She dropped an entire family's meal in the middle of the restaurant. The manager, who wasn't a kindly person to begin with, started reprimanding Alicen in front of the entire restaurant that was near to capacity. Nathan stepped in and took all the blame saying he wasn't paying attention. He paid for the family's entire meal as well as his own. After he approached Alicen, who was sitting outside waiting for the bus. After he had made a few jokes about him being a klutz, it was the happy ending you would expect.

Well, not as happy as Alicen would have liked.

A few hours went by, and Alicen had the apartment looking spotless as it once did, the worst part was what looked like a faded wine stain in the bedroom hidden under a pile of clothes. She still didn't feel like he old self and probably would never be that happy again. So as usual, she curled back up on the couch and watched her perfect family sitcom. The creaking in the attic started its usual movements again. Slowly moving to the left. Then moving quickly to the right and casually moving above her before suddenly stopping. The hair on the back of her neck would rise, and the chill of someone watching would send goosebumps up her arms. Then it steadily moved forward into the bedroom closet. There were three very loud bangs and had her jumping straight off the couch. She paused and muted the TV. The faint glow from it was the only light in the apartment. More bangs before what was clearly something heavy collapsing on the floor. Then she had to ask herself what she just heard. A slow, heavy wheeze came from the attic before completely stopping.

The apartment was quiet. Not the usual quiet one expects that still requires some sort of background interference like the pouring rain that was happening outside or the thunder that should have followed the flash of lightning Alicen just saw. No, she didn't hear any of that. She walked to the wall near the refrigerator and grabbed the flashlight from the wall. If someone was in the attic, she didn't want them to realize she was home. She picked up the phone and dialed emergency services before the power went out in the house. She looked toward the bedroom. Something in her felt the need to check out whatever was beyond that door. She was expecting the manikins dressed in moth-eaten clothes, the chests, and the boxes. Hopefully, that was that was up there.

In the closet, she pushed a bunch of stuff on the floor out of the way. She pulled down the latter and began to ascend with the deep sense of dread. She pushed on the attic door, it didn't move. She pushed on it again only a little harder. It still didn't move. Alicen took a deep breath and shoved the door and this time, it flew open to reveal the cold, damp darkness of the attic greeting her. She entered the attic and moved the light from her flashlight around to check if it was safe. Nothing moved. Nothing was in there at all.

She entered the attic and slowly moved forward a few steps before hearing a loud creek.

On the next step she took, everything went dark.

Darkness surrounded Alicen. She started to come to, but her vision was fading between black and blur. Slowly she started to hear the world around her. Seagulls, that was the first thing she heard. Waves and a soft, cold breeze blowing across what smelt like fresh water followed that. She sat up slowly, confused, and a little scared. As she regained her vision, the sights and smells were confirmed by what was the yellow hue. The entire world around her looked as if the was in the twilight time between night and the fading day.

She continued to look around at the water. She was sitting on a bunch of grass just in front of the rock-covered shore. No boats broke the surface of the water, no people sat on the docks fishing or played in the shallows of the water. She then noticed that there was some snow covering patches on the shore and grass around her. Not a lot of snow, not even an inch. She was still dressed in her pajamas, and she started to feel winter's cold touch.

When she stood up, she started to recognize some landmarks. A thick rope hanging from a tree that kids used to swing into the water. The small island, a popular one for boy and girl scouts during the summer months. A cabin where teenagers would go to for activities they shouldn't be doing. Lastly a tree, not just any tree, though. This tree was very old and had dozens of lover's initials carved into it, the one she noticed was "A.C. & N.C." her initials and Nathan's initials. She knew where she was.

This is the town her family lived in. The town was called Lakefront, named that because it sat on the shore of Lake Pensar. Alicen grew up here. Her family lived here. What she couldn't understand at this moment was how she got here from her home nearly five hundred miles away.

She turned around to head to her parent's house. She figured she had to be dreaming, but everything felt so real, the crunching of the snow and frozen grass under her feet and the freezing air. She hadn't walked five feet before she saw a little boy playing with a toy airplane. Baffled and with no adults nearby she approached the boy who was no old than four.

"Hey there, where are your parents?" She asked curiously wrapping her arms around herself tighter as the air got colder.

The boy stopped and just looked at her. He didn't say a word, which to Alicen was odd, but she tried to press him anyway.

"Do you live in town? Why don't we get you home, it's very cold."

The boy nodded and started to walk away. Alicen followed though she really didn't know where he was going.

They headed into town, and it looked exactly as she remembered it. The Shanty, a souvenir shop, was the first building that was on Main Street. Next to that was the Ice Cream Parlor that had a mini golf course that wrapped around the building. Old man Franklin's house was still the very well kept Victorian house, that even at eighty-seven, he worked on to keep it the best-looking house in town. The town was always so full of life and always busy. She knew during the winter it was a bit slower, but Lakefront was known for the bed and breakfasts which were busy all year round as it was a nice little honeymoon spot for young newlyweds and couples looking to get away for the weekend. Alicen couldn't shake the feeling that something was wrong as there was nobody around. Shops were closed, and parked cars were missing. The twilight tinted town started creeping out Alicen more and more the futher she and this mysterious boy went in.

He was a bit further ahead of her. Occasionally he would stop and turn around to make sure she was still following. He'd continue to fly his plane in silence making it a point to have it do a full circle before changing directions down a different street. Lakefront wasn't a big town, and Alicen knew all the streets. She saw houses of old playmates and remembered all the good and bad times of high school life. They made one more turn down another street. Alicen froze when she realized what street they had just turned down. It was the street her parents lived on. She could see the light purple house and brown picket fence from the place she was standing. Conflicted she stopped the boy.

"Hey, we need to make a stop real quick." She started before trailing off.

The boy stopped and turned around to give her a quizzical look. He then let her take the lead as she slowly approached the house she wasn't even sure if she would be welcomed at.

Alicen remembered the fight very clearly. She had brought Nathan home twice. The first time was at Thanksgiving during their first year together. Her parents did not approve of Nathan. Her father was an old world man where you had to work for the money you had, not just live off the hard work of others. Her mother didn't like the idea that Alicen's school work was being disturbed by this man who seemed to only buy Alicen's affection. It was a hard holiday that year, but Alicen insisted that Nathan wasn't like that. He was a gentleman and would always be there for her.

The second fight was after the wedding late last year. It was in the holiday season before her baby would have been born. She wanted to tell them in person that they would be grandparents and wanted to try and make amends so they would be a part of their grandchild's life. She was still mad that they had refused to attend the wedding because of how much they disapproved, but it was Nathan who insisted they visit. While

Alicen had graduated college with high grades and was offered a job straight out of college, her parents were still unimpressed with Nathan. They told her that she was welcome home when Nathan would eventually leave her but until then they didn't want to be near him.

The falling out became worse when her parents came to the hospital for the birth of her little boy. Alicen was in the room crying for hours holding her stillborn baby. Nathan caught them up on the situation with tear filled eyes, but Alicen could hold in the anger.

"Alicen, baby, we are here for you. We are so sorry about everything." Her mother said as she too was breaking down into tears. Alicen's father stood in the entry of the room, he clearly had been crying and trying to put on a strong face for his daughter.

"Now you're sorry?" Alicen contested. "Now, not when we came to give you a chance to be a part of your grandchild's life. Not when I found someone I truly love. Not when you missed the most important day of my life and I spent the day crying because you wouldn't come? Don't give me that I'm sorry, you didn't want to be a part of my life so you may as well leave now." Alicen was worse than her mother had ever seen her daughter in her life. She didn't know this was a moment to even prepare her for. She didn't know what to do so they left. While they attended and helped pay for the funeral, they gave Alicen the space she clearly needed.

Alicen hadn't spoken to her parents in nearly four months.

She walked up to the door, nervous and shaking. She gave the door three solid knocks before waiting in silence. What was really only thirty seconds felt like an eternity. Finally, she heard a voice approaching the door. A woman in her fifties speaking loudly to an older gentleman further in the house opened the door.

"Yes, hello," the portly woman said, "Who are you miss?"

"Mom? It's me Alicen, your daughter." Alicen gave a really confused and upset look.

"Oh dear, I'm not sure if this is some sick joke she is playing on us, or you are suffering from hypothermia." She gave Alicen a look up and down realizing she was dressed in pajamas. "Do come in though and warm up."

"Thanks, mom, maybe you can tell me about this boy."

Alicen's mom looked around, but she didn't see the boy that was hiding behind Alicen's leg.

Alicen stepped inside and looked around. The house hadn't changed at all save for the new carpet that sat in the middle of the hallway.

"Well Francine, who was at the door at this time of the day?" said the man.

"One of Alicen's friends. She isn't dressed for this weather so she's going to warm up before leaving."

Alicen walked into the living room where her father sat in his normal spot, a blue reclining chair next to the fireplace. The lamp behind him lit up the bookshelf and his chair so he could read the paper. He looked up from his paper, a sour look on his face.

"What the hell does she want?"

"Dad, it's me Alicen." She pleaded, tears now forming in her eyes with the thought that her parents didn't want anything to do with her. Alicen's father didn't reply he just went back to reading his newspaper.

"Don't mind him, he hasn't been the same since Alicen told us she didn't want us in her life. Poor thing, she's due to have a baby any time now, and I fear she won't let us into the baby's life." Her mom explained with a very sorrowful look in her eyes. "What little boy were you talking about?"

The boy, who was hiding behind the door to the living room turned and ran upstairs. Alicen turned to look at him, but he was gone.

"I woke up on the beach, and this little boy was just playing. He didn't have any parents with him, so I was going to walk him home. He won't talk though so I don't know his name or where his house is."

"I didn't see anyone with you. You still must be cold." Francine looked over Alicen again. Her pajama pants were wet up to the shin, and she was wearing a thick black tank top that left her sleeveless. "Why don't you go up to Alicen's room, you look about her size so there should be a coat and pants that you can have. Just be sure to return them to her when you tell her this little prank failed."

Alicen looked at her mother and wanted to say something, anything, but didn't at the cost of looking crazier than they already thought she was. She turned and walked up the all too familiar stairs.

She reached the top of the stairs and looked down the hall. Still, nothing had changed. Pictures of her and her parents hung on the wall. A silly six-year-old Alicen was making a funny face in one picture. She saw her picture with her first car and her high school graduation picture. Everything was dusted and in perfect order. Even the door to her room was untouched. Pictures of her high school celebrity crushed hung on the door, and a handmade sign read: Alicen's Room: KEEP OUT.

She entered the room to the rush of memories and emotions. She kept asking herself why her parents didn't recognize her. She saw a letter on her dresser that wasn't there before.

Dear Francine and Richard,

Alicen isn't doing well. It seems there were some complications with the pregnancy, but the doctors are assuring us that everything is fine. I know we haven't been on good terms, but she refused to call. I'm writing this to let you know what is going on. Alicen needs you, even if she won't admit it.

Nathan

Alicen sat on her bed. She couldn't believe that Nathan had gone behind her back. That letter was a lie. Alicen could recall clearly how the doctor said everything was fine, and so she decided not to get yelled at by her parents for forcing her out of their life. She still never understood why they wanted her out so much. She remembered all the great memories and vacations.

She went to the closet and changed into some jeans. Then she found her favorite jacket tucked into a corner. She put it on and sat on the bed once again to take in the comfort of her room.

In the last four months, she couldn't remember when she felt this comfortable. The punk aesthetics of her room reminded her of the fun times of being a teenager. When she left for college her entire taste in music and style changed, but her parents never changed her room or turned it into a guest room.

She got up and left the room to head downstairs. The boy was standing in the hallway staring at a picture of Alicen from their trip to Washington D.C. She was dressed in punk attire and had the worst scowl on her face standing in front of the White House.

Alicen walked up to the boy and saw the smiling girl.

"Alright, we need to find your home." She said with a genuine smile that she got when she looked at the boy.

They went downstairs and stood by the door thanking Francine for the hospitality. Francine looked down at the child and froze.

"J… James?" she looked as if she just saw a ghost.

The boy took off without a reply. He ran down the street as fast as he possibly could. Alicen in a moment of panic took off after him. It didn't seem like he was going in any specific direction but that he was just running and not from Francine but from Alicen. She yelled to him trying to catch up or hoping he would stop to catch his breath. Alicen was losing hers very quickly until she slipped on ice.

Darkness. That's all Alicen could see in any direction. The faint echoes of James rung loud and clear. She could see the child running like he was just before she fell. She couldn't move, but she could sense that she was still on the ground.

She was starting to realize that she was in some sort of nightmare. Her parents didn't recognize her, and that tore through her worse than the falling out in general. James was a pretty common name so that came to no surprise for Alicen. It was the reaction of her mother that really surprised her. She looked at him as if she knew him and hadn't seen him in years. Alicen was feeling sick to her stomach.

The shock, the confusion, and the contained emotions made Alicen want to vomit and cry. She couldn't, she needed to wake up. She was determined to wake up. She had no time to cry. The world was spinning around her. Finally starting to move she tossed and turned. Then she woke up.

Opening her eyes suddenly she looked around. She was back in her apartment, and it was dark. She gave a sigh of relief before sitting up on the couch. As she did, Alicen realized that she was in the clothes she had just changed into. She was over this sick, cruel joke that life was playing on her. Never acting violent before, for the first time she kicked the coffee table in anger. The apartment was looking untidy. A few whiskey bottles lay about, and she heard someone's voice in the bedroom.

Nathan? She thought to herself.

There was another voice replying to him. A familiar voice, one she couldn't quiet place.

She approached the door. As she was about to open the door, a muffled shuffle startled her from behind. She turned to see James sitting in the corner of the living room. He looked like he had just cried, his clothes worn and torn as if nobody had taken care of him in months. She gave a caring look at him before giving her attention to the conversation in the room. She pushed the door open, and neither Nathan nor the other woman in the room noticed her.

"I told you for the last time, I'm going out," Nathan said in a stern voice.

"Fine, go! Go be with those bar whores," the woman replied. She was lying in bed turned to the wall so Alicen couldn't get a good look at the miserable looking woman.

"I don't talk to anyone babe. But I can't take this anymore. All you do is mope. It's been two months."

Alicen was starting to get déjà vu.

"Do what you want, you never cared about our baby or me," the woman said, as Alicen silently mouthed along with her. Alicen realized, and felt a bit dumb, that the woman in the bed was she. This was the night her husband disappeared.

"Oh, I don't care," he started knocking over some whiskey bottles. "Yes, because I was the one who made you reject your parents. I was the one who didn't listen to the doctor when he said to go on bed rest a month before you were due. I gave up everything…" he trailed off.

Alicen stood up from the bed with a venomous look in her eyes. She had no words to say to what she was taking as a betrayal.

James started to get restless behind the Alicen that watched quietly as she was trying to fight back the tears.

"If you had only gone to therapy then things could be better. You could have help." Nathan said trying to pacify the argument.

"So you think I'm crazy?"

"I didn't say that, I went to therapy."

"Like that did any good, look at all the bottles," Alicen said picking one up and smashing it into the wall.

"Alicen stop, there is no need for any of this."

"There was no need for my baby to die, there was no need for my parents to shut me out of their life, yet here we are Nathan." Alicen was shaking.

"You need to accept that James is dead, nothing can change that."

Just then the boy that was curled up in the corner holding his ears to try to ignore the fight started to scream at the top of his lungs. Alicen turned from the argument. She rushed to him to try and quiet him down.

"Shush, it's okay. I remember this fight," Alicen said trying to calm him down. "Any second Nathan will be passing by and…" she stopped.

Nathan didn't walk by them. The argument stopped, and the apartment was deathly silent. Alicen looked back toward the bedroom.

Nathan was lying on the ground, he wasn't moving. The other Alicen knelt next to his body with blood covering her shirt and hand holding the broken bottle.

"No, no, no!" Alicen heard. "Nathan!"

Now Alicen was shaking along with the boy she was holding. This isn't what she remembered. Nathan wasn't dead. She continued to watch in disbelief, and the other Alicen was in a panic trying to figure out what to do. She looked toward the closet and the entrance to the attic.

Alicen pinched herself. She couldn't take this twisted nightmare. She couldn't hurt a fly, and now she sees herself kill Nathan. It didn't make sense.

Other Alicen had wrapped Nathan up in a tarp. Once she dragged his corpse up to the attic, she shut the door in a panic. Getting the stain remover and a bunch of towels she started to scrub the blood off the floor.

After a half hour of scrubbing what was left was a faint red stain. Numbly she put some clothes on top of the stain and quietly walked over to the fireplace. Placing the clothes in it, she walked past Alicen and

James to sit on the couch. The room turned dim as the TV went on and this other, fake Alicen turned on the sitcom of the perfect family.

Alicen couldn't remember the last time she cried after her baby's death. Even in the twisted memory, she didn't cry when she murdered her husband. She couldn't hold it back anymore.

She started to cry uncontrollably. The boy looked up at her curiously. Alicen was having a hard time catching her breath, but this meltdown made her feel good. She felt genuinely good like she wasn't holding anything in anymore. She knew she had to start accepting that James was gone. After some time she started to stop.

"Alight James, let's figure out how to get you home." She said still sniffling. She got up and led him toward the door. As she opened the door, she looked at him again. "I guess I have some help I need to get as well. Accept responsibility."

For the first time the boy smiled and as he exited the apartment the spotlights on the porch blinded her.

White surrounded Alicen. When the bright, blinding lights started to fade and the world started to come into focus that feeling of shock and dread she had felt all night rushed back. The room she was in was all white. Machines connected to her finger, chest, and head. As her focus started to come in clearer, she noticed the IV winding its way down to her arm. Realizing she was in a hospital, she lurched up only to be stopped because of a pair of handcuffs that linked her other arm to the bed. Her head started to throb in confusion or possibly from the tight bandaging wrapped around her head.

"Hey! What is this!" she screamed, and several nurses rushed in to calm her down.

They managed to fairly quickly, though not by any forced effort on their part. A man walked into the room escorted by another man holding a baby. Alicen's eyes widened.

"N… Nathan?"

"Yes, good you seem to remember," said the doctor. "You took quite a fall. Do you remember falling through the attic floor?"

She shook her head in confusion. Her eyes didn't break from the four-month-old baby in her missing husband's hands.

"Let me introduce myself, I am Dr. Clarke, a psychiatrist. Your husband and a Dr. West called in regard to your health."

"Dr. West? I haven't seen her since James died."

Nathan and Dr. Clarke gave each other very concerned glances. It looked as if they were silently talking to each other.

"Babe, listen," Nathan tried to start before being cut off.

"Listen to you now? You disappeared Nate and who's baby are you holding?" Alicen snapped.

"Alicen, this is going to be hard to hear so I need you to stay as calm as possible," Dr. Clarke started pacing back and forth at the foot of the bed and took a deep breathe. "You have had serve depression after your son James was born. So severe in fact that you built an entire reality around yourself believing that James, your son, had passed away at childbirth, and Nathan had left you."

He paused for a reaction but Alicen waited for more.

"It was when I was called you were already here. You attempted suicide after abandoning your child for several hours unattended. From what your husband tells me, you tried to jump out of the highest window which was in the attic and fell through the floor due to some weak boards."

"I… I don't believe you. I saw him. James was dead." She tried to protest by sitting up only to be reminded of the metal cuffs. She started to pull harder and harder at the cuffs even though the effort was futile.

"Nurse, would you please come in." Dr. Clarke yelled into the hallway.

The nurse came in and injected Alicen with a sedative. As she was fading and falling asleep, she heard Nathan and Dr. Clarke talking about her.

"Don't worry Mr. Carter, now that she has become aware of the situation she'll begin to talk and let go of everything she has been keeping to herself."

Alicen Carter fell asleep. She was beginning to remember all the times in her life she was asked if she was okay. Like most people in difficult situations, she numbly replied okay. She realized that it is okay to talk about what is bothering you, and people ask because they care.

THE DOOR

MICHELLE MONAGIN

I found the door the day after I moved into the house.

The newspapers had said I was running away from the failure of my last book. Or from the failure of my marriage. Or from a failed romance. Or from some other failure. Take your pick, I'd had enough of them recently; maybe it was true. I only knew that I wanted a change. I wanted to be away from the City, away from everyone I knew, away from every place where I was known.

I heard about the house from a man in a pub. I was alone in the pub—I had gone deliberately to a pub I had never been to before—so I could drink alone. I was about half drunk when I heard someone talking in the booth behind me. It was a man—I couldn't tell who he was talking to, but he said his friend was trying to sell a house out in the wilds of Michigan.

"Right out in the middle of the woods," he said. "The nearest neighbor is five miles away."

That statement was what attracted my attention. I started listening in earnest then, although I didn't at first turn to join into his conversation. He went on talking about this house. According to the man, when he said 'the middle of the woods,' he meant it. He said you couldn't get a satellite picture of the house, even if you had a satellite perched above the woods. It seemed that his friend was selling it furnished, taking nothing before closing.

"I've seen a picture of it, and it is lovely," the man went on, talking the house up. "It's a Tudor cottage, looks like a real one, rather than one of the Tudor revival houses we got in the 'twenties'."

"I don't know what a 'Tudor cottage' is," someone said, some girl. There was a murmur of agreement from two other people.

"It's got dark wood beams showing on the outside, with white-wash between the dark beams. And it's got little, bitty panes to the windows and none of the angles match." He paused for a moment as if for more commentary, but there was none, so he went on, "Well, anyway, I thought it was pretty. He says there is a lot of old furniture in it, but he's not interested in antiques."

It was shortly after this that I heard the man and his friends start to move out of the booth. I turned around to see what he looked like: a short man in a nondescript grey suit, he had average length brown hair, a totally forgettable face. I stood up and approached him to ask about the house and who was selling it. For some reason, his description had intrigued me. It just sounded so odd. Who would build a house in the middle of the woods, whatever style they had built it in. I asked why his friend was selling.

"Oh, it wasn't his house," he told me. "It belonged to an uncle of his, I think. Anyway, the owner died and left the house and the land to my friend."

I asked how much land and if his friend was selling the land with the house, but he was vague with his answers. I got the idea that he didn't know but that he was one of those men who can never admit that they don't know something. I decided that I had gotten as much as I was going to from this guy, so I asked who the realtors were who were facilitating the sale.

When I got home, I decided to check out the website for the realtors. I was a little surprised at the price they were asking. Of course, I knew it would be less than in the City, but I didn't think it would be that much less. It made me pause, just for a few moments, and think about taking a trip to Michigan to see the place. But I wasn't sure I'd have the nerve to come back if I left the City now, so I decided to go ahead with the sale.

I bought the house sight unseen, other than a small picture—a very dark picture—that really didn't show very much of the house. But for some reason that picture attracted me. It showed a lot more of the trees than the house, and they were beautiful trees. Looking at them, I imagined walking along for hours, seeing no other human being. It sounded like heaven at that moment.

Two days after the closing I packed up everything I cared about from my apartment, bought a used car, dropped the keys off at my friend's place for the friend of his who would be subletting it, and drove off to find solitude.

The house may be five miles—as the crow flies—away from the nearest neighbor, but by road, it's quite a bit more. Most of those five miles are through a dense wood that reminds me of the old Robin Hood movies. The road—or the track, rather—twists and circles around so much I would have gotten lost if there had been any other roads intersecting it. And it was dark enough so that I needed my headlights almost from the time I went in under the trees because the branches of the trees met above the track.

The old car was starting to make tired sounds before I even reached the trees. By the time I found the house I could see a little bit of steam coming from beneath the hood, so I was glad to stop.

The house, when I finally found it, was small. The listing had said that it was a two-story house, but if I had had to guess looking at it, I would have said there was only the one level with rooms while there was maybe an attic under the eaves. I could have reached the roof shingles without stretching on the side where the roof came down lowest. I would, maybe, have to jump to reach the roof at its highest point, but I don't think it would have been out of my reach.

The doors were less than six feet high and rather narrow. I had to bend my head a bit to go in the front door. I was tempted to go in sideways, but I decided I wasn't wide enough to make the door impassable. The ceilings, once I did get in, were no more than four inches above my head. The living room, into which the door opened, was very dark—a dark color on the walls and ceiling that I couldn't identify right away—dark wood floor and very small windows.

I had bought the furnishings along with the house and, looking around, I thought it looked like the owner of the house had just gone off shopping or something. It probably wouldn't have been my choice of furniture, but it wasn't bad.

There was a good sized couch upholstered in a sage green fabric with some kind of pattern to it and two comfortable-looking chairs in a solid fabric of a darker green. There was a heavy coffee table between the two chairs and the couch. Each of the chairs and the sofa had what my great-aunt used to call antimacassars—large crochet doilies—over their arms and backs. There was a sort of large place mat on the coffee table, with a basket of wax fruit in the middle of it.

There was a table with four chairs around it on the other side of the room, not really formal, but not like a farm-kitchen, either. A sideboard-style of cabinet and a china cupboard stood side-by-side on the other side of the table. Inside the china cupboard, visible through the glass doors, was what looked like a full set of china along with various baskets and vases. I went over and opened the drawers in the sideboard to see what might be there. There was one whole drawer full of silver, another held serving utensils in the same pattern.

All of the furniture and nick-knacks were old—I'm no expert, so I don't know how old—but well kept. Nice. There weren't any dings or dents in the wood. Nor were there any snags in the fabrics. I wondered why a businessman from the city wouldn't have gotten the stuff appraised. He could have gotten a lot more out of this stuff than the pittance I had paid for the house.

And there wasn't any dust. I wondered who came around to dust the place since, as the first man had said, this house was a long way away from any other humans.

After I had looked around for several minutes, I realized there was no light switch, nor, in fact, any electric lights. There were what looked like hurricane lamps on a few of the tables and a large fireplace on the south wall. I went back out of the house to look around, and I realized there were no power lines. I stood there, looking around at the variable greens and browns of the woods, and reminded myself that it was a good thing not to have television, that I was here to work. I only half convinced myself.

The woods gave me a strange feeling, like I was the only person left alive on the entire planet. I couldn't hear any of the noises I associated with living around a lot of other people. No trucks driving on concrete roads. No honking or yelling from irate drivers. No people talking. I'd never been so completely alone in my life, even before I moved to the City.

I went back into the house and on into the kitchen—which was the only other room on this level—next. Here, too, I found cupboards full of the usual dishes and utensils. The dishes were sturdy pottery painted with blue flowers that echoed the towels hung on the rack by the sink. The whole effect was strange, at once awkward and comfortable. I felt like I was visiting a favorite relative for the first time. An old relative.

There was a key rack by the back door with two sets of keys on it. One set was just the same as the one I'd been given by the real estate people; front door key, backdoor key, and several smaller keys, obviously for luggage or furniture. But the other set was different. It consisted of one very large, antique-looking key and a heavy fob in the shape of a badger. I hadn't seen anything that would take such a large key so far. And why wasn't it on the keyring with the other house keys.

I took the antique key off the rack and looked more closely at it. It was definitely old, not a new key that had gotten dirty and stained. It looked like tarnished silver, and it was heavy. It made me feel very odd, holding this old key. I wondered what it went to, if I had whatever it would open—a door, I was sure—not a cabinet. I'm not sure how long I stood there looking at that key, but when I looked up, the shadows had crept into the kitchen.

I looked around for some way to light the kitchen, finally lighting a candle to aid me in looking around. I wasn't all that surprised to see a wood burning stove. The stove was cold although there was some wood in the container next to it. It took me half an hour to figure out how to light the stove, and I realized that I didn't want to let the stove go out overnight, or I would never have coffee in the morning. I would need a larger supply of wood, eventually.

I remembered seeing a shed of some kind behind the house, so I went out to look. Sure enough there was a shed, and it was full to the roof with wood. Large logs of wood. I wasn't sure I would be able to lift one of them, let alone carry any into the house. There were some tools hanging just inside the door. I looked and saw an axe, a hatchet about half the size of the axe, and a saw. I sighed and decided to wait until later to find out how I was at cutting wood. Got to save some fun for tomorrow.

My first evening in my new home was an odd experience. I could type on my laptop, but I didn't have anywhere to plug it in so I couldn't use it for long. There was no cellular service anywhere in the clearing so I couldn't call anyone to let them know I had arrived safely. And there was no television or radio, of course. I hadn't thought to buy a battery powered radio to bring along. I read in bed for about an hour, then I went to sleep. I remember that I had strange dreams, but I don't remember what they were about.

The next day, after I had gone back to the nearest town in order to buy supplies and a manual typewriter, I decided to look around at my woods. I went out the back door and along a path that started next to the shed. It was dim and green rather than dark, there under the trees. I could see well enough with the light that came through the leaves, it was only the curving of the path that kept me from seeing more than ten feet in front of me.

The wood was very quiet as I walked along the path, with only the buzzing of insects I couldn't see breaking the silence. I couldn't hear any traffic or any other human sounds. When I stopped, which I occasionally did, and stood still for a few moments, I could hear small animals start moving around in the underbrush. I never caught sight of any animals except a squirrel that seemed to be following me, jumping from tree to tree in order to keep up.

After I had walked for about a mile, the path circled a sort of hill. It was a very small hill, maybe around the height of my shoulders, and it was covered in grass. There were no trees growing on it or tracks of any animals on the top of it, even though I could see the tracks of several different sizes of animals around the hill. The hill gave me a strange feeling. It was perfectly round, as far as I could tell. It looked like something was buried underneath it. Something big.

I kept walking on the path around the hill, noticing now that the wood was even more silent than it had been. The insects seemed to have all gone away to another part of the woods, and the little animals didn't move in the undergrowth. The silence added to the strange feeling that had been growing in me for some time.

I began to wonder what was under the hill. I knew that Indians had lived in the area for centuries… millennia, maybe. I wondered if this was an old burial ground, with bodies buried under the hill. It might be thousands of years old. I thought of ground-penetrating radar, maybe I could rent a machine from somewhere?

I had walked about half-way around the hill when I realized that I wouldn't have to rent any machinery to find out what was there. Because that's when I found the door.

The door was perfectly round. Set into the side of the hill it looked something like a porthole on a ship. A really, really big porthole. It was a cool blue-green in color, with silvery bands running like spokes from the center out to the outside. There was a large keyhole near the center of the door and a doorknob next to it.

I walked up to the door and tried to turn the handle. It was locked.

I stood there for a moment, my hand on the doorknob, and heard or felt… something. It was something like a vibration, something like a pure note of music. It tugged at my attention and my heart. I wanted to stand there forever, listening and feeling. I wanted to run along the woods path laughing. It was soothing and at the same time exciting, like coming home to my favorite room and finding the great American novel that I had lost years before.

Some time later—I can't really be sure how long, I didn't have a watch, and I wasn't good enough at woodcraft to tell from the way the light fell—I let my hand fall from the doorknob. Either whatever had hold of me had let me go, or I had gotten used to the feeling. Either way, I managed to let go of the knob and step back away from the door.

At that point, I started to be afraid. I had never felt anything like that before. I didn't know what was going on. The door was just a door. It hadn't changed, it hadn't moved. From a few steps away I couldn't feel or hear anything. Had I imagined it? I stood there, telling myself that I only had to step over and touch the door again to find out.

I kept telling myself that for a few moments. Then I turned around and went back to the house without doing the experiment.

I spent the rest of that day trying not to think about the door.

I told myself I imagined things, that I could not have felt or heard anything there. When that didn't work, I told myself I should write down what I had felt, that it would make a good atmosphere for a short story or a novel. And I tried—really I did. I sat for half an hour in front of my new typewriter, then a further forty-five minutes with pen and paper. I couldn't think of any way to describe it—or maybe I was afraid to describe it—and I couldn't think of anything else when I tried to write.

I tried to read. I picked up my copy of *Pride and Prejudice* and sat in front of the fire I had started when I got back. I read the first page, but when my eyes made it to the bottom of the page, I realized that I could not remember what I had read.

Finally, I went into the kitchen and started cooking myself something to eat. I wasn't really hungry; I just couldn't think of anything else to do. The house was clean. My phone didn't get reception here. I didn't know the area well enough to drive around at night. I couldn't write or read, and I was too keyed up to sleep. So I decided to cook.

I started with coffee. My drip coffee maker wouldn't work here, of course, without electricity. But I had also brought a French press along with me, so I filled the tea kettle and put it on the stove. I added a bit of wood to the stove while I was at it. Then I looked around to see what I had and if any of it sounded interesting to me right then.

Nothing much sounded interesting, but as I was looking around my eyes fastened on the key rack by the back door. Three sets of keys were still there now: the house-keys my real estate guy had given me; the set that was here when I arrived; and the big key. I ignored the two sets of house keys and focused on the other one. It was really a very large key,

I thought, picking it up off the hook. It was exactly the same silver color as the bands on the Door had been, I had already started thinking of that door in capital letters.

I tried to remember how big the keyhole had been, but the vibration kept getting in the way of my memory. Everything else that had happened around that time seemed to be blurred. It was as if the sound or vibration was physically there and pulling reality away from everything else in my memory to make itself super-real. And that was an unsettling thought. I pulled my mind away from the memory, hanging the key back up.

As I cooked spaghetti though, I kept glancing at the large key as if I expected it to have moved or disappeared. Every time I caught myself doing it, I would shake my head at myself. Anyone would think I was losing my nerve, I thought as I finally took myself off to bed. It's not as if anything had attacked me.

It took me a long time to fall asleep that night.

I woke up the next morning with the sun shining in my eyes. I had forgotten to close the curtains before I went to bed. My phone told me it was seven thirty in the morning. I turned over to put my face to the wall and lay there for a few moments trying to go back to sleep, but it was no use. I was awake. So I got up and started moving around.

After breakfast, during which I couldn't keep my eyes from straying to the key rack, I tried to think of something to do with myself that day. I wandered around inside the house for a while, but nothing could keep my attention. I kept coming back to the kitchen and fingering the key—or just looking at it—wondering if it would fit. Finally, I decided I'd have to try the key in the Door since I couldn't make myself do anything else.

The wood was almost silent again as I walked along the path behind the house. It seemed an expectant silence to me, but that may have been because of my mood. I was feeling expectant, myself, expectant and excited. What I was expecting wasn't quite so clear. I tried to tell myself that the Door just led to a root cellar or something similar, but I didn't believe myself.

When I reached the Door, I found it even harder to believe it led to something ordinary. Why would anyone put a door on the side of a hill? I supposed it might be a root cellar, or something similar. It was such an elaborate way to block off an entrance to a root cellar, though. And why would anyone put a lock on a root cellar in the middle of woods that no one ever visited? Why would anyone build a root cellar in the middle of the woods so far away from the house, for that matter?

I walked up to the Door and stood there for a moment with my head on one side, just listening. I couldn't hear any noise coming from inside the door. Or from the outside of the Door, either. The insects had stopped buzzing around again, and the wildlife was apparently keeping very still. Even the wind had stopped blowing the leaves around. There was no sound of traffic from the road or planes going by overhead. It was as if the whole world was holding its breath.

I put the key in the lock and turned it—it clicked sharply as it turned smoothly—but that was all. The Door didn't open automatically when I turned the key. I put my hand out and turned the knob. It turned easily, and the Door opened smoothly and silently with barely a push from me. I expected—naturally enough—to see a dark space inside the hill, but as I opened the Door, light came from behind it. Under the trees, it was gloomy though not really dark, but the light from beyond the Door shone out as if it were a spotlight.

The light that came from behind the Door did not waver like candlelight or firelight does. Nor did it have the antiseptic quality of artificial light. This was the warm glow of sunlight coming in from the entrance to a cave, maybe. But I was outside the hill, looking in. This light was coming from inside the hill.

The light strengthened, and I could feel a light breeze coming from inside as I opened the Door further. Instead of the smell of wet earth— or even dry earth—that I had expected, there were the smells of cut grass and sage and thyme, as well as the smell of the ocean, all floating on the breeze. And there were sounds coming from the other side of the Door. There were no voices, but there was the sound of waves crashing on rocks, of seabirds screeching.

I stood there for a moment, looking from the woods I was standing in, to the bright sunlight on the other side of the Door. I stepped nearer and craned my neck so I could see around the Door without actually moving through it. I could see the seagulls wheeling around what I could only suppose was a cliff above the ocean. But the ocean is hundreds of miles away, I thought, I couldn't be seeing it here.

And I was right, of course. I couldn't have been seeing the ocean there because *there* was the inside of a hill. I couldn't have been seeing anything except the inside of that hill. But I was seeing it, as far as my senses could tell the coast of a continent was through the Door in the hill. I wasn't sure of what continent it was because I had never spent much time anywhere but the City. I was very sure it wasn't the coast that the City sat upon.

This can't be real, I told myself. I wondered how it could have been faked. I looked around the edges of the door, trying to find the edges of the screen I knew must be there. I tried to see some pixelation in the picture. It remained completely clear, whatever I decided. Clearer than the real world? Blue-Ray is clear like that.

But that was silly, I knew. You can't feel a breeze from a scene on television—not even Blue-Ray. And you can't smell the smells of herbs and grass and the ocean when they are on television. This was real. Either this was real, or I had really lost my mind. And I didn't think I had lost my mind. Though they say, that mad people never believe they are mad.

That last thought did something toward cutting through my fear, for some reason. I smiled to myself, thinking about what my agent would say about that. She had always insisted that I was crazy, that I must be a bit off to write what I did write. Of course, thinking about my agent led me to think about my latest book, which wiped the smile off my face.

So, thinking about my agent and my publisher and my fans, I stepped through the Door, into a shallow cave above the coast of some continent.

It wasn't the continent I had been living on, of that I was sure at once. There was no sign of any people that I could see. There were just the grass and the stones and the sea. Of course, since I was still standing in the cave, my line of sight was somewhat limited. There might be some sign of people off to the left or to the right.

When I stepped out of the cave, onto a sort of landing in a hillside—a much larger hill than the one in my woods—I could see almost three hundred and sixty degrees. There was no road, and no people visible, no houses or apartments. Nothing was moving except the ocean and the clouds, and the seabirds circling around and occasionally diving.

Off in the distance, toward the ocean, I could see what looked like a fairy-tale castle. It seemed to be sitting on a rock out in the bay with a sand causeway leading from the land I was standing on out to the castle. There was no movement anywhere around the castle that I could see, though. No one walked or rode on the causeway.

I breathed in deeply, enjoying what I could smell—and what I couldn't. I could smell grass and thyme and other herbs I couldn't name. I could smell some sort of flower, or maybe flowers. I'm not so good at identifying flowers even by sight, I definitely couldn't do it by smell. Over all of these was the smell of the sea, of salt water.

What I couldn't smell was car exhaust, or hot tar, or any of the other objectionable smells that I had been used to. I couldn't smell any people.

I turned around and looked up the hill. There was something there, on top of the hill. Some sort of structure, but I couldn't see exactly what it was, only the corner of its wall. I looked around for the best way to get up there. The hillside was steep, and I didn't want to scramble up if I could avoid it. I definitely didn't want to go rolling down this hill.

Looking around me, I found I was almost on a path that wound around the hill from its base about twenty feet below me to its crest somewhere above my head. I walked up it, finding it easy going. It didn't take me long to reach the crown of the hill.

At the top of the hill was my house. It was my house, except that it was not surrounded by trees. It was my house on top of a hill. There were the dark beams surrounded by whitewashed plaster. There was the low dark door. It looked even smaller, not being surrounded by trees. It looked as if I could climb easily up to the bedroom window on the second floor.

I tried to open the door, but I found that it was locked. I reached into my pocket and pulled out my set of house keys. There was no reason to believe my house-keys would fit in this house in a different world, of course, it had to be a different world and a different house. No reason, except that this was my house. I put the key in the keyhole, and it turned, the door opened.

I went in to find a room exactly like my living room in the house in the woods. The kitchen was exactly like the kitchen in the house in the woods. There was even a key rack next to the back door with a set of keys to the house on it. There wasn't a key to the Door, though. I looked at the lone key, which I still had in my hand, and I thought that I wouldn't want to have two of them either. What if someone else got hold of the key.

I started a fire using some of the wood that was stacked by the fireplace. It was a bit cooler here than it had been in my woods. Then I went into the kitchen to see if there was anything to eat in there. There wasn't. So that wasn't different from my house in the woods, either. I'd needed to bring food in there. I would have to bring food in here, too.

At that point, I stopped myself. What was I thinking? I wasn't going to stay here, was I?

I froze standing over the stove, holding the lit match I had been planning to use to start the fire in the kitchen. Did I mean to move over into this world? Maybe not permanently, I told myself. But there's no denying that I feel more alive than I have in a couple of years.

I came back to myself with a curse when the match burned down to my fingers. I shook the match out and looked around me once more. No one had lived in this house for some time, at least months and possibly years. Long enough for dust to have collected on the wood in the kitchen. Everything was put away neatly: there were no dishes in the sink waiting to be washed; nor were there dishes in the dish rack waiting to be placed in the cupboards.

I didn't light the fire in the kitchen just then. Instead, I went out to the living room and moved most of the fuel away from the fire I had started in the fireplace so that it wouldn't get out of hand and burn down the house while I was away.

I would need some supplies if I was going to spend any amount of time here. I didn't know what was around the house on the hill, if there was a town nearby where I could buy anything. I didn't know what currency they might use. So I decided that the best place to stock up was the town five miles away from the house in the woods. I figured it wouldn't be too hard to bring food and whatnot in from the Door on the side of the hill.

I am leaving this record of where I am and what has happened to me not because I don't expect to come back to the house in the woods. I don't even expect anyone to be worried about me. I expect, in fact, that I will be going back and forth between these two houses as the mood suits me.

But, just in case I don't get back…

THE HIDDEN WORLD

E. W. FARNSWORTH

"Franco, you imp, where are you?" Abuela asked, frantic to find her lost boy. She had searched the hillside down to the water's edge. She walked around the wide lake calling his name. She looked along the shore, hoping against hope that his small body would not appear lifeless among the freshwater greenery that bobbed near the water's edge.

A naturally beautiful woman, Abuela was so distracted by Franco's disappearance her hair had become matted and tangled. She wore the same dress as she scoured the countryside. Her dark, Spanish eyes were sparkling as they busily searched.

She did not know what to do except to tell all her neighbors that young Franco had disappeared. She felt ashamed, but fear of doing nothing overcame her shame. Her neighbors were no help, chiding her for being a neglectful mother and raising a wayward, daydreaming son. They knew all about the boy's fantasies. He was already the talk of the countryside before he disappeared.

Now that he was gone, everyone's eyes said, "I told you so." Each had secretly suspected Franco's life would come to a bad ending. Survival in Patagonia depended on keeping alert no matter what happened. Working as hard as humanly possible often was not enough to stave off disaster. No one but Abuela wanted to raise a child like Franco. His name was like a curse on everyone's lips. The words, idiot, dreamer, dolt, wastrel, madman, idler, and maniac, were whispered to daughters who so much as thought of making a friend of young Franco.

In fact, Franco was a good, obedient boy, but he was always talking about fairies and pixies. He was obsessed. He claimed to see the shapes of fairies out of the corner of his eyes. Abuela often found him lost in thought having imaginary dialogs with wee creatures. He informed his mother he was going to find the fairies and live with them if they would allow him admittance to their society. He was determined about this goal. He searched everywhere for the entrance to the fairy world, which he fancied lay beneath the surface of the earth.

Abuela herself believed in fairies and pixies, so she did not want to discourage her son in his quest. She answered his questions about the magical creatures. He had a vivid sense of what fairies looked like. He was so detailed in his description of pixies, Abuela thought he must have seen and even handled one of the small, green pointy-eared creatures. She borrowed a book about all sorts of magical creatures, but Franco cried when he saw the illustrations. They were not representations of what he thought he saw.

Back by the goat pen, Franco had dug a hole he claimed would reach to fairyland. By a small boy's standard, the hole was deep, but he struck stone. At Abuela's suggestion, he filled the hole back in and planted herbs in a special garden to attract fairies. He trained honeysuckle along the goat pen fence, but the goats ate the vines. He planted wild sweet pea, which flowered and grew small pea pods. During the night the pods would disappear. Franco was distraught until his mother suggested he might have provided fairies with food they liked to eat. So Franco made sweet pea his sole crop. The plants took over the garden. In the early morning after the rain, the sun caused small rainbows to appear in the sweet pea patch. Franco thought he saw fairies picking peas. The garden was his way of communicating with the magical creatures.

Abuela taught her son songs about fairies and pixies. She showed him how to pinch like a pixie. When he tried to fly like a fairy, she had to explain that fairies had special wings to help them fly. She was afraid he would jump off a precipice, so she said fairies were small and light weight as well as winged. They could be nimble and fly where humans could not. They could also hide while in plain sight and keep in a human's peripheral vision where he was not likely to notice them. Franco was not so daft as to try to fly without wings. He was frustrated that he could not cause wings to sprout from his back by willing them to do so. No matter how hard he tried, the wings never sprouted, though his back hurt for his trying.

Franco became intrigued by the fairies' and pixies' love of the night, darkness and shadows. When his mother noticed the goat pens had been cleaned overnight without human agency, she attributed it to fairies helping her as she was especially good. On the other hand, when the milk turned sour, she blamed the pixies for their nocturnal mischief. Franco resolved he would hunt the wee creatures by night. To do that he would sneak out the back door and keep watch over the back yard under the rocky outcrop behind the goat pen. Abuela would find him sleeping there and bring him back inside to his bed.

When Franco disappeared, Abuela at first thought he must have gone hunting for his creatures in some new place. She exhausted all the old places they had visited and all the places he had speculated might be conducive to fairy dwellings. Only when she was sure she had scoured the landscape that he knew did she suspect kidnapping or worse had occurred. Since Franco was her only son and since her husband had disappeared shortly after he was born, the boy was all that remained of her family aside from herself. She wept bitterly until she thought her heart would break. After six days of grieving, she realized Franco might never return. She was at the point of despair when she heard crying out back in the goat pen.

At first, she thought the sound was the bleating of goats. Then she heard her name.

"Either a goat has learned to call my name," Abuela said out loud, "or Franco has returned and is out in the back of the hut."

She raced to see what was happening and found Franco, dazed on the ground, dirty, hungry and calling, "Mother!" He was weeping profusely, sounding much like a baby goat.

She took the boy in her arms and wept, running her hands over his body to be sure he was real and uninjured. She hugged and kissed him saying, "You worried me so. Where have you been?" Her mind swirled with relief and anger. "Why did you leave me?"

Franco got a faraway look in his eyes and said, "I was taken by the fairies. I've been to fairyland. I saw fairies and pixies. I met the Fairy Queen. I lived with them. Mother, I was worried about you, so they brought me back home. Now I can never go back again to see them."

He began to weep inconsolably. She tried to calm him down, but finally let him cry until he decided to cry no more. She held him and rocked him back and forth. She wept for joy because he had come home. He wept for grief because he had left fairyland.

Abuela was ecstatic her son was returned to her. She was not sure she believed what he said about being captured and returned by fairies. Yet his descriptions of what he saw in the fairy world were so detailed and consistent, she thought either he had been subjected to a traumatic experience in which he envisioned fairies, or he actually had been taken by them underground to the hidden world.

Franco was in need of food and water, but he was not starving or dying of thirst. Abuela fed him goat's milk and bread for nourishment. For four days, the boy settled back into the routine he had followed before he disappeared. Then he began looking for the portal to the fairy world again. This time, because he had actually been there, he had an idea of what to look for.

He told his mother that the fairies had blindfolded him coming and going, but he remembered climbing up and down for a long time. By the light in her son's eyes, Abuela was certain he would disappear again, so she made him promise to let her know where he was planning to search so she could find him.

Franco promised to keep his mother informed. Each day he searched a different place. His mother waited each time patiently until he returned. Months passed, but he could not find the portal. Years passed. Then decades came and went. Franco never flagged in his belief that he had been abducted. He thought his inability to find the portal to fairyland was due to the curse uttered when he left to come back home.

Abuela did not know what to think. She was happy that her son agreed to tell her where he was searching. She told him she would let him know if she saw any of the creatures he described. She became an ardent searcher for fairies.

Abuela's neighbors, learning that Franco had returned with fantastic stories of the fairies and pixies, laughed at him. They muttered he was a dimwit whose fantastical visions nearly drove his mother mad. They thought him useless for ordinary work. Instead of an ordinary trade or farming, Franco took up fishing in the lake. He would be seen daydreaming with his rod off to one side of his boat or the other. Evenings he would return with a stringer of fat fish for dinner and breakfast. The land was rich with worms and grubs, so there was never a lack of good bait. All it took was a little digging.

Franco learned to navigate the lake. He used a pinnacle as his reference point. It was a promontory of an underwater lake mount forming a tiny island in the huge flat sheet of lake water. Some days he would row out to the pinnacle and tie a line to secure his boat while he dreamed and slept in the afternoon sunshine.

He dreamed the same dream—of fairies and pixies in their hidden world. A thousand times he retraced his handholds and footholds climbing up and down the rocky passage to the giant underground cavern where the wee creatures lived.

He stopped telling people what he was dreaming of. He knew from their expressions they would never believe what they had not seen for themselves. Their lack of faith was a guarantee they would see no wee creatures. Franco was convinced that the magical beings only revealed themselves to true believers. If he had not believed in them, they would not have come for him in the first place.

Becoming a recluse was Franco's way of dealing with the surface world. He was devoted to his mother, who never doubted his word about his kidnapping. She humored him whenever he talked about the adventure that had shaped his life and thought. She hoped he would never frighten her again as he did for those seven days when he went missing. Still, she knew if he ever did find the portal, he would descend on his perpetual quest.

"In the event you do find the portal," she told him, "I beg you to return to the surface because I love you. I don't know what I would do without you. Your father left us. You are my only son."

Invariably when she said this, Franco would tell her, "It pains me to think I caused you pain and anguish. Yet I know I have to find the fairies one more time in spite of everything. Maybe then you and the others will believe I was really with them when I disappeared so many years ago."

Fairies were the last things on my mind as our aircraft descended to land in Patagonia.

Racile and I had flown from Boston, Massachusetts to Patagonia, Chile on a whim to camp for the summer in the wild while I collected rocks and she photographed scenery around Lake Riesco, a wilderness lake we had liked on a previous visit. When we arrived, our surroundings were stunning with one exception: the lake Racile had come to photograph had vanished.

We hiked to a small hut on a hill overlooking what used to be the lake and asked the two elderly people who lived there what had happened.

Abuela, the old woman who claimed to be over one hundred years old but looked sixty, said, "The lake was there until a week ago. Then we felt a great rumbling of the earth. Overnight, the lake was gone. The morning afterward I walked all the way down to see if any fish remained. The fish were gone as well. I'll miss the water views. My son Franco will miss the fishing."

Racile was devastated. She asked the old woman's eighty-year-old son, Franco, "What do you think happened to the lake?"

"It was taken by the fairies." He said this deadpan, his eyes focused on a rope while his hands tied a difficult knot for a goat's halter.

"Don't be telling our visitors white lies, Franco," his mother warned. She was concerned their guests would think him deranged.

Franco persisted, "It's no lie, Mother. The fairies needed the water for their own purposes. Anyway, nothing else explains it." He shrugged and continued his knot-tying exercise, lost in his own thoughts.

Knowing how the lake's disappearance dejected Racile, I decided to explore the huge basin that had formerly contained the lake water. I thought as a geologist I might find the real reason for the mystery of the vanished lake. As a scientist, I did not buy Franco's theory about the fairies. I was convinced somewhere in the basin the secret of the lake's disappearance could be found. Without making a major issue of my decision, I was determined to solve the mystery.

I told my girlfriend Racile, "Cheer up! You'll be the first to photograph a landscape that's been covered by water for hundreds if not thousands of years. The revealed rock formations have never been seen by man, so I may make discoveries too."

"It wasn't what we'd planned for, Abel. I wanted to capture the pristine beauty of the water, not the chance to compose the photographic documentary of a natural disaster."

Franco interjected, "If you're going exploring, you'll need a guide. I'll go with you."

He turned to his mother and asked, "You can manage for a few days, can't you, mother?" He was already pulling on his cap and reaching for his walking stick.

"You go right ahead, son. I can do what's necessary while you're gone."

She turned to me and explained, "I do most things myself as it is."

Don't get lost out there, Franco!" She said this with an appealing look at me. It was clear that she wanted me to look out for her elderly son while we were out walking.

I held up my hand-held GPS navigator, "It's not likely we'll get lost with this." The device showed our latitude, longitude and elevation above sea level to nine decimal places.

Franco chuckled. "We'll see. The fairies inhabit these parts. They're always wreaking havoc on technology."

Almost as an afterthought, Franco threw together some camping equipment and stuffed his backpack full of beef jerky. When he was ready, he kissed his mother goodbye.

By noon the three of us were hiking down the hill to the vast, empty basin where the lake had lain almost a week ago. Franco took the lead while Racile and I followed close behind him. He used his walking stick like a third leg showing remarkable agility for an aged man.

I decided to humor Franco by asking, "How do you suppose the fairies stole all the lake water? And where do you think they hid it?"

Franco thought about these questions for a few moments. Then he guessed, "They must have taken it down under the earth through a fissure they made. The lake went through the opening. The water's bound to be underground now in a lake in the hidden world. Underground water gathers in sundry places, but nowhere as vast as the surface lake was. The fairies' dwellings are situated near those pockets of water. I don't understand where they would have put all the water that flowed down into their world."

Racile became interested in our conversation at this point. "Franco, tell us how you know about the hidden world."

"I know of it because I went there as a boy. The fairies took me there. I was down there for a week before the fairies let me come to the surface world again." He laughed. "I was frightened out of my wits most of the time on the trips down and back up again, but the fairy world is scenic and colorful. Of course, it's also full of wee creatures, fairies, and pixies too. They came from the Old Country stowed away in merchant ships that wrecked and foundered off the Patagonian coast. They discovered secret dwelling places throughout the land and made friends with the native birds and furry animals. All those creatures accumulated in settlements according to their kinds. Human settlers made them viable by believing in them."

I figured Franco for a crackpot or congenital prevaricator, but I could see from Racile's reaction to Franco's description that she envisioned a fairy world she would rather photograph than the dull gray and brown residue of the lake bottom that lay before us in all directions now.

She asked Franco, "Do you think you could find the portal to the hidden world?"

Franco's face became serious. "I was blindfolded by the fairies after they stole me away. All the way down, they made me grope in the blind. They did the same when I stumbled up again. They only took my blindfold off when I'd reached my own backyard where the goat pen lies."

"Surely, you must have wanted to find the gateway to the fairies again," Racile insisted.

Franco shrugged. "I searched for the portal after that, but I never found it. Life was hard. Sometimes I yearned to be with the fairies again. The trouble was simple. The fairies told me I could never find my way back to their special place after I chose to leave it the first time."

"Why did you decide to come with us?" I asked him.

"Just because I am forbidden to find fairyland again doesn't mean you can't find it. I thought with you I could find the portal in the basin of the lake. I've looked everywhere else but at the bottom of the lake. Maybe there's an entry way to the fairy realm where the water seeped into the ground. So much water could not have gone underground without a great fissure opening to receive it."

"Franco," I said, "you're making good scientific sense now. So where do you think we ought to look for this fissure?"

"Water seeks its own level. For all of it to have drained, I reckon the fissure's at the lowest point of the basin. If it was any higher, we'd see a small lake below where the fissure lies."

"How will you know how to locate the lowest point?" Racile asked.

"Miss, I've fished the lake for seventy-five years in all weathers. I know the bottom well enough. I took soundings to find where the great fish slept on the bottom. The deepest place was always next to the rock formation you can see right there before you: don't you see the pinnacle chimney?" He gestured to the evident landmark. An unusual rock formation stood up in the bottom of the basin like a giant obelisk.

We made the tower of rock our objective. It was not quite a half a day's hike away. When we arrived there, we pitched our tents at the obelisk's base. At nightfall, I built a fire from driftwood that spat water all night it was so soggy. The air was chilly and damp, but overhead the stars shone brightly except where the pinnacle blocked them from our view.

Franco said, "I'll tend the fire and stand watch in case of teasing fairies or pinching pixies." I argued to stand watch so he could get some sleep. He was at first adamant. In the end, we agreed to share the watches on an alternating basis. The night passed peacefully for all our watching. We saw no signs of magical creatures.

At daybreak, we went to the place where Franco said he had plumbed the deepest place in the former lake. He knew how to locate it because of its orientation due west in the shadow of the pinnacle. There we found a rock chasm. It appeared to be a giant natural tear through the fabric of the land. I thought of a tissue on a tabletop, torn by two giant hands that pulled it apart by pressing on both sides.

"The fairies took the water there," Franco announced pointing toward the gaping cavity. "It's plain to me how it happened now."

I thought Franco was probably right. My curiosity was piqued, so I examined the fissure carefully with my geologist's eyes.

"What do you think, Abel?" Racile asked me as I finished my initial survey.

"All physical evidence suggests seismic activity caused the breach. A hollow area underground is most probably the receptacle for the lake water. This drainage hole is large enough for the lake to have drained overnight."

Hearing this, Franco interjected, "The hollow area underground you speak of is the hidden world. If we climb down inside the fissure, we'll reach the land of the fairies. It's not far below the surface, judging from my trip down and up when I was a boy. If I could climb up and down in a blindfold, I can do it now as a man without one."

Racile asked me, "What are the chances that the seismic activity that caused this fissure is over?"

I shrugged. "Yours is a good question, Racile. Not knowing the seismic patterns for this area, I can't predict what will happen next. Aftershocks are likely even after a week has elapsed. My first thought is the land shifted and found a new balancing point. Often the new balance is more reliable than the one preceding it."

Franco did not care about further seismic activity. He said, "I don't know about you two, but I'm going down into the fissure right away. This is a chance I've dreamed of all my life. If I'm not wrong, I'll see the fairies again real soon." Franco did not hesitate further. He clambered down inside the opening grasping at rocks and jagged formations as he descended.

Racile and I looked at each other and at the eighty-year-old man gaining his footholds ten feet under the surface where we stood. I made a decision to follow Franco down into the fissure.

"Racile, you can stay here on the surface if you like, but I'm going to make sure Franco doesn't get hurt. Think of his elderly mother's reaction if we should abandon him now!"

"Abel, I wouldn't miss the opportunity of seeing the fairy world. It's the photo opportunity of a lifetime. Follow the old man closely. I'll be climbing down right behind you both."

As we three climbed down the fissure, I became convinced we were scaling a kimberlite pipe formation. I used my mining hammer to free a diamond that glittered from the pipe. I figured the pipe, if properly mined, was worth a huge fortune.

In fact, the pinnacle was probably part of the pipe formation too, an ancient volcano whose crater probably formed the lake's basin. I estimated modern mining techniques would make this site equivalent to some of the great diamond finds in Africa and Russia.

As we descended into the fissure, the sunlight faded. The deep fissure never completely darkened. From the bottom rose a different kind of light. It was fluorescent and at times iridescent with a fairy glow. The subterranean rocks were soon lighting our way exclusively. The temperature was not as cold as I had expected underground even though a breeze blew up from the chasm that lay below the fissure. I wondered whether a geothermal vent could be the cause of the warm temperature of the breeze. That was not an entirely happy thought. The last thing I wanted was to descend into a cauldron of molten lava or magma.

Forging forth ahead of me by ten yards, Franco never flagged. He was a man on the mission of his life. Three hundred yards of steep descent seemed easy for this rugged old man. After dropping another two thousand yards, he disappeared. The fissure ended in a solid, horizontal cavern floor.

Franco had ducked under a rock ledge and walked into an enormous cavern, illuminated by the fluorescent rocks that lined its walls and ceiling. I saw the light reflected on the surface of an enormous underground lake that lay before us as placid as a sheet of glass.

Ahead of me, Franco said, "Here's the lake that disappeared from above."

I could not see him, but my eyes were still accommodating to the special light.

He cried out, "Ouch. Ouch. Stop it. You bad pixies. Don't you remember me?"

I moved towards his voice and made out the octogenarian waving his hands and swatting as he said, "Ouch! That hurts!"

Then I felt the pixies pinching me. Pixies pinch very hard and insistently. I had no idea how those small creatures could pester and pinch as hard as they do.

I tried to warn my girlfriend. "Racile, can you hear me? We're being pinched by small furry creatures with pointed ears. They seem to be everywhere. Ouch. Ouch. Stop it."

"Grow up, Abel. I'm holding one of the pixies now. They like being scratched behind their ears. Pick one up, scratch behind its ears and see what happens."

I grabbed a pixie and scratched it behind its ears as Racile advised. Immediately all the pinching stopped. The other pixies seemed to be mollified by my being kind to one of their own.

I shouted out, "Hey Franco, pick up a pixie. Hold it gently and scratch it behind its ears."

He must have followed my prescription because his flailing and shouting stopped.

Now we walked around the edge of the underground lake, each of us holding a pixie. Racile was so enchanted by the light on the water, she stopped to take pictures. She had difficulty doing this while she continued to scratch the pixie she was holding. Still, she managed to succeed.

Ahead I heard Franco telling some creature, "I'm Franco. We met before, long ago. I visited your realm when I was a small boy. I had to leave your world to reassure my mother I was still alive. Now I'm back again." I squinted to discern the figure he was talking with.

The Fairy Queen, in full fairy regalia including her crown, stood in front of Franco assessing him and what he was saying. She was a commanding figure with flaming red hair, gossamer fairy wings, and a powder-white face, though she was much shorter than my friend Racile. Her wings beat like no other I had seen. She was constantly moving them to maintain her position. Each of her wings seemed to have a life of its own. Like a hummingbird, she could dart and wheel or rise and fall in an instant.

The Fairy Queen responded to Franco saying, "I remember you though you've changed, Franco."

"Your Majesty, the change is all in fairyland. Where are your dwellings now that the cavern has been flooded?"

"Alas, Franco, everything is under water now. All this new water has caused pandemonium here. Not long ago after a great tremor through the earth, the rocks ruptured, and the water filled our realm all at once in a great flood. Our fairy dwellings and the pixies' palace and grounds are now all under water. Miraculously, though, we all managed to survive. We're trying to make a new life along the edges of this lake. I only hope we don't get another deluge from above."

She spoke clearly in a steady voice, but she was upset and stressed to the breaking point.

I walked up then beside Franco and told her, "Your Majesty, the seismic activity may not yet be over, but the lake above you has completely drained. You don't need to fear more water filling your realm. Rain will cause some dripping, but nothing like what you've experienced."

Racile aimed her camera at us while we talked. The camera's aperture was probably able to capture Franco, the Fairy Queen, the hundred-odd pixies and me. The camera's flashes brought Racile to the queen's attention.

"What can we do to help you?" Racile instinctively asked the Fairy Queen.

The Fairy Queen appraised Racile and nodded approvingly. She answered, "My fairies are afraid to reveal themselves because you are strangers. They surround you, but you won't be able to see them until they wish it."

I said, "You shouldn't fear us. We'll not harm you. My name is Abel. This woman is Racile. The one over there, you know, is Franco. We three came alone. No one is following us. We'd like to help you. Were any fairies hurt when the waters came?"

"Fortunately, no fairies were harmed. We fairies are nimble. All managed to reach high ground though our dwellings were inundated by the rising waters. I'm grateful for your sympathy."

Franco said, "I want to thank you for revealing your world to me when I was just a boy. It was an experience I've never forgotten. You were good to me and kind. I stayed with you for an entire week. Is there anything at all we can do to help you?"

"Natural forces have always made us strong. This deluge is aberrant, but it will strengthen us too. Fairy dwellings are humble. Perhaps you can help us excavate new homes in the areas along the shore where the waters have risen?"

"I can help with home building," I volunteered. "How much space do you need for a single dwelling?"

"Fairies only need enough for sleeping side by side. I'll show you exactly what we need."

I had worked with Habitat for Humanity to fashion low-cost housing for the needy humans of the world. I had also investigated troglodytic cave-dweller sites such as the Barabar Caves in India and the yaa dong dwellings in the Loess Plateau of China. I never dreamed I would be fashioning underground dwellings for the fairies. Yet, the dimensions were the only difference between human habitations and the fairies'. Once I knew the queen's requirements, I was able to hew new dwellings at the rate of one an hour the rest of the afternoon.

As I worked, fairies appeared from the dark recesses. They were a curious lot and enjoyed watching humans work. As I chipped and hacked at the rock, they mimicked me. They jostled each other and pointed at me when I removed loose stones.

The fairies danced to the rhythm of my rock hammer's tones. They laughed and played while I toiled. Racile and Franco kept scratching the ears of the pixies. The fairies imitated them as well. A party atmosphere invaded the space while the echoing sounds of my labor brought out large numbers of small creatures. It seemed to me like an underground teenage concert with a natural light show.

I was feeling accomplished when I completed the last dwelling I was going to attempt that day. Then the Fairy Queen told me, "We'll need only fifty thousand more than you've been able to construct today."

I felt crestfallen to learn the number was so large. At my current rate, I calculated I would have to slave ten thousand consecutive days to build accommodations for all the homeless fairies.

The Fairy Queen understood my disappointment. She told me, "I believe you'll have to train the fairies to do what you do. With your industry and our magic, things will work out. Pulling together, we'll all rebuild our community somehow." She smiled.

She had an uncanny ability to buck up my low spirits. Having observed the effect of my work on her subjects, she marshaled the most intelligent among them to discuss how to achieve her aim of rebuilding rapidly. They stood in a group shouting, waggling their wings and pointing at me. In my judgment, not much was being accomplished.

I asked the Fairy Queen, "Will you gather your fairy multitudes this evening? If you do, I'll teach them what they need to know. The more fairies that come, the more I'll teach, and the more houses will be fashioned by the time I have to depart."

The Fairy Queen communicated her wishes that all nearby fairies attend my discussion. Her messengers went forth and returned with increasing numbers until all the banks of the waters and the air around us were filled with fairies. They made a lot of rustling noises and laughter until the Fairy Queen called for silence. When the grand meeting began in earnest, I did not speak much. My intention was to provide a demonstration, not a recitation.

The Fairy Queen announced me to her subjects. "This human, whose name is Abel, will tell you how to construct dwellings. He will also demonstrate what you need to do. Listen carefully as he will not be with us much longer. All right, Abel, tell us what to do."

I raised my voice and said, "Fairies, to make a home, little is required. Boundaries and a place above high water are all you need."

I paused while the echoes of my voice subsided. Then I continued.

"I'll show you how to fashion a place large enough for your basic needs. You'll have to make such a place a home."

I demonstrated not once but thrice, explaining each step as I went. The fairies watched attentively. They whispered among themselves, but none asked me any questions.

The Fairy Queen was pleased with my demonstration.

She commanded her subjects, "Go tell the others and do with magic as this human showed you how to do with his industry." No fairy gainsaid or grumbled about her commands.

Franco told me, "I want to help make the habitats."

I said, "Franco, I appreciate your wanting to help, but you have more fitting work to do."

"Tell me what to do, then," he told me.

I said, "Make sure as many of the fairies as possible observe what I'll be doing. That will spread the knowledge throughout fairyland."

"What about me?" Racile asked. "What should I do to help?"

"Keep taking pictures, Racile. I hardly believe what we're doing. Maybe having a record of it will remind us once we're done and keep the memory alive." I still had trouble believing we weren't all involved in a consensual hallucination. How much of our experience was real and how much was a dream, I had no idea at the time.

We slept that night holding, scratching and hugging pixies because then they would not torment us by pinching and playing tricks. By the time morning arrived in the world above us, we were all ready to begin making fresh excavations.

All through the working day, I labored building fairy dwellings. I improved my methods and increased the number of dwellings I made in an hour. As I did this, I found diamonds, which I put in the pouch that hung on my belt.

Franco efficiently organized the spectators for each of the fairy habitations. He discovered that the fairies could fly in ranks five high. Doing this, the number of fairies who observed me was multiplied by five. Franco, with the help of the Queen of Fairies, made sure that each of my new excavations was witnessed by an entirely new group of fairies. When a group had finished witnessing my method, it hurried off to imitate what I had done.

Racile photographed the underground world and the creatures that came to see our labors. She took pictures of the inhabitants of the tiny dwellings once they were completed. She captured images of the flying fairies observing my work. She also photographed fairies building their own dwellings after seeing what I had done. Where I used a hammer, they used wands. They built with a touch in an instant. I hacked and hewed relentlessly. Their results were far superior to mine in every respect.

We worked for days, then weeks, but we thought the time flew by. In that time, I gathered hundreds of diamonds. Racile took thousands of pictures. Franco helped group the fairies so thousands saw what I did to make the dwellings. He also talked each evening with some of the fairy elders about old times when for a while he had lived underground with them.

Each night the Fairy Queen wanted to share what was happening throughout fairyland to acclimate to the new conditions. She waxed philosophical with a long view of what was happening to fairies and fairyland in general.

"My kingdom is endangered not because of the ravages of nature and industrial depredations of humankind. My fairies are discounted in the land above. No one believes in anything, anymore."

What she said struck a chord with me. There was a disconnect between the beings of the surface world and the denizens of the magical world here underground.

The queen continued, a tear coursing down her cheek, "Once upon a time every human child learned about fairies and pixies. We were thought to be hiding under every spring hedgerow and in the green rushes along every stream. Children looked for us and liked the gifts we brought them."

She wiped a tear away. Then she looked at me grimly.

"Today even the Tooth Fairy is ridiculed. It's a sad time for them and for us."

Franco somberly confessed, "I've always believed in fairies."

The Fairy Queen nodded reflectively. "That's why you were brought to the hidden world to learn our secrets. But you decided not to stay with us even after our kindness to you."

"If I had stayed, what would've happened to me in this great flood last week? I'm no longer nimble. I would have probably drowned."

The Fairy Queen paused to think about what Franco had said. "You have a point," she said. "Now that you've found us again, what'll you do? Will you stay with us? You'd be welcome to stay if you wish."

"Thank you, Your Highness, but now my ancient mother needs me. Humans are lucky to live to the age of one hundred. My mother's much older than that. She hasn't long for the world. In fact, I must return to the surface as soon as possible to help her through her declining years."

The Fairy Queen for a moment forgot her own troubles. She rejoined him with new determination, "Then, Franco, we must let you finish your work and escort you back to the surface quickly. Meanwhile, I'll send fairies to help your mother with her work."

She immediately called a colloquium of fairies and pixies to explain the situation and issue her commands.

"We must all pull together to get Franco back to help his aging mother. Learn what you can from our guests. I'm going to be escorting them back to the upper world in three surface days' time. In the mean time, be sure that Franco's mother Abuela has everything she needs in her hut above the basin."

I was amazed at the industry of the fairies and pixies when they had been given a mission by their Queen. I soon was through demonstrating how to build dwellings. Now I observed and criticized the fairies as they worked to build their own dwellings underground. I first taught those who had experienced doing as I had done. I taught them how to teach the others. Then I observed them teach and watched the marvelous results they achieved.

Our last three days in fairyland passed as if they were hours. We left a fairy kingdom industriously rebuilding their homes with a combination of magic and instruction on the shores of their new underground lake. They were working cheerfully, confident that their labors would not be in vain. They had much to do, and I wished we could have stayed and helped.

When it was time for us to depart, the Fairy Queen gathered her people to wish us well. She made a speech that rings in my mind today.

"Fairies, over the last month we've worked together with humans as once we did long ago. These humans came not for their own gain but to help us in our time of need. We shall never forget them as long as they live."

The fairies beat their wings in a kind of fairy applause. When they settled down again, the Fairy Queen continued.

"If any of these three or their offspring wishes to come to fairyland, we'll give them a hearty welcome and let them stay as long as they desire. Meanwhile, we'll watch over them all their days as if they were part of our fairy family."

The fairies nodded and whispered to each other. They were excitedly taking their Queen's command to heart. Then the Fairy Queen moved to her valediction.

"To the humans from all the fairies, I say, Thank you for coming in our hour of need. We deeply appreciate your belief in us and hope you can spread that belief among your peers when you return to humankind. We'd also like you to help us protect our kingdom from the ravages of industry and thoughtless pollution.

"The deluge we suffered was, fortunately, one involving fresh water that had gathered in a lake. It would have been far worse a disaster if that lake had been full of viscous chemical waste." She paused for a moment for that thought to sink in.

Raising her wings, she commanded, "So fairies and pixies, let's give these humans three great Hurrahs."

They did say, "Hurrah, Hurrah, Hurrah." The cavern echoed for many minutes afterward.

Then the Queen of Fairies escorted us to the fissure and hugged us each tight in her fairy embrace. I still recall the feel of the veins of her sturdy wings and her fresh, sweet smell.

Franco, Racile and I climbed through the fissure accompanied by troops of fairies and pixies, who pinched us affectionately in a fond farewell. I had to help Franco frequently during the steep climb. An eighty-year-old man does not climb a mile straight up without assistance. At many points, we had to rest so he could catch his breath.

When on the surface again, we decided to rest for the night in our pitched camp and journey up the hill to Franco's hut in the morning.

That night no pixies pinched us, but I felt a fairy presence hovering protectively over us. Once I awakened from a frightful nightmare about a sea of toxic waste flooding the hidden world. When I looked frantically in the direction of the portal, I fancied I saw fluorescent light glowing in the fissure, but it may have been my imagination.

We broke camp at daylight and packed our kit for the hike back out of the basin and up the hill.

When we reached Franco's hut in the late afternoon that day, we found Franco's mother milking their six she-goats in the enclosure out back by the rocky outcrop.

She did not look up from her milking while Franco excitedly told her what we had seen and experienced underground. When he had finished his account of our journey, she smiled broadly.

She lifted her wooden bucket of milk by its rope handle and walked slowly back into the hut to her kitchen table. There she served us the warm milk in wooden tankards. It tasted sweet and pure.

"It was over a month you were gone, but I had no doubt you'd return," she said as we drank the milk. She wiped a tear from her eye, the first small sign of her immense relief at Franco's return.

The old woman turned to me and asked, "Did you find what you were looking for?"

Her question surprised me. I had to collect my thoughts before I replied. "I didn't expect to find what I experienced among the fairies. I was on a rock expedition, however, and I made discoveries." I held up my pouch with the diamonds inside as my example. She nodded and smiled with one eyebrow raised. Her expression indicated I had found a mixed blessing.

Addressing Racile, she asked, "Miss, did you find what you were looking for?"

Racile smiled. "I expected to be reduced to photographing a blasted landscape where once there was a lake. Instead, I took pictures of a fairy world under the earth where fairies and pixies struggled to rebuild their dwellings. I was glad we could help." I could see that she was transformed by our experience. She had an aura of peace about her I had never before witnessed.

"And Franco, my son," she asked, "Did you find what you were looking for?"

"Mother, all my life since I was taken by the fairies, I've wanted to return to them. You know this. Yes, I found what I was looking for. It was not as I expected, though. The lives of the little ones were disturbed by the ingress of the lake water. I was glad we could help, but there was so much left for them to do after we departed. I despair of their ever rebuilding what they had before the flood."

The old woman nodded. Then she said, "While you were underground, I received magical help. This hut and the animal enclosures were cleaned each night by fairies. I didn't see them though I knew they were responsible. The milk was sweeter than ever, as you have also discovered from drinking it. Weeds disappeared magically from the garden. From those and other things, I knew you must be faring well. As for the future, why don't Abel and Racile stay in our hut this night? They can decide what to do next tomorrow morning."

We slept soundly in that hut. I had worked so hard helping the fairies; my muscles were sore and cramped. My hands had blisters on blisters from wielding my hammer repeatedly. I reflected I was lucky the hammer had not broken under all the strain. I fell asleep dreaming of returning to the hidden world. All night in my dreams I worked to build new homes for fairies.

We awakened to the sound of the cock's crowing. During our breakfast of oat porridge, I asked the old woman whether we could do anything to make her life easier.

"Without the lake, I need some way to collect rain water. I don't want to trouble you. I know you're anxious to get back home."

"There's no trouble, Ma'am. I'll see what I can do to make a rainwater collection vat."

I spent the day making an oblong wooden basin to catch the water as it cascaded down the outcrop above the goat pen. Racile recorded my work in a sequence of photographs including the goats watching me build the contraption.

I was wondering how I could test my structure when an evening squall filled the basin demonstrating it would serve the purpose for which it was intended. I scuppered some of the water into the existing goat troughs. I devised a runnel to slough excess water into the woman's irrigation matrix for her garden. I showed Franco how to maintain and extend what I had built. At eighty, he was still capable of learning. I knew I was leaving the capability in good hands.

After another exhausting day, we stayed that night at the hut. The next morning Racile and I climbed down the hill and flew back where we came from.

In Boston, Racile developed her photographic negatives. She grouped her photos under four subject headings: the desolate remains of Lake Riesco, the hut on the hill, the hidden world of the fairies and Abel Johnston. I was surprised at the last category. I had no idea she had documented my work with special care.

We discussed how to use her photos at length in candle light over wine. I recommended she might categorize the commercial photos in two parts. One was for an article we would co-author for National Geographic Magazine. The other was for a book we would write on our experience underground tentatively titled, The Hidden World.

As for the photographs Racile took of me, I suggested that we take those out of consideration for publication while we re-factored our relationship. She heartily agreed. A month in fairyland will change people. So it was with us as we decided to think about the possibility of marriage, a subject we had studiously avoided addressing during our years of friendship.

I meanwhile took my diamond collection to experts who proclaimed my specimens unparalleled. They wanted to know where I had found the rough gems. I remained silent about their source. I received a large sum for the diamonds. In the process of selling the gemstones, I formed an idea.

The more I thought about the commercial viability of the basin in Patagonia, the less I liked the idea of having industrial mines dig up the kimberlite pipes I had found. I figured I could return to Patagonia to gather diamonds whenever I liked. No one else ever needed to know where I mined them. Money, therefore, was no longer a problem for me.

It also occurred to me that by publishing our book, The Hidden World, Racile and I would be violating the trust we had elicited from the fairies and their Fairy Queen.

"Racile, I'm sorry, but I don't think we should publish the book about the fairies. Let's make it our private portfolio of photographs and enjoy them."

"Abel, I was thinking the same thing. We're beginning to think like an old married couple. Maybe we should get married after all." She won me over with her crooked smile.

Racile and I did get married in a small, private ceremony in my living room. We later published our National Geographic Magazine article. We suppressed and privately shared Racile's collection of pictures of me at work and of the hidden world.

Once a year we return to see Lake Riesco as an anniversary present to ourselves. The old woman now lies buried behind her hut on the hill overlooking the basin. Her son passed peacefully soon after she died. His grave lies beside hers.

We purchased the hut and surrounding acreage and rented the farm to a Patagonian farmer who loves the land and keeps a close watch over the countryside. He and his wife also believe in pixies and fairies. They swear they never tend to the two graves on the property. Yet the little cemetery is always immaculate though covered with sweet pea vines, seasonal flowers, and herbs, possibly the result of fairy visitations.

Every time we go back to the place, we marvel at how nature has reclaimed the basin as her own. Dense overgrowth now masks the fissure where I still harvest my diamonds. An eagle's next graces the summit of the towering pinnacle. I'm working with the Chilean government to make the dry lake bed a national park, protected from corporate development. Diamonds go a long way towards getting such things legislated in Patagonia, Chile, and I have plenty of those.

Racile had the idea of naming the park, "Fairy Queen National Park," to commemorate fairies generally. The Chilean national legislature had other ideas and voted to fund the "Patagonian National Park of Chile." At least, we figured, the land covering the hidden world would be somewhat protected.

Racile and I have a boy Franco, named for old Franco, and a girl Abuela, named for old Franco's mother. They are fraternal twins. Both fervently believed in fairies and pixies from the time they were in the nursery. Both were brought up bilingual in English and Spanish. When they came of age, they both participated with Racile and me in Habitat for Humanity building homes for the homeless and disadvantaged of the earth.

When Franco and Abuela were twenty-one years old, Racile and I shared with our twins our portfolio of photographs of the hidden world and swore them to eternal silence.

Franco has followed in his mother Racile's footsteps as a professional nature photographer. He spends his time documenting disappearing and disappeared natural landmarks. If a river disappears suddenly, he flies out to investigate. He is a regular contributor to National Geographic Magazine. He is also an experimenter in what he calls paranormal photography. This is an art form purporting to capture spiritual entities often overlooked by observers with strictly scientific views.

Abuela has followed in my footsteps as a geologist and mining engineer. She is an expert in diamond formations, especially kimberlite pipes. She accompanies me on private expeditions to the fissure to harvest the diamonds we need to fund our many philanthropies, including the Children's Fairy Institute of Patagonia. Sometimes she goes with her brother to investigate natural aberrations, but he has a girlfriend now. Being fiercely independent, Abuela strikes out on her own to discover gem sites. She is always careful to consider the environmental implications of a site in case any wee folk are dwelling there.

Both our children have mentioned feeling as if they were watched over by guardian angels while they worked and traveled. This is not surprising to me. I have never forgotten the valediction of the Fairy Queen and the sacred obligation fairies have to protect Racile, me and our offspring.

Racile and I sometimes have had a yearning to visit the hidden world again. Each time events in the busy surface world have intruded on our plans. We reason we visited there for purposes we are still discovering. Besides, having connected once, we remain connected always.

THE LAST STRONGHOLD

PAMELA JEFFS

Laid out before me are the skulls of ten sons. My sons. Once, the blood of gods and kings ran through their veins, but now all that remains is bone and memory. And I am the keeper of both.

The skulls stare at me as I wait in my ruined hall. Their eye sockets are empty, but I imagine I can still see the spark of life that once animated them. Ten sons. It is a terrible thing for a father to lose so many. I touch the brow of each skull. The cold impregnated in the bone seeps into my fingertips. Diaprepes, Azaes, Mestor, Elasippus, Autochthon, Mneseus, Evaemon, Ampheres, Eumelus… Atlas.

Atlas. He was my first-born and the first King of Atlantis. A bold lad in his youth, he grew to become a king both respected and feared by all nations of the ancient world. But the human sycophants he kept company with betrayed him. Jealous of his power, they rose against Atlas and slew him, the final blow struck by a human he had honoured and called friend.

I loved Atlas, and his loss affected me deeply. In my grief, I set the ocean to rage for a full season. I razed clean the coasts of continents; I swallowed the ships and armies that dared to cross my waters. I taught the humans to fear me in a new kind of way.

They tried to placate me. The humans prayed to me and sacrificed their animals, but I paid no notice. Nothing could replace the son taken from me.

Then things unravelled further. Following the demise of Atlas, my other sons began to fall. One by one death claimed them, in ways neither quiet nor easy. My sanity frayed. I blamed humans for my grief and questioned why they were allowed to continue existing at all. Such cruel, selfish beings; they cared nothing of greatness nor higher purpose. Why should they prosper when my sons lay dead and cold?

My brother Zeus, fearing what I would do, called me before him. As our king, his word was law. So I pleaded with him to let me have my revenge, to let me flood the world. But Zeus disagreed. He was soft when it came to humans.

"They have such potential," he told me. "Given the chance, they will do great things."

I spoke my truth to him. "Believing such a thing, Brother, shows you to be both weak and foolish."

Zeus's temper is a forge easily flared, and my words brought the weight of his ire upon me.

"You shall be bound to Atlantis," he said, "And sit there with your sons until you can devise another option for the future of humanity."

And since then I have remained here. This dead island, this dead city. Atlantis.

Millennia have passed and the time has mellowed my anger. My imposed solitude has given me the distance I need to find clarity. I am now ready to leave this place, ready to reconsider Zeus's point of view. I think I have succeeded. My view now is that perhaps humanity just needs to be taught. And so I have devised a way.

With my trident, I carefully shaved shards of bone from my sons' yellowed skulls. I mixed the bone with my own blood in a bowl carved from stone. The vessel was passed through fire and doused with seawater. From this, I fashioned a glass egg and inside it placed the embryo of a child who will grow to be the Heart of the World. She will be a mother for the human race, a woman who can teach them to honour the gods and to value peace over bloodshed.

My reverie is broken. I hear footsteps on the beach. Yes. Another treasure seeker has found the deep crack in the cliffs on the mainland, the lost door that leads beneath the sea and here to Atlantis. I shift in my seat. Anticipation wars with my dread. Perhaps this human will be one worthy of The Heart and will help me win my freedom from Zeus's curse. I take a deep breath and test the currents of sea air. I scent perfume. It is a woman.

She is not the first to come here, but of the others only their bleached bones remain, filling the dry moats that surround this citadel. They were all unworthy, thieves, murderers and liars all. I display their remains outside to stand as a warning to the next that tries for my favour.

The treasure seeker is closer now, crossing the bridges that lead to this hall. Her hand is on the door, her shadow falling across the threshold. She enters hesitantly, a man-made weapon held at the ready. I do not look at her. Let her first see what is spread before me, the skulls of my sons and let me see if my loss moves her.

The woman stops. She seems hesitant to approach. I raise my head, seeing my image reflected in the pools of her eyes. I am immortal, but I look old now, hair white, brow weathered and wrinkled. I ask her the question that I ask all who come to stand before me. "Can you name the firstborn son?"

She is a slight thing, tough and wiry as if she has travelled the hard places of the world and lived to tell the tale. Her hair is red; her eyes blue like the ocean on a clear day. Hope rises in my chest.

The woman lowers the weapon in her hand and approaches. "May I?" she asks pointing to the first skull in the line.

I nod; impressed with her bravery. She is the first to ever ask permission. She picks up my beloved son's skull, and staggers beneath the weight of it, the bones of a demigod are heavier than those of men.

Her eyes start to move as visions from beyond the plane of normal sight are revealed to her. I know what it is that she sees. It is Atlas upon his throne resplendent in his blood red robes, his raven hair crowned with a circlet of gold. The woman's breathing becomes ragged, and she places the skull back down.

I taste her fear. It is metallic. My hope fades. Only a blameless heart could bear saying the name without fear. I ask her again. "Can you name the firstborn son?"

For a moment she does not speak. Finally, she whispers, "Atlas."

I hear the blood pumping in her veins. The blackness in her soul is revealed to me. I sigh. This woman is not the one.

Prying into her thoughts, I see images of a man… a husband. A husband named Conner. There is blood on his face; she is standing over his corpse. This woman is a murderer.

She looks at me, her eyes wide with fear. I feel the egg secured within my chest twitch. The child inside it begs for release, but she is too precious a treasure to be given to one not worthy. My decision is made. I grasp my trident and call forth my Spirits of Justice and Vengeance. The Furies.

They detach from the ceiling with a piercing cry, their talons outstretched and gleaming. But the woman is brave; I will give her that. She does not scream. Instead, she raises her weapon and spits fire from it at the circling spirits. Three shots and one by one they fall to the ground, wings thrashing a rain of green blood across the surfaces of my hall.

I reel with shock. The loss of the Furies is too much, the weight of their blood too heavy on my conscience. My fragile peace shatters. Ancient rage is reborn. I raised my trident again and backed with the full force of my anger I send it crashing to the ground. The floor splits, the crack running deep into the heart of Atlantis. The earth begins to tremble. The woman falls to the ground.

I reach into my chest, to the place where my heart once resided. From there I pull forth the delicate egg. The Heart of the World lays cradled within it, eyes closed and cupid lips serene. In her, I see the promise to humanity that will never be fulfilled. I see my chance at freedom delayed. But I know myself a fool to have placed my hope in the hands of men.

I hold the egg in my fist and squeeze. The delicate glass cracks and the fluid within leaks out around my fingers. The baby starts to gasp in the now empty egg. My daughter is dying, just like her brothers before her. "The Heart of the World," I say to the woman.

Her eyes widen in surprise. Perhaps she is thinking of the husband she murdered. No. I see she harbours no regret on that score. She is thinking only of herself; thinking only of escape. But it is too late.

Seawater begins to leak in from the crack in the floor. The foundations of Atlantis are broken and before long, my last stronghold will be consigned to waves. The water will not bother me. I can sit in this hall beneath the waves. I have the patience to await another chance at freedom. I will endure.

I am Poseidon.

THE PORTALS

YI YI DU

Ten hallways with increasing difficulty…
Ten portals…
Ten contestants…
One survivor.

Jack — The Mirror

The hydraulic door lifted itself up with a mechanical click. Jack stepped out of the cold sanitizing chamber and into an empty hallway. Fluorescent white lights that blinked and flustered hang low off the tiled ceiling. Dull grey paint laminated the walls around him. Several yards away the hallway ends with what seem to be a sheet of metal. Jack gingerly crept forward as his footsteps rang loudly. The door behind him hissed and tightly sealed itself. The image replicated sucked all the life out of the marrows of Jack's bones. In the mirror, he was stripped of his clothes along with his skin, exposing the red and fleshy muscles underneath. They moved in the mirror as Jack flinched. Biting his ash white lips with his teeth, Jack inhaled through his flaring nostrils and moved closer to the delusional mirror. The creature in the mirror copied Jack's movements. Veins filled with blue blood popped as Jack halted in front of the mirror. He reached out his hand and so did the creature.

Without a warning, the creature in the mirror reached out and pulled Jack in. His scream echoed in the hallway.

Wendy — The Void

The vine covered mossy stones surrounded Wendy's slender body. Her tank top flailed in the slight moist breeze. She looked up and saw a sky filled with sinister dark clouds. Ahead of her was a gap about the length of two cars. With her hand sticking tightly against the wall, she shuffled herself to the edge. Under the pressure of her foot, loose cobbles on the side of the drop loosened and fell into the dark void. Wendy's knees buckled and her body softened at the sight of an endless pit. She leaned against the wall and panted. Her vision was swarmed with dark patches while her mind blanked out. The essence of life and hope withered in her heart. Her right leg finally gave out on her, and she fell to the edge of the drop. Her body swung itself over the solid ground. Wendy grabbed the edge with her two hands as she swayed on the edge. Beads of sweat rolled down her cheeks and moistened her palms. She was losing her grip. No. With a wail and a slip of her hand, Wendy, flailing, was consumed by the darkness.

Leonard — The Mist

The wooden ceiling almost touched Leonard's head. His hair rubbed against the classy stained wood panels. He adjusted his white collar and unknotted it. The heat was unbearable inside the wood-paneled tunnel. His chubby face reddened and moistened when he moved his tree-trunk legs forward. It was like a sauna for Leonard. Beads of sweat merged into streams and seeped into his eyes as he shifted his body towards the steam in front of him. The acid inside his sweat burned against his retinas. A searing itchiness blinded him. The world twisted and warped in his sight. Must not scratch. Must not scratch. Must not scratch. He looked down at his hands which had metal claws bound to them with chain links. Their razor sharp edge sliced through the wooden panels as Leonard unleashed them on the walls, trying to distract himself from the pain and increasing itchiness.

Leonard inched closer and closer to the misty cloud of steam. Almost there. Must not scratch. Must not scratch. Must not scratch. The itchiness was uncontainable any more. Leonard's hands unwillingly curled up closer and closer to his eyes. The edge of the metal scraped against the corner of his right eye. NO. no. NO. He watched in horror as his hands turned into piles of dust along with his arms. Moments later, a pile of clothing silently sat on a pile of grey dust.

Alison— The Icicle Ring

Silvery icicles dangled above her head as she slid across the hallway in her slip-on shoes. The air around her chilled her to her bones as her teeth clattered. The hot air exhaled around her face instantly froze as mists and fell to the floor. As dry as sheets of paper, the skin of her hand turned white and slightly flaked. Cracks appeared around the joints. Alison pulled her gaze from her hands and looked behind her. The buffer room between portals now seemed to be luring and attractive to Alison. The gears of her mind slowly turned as she looked in the other direction. The sight of a swirling blue mist in the middle of an icicle ring did not please her muddy mind at all. That's the way. The portal. But, warmth and… safety. Alison's mind completely froze in place. Submitted, she walked back towards the room one step after the other. Her vision dimmed as she half walked and half crawled back into the doorway. She wasn't moving when the door closed back on her.

Thomas — The Bottom

Walking in knee deep water tired Thomas out. The stink was unbearable as he attempted to bring his head underneath the surface of the yellow and murky water. It was like fermented dead salmon mixed with some century-old cheese. His face contorted in disgust as he gagged. It's down on the bottom. Just hold your breath. Several meters ahead, the hallway dipped, and the water became several meters deep. Thomas, having no choice, gulped a big swig of air into his lungs and plunged himself headfirst into the water. Deep gurgles boomed in Thomas's ears as he tried to advance forward. The water felt strange as if it was ten times heavier. In his mind, he knew he was only two meters down into the water. His back, however, felt as if he was being squished by a hydraulic press. Running out of air and unable to locate the spot, Thomas swung his arms down to resurface but was met with strong resistance as the water seemed to be purposely pushing him down. He could see the hallway lights above the water but couldn't move an inch toward them while his lungs starved itself of oxygen. Gasping for air, Thomas frantically flailed around uselessly. On the surface, muffled screams dissipated through the air as a big bubble popped. The water became calm after.

Scarlet — The Fire Extinguisher

Don't touch the fire. It's not safe. That's one of the rules that Scarlet learnt during her early years. Standing on a suspended platform in a hallway filled with lava chunks free flowing on the ground that is now smoked completely black, Scarlet clenched her fist tight and stared at the far side of the hallway where another platform was. It had a fire extinguisher sitting on it. Heh. Jokes on me. Despite every single brain cells in her head screaming at her, she stepped off the platform and onto a dark red obsidian. Immediately, her feet felt a tingling sensation as the heat rammed at her soles. Move quickly and don't step on the lava. A timer extended out of one of the ceiling tiles and displayed 60 on it. 59. 58. How. Scarlet cursed as she hopped from one obsidian to another. It was at the last tile when the time bipped. Two big red zeros flashed at Scarlet. Underneath her feet, the lava started to rise up and crept onto the obsidian. She yelled and leaped to another obsidian. This time misjudging the distance and stepped square into the ankle deep lava. Her foot was instantly gone, not even a wisp of smoke remained. She, stretching her hands out for the platform, fell into the lava. With a loud hiss, Scarlet was gone.

Fergus — The Ladder

Right after Fergus stepped out of the room, an armored laser turret spun around and aimed its barrels at Fergus. The murder machine, with a matt black finish, looked right at home in the one-person-tall trench. The sky must be the ceiling of the hallways. The trench, must be the side of the hallway. The machine gun. Probably just a scarecrow. Fergus boldly walked up to the machine's barrel as it readjusts its position. The black end of the barrel followed Fergus's face. He grabbed the barrel and slapped it aside. The metal felt cold to the touch compared to the soggy dirt walls around him. He proudly walked past the turret, ignoring the whirring inside, and headed towards the ladder hang at the end of the hallway. Several popping sounds penetrated Fergus's body. He looked down and saw rings of red appeared on his shirt. He turned around and there it was. No, it can't be loaded. It must be an illusion… Bolts of pain brought Fergus to the blood saturated ground. The last thing he saw was the barrel of the turret observing him motionlessly.

Teresa — The Iron-barred Door

How cute. The dogs whimpered in their cages that lined themselves up along the two side of the cinderblock walls. A total twenty-four of them. German Shepherds, Alaskan Malamutes, Greyhounds… At the end of the hallway was an iron barred door that lead to whiteness.

The dogs, wagging their tails between their legs, stared at Teresa with their large and innocent eyes. They stuck their nose out between the wires of the cages and sniffled her white summer dress as she moved along the cages. A golden retriever looked up at Teresa's oval face and back down at the lock engaged on the cage door, clearly wanting to get out. Teresa bent over and stared at the dog then at the lock. A simple latch mechanism. What's the harm in opening the lock, hey? Teresa moved her hands in and grasped the lever on the latch. The retriever bounced around in its cage as it sensed the forthcoming freedom. A click and the gate swung open. The dog squeezed through the door and stood in front of Teresa, who stood up. Suddenly, the dog's face stretched. The mouth curled upwards sinisterly and revealed rows of its teeth. The fluffy body of the retriever enlarged as well. It puffed up to two meters. The claws pinned Teresa beside the cage, and the dog moved in. Teresa desperately squirmed. It's saliva dripped onto the silky white fabric as the retriever opened its massive jaws…

Finn — The Vault Door

There was nothing but drawers stacked high around himself. The numbers on the drawers faded long ago, and it seemed no one ever unlocked them before with all the dust collected on top of them. Finn rested his left hand on one of them and turned his head towards the other side of the wall where a steel vault door was. It was slightly ajar. The exit? Nah, can't be that easy.

He turned his attention back to the drawers. Beside each and every one of them was a tiny white sticker. Neat prints engraved on it. Authorized Only.

But what authority. The contestant? Me? Out of his curiosity, he pulled on the handle of the drawer, and it slid open with a grind. Inside, lighting up Finn's face, were bars of gold in plastic bags neatly packed away. Finn ran his hand over the bricks, feeling their weight and the power that radiated from them. Finn opened another drawer. It was filled with diamonds, sapphires, and rubies. Jack looked around, and after pondering for a second, he ripped open the plastic bag and dumped all the precious stones into his army pants pockets. He went back to the gold bars and slid one in as well. Who will know? It's here for me. Why not. Just as he was about to touch the vault door's brass handle, the ceiling tiles exploded. Gold bars, diamonds, rubies, and golden cups rained upon the hallway. Within five seconds, the gold buried half of Finn's body. Feeling the immense pressure on his chest, Finn blacked out as his lungs were crushed against his ribs. The gold bar still was in his pocket.

David—The Arches

He didn't enter the hallway on one end. He didn't really enter the hallway at all. There was no buffer zone for David, who was standing in the middle of the hallway with his tuxedo. On each end of the hallway was an arch with a white whir in the middle spinning. Underneath the arch on David's right side was a woman. And on the left was a man. Both whom David knew. Mother and Father, who passed away two years ago. Now they were smiling at David as he scrutinized them without moving a single strand of muscle in his feet. No, they are not real. They are dead. Dead. Yet, they looked incredible. His mother, with her soft tender skin and her blue eyes, brushed back her wavy and ruby hair. His father, hands on his waist, held his muscular chest high and his pointy chin tall. There were no ages on their faces. There were no wrinkles. There was no pain of last moments of their lives during the plane crash. It was just them. Mother and Father. David watched as they extended their arms out towards him at the same time. Both mouthing a single word. Come. But come to whom? David looked at his mother and then at his father. No. You are not my parents. No. The urge of taking his mother's hands or embrace his father gnawed at David's wary mind.

"No. I am not going to chose." David spoke with a raspy voice. "You are not my mother, and you are not my father." He stood his ground firmly.

The hallway instantly started to vibrate violently. The arch glowed brightly. The cozy warm light consumed the walls of the hallway as it moved towards David. The illusion of his mother and father faded away, and David dropped to his knees on the floor. Around him, there was nothing but the white glow.

"Have I won? Have I really won?" He collapsed and closed his eyes.

THE SCREEN

JAYNE MOORE WALDROP

"Clay, get in the car. It's time to go."

From the air, the boy watched his dad's mouth form the words. Clay's legs kept pumping. The swing's wooden seat rose higher with each point and flex, its chains rubbing the tree branch like small, steady blades. Chips of bark landed in his hair or fell to the grassless spot beneath the swing.

"Just let me stay here. I'll be okay," Clay said. He didn't want to move to Stanford.

"Don't be silly," his mother said, standing near their white Dodge sedan as she finished a cigarette. "They'd put us in jail for leaving you behind."

Clay pictured his mother behind bars, surrounded by murderers, kidnappers, and other bad people. It would be his fault if she went to jail, and he didn't want to be blamed again. Besides, he knew they couldn't stay here. The house was already sold; the new people were moving in tomorrow. Without further protest, he dragged his sneakers against the ground to brake, creating a cloud of dust as the swing slowed. He walked to the car and climbed into the backseat, as far as possible from his little sister Hayley. Silently, by running his finger down the middle of the deep red upholstery, he reminded her of the seat's imaginary dividing line.

As they drove off, he looked out the rear window to say goodbye to the old house and life in Lone Oak. They were moving to Stanford, about an hour away by the two-lane roads that connected the Kentucky towns. They'd start new lives there, according to his parents. A fresh start. But Clay didn't want a new life. He wanted his old one back, his life before Sam died.

From behind his mother's seat, he watched her head bob a few times as she dozed. She always fell asleep on long rides. When she shifted her body to lean against the door, Clay checked to make sure it was locked.

When they pulled into the driveway of the new house, the moving van was nowhere in sight.

"Maybe the driver got lost," Dad said.

"Or maybe he stole all of our stuff and sold it at a pawn shop," Clay said.

"He did nothing of the sort," Mom said as she straightened herself from the nap. "Go on, scat. Look around the place. You're going to like it here."

Clay nodded. He'd look around, but he didn't have to like it.

Hayley hopped from the car and followed Dad toward the front door. Clay got out and surveyed the house and yard, squinting to see it better in the bright sun. His summer-cut hair, so short its blondeness had disappeared, spurted a few beads of sweat. His hand-me-down blue-checked shirt, untucked, billowed in a light breeze.

Studying the house from the gravel driveway, Clay thought it might be made of gingerbread, like in the fairy tales he read when he was little. It had a pointy roof, with upstairs windows sticking out like small doghouses. Giant oak trees lined the driveway and the street that went along the front. Beneath them, little tufts of dry grass struggled to grow in the summer heat. Worn-down dirt exposed thick roots that fastened the trees to the ground. Acorns were plentiful, making it rough on bare feet but a haven for squirrels. Maybe he'd hunt again with the little .410 shotgun that Gramps gave him for his last birthday, his ninth.

"Come on, Clay," Hayley yelled as she ran through the open front door. His six-year-old sister had a head start so she'd probably choose the best room for herself. Running as fast as he could, he hurled himself onto the half-moon brick stoop. Through the storm door glass, he saw Hayley reach the top of the stairs. He decided to take his time and act like it didn't matter.

He opened the arched front door slowly and noticed a brass knocker with a fancy dragon head with red eyes. It looked old and scary, and it produced a surprisingly loud sound that echoed in the small entryway, where there was a built-in seat below a mail slot. He put his hand through the slot to see if he could reach all the way to the outside. He'd never lived in town before. They'd lived in the country and had a mailbox at the old house.

"Are you coming?" Hayley called from upstairs.

"Wait a minute," he barked back. He'd make her wait, hoping to squelch her excitement about getting her choice of bedrooms.

He wandered through empty spaces painted a dull green and into the kitchen with cabinets that stretched to the ceiling. The flecked linoleum floor popped and creaked as he crossed it. Everything smelled like mothballs and talcum powder, the way old people smell when they dress up for church. He hated it all. Their house in Lone Oak had been newer and not so creepy. As he started up the stairs, he saw another empty room, maybe his parents' new bedroom. Two open closet doors revealed a few stray hangers left by the previous owners.

"Look at my new room," Hayley chirped as soon as she saw him reach the landing. She stood in the doorway of a room coated in pink. She could have it, he thought. He shrugged and walked into another room, painted deep blue, his favorite color.

Along one wall of the room was a row of windows, and below them, an equal length of empty bookshelves. It was a long, skinny room, with a closet on one end almost as big as another room. The closet had a tiny round window on the far wall, like the one over the front door. He plopped down on a built-in window seat and saw an old barn in deep green woods behind the house. It was a small barn, its roof high and pointed in the middle, with an open loft door and walls that wore a faded coat of red paint.

He ran downstairs and bumped into his dad, who was carrying an armload of boxes. Dad wouldn't start his new job at the hardware store until tomorrow.

"What's the rush, buddy?"

"I saw a barn out there. Is it ours?"

"Sure is. This used to be a farm until they sold the land to build the new houses all around us."

"Can I go?"

"Yeah, but it looks snaky back there. Watch where you step."

Clay looked for a back door and found it halfway down the basement stairs. The old wooden storm door was swollen and stuck, requiring him to push with his hip and shoulder. When it finally gave way, he ran through the backyard where the ground grew mossy. An old road led to the barn, but the way was overgrown with blackberry bushes and wild roses that scratched Clay's legs and tore at his clothes.

In front of the barn, an old tractor sat, its red belly rusted and its rubber tires rotted. A Pepsi bottle, half full of greenish water, sat upright on its running board. Clay spotted a door with a metal latch with a rusty padlock he couldn't budge. He used a rock to pound the latch until it broke away from the weathered boards, then he pulled the door open, skinning over a ridge of dirt and weeds.

Watching for snakes, Clay made his way through a tack room hung with old bridles, halters and a variety of chains, thick with cobwebs. A rickety wood ladder jutted into the hayloft. Clay mounted it and climbed, pulling himself up and over the broken tenth rung. The loft was empty except for a few bales of hay. He climbed down and saw another door in the far corner, probably a feed room like in Gramps' barn. Feed had to be kept in a safe place where horses couldn't get to it. If they did, they'd eat and eat until they foundered. Gramps said they didn't know any better. Clay slid the wooden handle from left to right until it opened. The only light in the room came from wide cracks between the boards that formed its walls, which were lined with old barrels. He pried one open and smelled the familiar molasses scent of sweet feed, the kind Gramps fed his horses. He closed the lid to keep out the mice.

He scanned the room until his eyes landed on something large and dark, propped against a wall but easily missed in the dim light. Dull metal hinges on its side were attached to panels. As he examined it, he saw a dull brass doorknocker like the one he'd seen on the front door. He lifted the clapper and heard the same clear sound as it hit the strike plate. He decided that the hinged panels must unfold, so he carefully moved the first one and then the second one. With the three parts unfolded, it stood by itself, despite the uneven barn floor. He walked around it, wanting to figure out what he had found.

The back was plain and unpainted, but the front had fancy carvings, bright colors, and several small, framed photographs. The largest one was a picture of a man who looked like a magician, wearing a black cape and holding a magic wand as a dove flew from his top hat. He had a pencil-thin mustache and slicked-back hair. The other photographs showed the same man performing magic acts, surrounded by pretty women who looked like his assistants. Old-fashioned gold letters across the top of the panels read "Gregory McGregor and his Highland Flings." It looked very old, matted with spider webs, but the photographs were behind glass, clear and undamaged.

Clay studied the images. There were three different women, all blondes but with distinctive faces that he analyzed and memorized. They were lovely, he thought, maybe the prettiest faces he'd ever seen. They wore different exotic costumes in each of the pictures. He felt like their sharp eyes followed him as he moved around the panels.

He heard his mother's distant voice, calling from the yard.

"Clay, where are you?"

"Coming, Mom." He slid the feed room lock back in place and shut the outside barn door.

"Coming," he called again as he navigated the thorns to get back to the mowed yard. The moving van had pulled up to the house; he recognized the things being hauled into the house, including the twin wagon wheel beds from his room. Maybe the movers were alright, after all.

Clay had a hard time falling asleep that night. He wasn't used to the new room and the strange shadows that swayed across its walls. He got out of bed and looked out the windows, seeing plenty of stars and twinkling lights in the dark sky. He didn't know if the lights were airplanes or satellites or UFOs.

He moved over to the window seat and looked toward the barn. He thought he saw a light flickering between its old boards and through the loft door, but he knew that wasn't possible. The barn didn't have electricity. Besides, who in the world would be down there so late, anyway? Maybe Dad went out with a flashlight to check something. He jumped into bed, pulled the covers over his head, and decided to ask about it in the morning.

"Have you ever heard of somebody named Gregory McGregor and his Highland Flings?" Clay said at breakfast. A stack of pancakes sat swimming in syrup on the plate before him.

"Sounds like a vaudeville act, or maybe a circus," Dad said. "Vaudeville was way before my time."

"Gregory McGregor. Who would give a child a name like that?" Mom said.

"It's a silly name," Hayley said. She used her fork to move a bit of pancake in circles before popping it in her mouth. Clay watched syrup roll down her chin.

"Why do you ask?" Dad said.

"There's an old piece of wood down in the barn, and it stands by itself when you unfold it. It has his name on it and pictures, and he looks like he was a magician," Clay said.

"Sounds like a dressing screen. They used to use them on stage and in old movies," Mom said. "They'd go behind the screen and change costumes."

"I've heard that name before," Dad said. "Wasn't it on the old deed to this place?"

"I'll get the papers," Mom said. She rose from the table and headed toward the living room.

"What did you think about the barn?"

"I didn't see any snakes," Clay said. He thought about the lights he saw last night. "Are you sure it's ours?"

"I'm sure. Why do you ask?"

"I saw lights down there last night like someone was in there."

"Maybe lights from the subdivision behind us."

Mom came back to the kitchen.

"You're right. That's where we saw the name. The title search says he owned the property until the Morrises bought it in 1959. That was eleven years ago," she said.

"Do you think he's still alive?" Clay asked. "Maybe he'd want his screen back."

"I doubt it. That was a long time ago," Dad said. "He'd probably be in a nursing home if he's still alive."

Clay jumped up from his seat. "May I be excused?"

"Yes, but before you wander off, you need to unpack your toys and books," Mom said. "I've already put away your clothes."

Upstairs, he worked quickly. He noticed how his hanging clothes created a divider in his big closet, blocking the back section from view like a secret hiding place. Hayley couldn't find him back there. If he were quiet, no one could find him.

From a box in the hall, he found an extra blanket and small pillow to make a pallet in the closet. He positioned the pillow so he could look out the small round window to survey the back yard, like a sentinel. The window provided enough light for reading during the day, but he would need a flashlight at night.

He unpacked his cars and trucks, the wheels still dusted with traces of the little dirt towns he and Sam had built with toy bulldozers and excavators at the old house. He placed them along the top of the bookshelves beneath the row of windows. The blue Jeep had been Sam's favorite – he always chose it. He missed his older brother and the hours they played together in the side yard. Now he was stuck with Hayley, who didn't know how to do anything and cried if she got dirty.

At the bottom of the first box, he found his books. He picked up The Call of the Wild, with a bookmark on page 45, and tossed it onto the pallet in the back of the closet. Another box was filled with worn stuffed animals. He didn't want to display them; he was too old for that. He put his favorite one—Wolfie—in the back of the closet and shoved the others into storage under the window seat. He took the empty boxes downstairs to the kitchen where his mother washed dishes.

"Where should I put the boxes?"

"Throw them down to the basement for now," Mom said. "We may need them later."

"Are we going to move again? Are we going back to Lone Oak?"

Mom looked up from the sink and turned around.

"Clay, we're not going back. You need to accept that."

"I hate this place."

"We're starting over, here. It's for the best."

"It's not best. I want to go home!"

Mom dried her hands on a dishtowel and walked over to the table. She sat down and patted her leg. "Come over here and talk to me."

Looking down at his shoes, Clay dragged himself to his mother's lap. She wrapped her arms around him and pulled him close. She didn't say anything for a few minutes. He felt her release him a bit as she moved her right hand to her face, but her arms returned to encircle him.

"Our lives changed when Sam died. We can't bring him back. Being in Lone Oak makes me very sad, and the same for your dad. We need a fresh start."

"It's my fault. I ruined everything."

"Honey, it's not your fault. Please don't say that."

Clay broke free and ran down the stairs then out the back door. He didn't want to think about it anymore, or hear his mom talk about it. Or see his parents cry. They weren't supposed to cry.

As fast as he could go, he headed toward the barn. He hoped whoever had been there during the night was gone. He saw no sign of disturbance, but once inside, he thought he heard something in the direction of the feed room. Probably a mouse, tracking its way to the sweet feed at the bottom of the barrel. He headed toward it, taking down a pitchfork from the tack wall, just in case. He slid the latch and stepped inside.

The room's transformation surprised him. It looked more like a theatre stage than a place to store feed. The dressing screen had been moved to the left of the stage. One of the feed barrels was draped to the floor with a black-and-white checked cloth, its original purpose unrecognizable. It served as a table for a hat and birdcage. Costumes hung all around the room on nails hammered into the rough walls. He recognized the costumes—the harem outfits, the wooden shoes, the sailor suits—from the photos on the screen. There were three of every costume, just like in the pictures. He no longer smelled hay and molasses, but a faint fragrance of perfume and oranges.

"Hello?" he said. "Is anybody here?"

There was no response.

"Hello? Anybody?"

He heard shuffling from somewhere behind the dressing screen. His fingers tightened around the pitchfork as he saw a shadow move between the screen's panels. When a man emerged from behind the right panel, Clay dropped the pitchfork and screamed. The man, just as startled as the boy, screamed back at him. They sized up each other.

"Who are you?" Clay said.

"Well, son, I could ask the same of you. What are you doing here? There's no matinee today."

Clay looked at the man, and then at the photograph of the magician on the screen.

"Are you Gregory McGregor?"

"The one and only," he said, with a sweeping bow. "So you've heard of me?"

"I read the sign."

"A smart lad, this one," the magician said. "What's your name?"

"Clay. Clay Blackwell."

The magician extended his hand. "Pleased to meet you, Clay. I like that name."

They shook hands, and Gregory called out toward the dressing screen.

"Girls, we've got company."

Clay heard more shuffling sounds, and suddenly legs wearing high heels walked across the weathered floorboards. Three women with blonde hair and beautiful faces appeared from behind the screen. He recognized them from the pictures.

"Who's this?" one of them asked.

"This is our friend, Clay Blackwell. Great name. Clay, I'd like for you to meet Deb, Dot and Linda, the Highland Flings."

Clay shook hands with each woman and decided they were even prettier in real life.

"You coming to the show tonight, kid?" Dot asked.

"Uh, I don't know if my folks will let me."

"You should come. You'd love it," one of the other women said. He wasn't sure if she was Deb or Linda.

"Yes, Clay, you should," Gregory said. "But now we have to rehearse—this is our first show since we got back together—so we'll have to ask you to leave. You know we can't give away our secrets."

"Run along, kid," Dot said. "And shut the door when you leave."

Clay nodded and backed away. He slipped out the feed room door and slid its handle, locking them in. He also locked the outer door and leaned the pitchfork against the tractor. He'd check on them later. He didn't know where those people came from, but with two doors, locked from the outside, he knew they couldn't get out.

Clay smelled food when he walked through the back door.

"I was just going to call you," his mom said. "Lunch is ready."

He didn't feel hungry, but he sat down at the table. Hayley was already there.

"You okay, Clay? You look pale," Mom asked.

He nodded but barely looked up. He ate the grilled cheese sandwich and chicken noodle soup in a hurry and went upstairs to his room. He looked out the window toward the barn. Nothing looked different. There was no sign of what he'd seen inside.

He crawled into his secret place in the closet, careful to close the gap in his hanging clothes, and curled up on the pallet. He fell asleep while stroking the worn pink satin lining of Wolfie's ear, and slept most of the afternoon. He woke to the sound of Hayley calling his name.

"Clay, where are you?"

He decided not to answer, to see if she would discover his hiding place. He heard her moving around his room, grunting as she looked for him under the bed and behind the doors. The closet door opened. He held his breath.

"Mom, I can't find him," Hayley yelled. Her footsteps on the stairs told him it was safe to come out. She had given up. Clay waited a few minutes before heading to the bathroom and then downstairs.

"Where were you?" Hayley said, scowling when she saw him.

"Taking a nap."

"You were not. I looked in your bed."

"You probably need glasses, stupid."

She stuck out her tongue and walked away. He smiled. It had been a good test run for his secret place.

He heard a car pull into the driveway and went to look out the dining room windows. Dad was coming up the sidewalk, already home from work, and wearing a new tan uniform. Clay realized he must have slept a long time. When his dad came through the front door, Clay noticed his name, Jim, embroidered on one of the front pockets of the new shirt. The other side said Stanford Paint and Hardware.

"Had a good day?" Dad asked as they hugged.

"Guess so."

"Glad to hear it."

"Do you have to wear that uniform every time you go to work?"

"Yes, they gave me a stack of new shirts today. Six of them. A whole week's worth."

"I thought a week was seven days."

"I get Sunday off," Dad said. "You know, the day of rest."

"Maybe we can we go squirrel hunting on Sundays. I've seen a million of them today. They're everywhere."

"We can't hunt around here. Too many houses. And, you know Gramps is keeping the guns for now, down at the farm."

"Right. I forgot."

Clay watched his dad's face change. Was he mad or sad or ready to cry? Clay never wanted to see that look again.

"I'm going outside," Clay said and bolted for the back door.

As he walked through the yard, he heard something and turned around. A squirrel ran past him and up a hickory tree. He watched it scamper up the trunk, its claws clinging to the tree as it spiraled to the top. He pretended he had his .410, butted up to his shoulder, and took aim. With his mouth, he made a sound like a shotgun blast. Instead of seeing the squirrel fall from the tree, he saw Sam's face, eyes wide from the loud sound and the pain, a hole in his chest the size of a baseball, his green plaid shirt instantly soaked in blood. Clay's ears were still ringing when he saw his brother hit the floor of their room, near the end of their matching wagon wheel beds. He hadn't known there was a shell still in the chamber, left from the last hunting trip to Gramps' farm. No one knew. He saw his mother crying and rocking on the floor, as she cradled Sam's head in her lap.

"What have you done? What have you done?" she said again and again as she sobbed and rocked.

Clay watched as the squirrel continued climbing to its leafy nest at the top of the tree. His arms released the imaginary gun and fell back to his sides. He walked back to the house, slipped up the stairs and made his way back into his secret place.

With night coming, Clay looked for a flashlight in one of the boxes waiting to be unpacked in the kitchen. When he found it, he put it in his jacket pocket, next to Sam's blue Jeep. He slipped out the back and headed for the barn. He grabbed the pitchfork and unlocked the doors.

The feed room was lighted with candles in old coffee cans, rusty from years in the barn storing nails and screws. The room was empty; he took a seat in one of the five folding chairs set in a semi-circle in front of the stage, near the dressing screen. As soon as he sat down, the Highland Flings came out: Deb on kazoo, Dot on recorder and Linda with a tambourine.

"And, now, presenting the world's finest magician, Gregory McGregor, and his famous Highland Flings," Linda announced. Clay clapped. As the sole member of the audience, he wanted to show his appreciation.

Gregory stepped out, dressed in a tuxedo and twirling his cape as he spun around in the small space. He was wearing the top hat and flashing a wand in his right hand. For the next hour or so, Clay was lost in magic from disappearing doves to a reappearing rabbit. The Highland Flings provided musical accompaniment and assistance on tricks that needed an extra set of hands or a volunteer to levitate. Clay lost track of time, but he knew it had to be close to his bedtime. He didn't want the show to end.

He applauded loudly as Gregory and the Flings took their bows. The women went back behind the screen; Gregory sat down in the chair next to Clay. His face looked red and shiny.

"So you liked the show?"

"Yes, very much. Can I come again tomorrow night?"

Gregory smiled, causing wrinkles to form around his eyes. "Sure, kid. We'll be in town a few more days." He wiped his brow with a multi-colored handkerchief, frayed around the edges, and stuffed it back in his pocket.

"We're just putting our show back together. We've not worked in a long time, but suddenly a door opened, and we saw this opportunity," he said. "Kid, when opportunity knocks, you have to open the door and let it in."

Clay wasn't sure what Gregory meant, but he thought about what the magician had said as he walked toward the house and went in the back door.

Over the next few weeks, the family unpacked most of the boxes, bringing out familiar items like the mantel clock and the baby pictures. Each night before going to sleep, Clay looked out toward the barn to see if lights were on. Every few days he slipped away to see the show. He never mentioned the performances to his family.

Near the end of summer, he saw a letter addressed "To the Parents of Clay Blackwell" under the mail slot in the front hall. Another one was addressed "To the Parents of Hayley Blackwell." He scooped up the letters and headed to the kitchen. Mom and Hayley sat across the round table from each other; Mom looking through her recipe box and Hayley coloring on leftover packing paper.

"The mail came," he said, handing the stack to Mom, who opened the one about Hayley first, scanned it, then opened the one about Clay.

"How exciting!" his mother said, her voice pushed to a cheerful range like a television mom. "School starts next Wednesday. We'll meet your teachers on Tuesday and get your supply lists."

Hayley put down the crayons and clapped her hands.

"Who's my teacher?"

"You have Mrs. Holland for first grade and Clay has Mrs. Berry."

"Is she pretty?" Hayley said. Clay rolled his eyes.

"I don't know, honey. I haven't met her," Mom said.

"Have you ever heard of Mrs. Berry?" Clay asked.

"No, I don't know the teachers yet," Mom said. "But the fourth grade is a wonderful year. It was Sam's favorite."

Clay winced when he heard his brother's name. No one had said it for a while. From Mom's expression, he thought she looked surprised, too. Her fingertips moved to cross her lips. Her eyes looked wet and full. She rose from the table and stood against the countertop near the sink, her back to the silent room. Finally, Mom spoke.

"We need to shop for new school shoes. We'll go this afternoon after lunch."

Clay watched as she walked out of the kitchen without looking his way. He heard her bedroom door close and its lock click. As quietly as he could climb the bare wooden stairs, he made his way to his closet.

Lying on his back on the pallet and looking up at clouds through the small window, Clay thought how strange it felt to be going to school somewhere other than Lone Oak Elementary. To a building he'd never seen, to teachers they didn't know, to a place that Sam would never know. Sam had always done everything first, being the oldest. Clay didn't want to be first; he had always depended on Sam to show him how. He liked the middle, wearing hand-me-downs and letting his brother lead the way. He didn't know if he could make it without Sam.

He drifted to sleep until his mom called him to lunch, which was followed by going to town to look for new shoes. Unlike Hayley, who eagerly tried on a pair with purple laces, Clay took no pleasure in the shopping trip. He told his mother he would rather wear Sam's old shoes, the ones from fourth grade that were packed away in the basement.

By Tuesday he couldn't muster much energy for going to the new school, but Mom said he had to go and meet his teacher. Mrs. Berry looked nice enough, but the classroom was filled with people he didn't know and didn't want to know. He dreaded Wednesday.

After dinner and baths, Clay and Hayley were sent to bed.

"You've got to go to sleep early so you'll be ready for school tomorrow morning," Mom said. But Clay couldn't sleep. He got out of bed and saw lights in the barn. In his seersucker pajamas, he crept down the stairs, past the living room. The television was on; he saw his dad, legs stretched out from the sofa, staring at the TV but not responding to its laughter. His parents' bedroom door was closed, so he guessed his mother was in bed. He tiptoed across the kitchen linoleum and out the door. When he got to the barn, he took his seat just as the show began. With rehearsals and performances, Gregory and the girls had perfected their act. It was even better than the last time he saw it.

He applauded loudly when it ended. Gregory came over to chat.

"Good to see you back, kid. We've missed you."

"Sorry I haven't been here for a while," Clay said. "The show's gotten even better."

"We're glad to be back and working hard. Thanks for giving us the chance to work again."

"Me?"

"Yeah, kid. You gave us the chance," Gregory said. "Like I always say, when opportunity knocks—"

"—you have to open the door and let it in," Clay finished.

"That's right. It's all about taking the chance to do something you've been wanting to do. Simple as that."

"What if the door closes? What if the screen gets folded back together?"

"Then we wait. There's always another opportunity if you're patient."

"What happens if I go behind the screen, like you and the girls?"

"Then you stay with us. We could use some help, if you're willing to work."

"Can I come home if I change my mind?"

"Sure, kid. It's a free country."

Clay thought it over. "Do you ever do any shows over in Lone Oak?"

"Oh, yeah, a while back. We loved the crowds in Lone Oak. Hope to get back there soon."

Suddenly, Clay heard his dad calling, up near the house. It was dark, and they must have figured out he wasn't in his room.

"Clay, where are you?" Dad called. Then he heard his mom's voice, too. He didn't answer.

"I'd like to go with you."

"Great, kid. Pack your stuff. We'll head out tomorrow."

"I don't have much to pack. I could go now," Clay said. He heard opportunity knocking.

"I like your style, kid. Eager to work. Girls, let's get on the road. Clay, blow out those candles and follow me."

Clay heard his dad's voice getting closer. He quickly put out the lights and walked to the other side of the screen.

"Son, are you in here?" Dad called as he came into the barn.

He carried a lantern, holding it high to see into the corners. He saw the feed room door open and crossed the barn in a few long strides. By lantern light, he read the screen and remembered that Clay had mentioned it. Fearing the old screen would topple over on the uneven floor, he folded the panels until they closed and leaned it against the barn wall. He left, mindful to latch the feed room door, and returned to the darkness, calling his son's name.

THE VERY SMALL DOOR

CALVIN MILLS

On Tuesday, November 3rd, 2007 several very small people appeared in our apartment. On the same day, my wife, Lizzie, disappeared.

I came home from work to our small loft apartment in a converted, century-old cathedral downtown. The cathedral had burned under mysterious circumstances during a Catholic singles mixer, and several people were killed. The eviscerated stone and mortar skeleton of the historic building sat abandoned for many years and had only recently been renovated into an apartment complex for artists. Lizzie showed the manager a portfolio of her artwork along with the normal references and my pay stubs, and we were allowed to move in.

Just as we were settling in, just when things were getting good, Lizzie's mother passed away. Although her death was certainly expected after a long battle with a rare form of cancer that attacks the heart, it wasn't easy to let go: not for her mother, not for Lizzie, and not for anyone else who knew her. Not knowing her mother well, I learned instead to let go of the Lizzie I had known and loved.

Two and a half months later, I almost dreaded coming home. I hated seeing the new Lizzie, the Lizzie who was no longer easy to laugh, the Lizzie I could do little to comfort in the long line of numb days that followed the death of her mother.

When I first arrived home, I thought Lizzie had simply gone out. I figured she'd be back any minute. I came in, dropped my briefcase and my keys on my desk in my office, and kicked off my shoes. I called out her name and didn't hear an answer. I went to the kitchen cupboard and stared inside. I wondered if I should make her something for dinner. Or should I go ahead and eat? Maybe she was out with her girlfriends. Maybe they were trying to cheer her up.

I scarfed a handful of bland pink and white animal cookies with sprinkles before I turned to the sink to pour myself a glass of water. When I reached down for the faucet handle, I was startled by the figure of a very small woman with wet hair standing against the backsplash, near the sponge—just to the right of the faucet. I jumped back, pulling my arm away, as if from a sprinting cockroach. I felt my pulse thumping in my throat.

I laughed when I realized the little woman was only two-dimensional. She was completely nude: her bronze breasts somewhat balloon-like, her bare crotch a pale triangle. There was something familiar about her. I stepped slowly forward to get a closer look. Then it hit me. I did know her—at least in a manner of speaking. I had seen her in a men's magazine I kept in my office. But now she had been carved out of the magazine with surgical precision and carefully decoupaged to the wall. Even the minuscule spaces between her tiny toes and fingers were skillfully incised. A few errant locks of hair seemed to curl into the air in the most natural manner possible. Tracing her silhouette were neither dark nor light lines; only her flesh and its own subtle shadow play were apparent along her outer curves. She looked very real, more like a pleasantly surprised miniature roommate than a two-dimensional illusion. And she seemed to be laughing—her head tilted just so, her top row of white teeth glinting like dew drops in crisp sunlight.

I looked closer and discovered very small bottles of shampoo and conditioner that seemed to be sitting on the counter an inch or so away from her feet and a very small towel rack with a yellow towel "hanging" from the tile within her miniature reach. The towel was cut with curved lines along the bottom edge so that it seemed to be simply draped there, waiting for the paper woman to take it in hand and use it to blot away the tiny droplets of water that sparkled on her airbrush-smooth skin like clusters of rhinestones.

I felt myself smiling. I was profoundly relieved by the assumption that Lizzie's frame of mind had improved. The evidence seemed inherent in the existence of the whimsical woman who now lived in a state of perpetual cleanliness by the sink.

Then, as suddenly as I had felt relieved at the possibility of Lizzie's improved frame of mind, I was stricken by a pang of guilt, of embarrassment because of the very small woman's publication of origin. I hoped her existence wasn't just an elaborate stab at my masculine weaknesses during a time of sexless mourning. My desire to make a thorough investigation of the entire apartment suddenly doubled.

The rooms were graying in the approaching darkness. I turned on the kitchen lights and eagerly scanned the walls for any other very small people who might be waiting to startle me. My forehead almost tingled. My stomach was a dull lump. With this peculiar blend of joy and paranoia, I embarked on a detailed inspection of each room. I hoped to discover that the very small woman was an expression of artistic joy rather than a carefully executed criticism.

In the bathroom where the corner of the fiberglass tub met the corner of the wall, there was a very small man with sandy blonde hair, blue coveralls, and a push broom. He was fixed to the wall in such a way that he seemed to be standing on the white linoleum floor, leaning against the mopboard. Somehow, Lizzie had cut the very thin miniature broom handle and bent it where the wall met the floor so the wide broom head was at an angle across the linoleum, as were his boots. These details greatly exaggerated the illusion that the little man was indeed standing there, that he was three-dimensional. Lizzie had even gone so far as to leave a pile of real dust and grit in a sharp line along the floor in front of the broom. Like the nude woman by the sink, our new janitor was roughly four inches tall. When no plausible insidious psychological message asserted itself in my conscience in regards to the little man with the push broom, the dull pang in my stomach lessened. But what did all this mean?

On the windowsill in my office, a pair of very small bird watchers stood staring out through binoculars. They were elderly, neatly dressed, and as still and patient as I assumed real birdwatchers must need to be. I too, looked out the window awhile, hoping I was meant to see something there. But by this time it had grown quite dark. All I could see was a sulfur yellow bulb on the opposite side of the courtyard. Peeking out from beneath its sconce, the bulb illuminated nothing more than a triangular section of a brick wall.

Squatting atop a broken light switch near the bedroom—that is to say the light switch that, when flipped, seemed to do nothing at all—was a very small muscle man wearing a construction helmet and tool belt. To me, without his shirt, and with his pleasant facial features and sparkling eyes, he looked more like a male stripper than a real construction worker. Maybe this was just my jealousy talking, because the very small man was tan and rippled with muscles.

I discovered several other people in various locations around the apartment, including a couple asleep on what appeared to be a futon mattress lying flat on the floor in a dark corner behind the television. In each case, the people seemed to be minding their own business, not at all concerned or worried about me. I coughed a single syllable of laughter every few minutes and glanced at the front door, anxious to see Lizzie again, but she never walked through the door.

The detail that really puzzled me about her artistic installation was a very small door pasted to the wall behind the dresser in the bedroom. It was a red door with a shiny black doorknob. The section of wall that it was glued to was sheetrock on the lower half, and brick on the top. High and centered on the brick wall, directly above the very small door, was an antique stained glass window that had inexplicably survived the fire. By the time I found the door, it was after midnight and Lizzie still wasn't home. She rarely stayed out late without calling me or leaving me a note.

Initially, when I found the figures around the apartment, I was more or less amused. When I saw the very small door, I began to worry.

It was not until I attempted to go to bed around four a.m. that I spotted the skydiver on the ceiling directly above our bed. Her arms and legs were spread wide. She stared out through aerodynamic goggles with terror and ecstasy in her eyes.

I watched the skydiver wide-eyed for what seemed like hours. Then, for an hour or so I fell into a variety of partial unconsciousness one can hardly measure as rest, let alone sleep. Unable to keep my eyes closed, I stared up at the skydiver again. When the clock finally agreed that I could begin making calls without startling anyone too much, I called her best friend, Erin-Kate. Erin-Kate hadn't heard from her. Now she was worried too. I called in sick to the office. When I reached her father, and he hadn't heard from her, I decided to call the police. I hated telling her father she was missing, especially because he had so recently suffered the loss of Lizzie's mother.

Two detectives arrived at the apartment on Wednesday a little after eleven a.m. I showed them the grim discovery I had made that morning after making the calls to Erin-Kate and to Lizzie's father: Lizzie's keys on the shelf by the door, right next to her wallet and cell-phone.

"Yes," I said. "The door was definitely locked when I came home."

The detective with meaty cheeks asked, "Can it be locked from the inside and then closed?"

"Yes."

When they asked me if I had any idea what might have happened to her, I said, "I don't know, but I think it probably has something to do with this." I stood up and motioned for them to follow. I proceeded to lead them on a detailed tour of each of the paper cutouts. Then I showed them her desk, where I'd found scraps of the same magazine pages. They didn't seem to know what to make of the very small people or the very small door. In fact, they looked at me like I was nuts for placing emphasis on the fact that they appeared on the same day she disappeared. A change was apparent in their demeanor after that. During the remainder of their visit, they avoided turning their backs on me.

They walked nearly backward through the door when they left. The one with the meaty cheeks said, "Don't leave town."

The quiet partner was lanky and balding and smelled of cigarette smoke. He said, "You'll let us know if you hear anything. Meanwhile, keep an eye on your bank accounts. She probably ran off somewhere. Sorry to say, it happens all the time. In these situations, it's usually some kind of misunderstanding. Maybe she left you a note and it fell under the fridge, or maybe it's revenge over a fight." Here he paused. I could feel both men studying my reactions. When I didn't respond to their queue, he said, "If you don't hear from her tomorrow, call us, and we'll step up our efforts. We'll speak with her father in the meantime and see if he wants to file a missing persons."

"Can I file one?"

"Immediate family only."

What could I say? So I repeated the only thing he said that stuck with me, "Only a misunderstanding? I hope you're right about that."

They spoke to each other as quietly as old women in church as they walked down the hall and descended the single flight of stairs. They seemed to have a lot to say, but I couldn't hear a word of it.

Three days passed. Other than answering frantic calls from her father and Erin-Kate, I had little idea what to do. Every time the phone rang, I leapt to catch it on the first ring. In hopes of passing the time quickly, I tried to sleep, but it proved impossible. I was filled with the desire to do something, anything, despite the nauseous exhaustion that had a stranglehold on me. I had to think the situation through. I had to look for clues. I had to solve the mystery of the very small people. The police certainly weren't going to.

When the following dawn slowly illuminated the apartment, I watched the clock. I saw every single minute pass and checked them off in my head. I had to wait until nine a.m. to call my boss. I gave him an update and asked to take the week off. I ate very little, and wandered around the apartment studying and restudying the figures to see if I could find some detail I had overlooked. On the third day, I did discover, near the very small door, a sticky spot on the wall. Other than that, there was nothing new to go on. The calls had been made to the police, but so far they had absolutely nothing helpful to report.

When Lizzie's father came to the apartment, I pointed out the same things I had shown the detectives. He wandered around the place solemnly and raised his eyebrow when I insisted on the importance of the very small people and the very small door. Her father was beaten, broken down already by the death of his wife, and had already been suffering from what he called 'melancholy.' He said, "I have trouble getting off the couch. I'm exhausted, but I still have to take sleeping pills. I can't get out of bed. It's from the bed to the couch and back again for me. That's pretty much it."

I said, "I understand," and I meant it.

After a long pause, I said, "I didn't have anything to do with her disappearance."

Her father looked at me, the pockets of skin beneath his eyes succumbing to gravity. The eyes themselves were remarkably bright for his age. "I know son," he said.

He even embraced me briefly and gave me a manly hard pat on the back just before he left. After he was gone, I realized that he had called me 'son' for the first time. My vision blurred at the bottom edges with prospective tears.

I felt better knowing that at least one person didn't suspect me, and even more, that he felt the loss as much as I did. I had given him time alone in her office. I had heard him weeping in there, breathing hard, his stuttered inhalations and whispered moans.

Erin-Kate's visit was less pleasant. She brought her new boyfriend, who because I'd never met him before, had absolutely no allegiance or sympathy for me. He stood most of the time with his arms crossed and kept himself within sight of Erin-Kate. I thought I saw a bulge in the back of his waistband under his shirttail. Erin-Kate must have heard some vague complaints against me from Lizzie somewhere along the way, because, when she was leaving, she said, "Of course I don't blame you. You and Lizzie had your problems, but I know she never would have stayed with you if she didn't feel like she could trust you."

I didn't know what to say to that.

She too studied my reaction to her words carefully. Her boyfriend turned a little sheepish toward the end. She walked out first. I could see she was tearing up again as she turned away. The boyfriend shook my hand with his long hairy arm stretched half way across the hall. He nearly crushed my hand in his while he nodded his head gravely.

I called my parents on the second day. They called me thereafter twice a day to ask if they should fly in from Florida to stay with me. I discouraged them. I didn't want them trying to cheer me up. I didn't want them distracting me from my somber meditations on the meaning of the very small door. I paced. I let myself feel the constant pangs of hunger. There seemed some small justice in the sensation that I was diminishing, growing smaller. If I were much thinner, the emptiness I felt would have less room to expand. It could only grow smaller with me.

I had so far calculated only one plausible solution in regards to the symbolism of the figures she had chosen. Perhaps the nude woman represented my inability to love Lizzie as deeply as she desired because I had such vague notions of femininity and an inherently idealistic view of the opposite sex. Therefore, though we had spent some time together in an intimate setting—such as that of the couple lying on the futon behind the television—there was work that needed to be done, as evidenced by the construction worker on the broken light switch. Therefore, she had chosen to leave through the very small door. In her absence, she believed I would live an unfulfilled life; continuing for a time in my personality-smothering—however well-paid—para-legal employ, but I would eventually end up a janitor. I would have thrown away the chance for us to grow old peacefully together like the elderly birdwatchers. Meanwhile, without being tethered to me, she would live life to its limits, as I was to gather from the ecstatic lady skydiver. Could this be true? Could this be her parting message to me?

At one particularly desperate moment near midnight on the third night, I slumped into the couch and began to sob. I was exhausted but still couldn't sleep. Through the wall of liquid distorted images before me, my fuzzy gaze settled on the photo album on the coffee table. I had brought it out when the detectives asked for a picture of Lizzie.

I picked up the album and took a shaky breath before opening it. The first group of pictures we had taken on a vacation to Oahu. I blinked fiercely and wiped away the water from my eyes. There was a picture she took of us, cheeks pressed together, the camera held out at arms length. We were soaking wet after being caught in a mid-afternoon rainstorm. We hid out in a parking garage until it passed. In this picture, her hair was darker than normal, but shapeless. Her eyelashes were emphasized, her cheeks pink. I slowly turned the pages, reliving the trips we had taken, the birthday cakes she had baked me, carefully decorated, then photographed, before I was allowed to eat them. There were pictures of her with her girlfriends at an art opening, all of them sufficiently photogenic. Although they were artists, and therefore a little edgy, they were wearing pretty dresses. I remembered that night. I was invited but had stayed home and ordered pizza. Meanwhile, as the photograph recorded, she and her friends were laughing and pleasantly blurry-eyed from art gallery boxed wine. I had pizza. They had friendship, a social life.

There were pictures of murals in cities we'd visited, pictures of her art projects, drawings, and paintings. There were pictures of her mother. In one, her mother, her hair dyed black and her cheeks round as plums, was sitting across the booth from Lizzie and Lizzie's sister at a Mexican restaurant. Lizzie's sister was wearing a sombrero, so I assumed it must have been her birthday. I didn't often go to see her mother and wasn't there when the pictures were taken, so I couldn't be sure.

On a page three-quarters of the way through the album, I saw that one photograph was missing. It was one of my favorite pictures of Lizzie. I had snapped it myself. She was walking in Washington Square Park in Manhattan. We took that trip because she wanted to see the art museums. Other than the portrait I took out for the detectives, it was the only empty slot in the book. The album was made up of black paper pages on which old-fashioned black stick-on corners held the photographs. Here there were four triangular corners holding nothing. Next to the empty space she had written in silver gel ink on the black page, "Happy in New York."

I went to her desk, which was in a room we called her studio. The desk was covered with cut up magazine pages. There were scraps of magazine paper in her trashcan. The desk drawers were full of art supplies, brushes, pencils, pens and quills, charcoal, stretchy grey erasers, and a neat row of X-Acto knives and replacement blades. On the desk, under a stack of ravaged fashion, tabloid, and news magazines, I found my men's magazine. I also found the missing picture of Lizzie from the album. She had removed herself from the picture. Her outline was there, from head to toe in crisp detail. The arch in Washington Square Park was there. But Lizzie was gone.

I grabbed the photograph in which she was nothing but negative space. I took it to the bedroom and pulled the dresser away from the wall. With my fingers, I found the sticky spot. I hurried to the kitchen, where I found a bag of flour. In the bedroom, I put some flour in the palm of my hand and blew it against the wall. The flour stuck to the glue residue. The pale shape I found on the wall was identical to the shape and position of Lizzie's body in the photograph. The ghostly flour outline of her body seemed to be walking toward the very small door. I held the photo there tenderly, lined up the two images. Sadly, a perfect fit.

If her picture were there, I'd think the solution was simple enough. I'd assume she wanted me to know that she had walked out on me. But what had happened to the actual picture? And if she truly left me, why did she take nothing, not even her money, her identification, her toothbrush, the pictures of her mother?

I suddenly hoped she had left me. That would be infinitely better than the other common explanations for the disappearance of an attractive young woman like Lizzie.

It was cold in the apartment, so I slipped my stocking feet into a pair of house shoes and put on a sweater. I didn't want to turn up the heat. I needed to suffer. She was missing, probably suffering. I drank the last beer in the fridge and prepared a bowl of Ramen noodles, of which I could only eat a few bites. Standing by the stove, I remembered the moment I fell in love with Lizzie. We'd only been seeing each other a week or so. We hadn't yet slept together. I was at the apartment she shared with Erin-Kate. Lizzie was wearing a baggy shirt without a bra. She leaned over the stove while reaching for a pasta strainer and her shirttail caught fire. But she was quick, tearing off the shirt and throwing it into the sink, then covering her braless breasts with one arm while turning the spigot to douse the flames with the other hand. She laughed wildly when she realized the danger had passed. Running out of the room, she apologized for the peep show. When she went to her room for another shirt, I stood in the kitchen, leaning against the cool Formica countertop like an idiot, wishing I'd tried to save her. But she had been able to save herself before I'd had the chance to react in the slightest. I wasn't the same after that. I was hopeless. I really was. I didn't always show it well perhaps, but I was certainly hopeless for her.

After my sad attempt at dinner, I slid into the fake Eames lounge chair and ottoman set Lizzie bought me for Christmas two years before at a vintage furniture shop. The wood was scratched, and the fake leather was worn and cracked, but soft. I stared at the album. I could feel myself growing thinner. I couldn't stop thinking about the very small door and her missing picture. It had to be important. It was the only thing that stood out. In the book there was a picture of me standing by a three-dimensional number nine, a steel sculpture painted red. We had seen it somewhere in Manhattan. We had been walking down the middle of the sidewalk when we nearly crashed into it.

I took the picture out of the book.

In her office, I cleared a space on her desk. I picked up one of her X-Acto knives, and as carefully as I could, I cut myself out of the photograph. When I was finished, I realized I had cut into the surface of her desk. I felt the sharp edges of the cuts I'd made in the wood. I rubbed them hard with my fingertip trying to smooth them. "Shit," I said, looking at the outline of myself on her table.

I took the picture to the bedroom. I had left the dresser pushed to one side so I could see the very small door. Sitting cross-legged on the hardwood floor, I was glad my ankles hurt, glad they were pressing against the wood under my weight. I wanted to be uncomfortable. I wanted to hurt. I pressed my picture to the wall near the door, careful not to cover the spot where her flour ghost stood. By placing myself between her image and the door, I felt like I might be able to stop her. It might give me the illusion she was walking, not toward the door, but toward me. I decided this was where my photograph would go. I set the photo on the floor while I went back to her office for a metal canister of rubber cement I had seen on her desk. I took it to the bedroom and twisted off the cap. I leaned over the canister and inhaled deeply. I was already sick with hunger and exhaustion, and the ammonia-like fumes from the glue canister burned my nasal passages, making me jerk quickly backwards. When I did this, I had one hand on the photo. I reached for the photo, but pushed it toward the wall. When I did this, everything went black.

I thought I'd passed out from the fumes, but I soon realized that I was not unconscious. I could still feel my ankles pressing into the floor. I could feel the glue in my right hand. But my head was numb. I could see nothing, hear nothing. I couldn't even smell the glue fumes. I dropped the glue but did not hear it hit the floor. I tried to look down. I felt my chin touch my chest; still darkness. Then, feeling the floor in front of me, my fingertips came to my photograph. I slid it toward myself, and I could see again. I shook my head and touched my cheeks, my eyelids. There was a crack beneath the mopboard beneath the very small door just beyond where the head of my photograph was resting.

Frightened, I pushed my photograph beneath the door again, head first. Everything went dark. I began shaking but pushed further. Suddenly I could see something. I could see a bit of light, amber light, a surface like a wall, and a long yellow tube of some kind with mechanical looking writing running its length. With my right hand, I touched my face, but I could not see my hand. I could feel my stubbly chin with my fingers, but I could neither see nor feel my hand with my chin. It was as if my body had been split in two. From the head down, I was myself. I moved my head. The back of my head struck something hard. Of course in my seated position, my head was a long way from anything solid. But my head in the photograph would be hitting the floor under the crack.

When I pulled the photograph out again, I could see the wall in front of me, the very small door, and Lizzie's flour ghost.

Still unbelieving, I pushed my picture beneath the door again, a little further this time. The sensation was the same. This time, I took a deep breath in the darkness. I could smell dust in the wall cavity. I let my eyes adjust to the dim yellow light, and I saw something on the wall, a simple drawing—an arrow pointing to the left. I removed my picture from the crack, and everything felt like it always had. My senses were dull but familiar.

I was so sick and so utterly exhausted, I reached up from where I was seated on the floor, jerked the blankets and pillows from the bed, and in one motion I swathed them around myself, situated my numb corpse in the fetal position, and let the unconsciousness my body so badly needed take me. I would sleep if I could. With a properly functioning mind and something to eat to provide a little energy, I would go into the wall in the morning—that was, if the world behind the wall proved to be anything other than a figment of my devastated mental state. With rest, I would know more. I would go there. I would find her.

Not long after I closed my eyes, I saw, in one of those pre-dream hallucinatory flashes, an image of Lizzie tearing off her flaming shirt, laughing, her breasts bouncing heavenly once, then twice, before her forearm and hand could cup and cover them.

I woke up feeling as if I had a severe hangover. Despite the state of my head, the dizziness, the thick, dull senses, I quickly repeated the experiment. Finding that it worked, I was delighted, not only because the experiment seemed to disprove my doubts regarding my sanity, but because it supplied me with my first real sense of hope for Lizzie's well-being. But there was a sense of terror too. I was faced with entering a world that existed outside the boundaries of the known, of the possible. I knew there was a healthy chance I was simply losing my mind, so I decided not to call anyone to tell them what I knew. Without a doubt, they'd lock me up. And worse than that, if I didn't go in looking for Lizzie, no one would.

After stuffing myself with six links of sausage, three microwave pancakes with syrup, two slices of toast with butter and jelly, and two scrambled eggs, I went to Lizzie's office to outfit myself for the journey. I found her digital camera and used it to take pictures of a few items that might prove useful. I photographed the following: a flashlight, a coil of string—because I didn't have any rope—a bottle of water, a box of granola bars, a backpack, and a chef's knife. I then used her computer to print out the pictures, shrunken down to a scale that seemed appropriate to myself in my photograph. The string, I decided to leave somewhat larger in scale, so it might function as rope. I cut out each object as carefully as possible—the careful coil of 'rope' was the most difficult— and brought them to the bedroom. I made a stop at the bathroom and evacuated my bowels and bladder so I might begin my work behind the wall with as much endurance as possible. As I was leaving the bathroom, I turned back and brushed my teeth and quickly applied deodorant. I stretched my arms and legs and cracked my knuckles, then slipped all the photographed items beneath the crack, before taking my picture in my hand and pushing it far enough through that my photographed arms could push against the inner wall to drag the remainder of my body through to the other realm.

For a few restless moments, I laid on the floor to allow my eyes to adjust. Again, I saw the long yellow tube with the mysterious writing. I stood and found myself at eye level with the tube. There was a staple to my right. What I had seen was nothing mysterious. It was plastic coated electrical wire, but it was thicker than my thigh now that I was so very small. I turned around and found that someone had drawn a black outline of a door on the wall where I entered. I reached out to touch the drawing, to see if it might be a functioning door, but I stopped short when I saw that my hand was flat. Light streamed in through the crack beneath the door. I patted my chest and brought my hands to my head. I gave myself a good feel. I was entirely flat. I was the image I had cut out of the photograph. I looked down at my feet. My carving wasn't as artful or precise as Lizzie's. My feet were blockish, and the souls were thick so that when I took a step forward, and a step back, I clomped a bit. I put my hand to my mouth, breathed out, then sniffed my hand. Toothpaste. Fascinating.

I picked up the backpack and stuffed the other items inside. Clomping awkwardly, I hiked what must have been one or two real feet, before I reached a giant 2x4 stud and another arrow. The pointed arrow indicated I follow a straight course into the stud. I felt the wood. It was solid. I suddenly became frightened. What if I became trapped in the wall? What if I was already trapped? I hadn't thought to experiment by sliding my head back out under the door. Ah… remembering that I was now flat, I reexamined the thick wood and the adjoining sheetrock. There was a slim crack between the two. I stood sideways and shimmied into the crack. After a brief moment of pure darkness and claustrophobia, I saw a dim sort of light and passed into another corridor. I took a step, then stopped because I thought I heard a sound. I tried to step again, but something held back my foot. I reached down with my hands in the darkish hall and felt a piece of line caught around my shoe. I yanked on it and thought I heard a distant sound again. I listened intently and tried not to move or even to breathe.

There was perhaps a distant sound, not like the first, then silence. I stepped over the line and continued to clomp along the corridor. It grew darker, and I was forced to bring out the flashlight. I was amused when it came to life at the touch of the switch. My beam of concentrated light greedily consumed the corners and far reaches of the corridor, but there was nothing of any interest there. It was simply the inside of a wall: 2x4s, sheetrock, sawdust, and wiring. I did note, though, that the line my foot caught disappeared through cracks on either side of the corridor.

I came to another 2x4 and found another arrow pointing in the same direction. From somewhere behind the wall came a distinct sound. It was clearly the barking of a dog. And it was a small dog by the sound of it. I had no way of knowing where the sound was coming from; the real world beyond the walls, or the world within the walls themselves. I stood very still and listened to the dog.

The barking grew louder, then from the thin crack, a ball of dark fur came snarling and spitting, bouncing from side to side and up and down almost simultaneously. I fell backward in my surprise and dropped the flashlight. With the snarls and throaty snorting sounds boiling around me I was afraid at first to reach out for the light. The creature bounced and leapt, all a blur of teeth and glinting eyes and flowing fur in the indistinct light outside the beam of the fallen flashlight. I heard its claws scratching and sliding against the wooden floor. Then, just as violently as the creature had burst into the corridor, it rushed out again. It disappeared behind the 2x4. I grabbed the flashlight and thrust its beam at the crack. The dog's snarling face appeared again, and it bared its teeth. I could see that it was, in fact, a Pomeranian. I could also see that it would like very much to kill me.

I jumped to my feet, but the dog held its ground. It barked and growled and wailed as if all at once. Now standing, I could see that it was a mere fraction of my size. If I was four inches high, the vicious Pomeranian was certainly no more than half an inch. And even more incredibly, it was entirely flat. But it was moving fast, and could somehow appear from different angles. Each time it turned I saw a different part of the dog, but ultimately, it remained two-dimensional.

My beam of light retreated from the tiny dog to shine on my empty hand. I turned the hand, and though it was flat, I could turn it to any angle . I could see the palm or the back, the cupped profile, the wrist. I turned my attention to my feet and found that though my front side displayed the tops of my shoes, I could also twist my legs enough to see the souls of my shoes.

The dog yipped, barked, snorted and bounced with no less violence than when it first appeared but seemed to be maintaining a perimeter at the threshold to the next corridor. I felt encouraged by the discovery of the Pomeranian. It was certainly a good omen. It was Lizzie's favorite breed of dog. She often talked dreamily of owning a dog one day. I had never encouraged this idea. I hated to think of our nice clean apartment full of dog hair.

Then, standing nearly motionless, considering how best to proceed, I heard a voice, a man's voice shouting, "Who's there?"

I pushed my shoulders back and widened my stance. I tightened my grip on the flashlight. Who was this man? I had to assume he could somehow be responsible for Lizzie's disappearance. Until that moment, I hadn't considered a kidnapper from the world behind the wall. I decided not to answer.

The voice came again. "We know you're there. You tripped the alarm."

I didn't know whether he meant the dog or the line I stumbled over, or both. Still, something told me I shouldn't answer, particularly because the voice was vaguely familiar, deep but nasal.

"Look," called the voice. "If you are who I think you are, you'll want to give me a minute to tie up Sparky before you come in." He paused, waited. When I didn't answer, his voice twisted with frustration. "Agreed?"

I cleared my throat and shouted, dropping my voice, "Agreed." My voice had the awkward effect of creating a near echo of his. My mind raced with the possibilities.

"Okay buddy," he said. I bristled at the word. There was certainly something creepy about the man with the familiar voice. I remained in what seemed like a logical attack stance. At first, I thought maybe I could use the flashlight as a club. Then I took off the backpack and dug around in it until I came out with the knife. I moved the flashlight to my left hand so I could handle the knife with my right.

"Okay buddy, you can come in," he said.

I thought about it. "No way am I gonna let you trap me in that narrow crack. You come out here."

There was a pause. Then the voice said, "If that makes you feel better. Personally, I wanted to kick your ass, but Lizzie wouldn't let me."

I twitched at the mention of her name.

An arm appeared through the crack, pausing long enough for the hand to get a grip on the wall so the man could pull himself through. My beam shone steadily on the hand. It was thin and a bit pale. It made me want to vomit. He would be through the crack in a second. Because he seemed at home in the world behind the wall and because he appeared to have some knowledge of Lizzie, he would have every advantage. I reacted purely on instinct, lunging at the hand, raising the knife well above my shoulder before bringing it down with all my force upon the back of the hand. A voice, muffled because it came from between the sheetrock and the 2x4, screamed out in pain, but I held the knife steady, attempting to keep the hand pressed to the wall. With a sudden bout of force, the flat hand pulled away, tearing itself in half in the process. "Fuuuck! Motherfucker," the voice howled. Then another voice answered, a woman's voice, calling my name, "Jeffery, I told you this was a bad idea." The voice was Lizzie's. My eyes grew wide, and my breathing quickened. My body was numb from the adrenaline of the attack, and now from the joy of hearing her voice, and recognizing no real fear in it. I wanted to call out to her but was emotionally choked, unable to speak.

The man's voice answered her before I could speak. "Damn right it was a bad idea." I understood then that the man's voice was mine and that the hand I impaled was also mine. He said, "You should have let me kick his ass. Now you can see exactly how much he deserves it."

She said, "Christ, let me see your hand."

"Shit, shit, shit, it hurts," he howled.

"I know it hurts baby, but I can fix it. We just have to get you back to my studio."

"Do I get to stab him at least once now?"

Lizzie's voice called again, this time much louder, "Jeffery, it's me. You just stabbed yourself. No more craziness. It's going to be okay. We're coming through."

Then the other me shouted, "Put the blasted knife down." Then softly his voice pleaded, "Don't go out there until he puts the knife down. I don't trust him."

Lizzie's voice came again, "If you would have let me go first like I said, this never would have happened." Then her voice doubled in volume. "I'm coming through, okay?"

I managed to let out a soft, "Yes."

When I finally saw her squeeze out through the crack and turn to face me, I was inundated with so many feelings and thoughts and questions that I couldn't settle on any one of them in particular. She hugged me. She hugged me, and I felt her ribs with my fingertips, her breasts against my chest, her arms wrapped around my sides, her hands caressing my back a little, her hair tickling my cheek. I squeezed her, hard. Then I moved back just a bit so I could kiss her. Before my lips reached hers she turned her head and said, "Don't."

I leaned back amazed and a little disgusted. "What?"

She smirked and said, "You wouldn't understand."

"Why wouldn't I?"

"I mean Jeffery, the other Jeffery, the one I'm with now. He wouldn't understand."

I looked over her shoulder and saw him standing there with his injured hand clamped in his healthy one, his face, my face, somewhat less attractive than I had thought it was up to that moment. His chin wasn't as definite as I imagined it. His eyes seemed lazier. One squinted a little more than the other. I recognized in him all the things I disliked about myself in certain photographs, the ones I always threw away. I could edit the photo album, but I couldn't edit this other version of myself living, breathing, annoying the hell out of me in the flesh.

A hot stab of jealousy pressed into my chest like a sharp-edged stone, yet I simultaneously felt something like remorse for stabbing him. Or was my rising blood pressure simply the result of a manifestation of pain sympathy, the sick feeling I got when I saw someone seriously injured or bleeding, like when I heard a thump like a melon as that old man fell and hit his head on the icy concrete steps outside the mall that time?

I stared at Lizzie, felt her familiar touch on my shoulders, and I said, "I don't understand."

"Of course, you don't, baby," she said, probably choosing her words unwittingly. The term of endearment filled me with joy. But he grumbled, pretending the wince was the physical pain he was enduring.

Then there were shuffling sounds and other voices. The dog, what had he called it? Snuggles, snuffles, sparkles? began to bark again behind the 2x4. Startled, my eyes shot to the crack and my arms involuntarily raised out from my sides.

"Whoa, whoa," she said. "It's okay." She paused. "In fact, it's better than okay. You'll see. Just promise me you'll keep an open mind?"

Already feeling stressed at the prospect, I asked, "Who is it?" And I heard a tinge of whining in my voice.

The other me said, "Oh brother."

She looked into my eyes fiercely, standing in front of me, moving her head from side to side to block my view when I moved. She didn't answer. I finally focused on her gaze. She was still. I was still. She smiled. I wanted to glue my flat self to her flat self and be stuck to her forever.

Then, in the dull light of the world behind the wall, a number of people shimmied through the crack and turned to face us, taking on an eerie illusionary three-dimensional quality. I saw a young blonde, but my mind refused at first to recognize her as Erin-Kate. Lizzie's friend Pamela was there too. Then Lizzie's father came out of the crack. He hurried directly to the other me when he saw he'd been injured. Then Lizzie's mother was in the corridor. She alone ignored the other version of myself and smiled warmly at me. I fixed my eyes on her. I said nothing, my mind feeling now that I was either dead or insane.

With a smile like that on her face, I assumed she was not the mother who had passed away. She had never even been sick. She seemed younger than Lizzie's father, because she was. She was a younger version of herself. Lizzie dug her fingernails into my arm. I started to speak, but her shaking head stopped me. She didn't have to explain. This mother would know nothing of her death; the past, present, or future. And there was probably no reason to warn her now, not here in this place. Considering this, I studied the other version of myself again. I could see things in his face, my face, small differences. Less small spots on the face, fewer gray hairs? The other me was younger. Was the other me immortal, captured in emulsion on paper forever?

As a group, we traveled through the walls to the place they had settled, up near the attic, where they had a view of the world through a louvered vent in the outer wall. The drastic height was phenomenally higher still when compared to our size. In order to repair his hand, Lizzie carefully and completely removed the injured hand first. Then she dragged a life-sized photograph, a double, and removing only the hand from it, reattached it to the neat stump line of his wrist. He gritted his teeth against the pain and stared coldly at me. Only by looking quite closely could you detect the seam on his wrist. When it was finished, his painful glare turned to a softer kind of hatred. I felt a little proud of him for his tolerance of the pain, the relaxed way he had of hurting.

She whispered a few words to him, and he reluctantly let her go alone with me into the next corridor. The long, narrow, and high-ceilinged 'rooms' had been furnished with pictures of fantastic colorful furniture, carpets, and art cut from magazines. The walls were plastered with paintings, art prints, and some seemed to be living photographs. Behind the glass of a golden picture frame, a capuchin monkey swung on a branch, tore off a handful of leaves and stuffed them into his mouth. He stared out at me pensively while he chewed. "Can he bite me?"

"No, he lives behind the glass."

I reached out slowly and touched the cold glass. The monkey, startled, leapt from the branch squealing and disappeared. I could see the leaves he'd torn away budding, the buds growing, little pale green leaves appearing, broadening, darkening, appearing just as they were before he'd plucked and eaten them.

There was a wall that had plastered to most of its surface a large magazine spread of an ocean. The waves moved. When I dipped my hand into the wall, it came out warm, wet, and with the taste of salt.

When she offered me a drink, she did so by bringing out a homemade menu book full of beautifully colored beverages from magazines. I chose a blended mango and rum concoction in a martini glass with a slice of starfruit. It was cold and sweet, yet tart, and the glass chilled my fingertips with icy condensation. It smelled a bit like her favorite shampoo.

"I'm glad you came." She kissed my forehead, "You get it now, don't you? You understand why I can't go back?"

I paused. Then I slurped a long draw from my drink and stopped only when I felt the cold pain in the roof of my mouth move to my temples and settle there. I tried to say something. I tried to tell her one of the thousand things I was thinking, but it all seemed useless now. And suddenly, I felt my numbness turn to anger. "I can't believe you're doing this to me."

She frowned, her eyes narrowing, darkening. Her smile faded.

I was suddenly furious. I knew I should be happy, but I wanted to shake her. "What about your father? How can you do this to your father?"

"I'm going to ask you to bring him to our apartment tomorrow at midnight. I'll come out just long enough to explain everything to him."

"And the police?"

"I'll write a note in my own handwriting that says I've gone to California. I'll leave here long enough to call the station if necessary. Dad can go to the police and corroborate my story."

"But how can you leave me? How can you leave the whole world?"

Lizzie smiled a smile like the one she smiled the time she tore off her burning shirt. "I have the best of the world here," she said, waving her arms toward the photographs of tropical islands, Persian markets, snow-capped mountains. "And none of the bad things." Everywhere I looked there were pictures of comfortable and elegant rooms, stylish clothes and cars and exotic tourist destinations. There were pastries and burgers and even a table crowded with an elaborate Thanksgiving dinner. It was her mother's table, her mother's cobbler, her mother's clove and pineapple ham. It seemed Lizzie had thought of everything.

"But how is all this even possible? How did you find the door?"

"The same way you did, I guess." She sat on the ottoman of a Mies Van der Rhoe Barcelona chair covered with white leather. The ottoman let out a pleasant sigh as the air escaped the compressed cushion.

I studied her face, her dark eyes, her near blue-black hair, the dimpled lines where her cheeks became her upper lip. "I can see why you'd want to stay. You can literally live in your own little world here can't you?"

"It seems that way so far."

"You can have your cake and eat it too?"

She stared at me, and for the first time since I'd found her, anger came into her eyes. "Don't say it like that."

Part of me wanted to apologize, but I shook my head. I gritted my teeth.

"I can't believe the way you let us all suffer on the outside. The real Erin-Kate, the real Pamela, the real me, and your real father. At the least, at the absolute least, you could have let us know sooner."

"Sooner?" She squinted.

"It's been five days Lizzie! I thought you were dead. Your father is a disaster."

Her lightness faded. "Five days? I've barely been here a day!"

I was dumbfounded. Then I said softly, "It's been a hell of a lot longer than that out there." My breathing stuttered.

"Here," she said, jumping up from the ottoman. She thrust against my chest a photograph of her mother. I looked at it. I bent it, and nothing happened. It remained static. "You've got to leave right now. If time moves that much faster out there, you have to get my father here now, tonight, as soon as possible. Explain to him that I didn't know how long it had been. Wait," she said. "No, it's better if I explain it to him. Just get him to the apartment. Tell him I'm okay. I'll be waiting. All you need to do is knock on the door when he's ready. I'll come out. But I'd like to be alone with him if you don't mind."

With this she was rushing me back through the corridors, her little dog trotting along behind us.

At the door, she embraced me, and I knew that she no longer loved me, and I was so angry that I told myself I no longer loved her either. I took one last look at my Lizzie and wondered how long she would get along with the other me. It wasn't enough to know that she lived in a world of her making, a place strange and impossible, that I had only begun to see. Her possibilities were endless, as I had accidentally guessed during my attempt at deciphering the very small people in our apartment. "Hurry now," she said, and she kissed me just once on the lips. I didn't know what to feel. I felt a kind of love, but was jealous as well. I had been with her. Now a younger me still had the chance I would no longer have.

She chose him over me. She chose all of them over all of us on the outside. More than anything, I felt betrayed. She betrayed life itself. She was pushing me toward the door, shoving me almost violently. I was out of time. "You can't just give up death," I whispered. "You can't just give up suffering."

"You may not want me to. But I can, and I will. Can't you be happy for me? Don't you see? My mother's here. There's no reason to think she'll ever not be here. Another you is here too. And you have my word; I won't ever leave him. But to be with him forever, I need to leave you."

As I slid beneath the very small door, I let my mind flash back to the instant she threw off her burning shirt. That was the moment I settled on. That was the picture of her I was in love with. That was the instant I could gaze at forever. That was the photograph I would keep in my mind forever. If I wanted to give her credit, I could imagine that the picture of me she chose as my replacement represented just such a moment for her. He came from a time when my love for her was fierce. Perhaps he was me in the very instant she fell in love. But the sickness, the sadness that had morphed into indignation, into anger, told me I was no longer that man.

As I pulled myself back into our bedroom, I knew that it was terribly important that I find her father, that I bring him to the very small door. For this reason, I made my exhausted self continue to pull my flat body through the crack beneath the very small door until I was whole again. In the fullness of my real body, I felt a thrust of sadness, of anger, of betrayal. I felt pain. But still, somehow, I felt alive with that pain. I took the pain all the way inside and realized that there was something worthwhile, something tragically beautiful, something terribly human there.

TROLL WEDDING

E. W. FARNSWORTH

I flew into Norway in early spring through eerily dense clouds using Instrument Flight Rules. I didn't see the ground until my wheels touched down on the icy tarmac. I had entered a land of mist and snow, shrouded in mystery, a land my ancestors had known for at least a thousand years. My purpose was to solve a few software problems way up north.

I first had to receive a briefing in Oslo where I would be lodging with the military attaché and his wife overnight before flying to Bodo. The attaché was an old family friend whose wife collected trolls. So as I entered their small dwelling, I was not surprised that one troll stood on each step of the stairwell that led to the guest room. Mind you, I was amused by the figurines. Norwegians have a tendency to fantasize their way through long, dark winter nights. The shapes of the little statues were of every imaginable form.

I received my briefing the next morning. The King himself was present and asked intelligent questions that left his officers baffled in amazement. He always questioned why things were happening. Others were interested in what was going on. Only the King asked the fundamental questions. I had built the Crystal Ball software for him, and he naturally took a proprietary interest in how it was working for the good of the state.

Since I am a descendant of the royal family, several times removed, I viewed the monarch as more than a figurehead. On him depended the fate of the nation. Norway had survived World War II because the King was wise enough to allow his young officers to exercise their initiative. Hearing this King express his concerns for certain flying tactics of a major foreign power, I understood his concern perfectly in technical terms. I knew why he wanted the fix I could provide for his software. I would make the targeting algorithms faster and bring the real-time data on high-value targets to decision makers' displays thirty seconds earlier than usual. My mission was now clear. I flew as soon after I reached my small aircraft as possible.

Along the west coast of Norway, the clouds remained unbroken. It was as if I was flying in an aureole of light divorced from anything but the instruments that showed the presence of navigational markers and, of course, my flight data. There's nothing magic about IFR aerial navigation, but as I descended into the Bodo airport through the enveloping mist, I recalled the look of the trolls on the attaché's stairway, watching me climb, menacingly.

My ultimate destination was not actually the airport but a huge cave in a mountain, which I reached by Jeep transport with the good services of the duty driver assigned to me. Once at the cave, my transition through the security wickets was efficiently managed. My escort told me, "Just keep an eye out for the trolls!" The man was serious, but at the time I thought he must be joking.

The short version is I completed my mission successfully, but when I finished it was very late. I had no escort going out, and I had still to arrange my lodgings. I found my way through the night fog to a bus stop where an old, portly woman was waiting patiently.

"When does the bus come for Bodo?"

She laughed. "It's anyone's guess." She cocked her head and eyed me as if I were a laboratory specimen. I looked at my watch. It was ten o'clock.

"You know what happens at precisely this hour of the night?" the crone asked me. Without waiting for my answer, she said, "It's the trolls' time. And till morning's light, the King of Trolls rules."

I might have laughed at her outright except I saw a fierce gleam in her eyes suggesting she was not to be trifled with. I turned to look in the direction I presumed the bus would come. When I turned back again, the crone had disappeared. In her place was a svelte, blonde twenty-something woman making eyes at me. She was beyond beautiful, this maiden. Her hair was done in golden braids on either side of her head, and her eyes were so crystalline blue, they pierced me to the heart.

I told her, "I'm waiting for the bus to Bodo."

She laughed merrily and said, "Give up!"

I was not amused. I was exhausted after all my travel and work. I was impatient to gain my lodging and get some rest. I was unnerved by the increase of the fog and mist, which now made it almost impossible to see my hand in front of my face. "What do you mean?"

She answered, "Why don't you come with me? I know a warm place with food and liquor. It's back in the cave you just left. Follow me, but not too far behind. Otherwise, you'll get lost. Quickly now!" She tugged at my jacket. I grabbed her extended hand and followed her in spite of my reservations about following a stranger. I counted on the security guards in the cave as my protection.

My peremptory guide had no trouble getting through the security checkpoints. In fact, the uniformed guards snapped to attention at the sight of her as if she had a high rank. Inward we progressed until we reached a place in the cave I had not seen on the tour I had been given earlier in the day. The gateway to the place had special guards and advanced technology with biometric identification for admittance. My guide's palm print provided the magic key to our entry.

We were confronted by a blast of noise and interplay of lights. The cavern we had entered was expansive, with artificial lights flashing and music playing. People were dancing and having fun. Liquor was being served freely to everyone. My hostess gave me a tankard of ale and told me to drink up and follow her to the feasting table. I drank.

As an effect of the liquor, the colors and sounds amplified. I floated rather than walked to the groaning board where huge flavored pastes of fish were available for tasting with small crackers and toast points. I ate and drank, noticing that my hostess was closely watching me. It did not occur to me that I was being drugged. I fought the insight but concluded my only option was to focus on details.

"Why are you looking at me like that?" I asked her.

Her answer was surprising, "I think you must be royal. Are you?"

"As a matter of fact, I am distantly related to the crown." I did not say this to brag. It was factually true.

She smiled. "My father told me I would marry a royal one day. Maybe my future husband stands before me now." She leaned forward and kissed me full on the lips. It was a magical moment because she had the sweetest breath. If she spent all her time kissing, she could not have done better with her lips on mine.

I stammered, "We've only just met. I don't even know your name."

She replied with an enchanting smile, "No matter. What does matter is your heart. I look in your eyes and see your innocence. What do you see in mine?"

I answered slurring my speech, "Endless possibilities," She seemed to understand me.

She stood back and announced in a loud voice, "He has finally come, my groom! Call forth my father the King. We must make haste."

The guests were suddenly all in motion. They formed two groups on either side of a red-carpeted path that led from where I was standing to a gleaming, golden throne. My female escort led me forward to the steps leading to the throne. At the same time, a group of men came from the right side of the throne in front of a towering figure. I blinked twice to be sure I did not mistake. The men looked exactly like the trolls that lined the steps at the attaché's house. The huge man behind them wore a golden crown.

Applause burst out as the crowned man took his place on the throne. He did it with a flourish, whisking his robe and descending into the seat with majesty.

The king said, "Daughter and Princess, come forward. What have you found?"

She bowed low and said, "I've found my husband, Father, and King. He's everything I've always wanted. He's royal. And he's a human!"

I felt a frisson of fear and looked around at the crowd that had assembled. Looking directly at them I thought they must be ordinary courtiers like those who jostled for privilege in the King of Norway's court that I had left only this morning. By using averted vision, though, they appeared to be quite different. They were like the trolls on the attaché's steps, but in even more fantastical shapes.

I pinched my arm to be sure I was awake. I stepped forward to hold the princess's head with both my hands. I moved my face towards hers and looked her in the eyes. She kissed me and hugged me close. Then she stepped back, breathless and blushing like a maiden.

She appealed, "See, father, how he loves me! I demand an immediate marriage and consummation before dawn."

Trumpets sounded so my ears hurt. An enormous cheer rang out, the sound reverberating around the cave's interior. The tempo of the flashing lights increased. I had read how pulsating lights might induce a stroke, so I closed my eyes periodically to avoid the strobe effect. I could do nothing about the music and raucous merriment of the crowd. I felt paralyzed and could not resist what I was being maneuvered into. The King opened his arms, and his daughter flew into his embrace.

"Let the wedding ceremony begin!" he decreed with an animal's roar.

Now lovely maidens came to dress the bride and me in white and yellow spring flowers. A brace of magpies flew into the party and began jabbering as they hit the ground. The cavern's ceiling seemed to open to the heavens where no clouds blocked the shimmering stars of the spring night.

I felt a slight shiver until a robe of warming ermine was wrapped around my shoulders and a golden crown was placed on my head. My bride was now wearing a golden crown like her father's. Her hair was braided with snowdrops' flowers so white they shone as the cave darkened and the long white candles were lighted one by one. I watched mystified as the strobe lights dimmed and ceased. The candle light took over.

The King beckoned what looked like a high priest, a robed figure as tall as he, with fiery eyes and a great locked book with an iron key. He went to a podium I had not seen before and opened his book with the key. He bowed his head and waited until the crowd grew silent. Then he read from the book in a language I had never heard before.

I tried to understand what his speech meant, but I saw everyone else was following the meaning with no trouble. Some of the assembly's lips were moving in unison with the priest's lips. The whole crowd had become a congregation as at church.

The princess urged me forward with the flat of her palm until we were standing right in front of the priest, whose hands were extended towards us. He snapped his fingers and behind him appeared a pile of gold and jewels that reached what used to be the ceiling of the cave. He said a few words, which my bride translated as, "All these riches shall be yours as my dowry." He then motioned for my bride and me to join hands. We did so.

At that very moment as if synchronized to do so, lightning forked through the clear sky and thunder sounded in a continuous roar. The assemblage tried to outshout the storm. Then the storm ceased, and the roar of the assemblage took on a life of its own. The crowd's roar thundered, and the lightning flashed, a reversal of my expectations.

The priest intoned a few verses. My bride wept. She turned to me and buried her beautiful head in my chest.

She raised her head and with eyes filled with tears of joy said, "It's done. We are wed. This is the happiest day of my life. Kiss me, husband. Through me, you shall one day be the Troll King."

I kissed her but now instead of sweet her breath was sour. Her lips were cold, not warm. The candle lights all went out. In the pitch-black darkness, I heard a great rustling as of giant birds flying in all directions. Then the silence was profound.

My bride and I were finally alone. We had no clothes. She pulled me to the cold floor. There we coupled and slept through most of the night.

In the hour before dawn, I felt a rough nudge. A voice urged me, "Get up. There's no time. Get dressed, fill your pockets with trolls' gold and be gone. Terrible things will happen to a human who faces the dawn in this cave."

My clothes were thrust into my hands.

I did not hesitate or ask questions. I dressed. I groped my way to the back of the cave. There I felt the cold metal. I scooped handfuls of gold into my pockets, which now sagged under the weight of the yellow metal and threatened to fall down.

I turned and, as fast as I could, walked in the direction of the entrance hall. I had to correct my path when I slammed into a wall. My hands ran along the wall until I felt an opening. I went through the opening and kept my hand on the right wall as I passed through a sequence of gateways, which opened at my touch.

Finally, I fell down a short flight of steps and rolled. I heard a great clanking sound as of metal against metal. I heard birdsong. As the first light of dawn brought illumination to the darkness, I was in a small wooded area next to a road.

In fact, I was at the bus stop where I was the night before. There was no fog. Snow lay on the land as it had the day before. A hand gripped my shoulder. I whirled around and saw smiling at me the crone I had met when I first came here. She had a new sparkle in her eyes and took my arm. I jerked away and fled in the direction of Bodo. She followed me.

She cried out, "Please wait for me. We belong together, you and I. If you go, I must bear your child without a father. Look in your pockets for the gold."

I reached into my pockets and pulled out leaves and acorns by the handful. I threw them on the ground. The crone threw up her hands and screeched. She ran to pick up what I was discarding.

"What with difficulty has been gathered, you spurn and cast away. Beware you don't earn my curse, husband."

"Husband?" I exclaimed with a growing sense of dread. "You drugged me. I was tricked."

She responded, "You remember the ceremony. You remember the consummation. I chose you above all humankind. My father, the King of Trolls, blessed our marriage. The High Priest of Trolls officiated at our holy matrimony."

"You are a bad dream, a shape changer. Where is the beautiful maid I met last night?"

She was crestfallen. "I was the maid, but I'm now your wife. In my womb, I bear the future Troll King, your son."

"Ach! This is too horrible to imagine. Why are you tormenting me?"

She frowned and the skies clouded over. It began to rain. The snow fog rose in a mist. I jogged, with her jogging right behind me. She sang while she ran in the language used in the ceremony by the High Priest. She sang her nine stanzas. Then she sang the Norwegian language translation of those stanzas. I caught the gist though I could not understand every word of her translation. The song was a mix of a taunt and a curse.

The taunt reviled me for not being able to see the truth when it was right in front of me. The curse was that I would remain forever blind. One day, the song went, my own female child would return to marry the new Troll King and bear the first troll born in America.

My hair stood on end as I contemplated the haunting meaning of this song. I had no trouble envisioning the work of the spell. I believe I saw my future lovely daughter in a vision the crone must have induced in my head.

The crone cackled and threw back her head. "Do you see her? Do you see your daughter? It's really she. She won't be able to resist coming back to me. I'll have her marry your son. He'll be Troll King. She'll be Troll Queen. Then the game will come full circle."

My mouth became parched at the implication of what she had said. I swung around and shouted at her hoarsely, "What do you mean, crone, by 'come full circle'?"

She stopped. She cocked her head. A crooked smile came across her horrible face, wet and streaming with a mix of rain and tears. As the rain fell on her head and dripped through her tangled hair, she pointed a gnarled finger at me and laughed.

"You really don't know, do you? You think you came to this country of your own free will. Hahaha. I am the troll your grandmother bore to my father the King of Trolls. She was lured here the same way you were. She suffered the same curse. So here you are. And so it goes into another generation."

Now she was walking backwards as the rain increased. The fog increased too. I felt the rain trickling down my face and neck. My shoes were sodden with the running water of the street.

A claxon horn brought me to my senses. It was the bus with the roll sign "Bodo" coming from the direction of the cave. It stopped when I hailed it. I must have looked a sorry sight. The driver did not seem to mind. I was his only passenger. I noticed he had some of the features of the trolls at the attaché's house in Oslo.

"Been up to the cave?" the driver asked.

"That's right," I replied.

"I thought so. If you stayed there overnight and survived, you must be blessed."

"What do you mean?"

"People go into the cave. Many don't come out again. Those who do tell horrible stories."

"Such as?"

"Being scared out of their wits, mostly, by trolls. They'll torture you and eat you. They'll make bargains for your life or your soul or the lives of your offspring."

I was more than a little uneasy because he licked his lips when he said, "eat you."

"Do you believe all the lies you're told?" I asked boldly.

"Better to believe lies than remain blind to the truth, I say." He slowed as he moved through a slippery patch. The bus slid almost sideways. "It's a treacherous road this time of year."

The bus left me at the main bus station in Bodo. I took a taxi to the airport. Before I got on my plane, I removed the remaining leaves and acorns from my pockets. I climbed aboard my aircraft and taxied to the takeoff point.

At exactly the planned time, I took off and flew along the coast to the south. I flew above the rain clouds in the sunshine. The clouds below me looked like spun gold. I made it back to Oslo without incident.

Before I left Norway, I wanted to pay my respects and say farewell to the attaché.

"Welcome back to Oslo, Will," Captain Aalstaar said. "The King is most grateful for all you've done for the cause."

"I'm glad to know I was able to help."

"Why don't you stay for lunch? My wife has bought four new trolls for her collection. She'd like you to see them. She really is devoted to her collection. Humor her, please, and say something nice about her additions."

When I arrived at the attaché's dwelling, the first thing I laid eyes on was the arrangements of four new troll figures in the living room. A Troll King with a crown, a Troll Princess with her crown, a High Priest Troll with a locked book and iron key and a Male Troll resembling me with two fistfuls of gold were arranged in a wedding scene. The tableau corresponded exactly to what I had participated in the previous night. The attaché's wife brought in Aquavit to toast her new acquisitions.

"Here's to the parallel kingdoms in Norway. On the one hand, the Norwegian King and his court. On the other hand the Troll King and his court." So the attaché's wife toasted. We all drank though I admit my drink was hard to swallow though the liquor was first class.

"As to the relationship between the troll kingdom and the human kingdom, how to they relate to one another?" I asked.

She smiled and said, "Of course the troll kingdom is pure fiction. It bears as little resemblance to reality as these four figures do. The imagination is a marvelous conduit for our subconscious intuitions."

The attaché wanted to discuss a few matters with me in private before I flew home. When his wife set out on her daily shopping trip, we were alone for our discussions.

"Will, you've done wonders yet again. The King is delighted you've restored his Crystal Ball software to full operational effectiveness. This morning he asked me a question, though, I couldn't answer. Perhaps you can help. He asked why you disappeared shortly after you completed your project at the cave and didn't materialize until late the morning after. He's always asking why. So tell me the answer so I can satisfy His Majesty."

"Sir, it was late. I had nowhere to stay in Bodo. A kindly person offered to put me up for the night. I accepted her offer. The next morning I caught the bus to Bodo."

"I'm sure the King will be happy to hear your answer. Next time, perhaps, we'll arrange for your lodgings in Bodo in advance and provide transport to and from the cave."

"I don't want to cause any trouble."

"It should be no trouble for someone who is even remotely related to the royal family as you are."

"Earlier your wife made light of her troll collection saying it was all a fiction. From her obsession with trolls, I expected her to be insistent about their reality."

"If you ply her with enough Aquavit, you'd find she fancies herself to be descended from trolls on both her mother's and father's sides. She firmly believes that the reason I was selected as attaché was her troll heritage."

"Does she then believe that trolls and humans can intermarry as her new tableau implies?"

"I don't think such troll-human intermarriage would be entirely happy. Trolls live by night and thrive on deceit. Humans live largely by day and pride themselves on their truthfulness."

"I find it interesting that the male Troll figure in the wedding tableau almost looks human."

"I hadn't noticed, but if you say so, it must be true."

"Let's for a moment say trolls lived in Bodo."

"Many people say that's true."

"Where would they dwell?"

"Trolls, according to folklore, can be anywhere. They can change their forms. They like to meet in large underground areas at night. They drink, dance, eat and play all night until just before dawn. Not everyone can see trolls. Those who have the special gift are given it by the trolls themselves. Oh, yes, trolls are rumored to be vastly wealthy with gold and jewels. The catch is, the wealth can only be used within the troll kingdom. If you take the wealth out of their realm, all the wealth turns to worthless rubbish like oak leaves and acorns."

"I see. And how do trolls view history?"

"Pardon me."

"If a troll curses a human, can that affect the human's life?"

"Will, beware a troll's curse. It's said that a curse is the only truth a troll knows. Why do you ask?"

"I was just curious. Anyway, I'm going to fly home now." I felt the sooner I was airborne, the better.

"My wife says you'll be back. She also says your daughter is destined for greatness through her connection to this country."

"Sir, I don't yet have a daughter."

"We'll see about that. Once again, thank you for coming. The King looks forward to seeing you again when you return. Have a safe flight home."

I didn't know what to think about my experience in Bodo. As I reflected on it during my flight home, I thought I might have fallen asleep and dreamed about the troll wedding and the curse. Yet details come back so vividly in my recurring nightmares as if my mind is orchestrated by a lingering magical power.

My wife's first child was a wonderful girl. She had blonde hair and blue eyes. Her skin was a radiant white. She grew up to be a lot like her mother. She was obsessed with trolls from the first time she heard about them. She ached to travel to Norway to find the trolls. Nothing I said could deflect her from her wish.

In her college years, my darling daughter studied Norwegian language and culture. She delved deeply into troll folklore in the Old Norse sagas. She interned with a group from the University of Oslo who were avid students of troll lore. She even wore a sweatshirt with the word TROLL in capital letters on her chest. Wearing her signature sweatshirt, she caught the eye of the Prince of Norway. He instantly fell in love with her.

To cut to the chase, my daughter married the King's son. She conceived the heir to the Norwegian throne. So much, I thought, for the feared troll curse. All those years I feared an outcome that turned out to be the exact opposite of the troll's cursed intent.

When my dear human wife passed, I had the occasion to go on a pilgrimage to Bodo to find the troll wife who uttered the curse. The Norwegian King required another emergency fix of his Crystal Ball software. He requested me by name. So back I flew to the north. I went to the cave and again fixed the King's Crystal Ball.

It was late when I finished, so I ended up waiting at the same bus stop outside the cave wherein the King's command center was located.

A handsome boy was also waiting for the bus. He was the image of me in my younger days.

"Do you think the bus will ever come? It's very late." The boy remarked as if to himself.

It had begun to drizzle, and the snow fog rose from the ground. Soon the air was a shroud. We shivered in the cold and wet and stamped our feet as if that would provide warmth.

He smiled and turned to me. "I know a place where we can get out of the cold. If you come with me, I'll show you where you can eat and drink. There you can sleep through the night safely. Tomorrow morning you can take the bus to the city."

"I'll gladly go with you," I said, "if you'll tell me your name."

"You know my name, father. It's Will, the same as yours. My mother prophesied you'd come again. And here you are. I've been waiting for you. She said you'd bring your daughter for me to marry. Where is she?"

"Son, I'm afraid she's married to another man. I'm very sorry. Perhaps we can find you a proper match among your troll companions in the cave."

The boy looked downcast. All his life he had been primed for the moment of meeting me. Instead of my fulfilling his dream, I was a great disappointment to him. I believe he was as disappointed in me as I was happy that my daughter had married the prince of her dreams.

My son led me to the cave just as his mother had done. His biometrics opened the great, secret door. Within the great space, as before, a great many trolls were carousing and eating. The same lights flashed. The same songs were being sung. This time, I eschewed the food and drink for fear of drugs.

My son shouted out that he had an announcement to make.

"My father has returned, but without my bride."

A hush fell over the crowd as the news penetrated the entire community of trolls. Then the crowd began a great gnashing of teeth and rending of clothing. Moans and groans rang out in the cavernous hall. A roar filled the room, and a spotlight fell on the throne.

My son drew me along a direct path to the throne as the ferocious Troll King approached and sat on it. The High Priest of Trolls with his book and iron key stood beside the throne, lowering at me.

From the back of the cave the boy's mother, my hideous troll-wife, came shrieking and wailing that I had failed the entire troll kingdom by not bringing a wife for our son. She stood in front of her father sobbing and pulling at her knotted hair.

I stepped forward to comfort her, but she pushed me away viciously and hurled savage troll language at me, spitting her words with hisses and grunts.

The Troll King raised his enormous hands. The crowd became silent. The King spoke in a voice like low thunder.

"What should we do with this man and his son? They have failed us."

"We should tear them both to pieces and feast on their flesh. We should then grind their bones into flour and make bread from the flour and eat it," my troll wife said with venom.

I was horror-stricken to hear her name both father and son in her vengeful spite. Her surface beauty stood in stark contrast to her wicked troll's soul.

The Troll King silenced his manic daughter with a stern gesture.

"I decree your curse was the problem. It went horribly wrong. The man's daughter married the King of Norway's son. Your husband did everything in his power to raise his daughter to be the wife of a troll prince. She is still fascinated by trolls. So if anyone is to be torn apart and eaten, it should be you, daughter. High Priest, bless the feast so we can begin."

"Wait!" I said without thinking. I could not abide seeing my troll wife killed and eaten. "If I can provide a solution to this conundrum, will that satisfy the Troll King, the High Priest and the subjects of the troll kingdom?"

"Proceed with your suggestion," the Troll King said sitting back on his throne with a leer.

I stepped forward boldly and asked, "Is it not true that trolls can take many forms?"

"Yes, this is true," the Troll King admitted.

"And is it not true that the only requirement is that the prince has a suitable bride?"

"That also is true," the Troll King said.

"What could be more appropriate than this prince, my son, be married to a princess?"

My troll wife raised her head smiling, assuming I meant somehow to surrender my daughter to the troll kingdom after all.

I spoke rapidly to dash my evil wife's hopes.

"I, therefore, call on my wife, the troll princess, to assume the form of my daughter, the human princess, and in that form marry my son the prince. Thus the prophecy and the curse are in full accord. She will have a new husband. You will have a suitable heir."

The Troll King rubbed his right hand on his chin. The High Priest nodded and whispered in the Troll King's ear. The King rose to make a judgment.

"I the Troll King decree these things. My daughter, the princess, shall take the form of her husband's human daughter and this night marries my grandson the prince. If she does not do this, she will be killed and eaten by the rest of us tonight. As for my son-in-law who made this suggestion, he will be free to depart and return to the world of humans. He is, however, banished forever from the troll kingdom for having failed to deliver his human daughter as was planned."

The trolls applauded this sage judgment. While everyone disported himself for the wedding, I backed through the crowd to the exit, anxious lest the Troll King change his mind and make me part of the wedding feast.

I did a double take as I saw my troll wife transform into my daughter's shape. I saw my troll son gape in astonishment that his wife would be this beautiful girl who stood before her father blushing like a bride on her wedding night.

I was rudely jostled out the door by the natural movement of the crowd as they pressed forward to hear the High Priest begin the marriage rites. I passed down the dark halls, using my right hand to guide me through the blackness. I stumbled down the final stairs and knew I was free.

The night was clear. The stars were twinkling in the velvet black of the heavens. I thought I heard a cheer within the cave, but when I strained to listen closely, I only heard a night owl.

By starlight, I navigated down the road all night and reached Bodo at first light. My teeth were chattering. I was bone tired. I decided to go to the nearest open inn and get some sleep.

Ironically, the nearest inn was Troll Haven. Its moniker was a troll figure for which my son may have posed. Over the reception desk was an enormous formal picture of the prince and princess of Norway, my son-in-law, and daughter.

The woman at the desk signed me in. When her eyes met mine, I knew them. They belonged to Mrs. Aalstaar, the attaché's wife whose trolls had included my troll wedding tableau.

"Welcome to Troll Haven, Will. It's good to see you again. In the great room by the fireplace, you'll find the troll figures I showed you many years ago in my home. All my trolls are here. You'll recognize them, I think. Sleep in as long as you like. I'll have food whenever you awaken."

"Mrs. Aalstaar, did you perchance have anything to do with the way things turned out in my life?"

"Such questions are not for the answering. Rejoice if you think things turned out well enough. While you're here, you might spend a little time talking with my husband, the Admiral. He mentions you often. He decided we'd retire to run this inn in Bodo because it was the place where he could be near his cave and I could be near mine. Enjoy your stay."

I did enjoy my stay. Admiral Aalstaar played a wicked game of cribbage. It is a grand old Navy wardroom game. Now that he was retired, and I was a mere contractor and no longer a naval officer, it was our common ground. I don't always win at cribbage as much depends on the deal. In that the card game is a lot like life.

While we were playing, I asked him questions about the relations between the trolls and the humans in Norway. Since he was no longer attaché, he could be candid with his answers.

"You ask an important question, Will. Trolls and humans have cooperated in Norway as long as human memory. In the great wars Norway has endured and won, trolls have fought alongside humans to preserve the nation. This is one reason the cave nearby accommodates both species."

"Admiral, trolls eat people. They are known to be a threat. What keeps the balance between the species, as you call them?"

"You're one to ask. You're related on both sides of this equation. By the way, fifteen two, fifteen four, fifteen six, fifteen eight, a pair makes ten and four pairs make eight more." He pegged eighteen while I pegged my meager twelve. The Admiral refilled and relit his pipe before we continued both our game and my inquisition.

"So how does the relationship work in times of war?" I asked him.

"Between trolls and humans, you mean?"

"That's right."

"In the cave, a great door slides aside. The two command centers are joined as one. The Troll King and the King of Norway sit in adjacent thrones to command Norwegian forces."

"Yet my Crystal Ball software is used only by the human side."

"That's why the relationship works so well. The Crystal Ball software is what the trolls lack. By including the software in the command architecture, the joint operations can be controlled from a centralized perspective. Otherwise, we'd have chaos. It's your deal."

He cut the cards to me. As I melded the deck and dealt the cards, I felt I was beginning to understand the relationship of trolls and men. I still had questions.

"What I don't understand is how the trolls can control their own forces in any conflict. From what I know of trolls, they are subject to their Troll King alone. He is a supreme dictator. What he commands, they carry out without question, to the death if necessary."

"Again, your statement contains the solution to your problem of understanding. Yes, trolls are ruled by a dictatorial Troll King. In contrast, humans are ruled by a King with a democratic foundation and human initiative as its motive force. Trolls would be totally lost in situations where their command policy was upset. Likewise, humans would be totally lost in situations where their democratic tendencies were denied. Consider Norway's traditional common enemies Sweden, Russia and Germany were fended off except by trolls. It would have been unthinkable for humans to have made the sacrifices the trolls made."

"What did the trolls gain in the bargain?"

"Besides feasting well on the dead, they continued their cooperative venture with humans instead of going to war to the death, potentially to their extinction."

"Then the coexistence of trolls and humans is the foundation of Norway?"

"You could say that. Yes."

He cut the cards. I flipped the top card, and we began to play. Ours was a most illuminating game.

Looking back in my advanced age, I can't say for certain how everything turned out as well as it did. The former attaché's wife bought another troll marriage tableau that looked a lot like my transformed troll wife and princess marrying my half troll prince son in the company of the Troll King and Troll Priest. I never returned to the troll dimension of the cave, but then I was never invited.

My daughter, who became Queen of Norway, bore her husband an heir, who will become King some day. I have no idea whether my troll-wife, who married my half troll son, bore the heir for the Troll King. Perhaps it was enough that my son was in line to be Troll King. In any case, I do hope my son had the good sense to think through his problem of succession as well as his father had done in the last generation.

TWINS

DENNIS WINKLEBLACK

David had stayed too long. His mother had given him a pass last week when he was ten minutes late, but he wouldn't be so lucky this time. Early January days were short in New England – leaden gray by his curfew of four o'clock, a wall of black by four-thirty. He pushed his bike to its limit on the gravel-littered, uneven asphalt already betraying its wintry assault. Matt's Goth Butcher video game was awesome, he'd become lost in another time and place. He had to get it, after his grounding or whatever.

Usually, David relished the yellowed interior light welcoming him in his suburban white-shingled colonial as he raced the sun's last reach. He'd never admit it to his parents, but upsetting them in even trivial ways bothered him. Since his twin sister left for the mall and never came back two years ago, the three of them shared an uncommon tie, a jealous bonding, his mother still taking pills from the doctor. Her discipline was unpredictable, sometimes excessive, in David's opinion. His father avoided such unpleasantness unless it was a big deal, like when he and Matt put a thumbtack on Ms. Gammon's chair last year in ninth grade biology. Someone told, his parents met with the principal, and David was barred from the football team for a month. He would never forget the anguish shaping his folks' faces and the pall of sadness that remained in the house long thereafter.

David dumped his bike in the front yard, stumbling over a tree root in his haste to minimize his tardiness. Jumping up, he raced to the front door and grasped the brass knob. Locked. His punishment must have begun. He rang the doorbell, its familiar melody muffled in reply. David envisioned his mother pointedly opening the door, hand on hip, jaw set, eyes fixed. He'd have to look contrite. Mind-flipping, he thought again about Goth Butcher. He had enough saved, easy. He punched the doorbell again, passing cars marking time's creep. Curious, David walked to the detached two-car garage at the side of the house and peered through one of its square glass windows. Aided by the flickering streetlights, he saw both his parents' cars, a Camry and a Corolla, side by side. He must really be in trouble.

His parents hid a house key for emergencies underneath a rock in the flower bed. He found the key in a portable tin once packed with breath mints. He slipped it into the lock, turned the knob and shoved the door wide, its brush-sweep over the floor tile a normally comforting greeting.

"Mom? Dad?" he yelled. When no one answered, David kicked off his shoes and headed for the family room. Tossing the remote aside, SportsCenter sprang to life, and he launched his nearly six foot body onto the beige sailcloth-covered sofa. Feeling a chill, David draped himself with an afghan made by Grandma Betsy. He checked the clock on the cable box – 4:55. Not too bad. But, boy, they were definitely going all out to make a point. His stomach rumbled. He could grab a cookie, of course. But then he'd catch it for spoiling his dinner. He'd wait.

Sometime later David awoke. "Mom? Dad? Mom? Dad?"

David tossed the cover aside and sat up. Impelled by the same obsession to keep tabs on each other he shared with his parents since Sophie's vanishing, David set out to scour the house. He slipped his iPhone from his pocket and chose his mom's cell number. Voice mail. He tried his dad's. Same thing. David headed for the kitchen where the magnetic board named "Mom's Memos" held family messages. The beginning of a shopping list curved outward beneath a red ladybug presuming a day like any other.

Dining room, laundry room, bathroom – the first floor was tidy as usual, his mother a 'neat freak,' as Matt called her. He glanced at the basement door, its lure substantial, a stutter step required to continue his path. He chuckled aloud, his love of horror flicks was messing with his mind.

Upstairs, he came first to his folks' bedroom, its king size bed neatly trimmed. The bathroom sparkled from the morning cleanup, save for a splat of toothpaste clinging to the faucet's side.

His father used the adjacent bedroom for an office, its closed portal signaling, "Do not disturb."

"Dad?" David entered, observing the roll top desk with its stacks of papers, stapler, and jade plant bordering a closed laptop computer. A black-meshed ergonomic chair—his dad's gift to himself—was slotted tidily in front.

After a peek into his room, David stepped across the hall to Sophie's. The door was shut, its normal position since the police investigation. They had dragged the lake, combed the woods, staked out Sophie's usual walking and biking paths, interviewed scores of friends and acquaintances, plus issued a nationwide amber alert, to no avail. Sophie, his twin, his other half was gone. Now, nearly two years distant, the unspoken assumption in his family was that she wouldn't return. He knew his mother went into Sophie's room from time to time—he could hear her from his—but his folks seldom mentioned Sophie, at least in front of him. He sorely wished they would, he thought it might help all of them move on. A trespasser now, David reverently entered the sanctum.

Sophie's room appeared as he remembered it. Covers askew, a book splayed spine-up at the bed's edge, a stuffed bear from Grandma Jenkins on the dresser, the previous day's clothes shed on the floor, nothing had changed, the room's air stale with dust, but mostly with absence. The large closet—why Sophie loved this room—overflowed its opened doors with clothes and shoes, anxious to be donned by a teenager seizing the day. A rocking chair and its blue corduroy seat cushion inhabited the corner. "To rock my babies," his mother had pronounced its origin. He imagined her sitting there on the occasions he'd heard her in Sophie's room, rocking, remembering, pondering, wishing, maybe praying, surely weeping.

He had to leave. There was one more place to investigate.

The light switch at the top of the basement staircase snapped solidly, its click echoing below. Mildewed dankness wafted past David. The tug, the same perception David experienced earlier, bore him down the steps, one by one, though he had no protest. A single lightbulb broadcast nothing unfamiliar. A workbench occupied the right corner, cluttered with tools used, returned, but not rehung on the pegboard. A sump pump and pit was on the left, its necessity accounting for the clammy air. The oil furnace sprang to life behind him. The water heater was back there, too. Because of his fear of spiders, he'd refused for many years to come here alone unless a parent stood at the top of the stairs. Reflexively, he checked the cobwebbed studs above, he could touch the ceiling if he wanted.

As a moment before, David was delivered to the wall opposite the bottom step, a portion of concrete no different from any other. He was pressed against it, not painfully, but awkwardly. He sought to step away, but couldn't. Able to raise his hands, he pushed against the gray pebbly, unfinished surface, without success.

Panicking, David took a deep breath and tried again, this time lurching forward, the wall vanishing, the force abating, a world of light beckoning.

Adjusting his eyes to the brilliance, David noticed a rocking chair enfolding a dark-haired girl in profile maintaining a rhythmic back and forth. "Excuse me?" David announced. Inching nearer, he cried, "Sophie! Sophie!" and lifted her from the chair, embracing her with famished arms. The splintered stickiness fixed to her face ground against his. Appraising her, David said, "Sophie, what happened?" He attempted to pick off the shards of hickory from her head's indented left side and vacant eye socket, but clots of blood cemented them.

Sophie's lips stretched into a tender smile, her right eye warming to him. "Sophie, what's going on? Where are we? Do Mom and Dad know you're here?"

"Help Mom and Dad let me go. All will be well," Sophie said. Then, patting his shoulder twice, she returned to the rocker and its back and forth, back and forth.

David slumped to his knees, then crumpled to the floor.

"David, time to wake up," his mother whispered above him. "Dinner's ready. How long have you been home?"

David opened his eyes, beholding only the cushion of the sofa not three inches away. A lamp positioned on the end table illumined the room. SportsCenter's theme music clarified the moment.

He squirmed to see the numbers on the cable box – 6:30. "I don't remember," he said.

"Well, go wash up," she said turning to leave.

"Where were you guys?" David asked.

"Out back, over at Henry Pearson's. He had a cord of wood delivered. He asked your dad to help him stack it. I was the supervisor," she said laughing. "Your dad's finishing up. That man sure goes through his hickory."

His mother stepped to the window. "Is that your bike on the front lawn? How many times have I told you not to leave it there? Go put it away like you're supposed to."

As David fumbled with a shoe, his mother fixed him with a stare. "My goodness, David! You've got blood on your face!"

TWISTED

TONY CONAWAY

"Mr. Cerkez, we have ten minutes left in our session. All you've told me so far is that you think that your favorite pizzeria has switched to an inferior brand of cheese. Do you think that you might answer a few questions?"

"Don't call me that. 'Mister Cerkez' was the son-of-a-bitch who my mother remarried. I'm not even Polish, or whatever he is."

"What should I call you?"

"The guys in my outfit called me 'Circus,' but you never served, so you don't get to call me that. Call me by my first name."

"All right. Waldo. How is your job going?"

I think for a moment. Should I tell him that I finally figured out why my boss hired me, why he puts up with me?

Should I tell this pencil-neck that Victor chose me because no one would believe me if I talked? People would assume it was the PTSD talking. Or the drugs, or the alcohol. Hey, I self-medicate to keep the demons away. That's the American way.

No, I decide. This egghead doesn't get to know that.

Instead, I just say, "Fine."

As I walk home from the shrink's office, I pass a few people who recognize me. No one wants to talk to me, of course. I get a bottle outta my pocket and dry-swallow a few pills. Soon I imagine that I can hear people's thoughts as I pass them.

"What a shame. He was such a nice, normal boy before he went off to war. Now he's completely changed."

"He drinks, he gets in fights, he gets arrested."

"That pretty girl he married left him, I hear she has a restraining order out against him."

I wonder if I should be mad at the way Victor uses me. But the truth is that he's the only one who'd give me a job.

"He used to be a very good auto mechanic. And now, why, I wouldn't trust him to wash my car!"

It starts to rain, and I wish I hadn't lost my driver's license. Or that the court would've allowed me to see a shrink who was closer to home. The shop is closer, so I head there, even though I'm off work today.

I am the one-and-only employee of Gilded Age Furniture. If we're open, it's either Victor or me at the counter. Or both. One straight guy, one gay. Neither one has much life outside the store.

I work as many hours as Victor will let me. It keeps me out of trouble.

For no good reason, I imagine how I would explain the secret of Gilded Age Furniture. If I was going to tell somebody. Which I'm not.

This is how Victor got the mirror:

It began with this big-ass mirror I liberated from this museum in Iraq. Victor had passed the word that he'd pay good money to anyone who could get it across the border into Jordan. Not Turkey, he said. "The Turks are inordinately possessive about their antiquities." Victor talks like that.

So I got it to Jordan, then to Lebanon, then onto a boat bound for home.

Turned out nobody even cared that much about the damn thing. It looked old, but the mirror part was too perfect. They didn't know how to make good mirrors back in the old days. So everyone figured it was a modern reproduction.

That's how I met Victor, getting him his mirror. A few ragheads died in the process. Boo-hoo. Do ya expect me to have sympathy for people who are shooting at me? Leaving IEDs in my path? Killing my buddies?

Not a chance.

This is what the mirror does:

First, Victor buys a painting with furniture in the background.

Then Victor places the painting so that it's reflected in the big mirror.

Then, somehow, Victor STEPS INTO the reflection of the painting. No, I don't now how the hell he does it. Victor says he doesn't know, either, he just does it.

Victor then removes the shit he wants from the painting, and brings it into our world.

My job is to grab the furniture as it emerges from the mirror, and pull it all the way into our world. A lot of this fancy shit is real delicate, you gotta make sure not to drop it. I've broken more than one piece that way. And I have to wear gloves because sometimes the furniture is warm, hot enough to burn you. But the gloves make me clumsy.

'Course, the furniture is reversed, since Victor is 'stealing' a mirror-image. You can't sell anything that's obviously reversed, say if it had writing on it.

But think about it: most furniture is the same reversed and not reversed. "Bilaterally symmetrical" is the word; I looked it up.

And even furniture that ain't symmetrical, we just say "it was made that way." Yeah, that school desk was made for a left-handed kid. That fainting couch was custom-built to sit to the right of a room's entrance, instead of to the left.

What the hell. It's a living. I don't have to understand how it's done.

And if a genie offered me the gift of knowledge, I wouldn't pick How does Victor do his mirror trick? I'd pick How can I get the goddam VA to put me on 100% disability?

As Victor is always reminding me, the shop doesn't have zero overhead just 'cause our stock comes out of a mirror. We got rent, electricity, water, taxes, and shit like that. And Victor has to buy the paintings, because they can't be seen again after we steal the furniture. There's too much chance that someone will notice that "Woman with Lorgnette" has somehow lost her chair, table, bureau, jewelry, and her lorgnette—whatever the hell a lorgnette is. So we burn the used paintings.

And not everything we sell is 'mirrored.' Victor says we hafta have a paper trail of 'real' items that we bought and sold. At least half of our stock comes to us… 'conventionally,' is how he puts it.

Is all the stuff we buy legit? I'd bet against it, especially the small, easy-to-steal shit. But Victor checks the Hot Sheet on the computer, and anything that's listed as stolen gets turned into the cops. Good Citizen Victor, that's him.

Finally, there's the stuff that comes through wrong.

Usually, it's 'cause the artist is lousy. Usually. The item looks okay when you see it in the painting. But something—usually the perspective—is off when you get it in front of you, in the real world. Victor calls those his 'Cabinet of Doctor Caligari' items, which is a reference to an old German movie that puts me to sleep every time I try to watch it. All's I can tell you is that it's 'Expressionist'—whatever that means—and that it uses 'forced perspective' to look weird. Oh, and it's in black and white, it's silent, and there's no hot babe taking her clothes off. So I ain't interested.

Victor is the smart one in the store. He went to college, and was a reservist. I was regular Army. He was doing clerical work while I was away in the Big Sand, getting what brains I had addled.

It's a hot, humid Wednesday morning when Victor comes to me and says, "Tomorrow is the Fourth of July. We're closed. Any plans, Waldo?"

"You know I don't."

"Well, Caligari's Cabinet is getting full. What say we load up the truck and celebrate the Fourth with a barbecue and a big bonfire?'

"Long as we're away from fireworks, I'm there."

So, next morning, we pull the pickup over to the loading dock and start putting twisted furniture into it. We're closed for the Fourth, so no customers come in to bother us. It takes all morning to load up, partly because Victor hasta re-examine each item to see if there's any way to save it. We get a shitload of chairs, tables, and bureaus that are just a little off. Sometimes we can make them sellable if we can make their legs even, so they'll stand without rocking.

The other reason it takes forever is that Victor wants to make only one trip with the truck, but he wants it loaded with as much shit as possible. So every item hasta be placed just so in the truck bed, so's it'll all fit it in. And it takes Victor forever to figure out how all the shit should be arranged.

Meanwhile, it's hot as hell and twice as humid. I'm getting mad, while Victor just flits around, lookin' at this and that.

Finally, Victor points to a huge armoire in the back of the truck and says, "I'm afraid that we'll have to move that out. The only way we can get this big table in is to put it behind the armoire, standing up against the back of the cab."

That's when I freakin' lose it. I cuss Victor out and stomp off, looking for a drink.

Without a car, I'm lookin' for a bar within walking distance. Specifically, I'm lookin' for a bar in walking distance that I'm still allowed in. And open on the Fourth of July, which ain't easy to find.

I end up in a dive called the Paddock. I'm banned from there, too, but they had a new bartender, and they must'a forgot to tell him that I'm not welcome anymore. The new guy has no idea who I am, and none of the regulars rat me out. This is a gambler's bar, and most of the regulars have their nose buried in their Daily Racing Forms, trying to pick a winner.

Me, I just want to get out of the heat and have a cold beer.

After the third beer, I've cooled off enough to relax. I look around at the dingy walls of the bar.

And that's when I notice the paintings.

Some of them are what you'd expect. Dogs playing poker. Some Norman Rockwell thing with people saluting.

And a rainbow ending in a pot o' gold.

I got no need for a dog, card-player or not. Since my brain injuries, I'm a lousy card player. If I got beaten at cards by a dog, I guarantee there'd be one dead dog.

And I had enough saluting to last a lifetime.

But, I wondered, why were we doing the mirror trick on furniture when we could be doing it on gold coins? We hardly even take jewelry, and it's always small stuff.

I spend a few minutes thinkin' about how I could maybe steal that picture off the wall. Then I realized I didn't need to.

'Cause I had one at home, on my bedroom wall. A calendar with a picture of a bag of gold coins.

When I got home, I went to the calendar. That's when I realized that it wasn't really a calendar… it was a painting of a calendar! Maybe it was some sort of weird, Andy Warhol-ish painting of a calendar—is he the guy who paints panels of comic strips? Or maybe it was what Victor calls a still life, which is when an artist paints what's in his studio, without real people—I think.

It featured a half-dressed girl in a pirate outfit, holding a bag of gold coins. How I forgot the girl, I don't know. The calendar promoted some kinda flavored rum that I don't drink. I was sure I hadn't bought it… it was on the wall when I rented this apartment. There are a lot of artists in this neighborhood, and a lot of paintings for sale at outdoor markets. I'm sure I only kept it 'cause of the picture of the girl.

I was antsy and couldn't sleep, so I decided to act. I took the picture off the wall, checked three times to make sure I had keys to both my apartment and to work, and headed out into the hot, humid, Fourth of July night.

Victor was gone, of course. I expect that he hired some local teens to help him unload the truckload of furniture. The big table we argued over was still there, just inside the loading dock doors. He wouldn't be back until tomorrow.

I put the calendar painting on an easel and positioned it so the mirror caught it, just the way Victor did it.

Now came the hard part. I'd watched Victor step into the mirror dozens of times. But I never did it myself. All's I could do was imitate how he did it.

Turned out, it worked.

Don't ask me how. I just stepped into the mirror like it was... I guess a waterfall is the best description. Because something was happening at the barrier, and it felt like it was something that could carry you away if you didn't step lively.

So there I was, in the painting. Only now it was real as any photograph.

There was a nice sunset in the distance, over a calm ocean.

There was a palm tree overhead and sand under my feet.

And there was the girl with the gunny sack of gold coins. She was holding it so the mouth of the bag was open, showing a half-dozen coins. Several spilled out into the sand as I gently worked the sack free from her hands.

The sack was tremendously heavy with the gold, and I wondered how it hadn't ripped. Or, for that matter, how she even held it up.

But she was a big girl, as tall as I am. Plenty of muscles under all that beautiful flesh.

First things first, I thought. Get the gold back home.

I carried it to the barrier. The sack was so heavy that the best I could do was swing it in larger and larger arcs until, when I let go, it'd pass through.

Which it did.

Then I went back and knelt at the girl's feet and searched for the spilled coins.

The picture on the calendar was always at sunset. But here, inside the mirror, the sun was actually setting. Soon it was almost dark, and I had to feel for the coins in the sand.

I got as many as I could before the sun disappeared. It's like that, in the tropics. One minute it's light, the next it's full dark.

I was standing there, pockets sagging from gold coins, next to one of the most beautiful women I'd ever imagined. Or a mannequin of one. Yeah, I know the word. Victor puts mannequins on the furniture in our show window.

The stars were giving me just enough light to see her outline. Her only imperfection was a small, Y-shaped scar on her left cheek. Aside from that, she was perfect. Better than real. She had tits that could not be believed. As big as they were, they jutted straight out. Not like some cheap boob job, either. They looked like they naturally sat that way.

The closest I can come to describing her rack is from this artsy movie I saw on cable—before they shut it off for non-payment. It was called The Dreamers, directed by Bernardo somebody, and it was basically this three-character movie. This American boy was visiting Paris in the 1960s during some riots. He hooks up with this French boy and girl who live in this huge apartment and walk around naked all the time. The girl is played by a very young Eva Green, who later played a James Bond Girl when that series was rebooted. And the naked Eva Green has tits to die for. I mean, my ex-wife told me about this pencil test that women use to decide if they need to wear a bra. Eva Green has huge tits yet would pass the pencil test.

And this girl—the Pirate Queen, I named her—had better tits than Eva Green.

So, of course, I gave them a feel. Any straight guy would. Hell, even Victor probably would.

What did I expect? I figured that she must be stiff, like a plastic mannequin.

I never expected her tits to feel real. They moved. They were warm. And I swear I heard her take a breath.

So I knew I hadta bug out. I got the gold, time to go!

I was almost through the barrier when a hand came out of the dark and grabbed me.

I screamed. Who wouldn't?

So I jumped.

But the hand didn't let go of my arm.

Off balance, I fell forward. I hit the floor of the shop, face-first. I don't know if I knocked myself out, or just fainted.

But can you blame me?

I dreamt I was back in the Big Sand, where it was hot all the time.

I dreamt that someone was pulling my pants off.

Then someone threw a bucket of cold water over my crotch. That woke me up.

I open my eyes and see the Pirate Queen standing over me, holding a bucket. A reversed Pirate Queen, the Y-shaped scar was now on her right cheek.

Oh, and she was naked. And wet. It looked like those big metal buttons on her pirate coat had singed her, so she took it off and poured water over herself from the sink.

We were back in Gilded Age Furniture. I was lying on the floor, soaked, with my pants off.

Then she spoke. Her first words to me were, "Your trousers were on fire. I took them off."

And I realized three things:

The store was full of smoke.

The store alarm was ringing.

And my thighs hurt! The pain was just getting started, but it was getting worse by the second.

Then I heard the front door open, and someone turned off the alarm. Pirate Queen heard it too, and stepped back, out of sight in the dark and the smoke. A moment later, Victor stepped into the back room, holding a gun. He lives just two blocks away.

It only took a moment for Victor to figure out it was me, lying on the floor in the smoky back room.

"Jesus, Waldo. What, did you fall asleep while smoking and set your pants on fire?"

"I… I burned myself."

"Are you dying?"

"Just hurtin'."

"Then I'm going to open the loading dock door and let the smoke out. Then we can see the damage."

He pushed the button, and the big door rolled up. He also turned some more lights on. "I see you opened some windows. Did you forget that would set off the alarm?"

The day had been still and hot, but a storm was supposed to come through before dawn, and there was a cool breeze now. It started sucking the smoke out, pretty quick.

As the smoke cleared, the naked Pirate Queen became visible from where she had hidden. She stepped forward and announced in a strong voice, "I opened the windows. I knew not of your alarm. I beg your forgiveness."

Victor just stared at her for a minute. When he finally spoke, he said, "Blow me rigid!"

Which is kinda an odd thing for a gay guy to say to a naked Pirate Queen.

"You should go to the E.R.," Victor said to me. He'd gotten out the First Aid kit and sprayed burn ointment on my thighs. I had burns where my pockets had been – where the gold coins were.

"I'll be all right," I insisted.

"Okay. Look, Waldo. There are at least two reasons I don't bring gold coins through the mirror."

"First off, there is the heat effect. You know the furniture comes through warm. Any metal parts on the furniture are even hotter. Metal conducts heat better than wood. So, when you brought gold coins through, they were almost hot enough to set the store on fire. As it was, they scorched the floor and raised all this smoke. And the ones in your pocket burned you."

"No, I don't know why things come through hot. This mirror didn't come with an instruction manual. I just read about what it could do in an old book. But I know that everything on the planet has inertial momentum because the planet is spinning. And, if you could somehow teleport an object from a different place on the planet, you'd also have to deal with its momentum. Like, imagine you grabbed something that was moving at fifty miles an hour faster than you were. It might tear itself out of your grasp and smash against the wall. Or the energy might express itself in heat. Wherever our mirrored furniture comes from, I'm convinced it's from a spinning planet like this one."

That's when Victor saw that I wasn't getting any of this.

"Okay, forget that part. Now, the second reason we don't go for coins—and I don't know how you could forget this—is that they're reversed, your idiot! You know coins have lettering on them! When they came through, the lettering was reversed. You can't sell them!"

"Oh. I forgot. So they're worthless?"

"I didn't say that. They can be melted down, and the gold sold. But believe me, they'd be worth much more as three-hundred-year-old coins, than refashioned as gold ingots. So I have a guy who will do it, no questions asked. But he'll take a hefty percentage."

"Melting down gold doesn't sound that tough. Why can't we do it?"

"It's not just making ingots out of coins, Waldo! What do you do next? You need connections to sell gold. My guy is a registered, bonded, dealer in precious metals. So I'll take the coins to him, and we'll have the money for them in a week. He'll even pay us in cash, off the books. Let's hope he's not away on vacation."

"Us? I'm the one who got burned."

"In my store! That you nearly set on fire! Using my mirror! I get a cut."

"Yeah. Okay. I just wanna go home and soak my thighs in a tub full o' ice."

"And what about Ilsa, the Amazon Warrior Queen? You don't touch humans or livestock in the mirror world. It brings them to life."

I'd actually forgotten the Pirate Queen. We looked around.

But she was gone.

All summer, we've been gradually repainting Gilded Age Furniture, and I'd left my painting clothes there. So I had some paint-stained trousers to walk home in.

My burned thighs were hurting, and I was finally tired. I'd helped Victor clean up, and scraped the hot coins off the floor using a snow shovel that hadn't been touched since last winter. The still-hot coins went into an antique metal coal bucket, something Victor called a coal scuttle. I have a lot of terms for antiques rattling around in my head, but that was a new one on me.

It was long after midnight, and the cold front was making it chilly. I'd worn a tee-shirt today, but now I'd added the long-sleeve shirt I used to keep paint off me. I pulled it tight around me to keep warm.

I had plenty to occupy my mind, but all I could think about was What happened to the Pirate Queen? We looked throughout the store but never found her. Either she slipped out through the loading dock bay while Victor was yammering away, or she found some way to go back where she came from.

I stopped under a streetlight and looked at the image she— and the gold—came from. I'd insisted on taking it back, despite Victor's protests. I wanted to see if the Pirate Queen reappeared in the picture.

As I looked down at the painting, I saw it was still empty. It still had the images of a palm tree, a beach, the ocean and a sunset. But no gold coins. No Pirate Queen.

Then, as I raised my eyes from the painting, I saw her. The Pirate Queen, big as life. Standing under the light of the streetlamp, looking at me.

Apparently, the parts of her clothes trimmed with metal were not wearable. She was dressed only in her thigh-high leather boots. There was a large towel from the store's bathroom wrapped around her. And one of those goofy triangular hats like they wore back in the American Revolution.

She stood there, shivering in the cold. And I thought, if I live to be a hundred, I'll never see anything more erotic.

So gave her my paint-stained shirt to wear. And I invited her back to my apartment.

I mean, could you have done anything else? An almost-nude goddess, wearing only boots and a hat, trying to hide her nakedness with a too-small towel?

I spent the walk back with my arm around her, trying to keep her warm. She was almost as tall as I am. I always found a woman wearing a man's shirt sexy. It's something they do after you screw, instead of getting dressed, they put on something of yours.

And the Pirate Queen was so tall that the bottom of her ass stuck out of the bottom of my shirt. I couldn't see that from my position, holding her close to me. But you can be damn sure I looked at her reflection in every store window we passed.

And yes, I was trying to figure out how to get her to bang me.

That turned out not to be a problem. Inside my tiny crib, she immediately doffed her boots, towel, shirt and hat and jumped into my bed.

She got under the covers and said, "I'm still cold. Join me."

It was the best time I'd had since I'd got back home from the Big Sand, five years ago.

We screwed like animals. We screwed for hours. I forgot my burns, forgot my tiredness. We finally fell asleep after dawn. A few hours later we awoke again and screwed some more. She was everything a red-blooded American boy could want: completely uninhibited, experienced, and constantly horny.

Eventually, we had to eat. I didn't want to leave, so I ordered out, both Chinese and pizza. And we drank up every bottle of beer I had in the place.

I didn't have to worry about going into work. The place reeked of smoke, and Victor didn't expect any business on Fourth of July weekend, so he'd told me to stay home. He was going in to air out the shop over the weekend and do some paperwork.

Sometime in mid-afternoon, she got up and went to the bathroom. It was bright daylight—the rainstorm had come and gone—but she had no hesitation about walking around naked.

All of a sudden, the thought occurred to me: how the hell does a chick from the 17th century—or whenever—know how to operate a modern toilet? Or a sink for that matter?

The toilet flushed, the sink turned on and off, and she emerged, smiling. She went into the kitchen area—my crib is basically one big room, except for the bathroom and two closets. She picked up a slice of cold pizza and asked, "One of these machines heats food, yes?"

I just nodded. I wanted to see what she'd do.

She got a blank look on her face, then smiled again. "Yes! A micro-wave machine!" She opened my microwave—it has an obvious handle—and put her slice of pizza inside.

"Wait!" I joined her by the kitchen appliances. "Two things you need to know about the microwave. One, you can't put anything metal inside it. And two, it's shit at heating bread. Pizza's basically cheese and tomato sauce on bread. So we'll have to use the oven."

I opened the oven door and pulled out the metal tray I keep inside. I know, you expected a screw-up like me to live in chaos. But one of the few things the Army and I agree on is that life is easier when you're squared away. I make my bed with hospital corners, I roll my undershorts into a cylinder, and I keep my place neat.

As her pizza slice warmed, I asked her, "How did you even know what a microwave does?"

"What my creator knew, I know. But I have to… what would be the right word… access that information. I clear my thoughts of everything except what I want to know, and it is as if my creator speaks to me."

"Your creator?" I'm not religious, and I hoped she wasn't, either. And I hoped like hell that she wasn't… whaddayacallit… omniscient!

"The artist who painted me. And be thankful it was a woman, so that you will not have to explain to me the use of a Tampon!"

"Um. What did you use… back when? Where you came from?"

"I always lived by the sea, so sea sponges were easy to come by. What women who lived far inland use, I know not. Cloth, I reckon. I look forward to using many of your future conveniences!"

From the smell, her pizza was ready. I used an oven mitt to take the tray out, scraped the slice off the tray with a spatula, and put it on a plate for her. She watched everything I did.

"It'll be hot," I warned her. "Do you want some cold water? We drank everything else up."

"Water? Safe to drink?"

"Here, in this country, yes. As long as it comes out of a faucet, like this." I filled a glass with cold water while she blew on her pizza.

While her pizza cooled, she gave me a damp-eyed look and said, "Waldo, I have nothing here, not even clothes. I am at your mercy. Will you give me coin, that I might buy what I need?"

"Sure. I'm not rich, but I just got paid. There ought to be some stores open. We can shop for clothes today if you want."

"I do not even have women's clothes to wear to a shopkeeper. What excuse will I give?"

"Easy. Tell anyone who asks that the airline lost all your luggage, so you have to replace everything. They'll believe that."

She paused with the slice halfway to her mouth and got that blank look again. This time, it lasted for over a minute.

"Yes," she said when she came out of it. "Airlines, ships of the air. Marvelous." She took a big bite and smiled while she chewed. "Airlines. Pizza. Tampons. Yours is a world of wonders!"

"That's what our politicians keep telling us," I said. But something about all this was starting to worry me. I put it down to being sober, I hadn't taken any pills since last night, and we'd run out of beer hours ago.

I should've realized that I could never get this lucky.

She may have been nearly my height, but that didn't mean that my clothes would fit her. After some searching, we found that she could wear a workout outfit of mine. She could pull the sweat pants high over her hips and tighten the drawstring enough to keep them up.

She needed footwear, too. Last night I noticed that she had to keep tugging on her boots to keep them from falling down. In the light, I could see that she'd ripped the metal buckles from them, so there was nothing to hold them up.

Fortunately, it was summer. Flip-flops are pretty much one-size-fits-all.

We were about to head out the door when I realized that I still didn't know her name. When we were in bed, I'd taken to calling her "my Pirate Queen" or "my Queen." That seemed to amuse her, but she didn't offer another name.

But I was about to blow my paycheck on this chick, so I figured I was entitled to a name.

"Clotilda," she offered when I asked her. "Is that a common name here?"

"No, not really. And it would attract attention. People would ask questions. Do you have a nickname? A short form of your name?"

"Clo."

"Also not common. What about 'Chloe'? It's spelled differently, but—"

"Clo-ey?! That's a name for a mewling virgin! A cringing slave, fearful of kittens and shadows of kittens!"

"Okay, okay. Look, I've been calling you 'Queen,' why don't we just stick with that? 'Queen' or 'Queenie.'"

"Is that not conspicuous?"

"Nah. It worked for Dana Owens, it'll work for you."

"Who?"

"A singer named Queen Latifa. Her real name was Dana Owens. My ex-wife was a fan, and played her music all the time."

"As you wish."

Shopping with Queenie was weird. We constantly ran into things that didn't exist in her time, like Spandex or zippers or Velcro. She'd have to zone out for a minute until her maker's voice explained it. But once she understood it, she was often enthusiastic.

And who wouldn't be thrilled by elastic? Her people had to tie or hook or button or buckle everything for it to stay in place. Imagine underpants without elastic, that you had to tie onto your shirt for it to stay up!

Her shopping habits were typically female: she wanted to see everything. If she hadn't kept bringing me into the fitting rooms with her so I can see her naked, I would've left after the first hour.

Thankfully, the stores eventually closed, and we lugged a dozen shopping bags back to my car. I still had the car; I just don't have a license to drive anymore.

I hadn't gotten much sleep last night, and my burns were aching. I figured that I'd go straight to sleep, but she wanted to bang as soon as we got home.

And who was I to say no?

We banged like mad minks all weekend, stopping only to sleep or eat. When Monday morning rolled around, I wondered how she'd manage in the apartment without me. But she said not to worry, so I left for work.

I taught her the basics of using a laptop. Like all American soldiers, I used a computer. In addition to using them in our official duties, we used email to talk with our relatives back home.

I used to do that. But my folks are dead now, and my ex won't talk to me. I don't really have many people to email nowadays. I used to play video games, but since the brain injury, they give me a headache. Mostly I use my computer for downloading porn.

The truth was, I went to work because I needed the break. I never thought you could have too much sex, but she was severely testing my stamina.

The shop still smelled of smoke, but it was bearable. Summer is usually a slow time for us, but we had a steady stream of customers, enough to make the day move faster. That was a help to me since I hadn't even gotten buzzed once that day.

If for no other reason than because Queenie was spending most of my paycheck, I was cutting back on drugs and alcohol. Not completely, mindyou, but significantly.

Victor asked me if I'd seen the Pirate Queen. I told him no.

"Well, perhaps humans can't continue to exist if they come through the mirror into our world. I'm sure it's happened before. I'll see if there's any information on that in the old books."

"Fine," I said. Having Victor off poking around in the Rare Book Section of the Main Library would help keep him out of my hair.

I picked up some Vietnamese takeout on the way home. But I didn't rush home as fast as I could've. What was wrong with me? The hottest woman I'd ever screwed was waiting for me back in my place!

When I opened the door to my apartment, I found her naked on the sofa, watching television… and playing with my gun. I keep it in a locked case on the top shelf in my closet, but apparently, she'd gone through everything I owned.

She smiled when I came in. "Waldo! So much I have learned today." She raised my Glock pistol in the air. "This is a modern pistol, yes? I saw it used on your television dramas. My creator knew little of such weapons."

Gently, I took it away from her. Glocks are especially dangerous to play with since they don't have a safety. I checked; it was loaded but had not been fired.

"Yes, this is a modern pistol. And very dangerous. I will teach you how to use it properly, but you must not use it until then."

"Good. Show me now."

I sighed. What I really needed was to get stupid with alcohol and drugs. But all I had was a six-pack of beer and a bag of rice and pho.

"I brought food. First, we eat before it gets cold." I looked at the clock. It was early July, so the sun doesn't set until almost nine. "Then we can go to the range, a place where firing a weapon like this is permitted."

"There you will teach me to use this gun of the hand?"

"Yes."

"Good. All modern weapons I wish to learn. First, we eat, then we employ weapons, then we bang."

Well, at least her word choice was less weird. She was saying 'bang' instead of 'swive.' I suppose that was progress.

By Friday of that first week I'd discovered a number of things about Queenie; she wasn't just insatiable in bed. She had an insatiable desire to learn. She'd made me go get a library card, and she used it to take out entire stacks of books.

She was a born flirt. She pouted until I took her out, then flirted—or worse—with any man when my back was turned. One time in a bar when I went to the men's room, I heard a couple screwing in the women's room next door as I was leaving. I looked all over for Queenie but couldn't find her. On a hunch, I checked the ladies' room. And there she was, getting banged by the bartender, her ass on a sink.

She loved violence. She loved shooting anything; guns, rifles, bows and arrows. She threw a punch at the drop of a hat. The bars that had banned me had let me back in, seeing that I was with a gorgeous woman. She quickly got us banned again.

And after lunch on Friday I discovered something else. After I ate my sandwich, I went to the bathroom at the shop. When I tried to piss it felt like I had barbed wire in my dick. She'd given me the clap.

Victor gave me the afternoon off to take care of it. I didn't tell him who gave it to me. I stomped home, furious. But she wasn't in the apartment. I waited around for a few minutes—and changed into a clean pair of Jockey shorts—then headed out. She was coming up the stairs as I was going out.

I grabbed her by the arm and dragged her back out into the street.

"I can't believe you! You gave me the clap! A… disease of the dick!"

She shrugged. That wasn't the reaction I was expecting.

"I was a whore. All whores are poxed. What did you expect?"

"What? You were… I thought you were a Pirate Queen!"

That made her laugh. "A woman, leading a pirate ship? How would that happen? Rough men, following the lead of a female? No, I had advanced as far as a woman can go. I was a whore, then what you call a madam, if you like, Queen of the Whores, and finally, the lover of a great pirate captain. I influenced him, yes, but men would never follow me."

"And you never thought to tell me you had this pox?"

"Most of the men I swived had the pox as well. I assumed you did, too."

"Even if I did, I could've had a different venereal disease, or a different strain—"

But she had stopped to zone out again. Modern medicine must have been another thing she didn't understand.

The blankness ended, and she shook herself. "I am sorry. My creator was not expert in these things. You must teach me."

"Jesus! What I'm going to do right now is take both of us down to the Free Clinic and get us some antibiotic shots! That will take care of gonorrhea or syphilis."

"You can cure the pox? There was no cure in my time!"

"We can cure some kinds of pox. Just pray that we don't have AIDS or herpes. There is… medicine for them, but the medicine only helps. It does not cure."

"Many things I must learn," she said for the hundredth time.

Thank God for Free Clinics, who treat anyone, whether or not they have ID. All you have to do is fill out a questionnaire and donate whatever you can afford.

Queenie became excited when she read that question that asked if you were a prostitute. She asked, "Are there whores here? Which ones are the whores?"

It was a Friday afternoon, and the waiting room was only half-full. I wasn't easy to embarrass, but I never had to point out whores in a waiting room before.

There were two girls dressed as prostitutes in the corner. I whispered, "Those two blondes over there are probably whores, but—"

That was all she needed. Queenie was up and crouched in front of the two slutty blondes, bringing her face down to their level. "Hello. I, too, am a whore. I am from far away and have many questions. May I buy you food or drink whilst I learn from you?"

I put my head in my hands. When I was on my tours of Iraq and Afghanistan, they gave us all sorts of lectures about how to deal with the natives. They never covered anything like this, though.

After that, things got darker.

The Free Clinic cured both Queenie and me. The 400-year-old strain of pox she gave us couldn't stand up to modern antibiotics. She learned about making men use condoms, which was good... because I soon figured out, she wasn't just flirting with other guys. She was turning tricks while I was at work.

And she'd started to buy things. Books on everything; medicine, history, navigation, warfare, science. Add these to the stacks of library books—none returned to the library—and my apartment started to look like a bookstore.

Make that 'my apartment looked like the Texas Book Depository,' because there were weapons there as well as books. She'd gotten her own pistol. She'd met someone who knew someone who sold guns illegally, without ID she couldn't legally buy it herself. She had several modern bows of various types, and reams of arrows. She even got a bulletproof vest, designed for a female.

How did she pay for all this? Hookers make a lot of money, as long as they don't give it to a pimp.

I complained about her whoring several times, but she always responded the same way, by screwing my brains out. I had to admit, it was hard to put my objection into words after a marathon sex session.

Victor's research hadn't led to anything conclusive. "All I've found," he said, "are warnings against bringing through any living thing, human or animal, through the mirror. It never seems to end well."

"That's it?"

"Isn't that enough? Even small, usually harmless animals are said to turn bad. Flocks of sheep killing their shepherds. Birds pecking out eyes. That sort of thing."

"Right. No sheep, no birds, no bunnies. Just furniture."

"Oh," he added, as he opened up the office safe. "The cash for those gold coins came through. Your cut is over six thousand dollars. I hope it makes up for the burns."

I opened the envelope he handed me and gazed at the bills. I hadn't held this much cash in my hand in years.

"Try to spend it wisely, Waldo. Better yet, put it in the bank."

"Right," I said.

"Good," Queenie said when I brought home the envelope of cash. "I need two thousand."

"What? What could you possibly spend two thousand on? And aren't you earning enough? You must be making three times what I am?"

"I can show you if you wish. In fact, I would prefer that you come with me, so I am sure that I am paying a fair price and not cheated." She put her shoes on and her fanny pack. She thought that carrying a purse was an absurd bother. "Let's go. We need to take the car."

But our destination was only a few blocks away, in a loft neighborhood populated by artists.

Queenie pounded on a door at a loft. Someone buzzed us in, and we went up two flights of stairs.

She entered a door without knocking. I followed.

"Tilda, baby! If I'd known it was you, I'd have my pants off already! I... oh."

A fifty-something guy dressed all in black was inside, obviously surprised to see me. There were canvases all over the place. An artist's studio.

Queenie—'Tilda?' I hadn't thought to get 'Tilda' out of 'Clotilda'—was all business. "Gunther, is the painting I commissioned done? I need it."

Gunther waved at a large canvas on an easel. "Yes, yes. Just as you specified."

She went over to the easel, which had a large coffee-table book open next to it, sitting atop a small table. I joined her. The book was open to a seaport town, a ramshackle collection of weathered wooden buildings—shacks really—built atop piers in a harbor. Several of them were crossed out with a marker pen. I'd already learned that Queenie was no respecter of books.

The painting reproduced that picture, minus the crossed-out buildings. Since the missing buildings appeared to be newer, it looked like Queenie had commissioned a painting of a harbor the way it was, presumably, in her time.

"Yes, it's done," Queenie said. "Waldo, you need to pay. How much do we still owe, Gunther?"

"Uh, two-thousand."

This is what she'd brought me along for. Well, I'd bargained with more than a few raghead merchants in the Big Sand. I wasn't going to give Gunther his money without trying to beat him down.

"Two-thousand seems an awful lot for this, Gunther. Especially since it's right out of a photo. I could've scanned it in and erased the old buildings with Photoshop."

"Well, the painting is just seven-hundred. The rest is the mirror that Tilda asked me to order for her. It includes an extra hundred for shipping."

"Mirror?"

"Something I found with your computer, Waldo. It was on display in a gallery that also displays Gunther's painting. I hoped that Gunther could get it for a good price."

I'd planned to get all alpha dog about Gunther obviously banging my Queenie, and use that to get him to lower the price. But this mirror shit blew that strategy right out of my head.

I ended up paying the full two-grand. At least Gunther helped us load our shit into the car. The painting he did weighed nothing, but the mirror was big, old and heavy, although not as big as the mirror I'd stolen in Iraq.

As usual, Queenie calmed my anger by screwing my brains out.

We lay in each other's arms, recovering. In one way Queenie was like most women—she never shut up.

"Waldo, you disapprove of my whoring, yes?"

"Of course."

"But you were a soldier. You knew many whores, did you not?"

"Well, yeah. It's something a lot of soldiers do when you're far from home. Especially when you're deployed… uh, at war."

"It was always thus. What did you ask your whores to do? I will do it."

"Uh, you're doing everything I want, Queenie. The only thing we're not doing isn't something you can do."

"How so?"

"I suppose you'd call it humiliating my whores. I didn't really do anything… it was just that they had to be whoring."

"Because… they were women of good character, yet circumstances forced them to whore?"

"Yeah, that's part of it. Muslim women, supposed to be so chaste, covering themselves up. And the war… many families had to flee. In Iraq, especially. Whole families would flee over the border to Jordan, and suddenly they had no money. So one woman would have to become a whore to support the entire family."

I sat up and looked away. "And I can't tell you how much we came to hate them, the Iraqis. We got sent over there to help them in their hot, miserable country. And when they're not shooting each other, they're trying to kill us. So banging their women, that was one way to get back at them."

I looked back at her, but she had fallen asleep. I got up quietly. I didn't like thinking about the war. Yeah, I did some bad things, things I'd regret if I thought about them too much. So I didn't think about the war. But Queenie's questions brought it back to me.

I was keeping plenty of beer in the apartment now. I padded over to the kitchen area, sat naked on the floor, and went through a six-pack, draining bottle after bottle. Then I worked my way through most of another six-pack before I fell asleep.

>◇< >◇< >◇<

I was getting seriously creeped out, and it wasn't just because of memories of the war.

For the first time in my life, I hung around work after my shift was over. I didn't want to go home. Even getting the best sex of my life wasn't inducement enough.

"You're looking strung-out, Waldo. Go home and get some sleep." Victor shook his head sadly.

"I'm doing less drugs than ever, Victor. It's just…"

But I couldn't tell Victor that the missing Pirate Queen had spent the past month at my place. I'd been lying to him for so long, it didn't feel right.

"It's going to be a hot August. Dog days. It wears on all of us, Waldo. I'm going to close up the store, now."

"Yeah. Well, I've got AC at home. I guess I'll head there."

>◇< >◇< >◇<

I was soaked with sweat by the time I walked home. Maybe I should've taken the car, after all.

I had my own parking space, it came with the apartment. As I approached my building, I was surprised to find that my car was jammed full of gear. Clothes, books, backpacks, that mirror and the painting were all in the back seat.

And if those valuables were in the open, in back, what was in the trunk?

The weapons, I was sure.

Was Queenie leaving me? That wasn't the worst news in the world. But she didn't know how to drive!

She couldn't have secretly learned, could she?

She must have been watching out the window because she met me coming down the steps.

"Come, Waldo. We have an errand to execute."

"Run. Errand to run. And I'm tired. I just want to go to bed."

"This is needful. We need to go to the drugstore. Medicines I must have. You would not deny me medicine, would you?"

"What, you have a prescription? Where would you… no, don't tell me. We'll go to the drugstore, and then I'm going to bed."

We piled into the car. I didn't even bother to ask why there was so much gear in the car. She didn't offer to tell me.

DeHaven's Drugs was just a little too far to walk in this heat, so it made sense that she wanted me to drive her. It was one of the oldest drugstores in the city, in the same family for four generations. It actually had an old, unused soda fountain against one wall, from back when drugstores had such things.

I parked outside and followed Queenie inside. I didn't ask why she was wearing a windbreaker in this heat, or why she had a backpack on.

We walked inside. There was only one customer in the store, talking to Mr. DeHaven IV behind the prescription counter.

Queenie walked right up to the counter, pulled out her gun, and shot the customer through the head.

I shouted something. I don't remember what.

Then Queenie turned her gun on Mr. DeHaven.

"You have many drugs back there. We want them."

DeHaven raised his hands. "Sure," he stammered. "Oh, God!"

Queenie jumped up on the counter and slid down next to him. "Back up," she ordered. Then she doffed her backpack and put it on the counter. It was almost empty; all it contained was another backpack—empty—and my Glock.

She handed the Glock to me. "Stand guard," she ordered me.

I was too stunned to protest.

She filled up one backpack with drugs. Her choices confused Mr. DeHaven. "Those aren't narcotics," he noted. "They're just antibiotics. You killed a man, just to steal antibiotics?"

"Fine," she said. "Fill the rest of the bag with narcotics. And I want every condom and Tampon in the store in the other backpack. Now!"

The whole thing took less than three minutes. We were back out the door with our loot in four, and roaring away in my car in five.

"You know that there are security cameras in every drugstore. They know you shot that man. The police will be hunting you… both of us!"

"All is well, Waldo."

"What? How can you say that? Where are we going?"

"Back to the shop, of course. Quickly!"

When we arrived at Gilded Age Furniture, Queenie directed me to park out back near the loading dock. I used my key and opened the loading dock door.

"Everything inside, Waldo! Every bag, every item!'

We each went back and forth a dozen times, carrying the gear. We only slowed down to be careful when we carried the big mirror in. As I'd guessed, the trunk was full of weapons, but no guns. It only had weapons made of something other than metal: fiberglass bows, wooden staffs, shit like that.

"The police will come here as soon as they identify us, Queenie. We can't get away."

"We have no choice now. We will escape through the mirror, and go back to whence I came."

It was hard to think. I didn't want to live in some primitive, low-tech time. That would be like living in Afghanistan squared. But I didn't see any choice. With my record, the cops wouldn't believe that I hadn't been involved voluntarily.

The big mirror I'd stolen in Iraq was in its usual place. To my surprise, Queenie didn't put the painting she'd commissioned in front of it, as we did. Instead, she put the new mirror in front. The painting was angled so its reflection first caught the new mirror, then was reflected in the big Iraq mirror.

A reflection of a reflection. The image in the Iraqi mirror was no longer reversed.

She started tossing the gear into the mirror. Backpacks of medicines, books, weapons, all sorts of stuff. It went through the surface of the Iraqi mirror as easily as if you were dropping things into water.

"Help me," she said. I got up and started tossing gear in. In a few minutes it was all inside.

"Now come, Waldo. There is no choice. Come with me, or spend the rest of your life in prison."

When you put it like that…

We stepped into the big mirror. This time, it felt different.

It was dark in the port city where Queenie came from. I could smell the salt of the sea, and hear the tide and the squeaking of the piers as they flexed.

But something was wrong. I felt different.

It wasn't Queenie in front of me. The shadowy figure was too tall, too broad. It turned, and I saw it was a muscular man, bearded, with a cruel face. He was a foot taller than I was.

Then the moon came out from behind a cloud and illuminated his face. He had a Y-shaped scar on his cheek.

It was Queenie. Or had been. Now she was a Pirate King.

I had a terrible suspicion of why I felt wrong. I put my hands on my chest. Breasts. I had two breasts! And my hair, short a few seconds ago, now hung below my shoulders.

"Why?" I whispered. "Why would you do this to me?" Even whispering, I could tell my voice was so much higher. A woman's voice.

I bunched my hands into fists, but I could tell that my hands were now small. My arms seemed to have no strength.

Queenie's voice roared a strong baritone. "This was never about you. I told you my story. I was Queen of the Whores and had gone as far as I could go. Fate made me a woman, and a woman has no power in this world."

"But now I am a man, a strong, tall man, the kind of man who can rule! I will command a pirate ship if I wish. But I have treasures with me from your world. No metal weapons, alas. But the drugs!"

She laughed. "I can cure dozens of illnesses with these. Just having a cure for the pox will make me the richest man in the Empire!"

"The drugs will run out."

"I brought many, many books on how to make more. If I cannot make more, so what! A poxed lord will pay a fortune to be cured! And I have other books, on strategy, and how to make weapons, and so much more!"

I looked at myself in the moonlight. "And why did you do this to me?"

"We know of these mirrors here. For me to be a man, you can no longer be. I needed your height, too, so you are a small woman. At least be grateful that I made you young and comely. You will be a valuable whore, while your beauty lasts."

Only then did I understand the horror of the life that awaited me. I turned back towards the portal.

But before I could move, Queenie threw something heavy at the portal. It shattered, like a glass mirror.

Queenie gave a deep, rumbling laugh. "I will not waste these… narcotics and condoms on you. They are too valuable. You will have to deaden yourself with drink… and laudanum, when you can get it."

Then Queenie slapped me across the face with a broad hand. I fell sprawling atop the backpacks of supplies stolen from the future.

"And now, before you become poxed like every whore, I will take you myself." Thick, strong hands tore my clothes away. "Expect this to hurt."

I looked up at the moon and wondered if I had the courage to kill myself. And, if not, when I could get ahold of some laudanum.

TYPECAST

GARY WOSK

It was made to look like Dodge City, Kansas in 1868.

As usual, on this day, the good and bad were facing off against each other.

Actor Tom Mix as usual playing the good guy, this time as Sheriff Tom Morgan, ducked low for cover behind a large, wooden barrel near the blacksmith's barn. He needed to get out of the way of incoming bullets in the silent movie Revenge of the Renegades.

Realizing that the barrel would not protect him from the constant volley of gunfire, Tom began to run for the barn where he would be harder to find.

Bad Joe Mankowitz, in his role as Slade Perkins, however, had Tom firmly in his sights, but decided not to pull the trigger. Something came over him.

"What are you waiting for, Slade?" asked Tom beseechingly, his words conveyed to the audience in subtitles. "Follow the script."

"I just can't do this to you again, Sheriff, even though I only wound you," said Bad Joe apologetically. I just can't take this anymore. It's just not fair. When the movie ends, I just want to throw myself off a cliff."

"You're breaking a cardinal rule."

"Too bad," Slade said tersely before quickly fleeing the scene.

Moments later, Tom stood frozen in in his tracks. Moviegoers at the Orpheum Theatre in Los Angeles spilled their refreshments onto their seats, the floor and themselves. The organist's music came to a grinding halt. Everyone was startled by a loud ripping noise.

The audience was on the verge of panic.

"Stop the film!"

"House lights!" shouted members of the audience. The screen resembled a funhouse mirror with actors twisted, elongated and interconnected. The words on the screen were crooked. The ad-libbing continued.

"What in the hell was that? Did you hear that?" the distorted looking Tom mouthed to the outlaws. He was no longer concerned about being filled with lead. "We have an emergency, boys. Let's have a cease-fire. We'll settle our score later."

Tom pointed his index finger in the direction of the tear on the lower right side of the screen. "See that boys?"

"This isn't in the script," said Jake Simmons, the head of the gang that had just robbed the town's bank. "It's a trick. The sheriff is lying. Whatever you do, don't lay down your arms."

"I'm telling the truth," insisted Tom. "If I was fibbing, why would I come out here in the open and risk my life.

"Well, I reckon you've got a point there," said the pipsqueak Arnold James.

"Nobody asked for your opinion," Jake said.

"Slade has escaped the movie. And he left his horse behind so he couldn't have gone that far. Let's go look for him."

"Probably went to one of those modern day saloons," suggested an extra who emerged from behind a post on the wooden slatted boardwalk outside O'Malley's Bar and Grill on Main Street.

"Nah," retorted Tom. "That kid has something else on his mind. He's complained about it to the director and me before."

"Could it be a girl?" bartender Bob Clemmons inquired.

"Nope, that isn't it," said Tom. "No more guessing, boys. It's kind of confidential. We're wasting time."

"There is no fricking way me and the boys are leaving this movie behind," said Bob adamantly.

"It shouldn't take too long to find him. Maybe the projectionist can play the intermission reel."

"Okay," agreed Bob, "but we won't go on the other side."

Tom and the gang then scampered off the screen in search of the MIA actor.

With the theatre lights on, some of the audience members walked down the carpeted aisles and inched their way up to the screen to try to figure out what caused the puncture. They backed off as soon as they saw the six-guns aimed in their direction.

"Don't shoot," Tom ordered. "These are law-abiding citizens."

"Hold your fire," said Bob. "It looks like we've come to a dead end."

"You're right, Bob. We can't go any further."

Tom and the gang knew that if they entered the real world of 1927, they would probably never work in Hollywood again. They were also afraid that scores of theater-goers would do them great bodily harm, upset that the movie they had been enjoying ended so abruptly. And, of course, they were worried about a confrontation with the Keystone Cops if they were summoned to the theatre.

When the modern day sheriff's deputies arrived at the theatre fifteen minutes later, the actors had left the tear in the screen, but no one was sure of what had happened because the projector had been turned off and the screen was blank.

"Are you okay?" deputy Randell Gardener asked an elderly woman sitting on a lobby chair, slightly out of breath. She didn't need consoling. She was euphoric.

"Oh for heaven's sakes, yes," said Essie Weinberg. "It was so exciting. I'm going to tell all my friends to go see it. It was better than a Lon Chaney movie."

"What happened?" Randell was taking notes.

"There was this tearing sound, and then this strange looking cowboy with a stubby beard popped out from the screen," she explained. "He smiled, waved his hat and shouted, 'Yahoo. Howdy pardners, don't be scared, I'm not the person you see on the screen.'"

"You said he looked strange. What did you mean by that?"

"He was bright, and I could see through him."

Randell was skeptical of the account.

"What else did he say?"

"Oh, 'I wish I could stick around and sign some autographs, but I'm being followed. I also have some important business to take care of. Gotta get. I hope everyone enjoys the rest of the film.' He was really in a hurry and scurried through the emergency exit and didn't look back."

Randell decided the woman did not have dementia after others corroborated her version of the events. There was also a trail of dirty footprints that led from the screen to the exit.

"People will be afraid of going to the movies if we don't make some arrests," deputy Forrester Kelly cautioned.

"Apparently, you haven't been on the force very long," Gardener said. "It's common knowledge that if mortals like us enter into the movie, we never come back."

While the deputies and theatre officials scratched their heads, Bad Joe was well on his way to Fox Film Corporation. His real flesh and blood persona didn't have the moxie to confront director Raoul Walsh, but he sure did.

After stepping off the trolley, Bad Joe, now completely out of character, walked a short distance to the studio, ignoring gawkers along the way, startled by his glow.

"Go right in Bad Joe," said the security guard at the front gate. "Are you okay? You don't look right."

"Don't be alarmed. It's just make-up. They've covered me in silver nitrate. You see, I have this part in a science fiction film that takes place in the Old West."

"Strange. Really strange, Bad Joe. You're great in Revenge of the Renegades.

"Well, thanks," he answered. It was the kind of compliment he was tired of hearing.

Bad Joe moved as quickly as he could across the backlot not wanting to attract attention or possibly meet up with the real Bad Joe. He had heard that if such an encounter were to occur, the silver nitrate Bad Joe would instantly dissolve, and he would instantly be transferred back into "Revenge of the Renegades."

A few minutes later, the cowboy walked up a staircase, his boots clumping on the steps. On the second floor, he entered Raoul's bungalow office.

"You're tracking in dirt, sir," lectured the director's young buxom blonde receptionist, also irritated because he had interrupted her from polishing her nails.

"I'm Bad Joe and I'm here to see Raoul!" he said stridently. No woman in the Old West dared speak to him as she did, but this was modern times, and women were bolder, sassy, a fact that eluded him.

"Yes, yes, I know who you are," she said condescendingly because he wasn't a big star. "I'm sorry Bad Joe, but Mr. Walsh is in a meeting with Mr. Mix discussing the cast for their next film."

"I don't give a damn! I'm going in!"

"Suit yourself."

Bad Joe knocked loudly three times on the director's door and then barged in.

"What the hell are you doing here, Bad Joe?" an alarmed Raoul asked seated behind his mahogany desk in a black leather chair, holding a cigar in his right hand. His feet were comfortably propped up on the desk. "Where are your manners? You're not Bad Joe. You're Bad, Bad Joe. You should probably leave and get back into the movie."

Bad Joe didn't like the tone of Raoul's voice and instinctively reached for his holster and then realized he wasn't in a movie and that his gun only contained blanks.

"Calm down," suggested Raoul, lowering his tone several notches.

"What are you doing out here?" repeated Tom, seated across the desk from Raoul. "You're supposed to be in Revenge of the Renegades and not in the outside world. That's not allowed. You signed a contract. And the real Joe won't be happy about this if he finds out."

"Screw the real Bad Joe! I'm not scared of him. He doesn't have the guts to confront you guys like I do. He just complains about the roles he plays, but doesn't do anything about it."

"You do understand you're not real, don't you?" Tom inquired.

"I'm real enough," said Bad Joe defiantly.

"Don't push your luck," Raoul warned. "Now, what's on your mind?"

"I'm here to tell you guys that I'm not going back to that film. Enough is enough."

"What are you talking about?" Raoul asked, now nervous.

Bad Joe remained silent.

"Yeah, I know, I know, why you're here," Tom said. "You want to play a good guy for once. Well, kid, like I've told you before, you have to pay your dues."

"With all due respect Mr. Mix, I am not a kid. I'm thirty-six, and I've appeared in more than two dozen films as the villain. I can't do this anymore."

"How dare you walk out on me," Tom scolded. "It was me who gave you your big break, and this is how you repay me? Coming in here with a demand? If it wasn't for me, you'd still be selling newspapers on the corner."

"You need to go back into the film," Raoul urged. "If you don't, we'll have a public relations nightmare on our hands. You and the real Bad Joe will be finished. And Tom and I will be finished once word gets out we can't keep the talent on the screen."

"Don't get me wrong, Tom, I appreciate everything you've done for me, but don't hold that over my head," Bad Joe said." "I'm just sick and tired of being typecast. I'm a nice guy being asked to commit bad deeds. That's not who I am. Do you know what it's like to be reviled everywhere you go? Even by your family? To hear the hissing, see the revulsion on people's faces? Threaten me with a citizen's arrest?"

"I can only imagine," said Tom.

"That's right, you can only imagine," said Bad Joe. "You're Mister Goody Two Shoes. Why can't I be the one who gets the girl in the end for once? I'm good looking and nice. I want an image change!"

Raoul, though seething inside, tried to remain calm. He had to do something to make the actor happy. He decided that his best course of action was to commiserate.

"I understand completely what you're going through. I played John Wilkes Booth in the film "The Birth of a Nation" in 1915," Raoul said sympathetically. "Even to this day, people accuse me of assassinating Lincoln. They think they're being funny, but it gets old fast."

"Well, that's very nice and all, but that was only one time. I've been the villain for ten years now."

"You do realize Bad Joe that if we change your image, word will get around, and the other actors will be lining up outside my door making the same request," Raoul said resignedly.

"I won't tell anyone that we met. I promise. Gentlemen's agreement."

"I'll tell you what… I can cast you as a good guy in my next Western, Pioneer Women," Raoul said. How does that sound, Bad Joe?"

"That could be my ticket to stardom."

"I will do this for you on one condition," Raoul said. "You need to promise me that when you leave this office, you'll go straight back to Revenge of the Renegades. It will only be for a while because we're planning to pull it out of the theaters in about a week. We start shooting the new film in the Simi Valley in about two months. I'll let the real Bad Joe know so that he can start feeling better about himself too."

"Do I get the girl this time?"

"Yes. And you'll be in a kissing scene with her. Unfortunately, you get killed in the end by Comanches. Life isn't perfect."

"By bow and arrow?"

"Uh… huh."

"Scalped?"

"Yep."

"Yikes. Well… that's okay… I guess," Bad Joe said, a little disappointed, but then he perked up. "This is more of a star-vehicle film, right?"

"Exactly. And we'll change your name too," Raoul said. "Mankowitz just won't cut it. We should have changed it long ago."

"Do you have any suggestions?" Bad Joe asked.

"Let me see…" said Raoul. He opened the top drawer of his desk and removed a manila folder that contained a list of potential names reserved for potential stars.

"I don't usually do this for feature actors, but I'll make an exception in your case since you will soon be a star. How about… John Wayne? I had it in mind for someone else, I believe his name is Marion… Marion Robert Morrison, but if you want it, it's yours."

"So, do we have a deal, Bad Joe?" asked Raoul.

"To be honest, I really don't want to go back to Revenge of the Renegades.

"Come on, Bad Joe. Like I said, it's I just for one more week," Tom assured him.

"You'd be making a big mistake, kid," Raoul said forcefully. "You'll lose Marjorie forever."

"Marjorie?"

"Actress Marjorie Daw. She plays Alice, the clerk at the supply store. She falls madly in love with you and wants to reform you. Didn't you read the damn script?"

"Not really. Does she really fall in love with me?"

"Yes," said Raoul. "If you only would have stayed in the film for another fifteen minutes, you would have found out."

Bad Joe softened his stance.

"Maybe I should go back then."

"That would be a wise decision," said Raoul. "I'll tell you what. I'll also increase your salary to one hundred dollars a week. No, make it one hundred fifty dollars a week if you agree to go back and never to pull another shenanigan like this."

"You've got a deal!"

"Should we change your name to John Wayne?"

"No, that's all right. That doesn't sound tough enough. Maybe something with the word Chuck in it, like Chuck Calhoun. I'm not sure. We'll figure out something before filming on the movie begins."

"Yeah, cowboy, I'm making up new fake movie names every day. I'll discuss it with the real Bad Joe."

The revitalized Bad Joe shook hands with Raoul and Tom and left the office to catch a trolley. Once back inside of the Orpheum, he looked up to the projectionist.

"Hey Max, can you start the film again."

"Well, I could, but there's no one in the theatre except you."

"That's okay, Just rewind the film to the part where I'm just about to shoot the sheriff, and once I get there, turn it off."

"Sure, Bad Joe, but are you sure you want to? You look too happy-go-lucky to be playing a bandit. Don't you need to have a scowl on your face?"

"You mean like this?" Bad Joe asked gleefully.

"Exactly."

After walking back into the torn screen, Bad Joe was greeted by Mix, who quipped, "Welcome back pardner to Revenge of the Renegades. I've been expecting you. Now put your hands up. You're under arrest for robbing a bank and trespassing into the real world."

"Good try, Tom, but that's not in the script."

CONTRIBUTORS

ALISON THORNTON

Alison Thornton is from Port Moody, British Columbia. She has been writing stories since the age of sixteen and has always enjoyed it.

Alma Sinan

Alma Sinan is a Toronto writer. Some of her publications include: "Seabound" in the Lover's Lost Issue of Leannan Magazine, "Soul Glass" in Litro magazine/website, "The Beet Man" in Falling Star magazine, "Morpheus' Pen" on the Frame Lines website and "The Summoning" in All Rights Reserved magazine. Some of her other short stories have been published in Black Petals, Morbid Curiosity and Raven's Call Quarterly.

Alma is also the Chair of the Ontario Chapter of the Association for Gravestone Studies and gives talks and tours on the subject.

BETTY GABRIEL

Betty Gabriel is a mildly eccentric tea drinking Brit with a penchant for Devonshire cream teas, cider, curry and rock music.

Previous work has appeared in Bones II (2014), Slaughter House: The Serial Killer Edition - Volume 1 (2013), Infernal Ink Magazine (October 2014), Body Parts Magazine (May 2016) and Siren's Call Women in Horror Month eZine, (Feb 2016).

In her spare time Betty is a soup maker extraordinaire who likes to spend time with her husband and dogs. She lives in a small town by the sea, and if she isn't watching Ninja Warrior, can usually be found with her fingers poised over the keyboard with the intention of killing another character off.

Follow Betty via Twitter: @Thecushionlady

CALVIN MILLS

Calvin Mills is a writer of short stories, essays, and plays. His work has appeared in Short Story, Weird Tales, Tales from the South, Road Story, and other magazines and anthologies. His musical, "Freak Like Me", premiered in 2012.

Mills grew up behind the Redwood Curtain in Eureka, California and lived for a decade in Little Rock, Arkansas. He teaches English and art at Peninsula College in Port Angeles, Washington, where he is the faculty advisor for Tidepools Magazine.

DENNIS WINKLEBLACK

Dennis Winkleblack is a retired minister residing in Simsbury, Connecticut. The author of several articles in professional journals and the popular workbook for churches, "Who Cares For the Pastor?" he is enjoying a new season of life as a writer of fiction.

His book, After Church Mysteries: Rev. Richard Burgess, PI is available from Amazon summer 2016 (pen name, Dennis Martin).

DJ TYRER

DJ Tyrer is the person behind Atlantean Publishing and has been widely published in anthologies and magazines around the world, such as Disturbance (Laurel Highlands), Tales of the Black Arts (Hazardous Press), Amok!, Stomping Grounds and Ill-considered Expeditions (all April Moon Books), History and Mystery, Oh My! (Mystery & Horror LLC), Destroy All Robots (Dynatox Ministries), and Sorcery & Sanctity: A Homage to Arthur Machen (Hieroglyphics Press), and in addition, has a novella available in paperback and on the Kindle, The Yellow House (Dunhams Manor).

DJ Tyrer's website is at http://djtyrer.blogspot.co.uk/
The Atlantean Publishing website is at:
http://atlanteanpublishing.blogspot.co.uk/

EMILY LEEDHAM

Emily Leedham is a student in British Columbia, Canada. She sleeps far too little, sasses far too much, and is basically a cat.

E. W. Farnsworth lives and writes in Arizona. Eighty-three of his short stories were published at a variety of venues in 2015. Over seventy of his short stories are already contracted to be published in 2016. Also published in 2015 were his collected Arizona westerns Desert Sun, Red Blood, his global mystery/thriller about combating cryptocurrency crimes, Bitcoin Fandango, his John Fulghum Mysteries about a hard-boiled Boston detective and Engaging Rachel, an Anderson romance/thriller.

To be published by Zimbell House in 2016 are Pirate Tales, John Fulghum Mysteries, Volume II, and Love in the Time of Baro Xaimos.

Contracted by Audio Arcadia in England for publication in 2016 is DarkFire at the Edge of Time, Farnsworth's collection of visionary science fiction stories. His series of three superhero Al Katana novels will appear from Pro Se Productions starting in 2017.

E. W. Farnsworth is now working on an epic poem, The Voyage of the Spaceship Arcturus, about the future of humankind when humans, avatars and artificial intelligences must work together to instantiate a second Eden after the Chaos Wars bring an end to life on Earth. For updates please see: www.ewfarnsworth.com.

GARY WOSK

Gary was born in New York City. He earned a bachelor's degree in journalism from California State University, Northridge and reported for such newspapers as the San Luis Obispo Telegram-Tribune, Brawley News and the Newhall Signal. Other positions have included special sections editor for the Los Angeles Daily News, senior communications officer/spokesperson/editor for the Metropolitan Transportation Authority and media relations manager of The ALS Association.

His published short stories include "My Gym" (Trinity Gateways), "They Are Here" (Fiction Brigade and Dark Futures), "Bezillgo Versus the Allerton Theatre" (Grinning Skull Press), "Bubbe to the Rescue " (eFiction), "Flameout" (G.IS.G Heavenly Publications, "The Violation" (Perihelion Science Fiction) "Sugar" (Writers Haven) "Full Bladder" (Zimbell House Publishing) and "Perseverance (On the Verge Magazine).

Gary also freelances as a writer and media relations. He lives in North Hills, California with his wife Mina.

JAYNE MOORE WALDROP

Jayne Moore Waldrop is a writer, lawyer and contributing book columnist for the Louisville Courier-Journal.

Her work has appeared or is forthcoming in Appalachian Heritage, New Madrid Journal, Limestone Journal, Minerva Rising, Kudzu, Luna Station Quarterly, and Deep South Magazine.

She lives in Kentucky.

Jeremy Kratka

Jeremy Kratka is a writer with a passion for the unknown. He lives in Massachusetts and writers video game reviews in his free time.

JOHN VICARY

A contributor to more than sixty compendiums in his career, John Vicary is the submissions editor at Bedlam Publishing and also co-founded the editing business, The LetterWorks.

He enjoys playing piano and lives in rural Michigan with his family.

You can read more of John's work at: keppiehed.com.

Jon Alston has an MA in Creative Writing. Good for him. He writes things from time to time, and sometimes people publish them. Good for him. On occasion, he will photograph things (or people), and maybe write about them; sometimes there is money exchanged for his services. Good for him.

He is married and has two children of both genders. Way to reproduce. He is the Executive Editor and founder of From Sac, a literary journal for Northern California. How about that?

Currently he teaches English at Brigham Young University, Idaho among the frozen potato fields and Mormons. Good for you, Jon.

MATTHEW MCKIERNAN

Matthew McKiernan has just completed his thesis, and received his MFA in Creative writing, from Rosemont College. He graduated from LaSalle University in 2013 with a BA in English and History.

His first short story, "A Leap of Faith" was published in "Skive Magazine" in November 2013. Another short story, "Dragon Slayer" was published in the Anthology, "Of Dragons & Magic: Tales of the Lost Wolds" in May 2014. His short story "Trapped" was published in the Anthology, "Of Dead and Dying: Tales of the Apocalypse" in October 2014. His latest short story, "Real" was published in the January 2015 edition of "Beyond Science Fiction."

He is currently editing his science fiction novel, "Human" which he hopes to publish next year.

MICHAEL EVIS

Mike Evis lives just outside Oxford, England. He is a former software engineer, with a chronic inability to pass any bookshop without entering and buying a book.

A wide ranging reader, his interests include modern literature, science fiction, fantasy, and crime. He also likes obscure indie music no one has ever heard of.

He has had stories published in several anthologies: *When The House Whispers,* Oloris Publishing, *It's about Time*, Main Street Rag Publishing Company (due Summer / Fall 2016), and *The Key*, Zimbell House Publishing.

Michelle has been writing science fiction and fantasy for many years. She has had several short stories published recently.

She lives in Michigan, and is currently working on her first novel. To follow Michelle, check out her blog:

http://www.michellemmonigan.com

Pamela Jeffs is a prize-winning speculative fiction author living in Queensland, Australia with her husband and two daughters.

She is a member of the Queensland Writers' Centre and has had her short fiction published in recent Australian anthologies. Pamela draws upon the natural world for inspiration in her work.

Visit her at: www.pamelajeffs.wix.com/pamela-jeffs

Sammi Cox lives in the UK and spends her time writing and making things. She has been interested in history, archaeology and the natural world since she was a child.

However, it is tales of myth, magic and folklore that have captured her heart, and where she finds the greatest inspiration.

Born in Philadelphia, Pennsylvania, Tony Conaway has written and ghostwritten everything from blogs to books. He has co-written non-fiction books published by McGraw-Hill, Macmillan and Prentice Hall.

His fiction has been published in six anthologies and numerous publications, including Blue Lake Review, Danse Macabre, qarrtsiluni, Rind Literary Magazine, the Rusty Nail, and Typehouse Literary Magazine.

He has also sold jokes to "The Tonight Show" which Jay Leno performed on air. Unfortunately, Stephen Colbert won't return his calls.

Yi Yi Du is a senior student studying at Dr. Charles Best Secondary School in Coquitlam, B.C.

In his free time, he likes to bike with his friends in the mountains and enjoy the scenery.

He often takes inspirations from things around him to write sci-fi and fantasy short stories.

A Note from the Publisher

How to Thank a Contributor

Dear Reader,

Everyone at Zimbell House Publishing would like to thank you for reading *The Lost Door*. If you would like to thank a particular contributor, the best way is to leave a review for them. You may do so by leaving one on our Goodreads page, under the *The Lost Door* title, by using the link below:

http://www.goodreads.com/ZimbellHousePublishing and be sure to mention the contributor directly.

Why leave a review? Reviews help budding authors build their credibility in the book industry. By posting a review on Goodreads, you help other readers find new authors they may wish to follow, and you never know, your review may end up on an author's website one day.

Friend us on Goodreads:
https://www.goodreads.com/ZimbellHousePublishing

Visit our website:
http://www.ZimbellHousePublishing.com

Follow us on Twitter:
http://twitter.com/ZimbellHousePub